ASHLYNNE KRISTINE

The Goalie and The Teacher

This novel is entirely a work of fiction. The names, characters and incidents portrayed in it are the work of the author's imagination. Any resemblance to actual persons, living or dead, events or localities is entirely coincidental.

Trigger Warning:

This book contains explicit sexual content, explores sibling loss, and grief is depicted. Anxiety is also mentioned, and an on-page anxiety attack takes place.

First edition

ISBN: 979-8-9895460-1-5

Cover art by Love Lee Creative

This book was professionally typeset on Reedsy. Find out more at reedsy.com

To the people who told themselves they didn't need another grumpy, tattooed book boyfriend.
You can file Townes McCarthy under "Hockey Daddies"

Contents

1

Townes

I couldn't remember the woman's name. Carly? No...
Janice?

Yeah, that sounded right.

Soft, classical music drifted through the upscale restaurant, but it was drowned out by the voices of the other people surrounding us. Men dressed in suits and gleaming watches chatted with women who were as well dressed as the one in front of me. The red, satin dress hugged tight to her lush frame, exposing every dip and curve. The gold necklace she wore dangled above her cleavage, and her perfume–some kind of floral scent–lightly invaded my nose. All of it was meant to entice me, and none of it was working.

A pink manicured hand tossed long, curled brown hair over a bare shoulder and she smiled. "So, hockey, huh? I've never dated an athlete."

Most women hadn't, or if they did, it was some middle-aged man playing on a community baseball team as a hobby. Not a professional goalie for one of the nation's biggest hockey teams.

I tapped a finger along my water glass and debated even responding. These dates always started the same, and I was growing tired of the repetitive questions. Women seemed to be more interested in my occupation and what it could mean for them. I needed someone whose first question wasn't about my job, or if my salary on Google was accurate. Because then, it would mean they were at least a little interested in me as a person, and that would make it significantly easier to ask them to marry me. I didn't need to be worried about my future fake wife saying something suspicious at the immigration office.

When I didn't say anything, Janice widened her smile and rested her chin on a fist. "So, what's it like? I'm sure you're busy during the season obviously, but what do you do in the offseason?"

Hm, maybe I judged her too soon.

I looked her over again and kept my answer vague when my eyes met hers. "Relax mostly. Play video games, hang out with other guys on the team."

"That's it?" she asked, raising her brows like my answer shocked her.

What had she expected me to say? That I spent my offseasons in a beach house in Florida? Drinking beers on the deck when I wasn't partying on a yacht?

I was too old for that.

My water met my lips as I shrugged, hoping she'd change the topic. The truth was that my offseason consisted of taking my niece to dance classes and swim lessons before we cooked dinner every night. Well, I cooked–she sat on the counter and taste tested everything.

I wasn't going to tell Janice that, though.

2

No, Hayley was someone I kept from the spotlight, and from anyone who wasn't a part of my close circle. I promised myself I would do that when I took her in four years ago–through circumstances I hated thinking about. It wasn't that I was unwilling to introduce people to her, it was about privacy.

She opened her mouth to speak but was interrupted by the waiter. After the man took our orders, Janice sipped her wine and sighed when she put the glass down. "So, when are you going to ask about me?"

My ability to make small talk, or lack thereof, was likely one reason these dates were horrible. I didn't care for personal questions, no matter how deep or shallow. However, the night was still young, and Janice hadn't done anything to raise any red flags. I leaned forward and braced my forearms on the table. "What do you want me to ask you?"

"You don't do this dating thing often, do you?" she asked through a choked laugh.

Instead of telling her she was my third date this week, I shrugged. "Often enough to know I get tired of the basic questions. Have you ever broken a promise?"

She didn't miss a beat. "Once. In third grade, I promised my sister I wouldn't tell our dad about how she cut our brother's hair. But he promised candy to whoever fessed up."

I think my smirk surprised her as much as it did me. "I can't believe you betrayed your sister."

"It's what siblings do," she shrugged. "Do you have any?"

Yeah. Not going there.

"Your profile said you work in accounting? Is that the freelance kind or the kind where you wear clothes and go into an office?"

3

I was relieved when she laughed and didn't press me about not answering her question. "The office kind."

This was kind of…nice. It was the most relaxed date I'd been on since I started a month ago. When I realized my knees likely wouldn't last much longer as a professional goalie, I knew my retirement was coming soon. The only problem with retirement though, meant I would have to go back to Vancouver.

And that meant Hayley would stay here with her grandmother. That wasn't something I could let happen. Two months ago, after a game, I popped some pain medication and downloaded a few dating apps, with the intention of finding a woman who wouldn't mind letting me use her for a green card. I should have realized though how hard that would be, given who I was. Again, most women wanted to be with me because of what I could give them materialistically. They wouldn't want to stay out of obligation when my name wasn't making headlines and I wasn't getting deals for underwear calendars.

By the time Janice and I had finished our food, I found myself relaxing back into the faux leather chair. Her cheeks were red from her wine, and her smile was just as kind as when we met outside earlier. I thought *this could work*. I just had to ask her one more question.

Our waiter came back though and asked, "Are we getting dessert tonight?"

I looked at Janice, letting her know it was up to her. She nodded, and as she ordered her food, I traced over her features. I didn't do it earlier because, well, why? There wasn't any guarantee this date would have gone as well as it did, and looks didn't matter in the grand scheme of things.

Her jawline was soft, and her button nose was cute from her profile. I wondered what Hayley would say if they ever met. She'd probably try to compare her to whatever Disney princess she was obsessed with at that moment.

When the server walked away, I cleared my throat to earn Janice's attention. "I do have one more question."

"Just one?" She raised a brow and finished the last of her dark wine.

"Yeah. Well, your answer is going to determine if there's more."

Her posture changed. She sat straighter in her chair and her expression hardened into concern or determination, I wasn't sure. "Okay, shoot."

I leveled her with a stare, and in an even tone asked, "What's your opinion on kids?"

Her mouth opened and shut a few times before settling on her next question. "Do you have any?"

"I'm just curious."

She stayed silent for a moment and looked me over. I hadn't given any indication I was responsible for a child, and my question was common enough. So, her answer shouldn't be swayed by anything.

"Honestly?" The light in her eyes shifted to something darker as they darted from the table to me.

A knot formed in the pit of my stomach, but I pushed past the uneasiness. "I wouldn't ask for anything less."

She sighed and tilted her head to the side as she forced a nervous smile. "I like kids, but I don't want them for myself."

I nodded in understanding as I unfurled that knot and tossed aside the disappointment. It was my fault, the last thing I should have done was get my hopes up, no matter how small. Our server came back with her dessert, a slice of chocolate cake, and before he walked away, I asked, "Can we get the check?"

Janice was staring at the cake in front of her, worrying her bottom lip. "That's not the answer you wanted, is it?"

We fell into silence as she picked at the cake, and I waited for the check. I wasn't going to sit and offer words of encouragement. No niceties of, *well sorry this didn't work out,* because it didn't matter. I was back to square one, and she was going to continue her life, she'd forget about this night soon enough. I didn't shame her for how she wanted to live, there was no point.

It was easier for us both to say nothing.

When the server came back, I looked at the amount and placed cash on the table. I stood and took in the way her hair seemed flatter, her shoulders slumped in. I was a dick, I knew that, but I had some manners. "Have a good rest of your night, Janice."

She glanced up and blinked before she whispered, "My name's Jamie."

Fuck.

I turned around and walked out of the restaurant.

As I drove home, I thought of how close I was to ending this stupid fucked up mission of mine. If she had given me any other answer, this could have worked. She didn't though, so I was back to square one.

It didn't take long before my townhouse came into view, and a familiar green sedan sat in the driveway. I groaned and shut my door a little harder than necessary as I got out and stalked toward the door. As soon as it clicked shut behind me, a tiny, curly haired Hayley was running around the corner.

"Uncle T!" She jumped into my arms, and I caught her before she dropped to the floor.

"You should be in bed."

She put out her bottom lip. I hated when she did that. "I wanted to see you when you got home."

"And here I am. Come on, you have school tomorrow." I set her down and watched her walk back upstairs. Before she disappeared into the darkness I called after her, "Be there in a minute."

Light from the kitchen illuminated the end of the dark hallway, and the closer I walked toward it, the more I could hear voices. Both were familiar. One belonged to Scottie, the team's rookie who started last year, and the other belonged to someone I tried not to think about.

I rounded the corner and found Scottie and the blonde woman hovered over the kitchen island, papers littered the granite countertop and they each had a red pen in hand. She saw me first, her baby blue eyes snagging onto mine as her head snapped up. Wild, curly hair bounced as she smiled wide–exposing two snaggle canines–and her eyes roamed over my dark slacks and white button up.

"Well, don't you look fancy."

Hollis had been coming over for a few months now, a couple times a week. Scottie offered to help her grade papers when she didn't want to do it by herself. And if she wasn't doing that here, she was doing it with Basil–her best friend, and my best friend's fiancé. I didn't really care if she came over.

I did care, however, that when she did, I couldn't stop looking at her. It was a problem I didn't need, and one I dealt with the only way I knew how.

Scowling and staying quiet.

I was just waiting for it to finally work.

Hollis directed her smile toward Scottie and started gathering her stuff. "It's late, I should get going."

The rookie raised a brow, and a teasing smile plastered his face as he brought a beer bottle to his lips. "Are you sure? Don't let him scare you off."

"Oh please, he wishes he was scary," she said before looking back at me and winking. That fucking wink. I hated how seeing it made blood rush to my ears, and made me want to keep looking at her, yet turn away at the same time. I preoccupied myself with grabbing some water from the fridge.

The island had been cleaned in record time, and I watched as Hollis and Scottie exchanged goodnights before she made her way to the door.

When I heard it shut from the kitchen, I looked at Scottie. "How long was she here this time?"

"Uh, a few hours probably. Honestly, I lost track of time between the third and fifth mountain of papers."

I sipped my water and hummed. Not that it was my business, or that I wanted it to be, but I wondered what her boyfriend had to say about her coming over. I didn't like the asshole, and Hollis could do better–again, it wasn't my business. But I had some opinions.

"How'd your date go?" Scottie asked with another swig of beer.

"Could have gone better. I need to go get Hayley to bed."

He raised a surprised brow and lowered his drink. "I told her to go to bed an hour ago, I swear."

I sighed. "I know, she stayed up anyway."

He nodded in understanding and brought the bottle to his lips once again. Ever since Scottie moved in last year, he'd taken it upon himself to be the "fun yet stern Uncle" for Hayley.

She'd taken to the fun bit, but she didn't listen to him *that* well.

I walked back down the hallway, past the dark pictures lining the hallway, and rounded the metal banister to head upstairs. When I walked toward Hayley's bedroom, ready to tuck her in, I was expecting her to still be awake. Sitting in bed playing with her stuffed animals or reading one of the new picture books she got last weekend. But when I inched her door inward, I found her asleep on top of her covers. My socks sunk into the plush carpet as I moved toward the white wooden bed, and without waking her, I tucked her in under the covers.

As I looked down at her and saw all the ways she was the mirror image of my sister, my resolve hardened.

I'd find a way to stay here with her, there was no other option.

2

Hollis

The door clicked behind me, and I plopped myself on the couch when my phone started ringing. I knew who it was, and like many other times these past few weeks, I was dreading answering it.

I threw my head back and sighed before I fished my phone from my pocket. "What's up?"

"Hey, you never called me back? We were supposed to join Aaron and Rosie for dinner. I had to go by myself and make excuses. What's up with that?"

I groaned and pinched the bridge of my nose. Tonight was my boyfriend's monthly dinner with his coworkers, and after months of begging to tag along, I couldn't make it. Not because I didn't want to, but because he planned it on a night I was busy. Ryan knew that twice a week I went over to my friends' houses so they could help me grade papers while we watched trashy television.

I was tired and didn't feel like having to explain myself again. "Can we–"

"I'm heading over right now, want me to grab you anything?"

"No." I hung up the phone and stared at my ceiling for a good, long while as I tried to think of how this night was going to end. I'd been planning on breaking up with Ryan for a while now, but there never seemed to be a good time. I mean, it wasn't easy to call things off with someone you'd been with for three years.

I'd be lying if I said it was hard because I still loved him–I was attached to the memories, the good ones that made my chest ache with what used to be.

A knock came to the door a moment before it was being pushed open, and Ryan walked in. He was still wearing his cream button up T-shirt and black slacks from the dinner, which eased something inside me. Knowing he didn't bother to change because he wanted to see me. He smiled, and I waited for the flutters to return in my stomach–but they never did.

It was the first time they hadn't shown up at all, and I knew he couldn't stay long. He reached the couch and bent down for a kiss, but I turned my head at the last second. When his lips met my cheek, a shutter went through me, propelling me off the couch and to the other side of the coffee table. He raised a questioning brow as I crossed my arms.

"You okay?"

"Yeah, what uh–what did you want to talk about?"

He scoffed and shrugged off his coat. "We can start with you bailing on me tonight."

God…when did his voice get so annoying? I missed when it sounded like silk as it caressed my ears. Sweet whispers of nothing while we laid under the thin blanket in his college dorm room.

11

"Are you going to gloss over the fact that you knew I was busy, and decided to make plans anyways? How can you blame me?"

He threw his hands up as if I was the problem. "We do this every month, god forbid you make plans that accommodate mine."

This man was ridiculous. I pinched the bridge of my nose to try and keep calm. "Ryan, I accommodate all of your plans. A stupid work event? I cancel girls' night with Basil. Golf with your family? I put off grading papers so I can laugh at your dad's horrible sexist jokes."

"That's you being supportive babe–"

I held up my hand and felt blood rush to my ears. "That's me putting aside my needs in hopes that when I ask you to do something, you'll do it."

This had been going on for too long–and I hated that I allowed it. I was too comfortable in our routine; weekly date nights with flowers and expensive dinners, small fights that resolved in the bedsheets. But I was also tired, tired of spending so much of my own energy to make sure we were both happy. Somewhere in the past year, things shifted, and I wished I caught it when it happened.

Because now, there was no turning back.

"Look, Ryan, I can't do this anymore."

He scoffed and pulled at a thread on the back of the couch. A habit I hated because I couldn't sew anything to save my life. "You're being dramatic."

I stepped forward, my hands fell to my sides. "I'm dramatic? You threatened to get a waiter fired for spilling a drop of wine on your pants. They weren't even expensive! I got those for you from a consignment shop."

He shook his finger. "See, this is what I mean. Look babe, I can leave, let you cool down. I can come back another time." He ran his hand through his hair and sighed. "Just text me when you're ready to talk like an adult."

That was it. All I had done the past year was talk, communicate my feelings, and try to find a middle ground where we weren't arguing all the time. I watched as Ryan walked toward the door, then took a deep breath.

"I don't want you coming back, Ryan. I—I can't do this."

He rolled his head back and pinned me with a confused stare. "Can't do what?"

I groaned this time, and he didn't bother hiding the shock on his face. "This. Us, Ryan. You can leave, but I don't want you coming back."

He clicked his tongue and scoffed. I wished things were different, but I knew it wasn't possible. A year of trying to change things proved that. When Ryan finally looked at me again, I paused. He seemed remorseful—or at least he realized I was serious. His brows were pulled tight and his voice broke when he spoke again, "Babe you—"

"Don't call me that."

"Hol, we can work through this—" He took a step toward be, but I backed away.

I leveled him with a stare and managed to keep my tears at bay. This was hard, loving someone who didn't put you first. But it was harder letting go of a person you confided in for years, who knew you in and out.

"Leave, Ryan. Please."

He shook his head and finally grabbed the doorknob. "I'll be back Hol, we can talk about this a different day."

I watched as he left, and flinched when the door slammed

shut. This day had been so nice. I left work on time and spent the evening with Scottie. I even ran into Townes, Scottie's grumpy roommate, who made me smile despite his permanent scowl and sour mood.

But even though I ended things with Ryan, I didn't feel like my night was ruined. I walked into the kitchen to grab a drink and wondered what the future held now that I was single. Not that I was looking for love or a relationship right off the bat.

I had a steady teaching job–even if the school wasn't the best, and I was almost ready to start some home renovations.

Things would be alright, and I was excited for what was to come.

3

Hollis

2 months later...

Mom was at the grocery store and set her phone on a shelf as she looked at the back of a box of organic, whole-wheat pasta.

"So, your dad and I were thinking about going to see your sister this weekend. We could stop by on the way and see you?" She put the pasta in her cart and grabbed her phone again. I could see where her foundation wasn't blended properly on her neck from the angle she held the phone.

I finished smoothing my hair back into its bun before I answered, "That could work, do you know what time?"

I'd have to ask Dave to pick up my shift.

"Let me check with Emma. She has a show we're coming up to see, I just don't remember when it starts. But it'll be before then."

I was happy she couldn't see me roll my eyes. She'd scold me otherwise. *You weren't meant to see your brain, stop it.* The only reason she was coming to the city was to see my sister, but it would be nice if she at least pretended I wasn't a simple pit stop. Maybe it was a middle child thing, or maybe it was being the middle child while your siblings were super successful. Emma was a violinist in one of Colorado's prestigious orchestras, and Lionel was in med school.

Then there was me, a *former* public school teacher. The termination email that landed in my inbox a week ago was still a sore spot in my professional career. I gave that school all my formative teaching years, just to be set aside like a sandwich you took one bite of and decided it didn't sound good anymore.

"Sounds good, but, next time could please let me know, like, a week before you plan on visiting? I'm pretty busy with work." I hadn't told either of my parents of my current job situation, because they would suggest I do something to be more like either of my siblings. I loved them both dearly, but living up to either of them was impossible.

Mom waved a hand and her bracelets jingled. Her thin, blonde hair was pulled into a clip and some pieces dropped to frame her face when she pulled her phone up. I looked into blue eyes much like my own and was grateful I reconsidered permanent eyeliner in college.

"I'll text your sister and let you know later tonight. Sound good?"

I nodded. "Sounds great."

"Perfect, we'll talk later. The store has a sale on strawberries, and you know all the good ones are probably gone. Gotta go hunting. Love you!" She air kissed the space between her and the phone before she hung up. I considered for a split second calling my sister and asking her why she didn't tell me about her concert. Sure, in her defense, I hadn't gone to

16

many of them, unlike our retired parents who went to every. single. one. But that didn't mean I didn't want to be invited.

I tapped my phone screen, contemplating pulling up our bare text thread, but thought better of it and placed my phone in my purse as I headed out the door.

* * *

Working at Al's reminded me a lot of the bar I worked at in college.

Small, dingy, and smelled overwhelmingly of sweat from men my dad's age who kept my tip jar full. Al's was a constant part-time summer job I'd had since my first year of teaching; when I realized my salary didn't cover basic living during those few months. So, when I got that damn email, Johanna was the first person I called. She was more than happy to offer me a full-time position until something else came along. I was good for business and knew how to make good drinks.

"Hey Hol?"

I glanced at Finn, an older man with glasses thicker than the sole of my shoe, and smiled. "Sup?"

"You think any of those ladies will say no to a dance?"

I peered over his receding hairline, and saw the women he was talking about. Abigail, Meghan, and Franny. All around his age, and more than willing to talk, flirt, and smile at anything that looked their way for more than three seconds. They were all divorced, in their early sixties, and just looking for a good time. They also started coming right after Finn had knee surgery, otherwise he'd have tried to talk to them by now.

"Finn, they've been waiting for you."

"They have?" His eyes went wide as a smile tugged on his thin lips.

I nodded. "Oh yeah, how do you think I've spent my time with you gone? I've been building you up with the ladies. I'm surprised there's not a line out the bar."

"In that case." He slicked the few hairs left on his head to the side and slid off his bar stool. I watched him walk over to them, and noticed how Abigail—a pretty woman with gray hair and glasses as big as Finn's—had the brightest smile. My eyes darted to the door as it's hinges creaked open, and I froze when I noticed who had walked in.

The brunette was—stunning, if I was being honest. She was tall, her hair so shiny I could see the light reflecting off it from where I stood, she could be a model if she wasn't already. My eyes shifted, even though I saw him first. He was imposing, all inked skin with a disgustingly attractive hard jaw, that was dusted with hair.

Townes's eyes scanned the bar, and I turned at the last second. Would it be horrible if he saw me? Probably not. But given how all he ever did around me was scowl and huff, I was sure seeing me might ruin his night. I busied myself with wiping down the counter and taking orders. All while avoiding looking in the small corner Townes and his obvious date settled in.

"A Sex on the Beach for the lady, Hol." Finn grinned, tapping twice on the counter. I smiled at Abigail, who had her arm wrapped around Finn's mid-section.

"Are you feeling okay, Abby? You're usually a red wine woman."

She leaned in while Finn started chatting with his buddy, Mitch. "I'm trying that manifesting stuff my granddaughter

18

talks about."

"We don't live near any beaches though," I said as I poured the vodka into my shaker.

"Dot said it takes a while, so who knows, maybe Finn will take me to Cabo."

I laughed, loud and hard enough to develop a stitch in my side. "I'll manifest that for you too. Here's your Sex on the Beach." We exchanged winks, and I watched them saunter off to an empty table.

The next hour went by as it usually did. I made drinks and watched people talk. In between having something to do, I scrolled job searching sites and updated my resume as needed. Right when I was going to call it a day with job hunting; I paused, blinked, then continued to stay in a state of shock.

White River Academy, a charter school with ridiculous retention and amazing test scores, had an opening for an English teacher.

When I graduated college, it was the first place I applied to, and was heartbroken when I got rejected. Was this a sign? I'd have to make sure my resume was amazing, so amazing that the hiring manager could tell when it landed in their inbox. I favorited the job listing and shoved my phone back into my pocket. My body tingled with anticipation as I started mindlessly wiping the counter again.

The school probably paid really well, and they probably offered support for teachers and staff, right? With less stress and more pay, then I could focus on–

"Get me whatever's on tap. I'm not picky."

The disgruntled voice pulled me from my trailing thoughts. I looked up, and made sure to keep my eyes on his, instead of darting back to the moth inked into his hand. I smiled, and batted my lashes, it made his jaw tick and a tiny part of me loved it. "Oh, hi Townes. It's so nice to see you, how've you been?"

We stared each other down for a moment, and I sweetened my next words as I tilted my head. "I'll do it if you say please, and I won't tell Basil you were being rude." He and I both knew Basil, my best friend, and his best friend's fiancé–would kick his ass.

Townes's nostrils flared. "Please." It was said through gritted teeth, but I'd take it.

"See, that wasn't so hard, was it?" I smiled and whirled around to get him the first beer I touched. When I turned back around, he was sitting down. My eyes darted to the corner and realized it was empty. Odd. "How'd your date go?"

"Why're you a bartender?" he quipped back as soon as the beer glass clinked on the bar top. I blinked, taken aback by the question, and irritated with his tone. Townes being in a pissy mood wasn't new to me, but he wasn't usually rude. He reached for the beer as I took it back, and his scowl deepened. "That's mine."

"Technically, you haven't paid for it yet, so it's the bars." I set it down in front of me and leaned my arms on the counter. "You want to tell me what crawled up your butt to make you extra grumpy?" He mumbled something and leaned back. "What was that? I can't hear you through the facial hair."

"I'm sorry. Okay? It's been a rough few months, and tonight didn't make anything better."

Rough few months, huh.

The words couldn't be more true. Besides losing the job I loved and breaking up with Ryan; I was drowning in student debt and my house was falling apart. Nothing about the last few months had been easy, but at least I didn't take my stress out on other people. I sighed and set the beer back in front of Townes, then nodded when he gave me a questioning look.

"Go ahead, you seem like you really need it."

When he downed half of it, he looked at me with soft eyes. They were brown, usually darkened with whatever made him so tense; but whether it was the beer or something else, they were lighter even in the dimmed light. "Thank you, Hollis."

The way he said my name, straightforward and in a voice so deep–it made my neck tingle. I wasn't ashamed to admit that even when Ryan and I were together, I thought Townes was attractive. I was in a committed relationship, but I wasn't blind. Besides, I knew nothing would come of it, even after our break-up. I swore to myself as I watched Ryan leave my house like a sad puppy, that I would focus on myself and wouldn't put up with anything I didn't deserve.

So–respectfully–would I like to climb Townes like a tree? Yes. It had been months and the only action I had gotten came from my purple vibrator.

But I was better than that. The next time I slept with someone, I'd be in a happy, committed relationship.

"You're welcome. Now, shall we try this again? How'd your date go?"

Townes downed the rest of his beer and groaned. "Horrible. She kept asking me if I had any beach properties and said kids were as lovable as fish."

"That's–horrible." I respected people who were child free by choice. There were a lot of reasons that had nothing to do with me, but when people acted like children were the worst things in the world? I couldn't stand it. Townes really

21

dodged a bullet.

"Yeah, so I'm back at square fucking one with no end in sight." He ran his tattooed hands through his hair before burying his eyes in his palms. I stared at him, trying to understand why he was so upset about one bad date. Well, not one; Basil had mentioned Townes suddenly deciding to enter the dating scene. It was weird though, I would think he'd have found someone good enough to see again.

I placed another beer in front of him, and asked quietly, unsure of how he'd take my question, "Can I ask why you're at square one? What's so important about all these dates?"

Townes was eerily quiet, and I was worried he wouldn't be there after I was pulled away to make a few drinks. But I came back and there he was, beer half gone and tired eyes staring at the glass. I leaned in. "I'm sorry if that was too personal of a question, you don't have to answer."

I took a step back, recognizing the tension in his shoulders and agitation in the way he tapped the side of his beer glass. He wanted space. I turned to find another spot behind the counter to take up space when he spoke up.

His voice was raw with frustration, a stark contrast to the words that came out of his mouth. "Thanks for the beer."

4

Townes

Me: *Can you pick Hayley up from dance? Practice ran over, just got out.*
   Marion Fenton: *Are you ever going to not ask? Lol! YES, I'll get her.*

I tossed my phone into my duffle before I finished what was left in my water bottle. Last night left me pissed off, the date was going so well at first. Regan, a physical therapist, checked every box on my list. She liked kids, didn't care about my money, and was a decent person.

Or so I thought. When Hollis's laugh reverberated throughout the bar, earning our attention, Regan scoffed and narrowed her eyes at the blonde. When I called her out on it, she shrugged her shoulders. "Even when I was broke, I would never have shown my tits and laughed for tips. I feel bad for her is all."

It costs nothing to keep your mouth shut, to be a decent person. So, be it because Hollis was my reluctant acquaintance, or something else, I ended the date and got a drink. From there, my mood plummeted. Between the abrupt ending to the date and the unexpected questions from Hollis, I ended up exhausted and ready to go home. To reevaluate how the hell I was going to find a wife…maybe it was time to try a different dating app.

Summer was just beginning, but my mind swam with everything I already had to do; get Hayley to and from dance, practice, find a date before our game Saturday, and find time to sleep. I knew it was a lot, but I also knew I could handle it. I'd been handling it since I was thrust into this situation four years ago. But despite the craziness that comes with caring for a child, I wouldn't change it for anything.

I hauled my bag over my shoulder and started for the front of the training center, when Scottie came up beside me. His red curls stuck to his forehead as he smirked. "You're in an exceptionally bad mood today. I take it the date didn't go well?"

I spared him a glance but kept walking.

"Damn T. Do you want me to ask anyone I know? I promise these girls aren't horrible."

"Scottie, no offense, but I don't think any of the girls you know are good candidates to be my fake wife." I had no qualms with any of the women Scottie knew, but they'd made it very clear relationships weren't in their cards. Besides, half of them pined for other single guys on the team.

He nodded. "Fair, fair. Still, let me see who I can talk to. Hm, I have a cousin?"

I rolled my eyes and broke off from our shared gait, and to my truck. Scottie waved as I pulled out of the parking lot and headed to pick up Hayley. I would take the drive to gain some semblance of control and squash the heat rising up my neck, to slow the pounding of my heart as I filtered through what-ifs. The feeling started a few months after Kennedy's passing, when I was in the thick of figuring out how to care for a three-year-old I'd only seen twice due to scheduling conflicts.

The team's behavioral health specialist identified it as anxiety, but that knowledge fell to the wayside. Hayley, and making sure she adjusted to her new life, came first.

I did read some books though, so I at least developed decent breathing exercises to calm down before it blew out of proportion.

The metal gates opened to the fifty-five and up community, and I slowed down as I drove past the well lived in homes. Almost every home had a pink flamingo planted in the front lawn–because old people loved those things–along with bird baths where the summer birds were enjoying afternoon baths. I rounded the corner and spotted my destination. The house was small, like all the others, but the lawn was free of decorations. Instead, it was perfectly cut and a flower bed sat underneath the front window. I could see the wind chimes from where I parked my truck along the sidewalk.

I stalked up to the dark wooden door and knocked. Small feet pounded on the other side before the door clicked open, and I was being run over by fifty pounds of child.

"Uncle T!" Hayley yelled as she tried to crawl up my body. I let out a huff when my knee ached as I picked her up and walked us both back inside.

"You have fun with Nana?"

Her brown curls bounced as she nodded before she dropped to the floor. She looked up at me with warm eyes. They were the same dark shade of brown as her dads had been, but they held enough warmth to make my chest physically ache. She might have gotten his eyes, hair, and even his darker complexion. But her attitude, kindness, and everything else–that was all Kennedy.

I followed her into the kitchen and found Marion sitting at the infamous glass table. I never questioned what the legs were made of, if they were painted gold, or if she spent her life savings on a single piece of furniture. Hayley ran toward her and grabbed a cookie from the plate.

"Go get your stuff, sweetie," Marion said, patting Hayley's shoulder. Her long braids fell down her back, and tiny gold jewelry adorned each one. Her bracelets created soft sounds as they moved against each other when she placed her arms on the table. Hayley nodded and ran past me toward the spare room Marion and Rodrick renovated into a bedroom for their only grandchild.

Her grandparents were nice people, and we never had any disagreements. That was until two years ago, when Rodrick passed away from heart surgery complications. Since then, Marion had wanted to be more involved in Hayley's life. Sometimes, I couldn't help but wonder if Marion resented the decision their son made. Making me Hayley's guardian instead of them.

Afterall, she and Rodrick had retired a couple years before Hayley's parents passed and they had more than enough time to care for a child. When everything happened, I questioned that decision too, I didn't think I would be able to care for Hayley.

I knew better now that I was the best place she could be. Hell, my home was the only place for her.

Marion rhythmically tapped her fingers against the table and gestured to the cookies when I met her gaze. "Want one?"

When I didn't immediately answer, she continued, "Hayley made them just for you."

I eyed the cookies and gave into temptation. I grabbed one off of the blue plate, and they were still slightly warm when I took a bite. Case—the team's captain—had done a damn good job teaching this kid how to bake, these cookies were delicious. Marion hummed when I grabbed another, and I looked at her with a curious brow. Her voice was gentle as she spoke. "How have you been, Townes?"

I shrugged. "Busy, but fine."

"You know that's not what I meant."

I didn't like the pity that coated her words, and I didn't need it either. She knew the predicament I was in, and had even offered to set me up on a few blind dates. While I knew she would love to have Hayley full time, she didn't want it to be at the expense of me leaving.

She clicked her tongue. "You're putting in a lot of effort for someone you're not going to be with forever. And I appreciate that you're doing it for Hayley, but wouldn't it be easier to just pick someone and get it over with?"

"No? Marion, I can't just pick anyone. You know that."

She shook her head, and a sly smile crossed her face. "You're not looking to fall in love, Townes. So that should really open up your options."

I clenched my jaw and stared down at the chocolate chip cookie. Falling in love had nothing to do with my decision to find a fake wife that lived up to my standards. Besides, even if it did, it wasn't any of her business. I glanced up at her, confused by both her interest in my love life, and how it had anything to do with getting a green card.

"I think you need to worry about yourself instead of my

situation."

Her mouth opened to continue, but Hayley, with her heavy feet, came back into the kitchen. Her backpack was hanging off one shoulder and was stuffed to the brim. She breathed a little heavier than normal and I raised a brow.

"What's in the bag?"

"Nothing," she said too quickly.

I stared at her for a moment before I sighed and grabbed her bag, along with another cookie. Arguing with her wasn't in the cards, I knew who'd lose. "Say bye to Nana."

Hayley ran past me and into Marion's outstretched arms. "Love you Nana, will you tell Papa I said goodbye?"

"Of course I will, sweet girl. I'll see you Saturday, okay?"

"Okay! Oh, don't forget Mr. Cucumber needs dinner," Hayley said, kissing her on the cheek.

I waved to Marion as Hayley grabbed my hand and started leading me to the door. Once we were outside and down the front steps, Hayley ran to my parked truck. Right up to the passenger side door. "Shotgun!"

"Not happening. Get in the back."

She crossed her arms and made an expression with her face. I didn't know what she was aiming for, but it looked like she needed to use the bathroom. "Uncle T, I'm a big girl. And everyone knows big girls sit up front."

I snorted and opened up the back door. "Not a chance, get in." We stared at each other until I finally sighed and kneeled to her level. "How about this, when you're half my height, you can sit up front?"

Her nose scrunched again. "But you're like, twenty feet tall."

"Better get growing then, Haybug," I said with a smirk.

28

Hayley thankfully didn't say anything else as she got into her seat. I shut the door and walked around to the driver's side to get in. She told me all about her afternoon with her grandparents as we drove home. They made cookies, she painted on the canvas set they bought her a few months ago, and she fed Cucumber–the squirrel that ate the bird seed–a few peanuts.

By the time we made it home, I knew enough about the squirrel's eating habits that I made a note to drop off a bag of various nuts the next time she went over. If my niece was intent on feeding the animal, the least I could do was cover the cost of food. I followed behind her as we walked to the door, and stopped short when she let out an excited, "Uncle Scottie I'm back!"

She ran to the kitchen, tossing her heavy backpack to the side, and I placed it in the closet before I continued after her. When I entered the kitchen, I paused. Hayley sat on the counter between Scottie, who was guzzling water, and Hollis.

Why the hell was she here?

She handed Hayley a pancake, and her gaze landed on me. But only for a second before her eyes darted to Scottie. "When did you guys want to leave?"

"Er ee oing?"

"Hayley, manners. Don't talk with your mouth full." I stayed in the doorway, not wanting to get any closer to Hollis. I already had one quick mouthed person to deal with, and my proximity might set her off.

Hollis smiled and soothed over a few of Hayley's wild curls. "Your Uncle Case and Basil invited us over for dinner." I glanced at Scottie, who looked as confused as I was, and Hollis caught on. "Did–did you guys not know?"

29

We both shook our heads and I wracked my brain to try and remember when Case told me about this, but then remembered I'd been so busy lately it was very likely I simply forgot.

Hayley plopped off the counter and rubbed her hands together to get rid of any food left on them. "I'm ready now!"

"I guess I am too," Scottie said, sliding his phone into his pocket. The three of them looked at me, waiting for a response. I hadn't showered yet, my hair was a mess and I needed some medicine for my knee.

My eyes were firmly set between Scottie and my niece, because I was sure Hollis was looking at me in a way that would send irritation prickling down my body.

"Give me ten minutes."

5

Hollis

Townes was pissing me off, like seriously, how hard was it to *smile?* You had those mouth muscles for a reason.

It was also making me mad because of the firm way his face rested, all tense lines like the faint evidence of past joy was too much. I was just past ovulation, and he wasn't doing me any favors looking as good as he did.

So, I tried my best to keep my attention elsewhere, unfortunately for me, my other option wasn't that much better.

Basil and Case sat directly across from me at the buffet style table, leaning into each other like the lovesick people they were. My heart ached for two reasons; I was filled with joy seeing my best friend happy, and because jealousy was a bitch. She had what I'd always wanted and seldom received. The kind of affection that made other people roll their eyes and say *it's so cute it's gross.*

I called things off with Ryan a week before we all went up to Breckinridge and watched as Case proposed to Basil. My heart hurt that whole weekend, and I ate so much ice cream

I became temporarily immune to brain freezes. I didn't tell Basil what happened until after we got home—not wanting to take attention away from her during her special weekend—and after assuring her I was okay, she helped me pack up the things he kept at my house. Then we dropped everything off at his condo, and I assumed that was the end of it.

But things were never easy. My phone buzzed from beside me, and I bit my tongue as I opened the message.

Ryan: *Can we talk?*

Another buzz.

Ryan: *Please Hol, it's important.*

I rolled my eyes and silenced the phone before placing it face down on the table. Albeit a little hard, because Hayley leaned in and loudly whispered, "Uncle T says we have to be gentle with our things."

I smiled and stabbed my fork into my salad. "Your Uncle T also says cookies aren't a good choice for breakfast. Are we really going to listen to him?"

"Don't try and influence her, she knows better." Townes spoke up from the end of the table. Hayley and I shared a giggle before Case straightened in his seat, clearing his throat. I faced him and noticed the way Basil stared. Her eyes wide, and her smile warm as she admired him.

"Thanks for coming guys," Case started, his green eyes darting between us all. "There was something Basil and I needed to ask." He took a breath, and his smile widened. "Would you all do us the honor of being our wedding party?"

I looked at Basil, who had met my gaze with soft eyes. I leaned in closer. "So, this is how you ask me to be your maid of honor? I get ambushed?"

"Case wanted to ask you guys, and don't worry, I have a

girls' day planned for us in a few weeks. That's when I was going to officially ask you."

My vision went blurry, and my voice was hoarse as I placed my hand on hers. "I love you, B."

"I love you, Hol." Her eyes were just as full as mine before we wiped away the unshed tears.

"So," I kept my voice just above a whisper. "Who's Case's best man going to be?" Between Townes and Scottie, I really didn't know who he'd pick, maybe he'd ask them both? They could share the responsibilities, I supposed.

"Can I be the flower girl!" Hayley jumped out of her seat and reached her hand up.

Case smiled and grabbed her hand. "You're jumping the gun Hayley, I was just about to ask you."

She gasped and sat back down, placing her hands neatly folded together in her lap. "Sorry Uncle Casey, you can ask now."

We all laughed, and I caught the way Townes was staring between them. His scowl was a touch softer, but those eyes were as intense as always. I wondered what he was thinking about now, and what had been on his mind since he left the bar last night. I might have tried to ask Scottie what was causing Townes to be more uptight than usual, but he had kept his mouth shut. I mean, he literally went through the motions of locking his lips and throwing away an invisible key.

It only made me more curious and determined to get an answer.

As Case chatted with Hayley, and Basil fought off Scottie from taking anymore of her food, I moved seats. I sat next to Townes and waited until he looked at me. When he didn't,

33

I resorted to the only thing I could think of. I pinched the underside of his arm.

"What the fuck was that for?" He hissed.

"You didn't look at me," I said plainly as he rubbed the spot I attacked.

His scowl returned, and he lowered his voice so we didn't attract attention. "So you had to hurt me?"

"It worked, didn't it?" I smiled.

Townes's jaw ticked, and my eyes dipped to the motion. His beard was growing in, light stubble decorated his jaw. Short enough for me to better gauge his facial expressions, but not long enough for me to wonder what it'd feel like to run my fingers through it.

Not that it was a regular thing that crossed my mind. It was perfectly reasonable to think that of anyone who had facial hair.

I cleared my throat. "About last night–"

"Uncle T! I gotta use the ladies' room."

Townes pulled his gaze as he turned around, but I was already standing. "I'll take you."

The small restaurant we were at was cute, with white linen cloths adorning the tables, and lush greenery hanging from the ceilings. However, it didn't have a family bathroom. I knew Townes's options were to wait in front of the women's room for Hayley to finish, or announce his presence and go in with her to make sure she was safe. It wasn't fair to him, and I felt horrible for all the fathers who faced similar problems.

Hayley hopped out of her seat and grabbed my hand as we walked to the bathrooms.

"Uncle T looked extra grumpy." Hayley found an empty stall, and I waited by the sinks.

"He did, didn't he?"

"It's okay, Hollis. He's always like that, but he's been extra this week."

Was it wrong to gossip with a seven-year-old about her mildly hot Uncle? *Eh.*

"Do you know why he's been so upset?"

She walked out of the stall and straight to the sink. When reaching on her tiptoes didn't get her to the sink, I looked around and grabbed a small stool nestled under a nearby decorative bench. "No, but it makes me sad that he's sad. I give him lots of hugs, but I don't think it's helping."

That made my heart hurt and sink into my stomach as we walked back to the table. Scottie perked up when we sat down, and threw an arm over the back of my chair. "We were talking about going ice skating next week, maybe Monday, you wanna come?"

I gave him my sincerest smile, but shook my head. I had gotten another notice in the mail about a late payment on my student loans, and I already picked up extra shifts so I could get back on track. While going out and having fun with my friends sounded a lot more fun, I needed to get my life together. The self-care routine I'd implemented helped a lot; I was buying face masks and taking up new hobbies. But it was only the first step to finding myself outside of my past relationship, and unfortunately, that came with money problems.

"I appreciate the offer, but I'm busy that day." I hadn't told anyone about the new job, and it was because I knew I'd be offered handouts. My friends were great, better than great actually, which was why I didn't want them to worry. Once I had everything under control though—and that included a new job–then I'd tell them the truth.

"Hollis, are you coming to my uncles' game?" Hayley asked.

I leaned toward her, already smiling. This was their first game in the playoffs, and while I hadn't gone to any other game this season due to work, I made sure to take that day off. "You bet your butt I am."

6

Townes

My ears rang from the roar of the crowd, my body was sore and aching as my teammates barreled me into a group hug. Sweat dripped down my face as I tried to take some weight off my aching knee.

We won our first game in the playoffs, and while I should be as excited as everyone else, I just wanted to go home. Scottie threw an arm around my shoulders, breathing heavily. I patted his back twice and let my arm drop as we started making our way to the locker rooms. When I looked over at his sweaty face, hair sticking to his forehead, I saw it. That glimmer of excitement in his eyes, and I knew mine was still there too. I loved this sport and was more than grateful it was my career, but I also knew mine were a shade darker.

I didn't know if it started with the ache in my knee, or when Hayley asked to start dance classes. But one day, after a winning game, all I wanted to do was go home.

The energy and excitement from the ice followed us into the locker room, and as I was busy untying my laces, someone walked over.

"Are you coming tonight, T?" I spared Riley a glance, his dark hair was cut short in one length, which did nothing to keep the sweat from dripping down his face. Before I could come up with an excuse to leave, Scottie planted himself next to me and threw an arm over my shoulder.

"We're coming Riles. Can't miss out on celebrating such a joyous night, can we Townes?" He patted my back and smiled at me expectantly. As much as I wanted to fight him, I knew it was useless.

Also, next season was my last, and what if we didn't make it this far?

I grumbled and yanked my skates off. "I'll meet you guys at the party."

Scottie and Riley nodded and headed to the showers first. I pulled out my phone and opened the text messages I'd accumulated during the game.

Marion: *Yeah!!!*

Marion: *Great block Uncle T!*

Marion: *Nana said it's bedtime but I can't sleep cause u were jus awsum! I love you!*

I chuckled at the excited messages. Since Hayley was too young for a phone, though it never stopped her from asking, she used Marion's during games. She wanted to come, but I knew how tense the crowd could get, and with the loud sounds and flashing lights, it was easier for her to stay home. Although, I told her if we made it to the finals, then she could come watch.

With damp hair and my duffle over my shoulder, I headed toward the physical trainer's office. Rachel usually was here late, and I knew she'd wrap my knee for me. It was something I'd tried many times and while I was getting better at it, I couldn't beat her. Wrapping my knee would allow me more time to try and enjoy myself tonight, instead of solely relying on medication. The hallway was quiet, almost everyone had left the arena, so I wasn't expecting to run into anyone.

Literally.

"Oof–" Hollis bumped into me, and I instinctively braced my hands on her shoulders to steady her.

Then, I promptly removed her from my body. "Watch where you're going."

She met my eyes, her mouth tugged at one end–the promise of another smirk that would send me reeling. "I could tell you the same thing."

"You're the one who ran into me."

"And given you've almost reached giant status with how tall you are, you should have seen me coming. Ergo, my statement still stands." Her smile was sweet as she batted her lashes.

The way she sparred with me so much recently, admittedly, left me speechless. This was a totally different Hollis than the one I got wrangled into helping move into her house a year ago. A tiny thought passed through my mind, one that had me dropping my hands.

Was she like this with her boyfriend?

I'd met the man once, and it was more than enough to determine I didn't like him. Not that my opinion mattered in regards to who Hollis slept with–but it didn't take a genius to know she could do better.

She cleared her throat, but her smile remained. "Have you seen Case or Scottie? I was gonna get a ride with one of them to the party."

Of course she was going.

39

"Scottie left already, and I haven't seen Case."

"Hm." She pulled out her phone and scrolled for a moment. "If I can't find them, could I catch a ride with you?"

There were a million reasons why I shouldn't let Hollis into my car, and they all had to do with my inability to talk to her without wanting to find ways to shut her up. It was the smallest urge, and one that had crossed my mind too many times for comfort. A quick gentle grab of her wrist before I found the closest wall to pin her too, or a quiet word against the shell of her ear. I shook my head, and furrowed my brows as I tried to convince myself that *those* thoughts weren't sexual in nature. I had no time for that, but they made my hands itch with temptation. How far would I have to go for her to understand that talking wasn't something I enjoyed doing.

Her phone dinged, and I watched her shoulders drop. "They're outside, I guess I'll see you in a bit!" She waved a hand and turned on her heel, leaving me staring after her for a second longer than necessary.

* * *

Scottie fucking blabbed.

I hadn't been at this party for more than five minutes and eight women had made some sort of move. Flipping their hair and bragging how well they can do household chores–amongst other things. Two of them winked with that promise, and I drank my beer so fast my head swam.

"Tell me exactly what you said." I pulled Scottie back by his shoulder, turning him around until that shit-eating grin was directed at me.

"I may have mentioned you're ready to settle down, is all.

That so bad?"

I pinched the bridge of my nose and tried to get a hold of my breathing. "It is when I was trying to be discreet, Scottie. There's a vetting process, too. I'm not going to ask just anyone to be my fake fucking wife."

Scottie's expression softened a fraction before he clicked his tongue. "Hey, man I—I'm sorry. I just want to help is all."

I sighed as I threw my head back to stare at the ceiling. "It's fine," I ran a hand through my hair and stared back at him. "But I need you to fix this, the last thing I want is to have women keep coming up to me all night. I'm tired and don't really feel like dealing with my problems right now."

He nodded, and the motion made his red curls bounce as his eyes flickered behind me and went wide.

"Excuse me, guys?"

As if this night couldn't be going any worse.

Scottie bolted in front of me before I had the chance to turn around fully.

"Hey Hol! Having fun? Have you met Dick? His name's Richard, but Dick is more fun." Scottie threw his arm over her shoulders and dragged her away. Her wide eyes lingered on me, and I knew that for some reason, she wanted to talk. I would thank Scottie later for giving me a little reprieve, but now I'd focus on finding someplace quiet. The sooner I got out of sight of all the women, the better. I made a b-line for the kitchen and grabbed another beer before I made my way to the backyard. The only people outside were along the fence line, playing a very competitive game of cornhole, and didn't even spare me a glance when the door shut behind me. I walked down the stone path that was nestled perfectly in the manicured grass until I was at the old bench Riley placed

41

on the side of his house.

I never questioned why he kept it here instead of the patio he built right after he moved in. But he kept the cushions clean, and that was good enough for me. I leaned my head back and closed my eyes, taking in the warm summer air.

"Ah shit–"

My eyes flew open just in time to see Hollis turning around, a phone to her ear, speaking in a hushed whisper. The words didn't reach me, but when she turned around I could tell something was off. The usual softness to her features were hardened, and her face was flushed as she bit her lip. "Sorry, I didn't know anyone was out here."

I stayed silent, hoping she'd take the hint and walk away. Instead, she walked forward and took a seat next to me. I told myself the only reason I didn't leave was because she was busy staring at the stars. It had nothing to do with the fact I was the tiniest bit curious about what bothered her. I'd seen her plenty of times at the after parties. She was always dancing and trying to beat someone in a drinking game.

She never seemed unhappy before, so why did she now?

But asking that wasn't my problem. She was a grown woman and could handle herself. I had enough on my plate to start worrying about anyone else.

"Penny for your thoughts?" Hollis turned to look at me, but I kept my eyes forward. "I'll tell you mine for a quarter." She adjusted herself on the bench until she was fully facing me. One knee was pulled to her chest, which she rested her head on, while the other swung below. "I'm drowning in student debt, I'm pretty sure my ex-boyfriend wants to get back together, and my parents want me to attend a mandatory family dinner."

42

I was silent as I took all the information in, and finally looked at her. "Why are you telling me all of this?"

She shrugged. "Because sometimes it's easier to get things off your chest when someone else does it first. And, well, I heard what's been said about you tonight, and I think getting the truth from you would be better than anything Scottie said."

"So you came out here, told me a bunch of shit going on in your life expecting me to suddenly open up?" The words came out clipped, but Hollis stayed steady.

Her smile grew softer. "I told you because you're grumpy enough to not give me pity. And it was either tell you or go home right now and scream into a pillow. Which honestly isn't as therapeutic as I've heard."

She went back to being quiet as I stared at the grass. Hollis had no reason to tell me anything that was going on in her life, and I made a point to gloss over the boyfriend comment. I appreciated that, even though it wasn't my business, she trusted me enough to tell me. Maybe I could give her the same courtesy. I might not know Hollis that well, but I knew she wasn't going to tell anyone about my problems.

"Next year, after my contract ends, I'll have a few months before I have to move back to Vancouver."

I kept my gaze forward but was aware of Hollis inching closer to me. "I didn't know you were from Canada."

"It's not something I feel is worth everyone knowing." I took in a breath and kept my gaze forward. "Anyways, moving back was the plan for the longest time. But it changed when Hayley came to live with me. I decided to stay for her. I can't take her back with me because I haven't formally adopted her, which is a whole other process."

The truth got stuck on my tongue as I tried to pry them away. Hollis, thankfully, found the words I couldn't say, and said them for me, "You need a green card, so you can be there for her?"

It was exactly how I would have said it, but hearing the truth from someone else did nothing but make me angry. Because it was so fucking hard, and I was running out of time.

I needed to go home. There was no point in wasting my time sitting here, when I could be working on a solution to my problem. Maybe there was another dating app I could download, or maybe I could–reluctantly–ease up on my requirements.

I thought through how the rest of my night was going to go as I left Hollis sitting in the dark.

7

Hollis

When Basil and I were college freshmen, we were invited to a fraternity party, and because we didn't know any better, we went. Only to be bombarded with attention, and Basil sustained an unwelcomed butt slam from Theodore Anderson—some jock we unfortunately shared most of our classes with.

The next morning—while I was violently hungover—I made a last minute to my project for our communications class. Instead of presenting an argument on the benefits of being vegetarian, how it would affect the food industry if less people relied on meat—I went for something just as relevant.

How men are babies, and should always be scared of their moms.

With Theodore sitting in the front row, I read screenshots of messages I sent to his mother–who was a lawyer–informing her of how her son treated barely of age women on campus.

He left the room when his phone rang, and I received an eighty for the assignment.

All that to say, what I was about to do was a lot less stupid.

I stared at the dark wooden door, my fist ready to make contact as I mentally went through to motions of knocking. Now, if only I could actually do it. Townes's words from the party a few nights ago stayed with me, and my stomach had been tied in knots when I realized I could do something to help. It was crazy, but it would be mutually beneficial. I just had to talk to him.

My hand fell to my side as I took deep breaths, steadying myself as the kiss of warm summer air kissed the back of my neck. All I had to do was talk to him, it wasn't like I hadn't done it before. I stared at the door another moment...

I turned on my heel and started down the concrete steps. There was no way he would agree to my idea, and it was silly of me to even consider it. My foot reached the bottom step, and I paused when the door hinged open.

"Hol? What are you doing?"

"I–uh–you know what? I thought I left something here but remembered where it is at home. I'll see you later, okay?" Without wanting to risk any more questions, I moved to turn around again. But stopped when beads clanged behind Scottie, and Hayley popped her head out.

"Hollis!" She barreled into me hard enough to force the air in my body to escape. I looked down and was met with a smile. "Are you here to come bowling with us?"

Was I there to willingly put myself in a position where Townes and I couldn't escape each other? No.

"Please? We can do boys against girls and kick their butts!" She pointed back to Scottie, who chuckled.

"You can try, but you'll never win. Your uncle and I are master bowlers."

46

Hayley grabbed my hand and stuck out her tongue, a gesture Scottie happily copied.

"Your face will get stuck like that if you don't stop." Townes leaned against the doorway, his arms crossed and his scowl in place. He didn't look at me as he locked the door and walked to his truck. "If we don't leave now, we can't get ice cream afterwards."

"Oh! Hollis, ice cream! You have to come now, please? I'll share mine with you." Hayley didn't wait for an answer before she started dragging me to Townes's truck. But he stopped in front of her, his eyes darted to me and held mine for a fraction of a second before he looked back at his niece.

"No. She's busy. Aren't you?" This time he held my gaze in a challenge, like he was waiting for me to back down. Did opening up leave him feeling vulnerable and unwilling to be in my company more than usual? If so, tough shit.

I smiled down at Hayley. "Actually, my schedule just opened up. I'd love to come."

Townes's scowl deepened and his nostrils flared slightly as we walked to the truck. We piled in, and I busied myself with Hayley to keep my mind off my nagging question for Townes. She asked me a lot of questions on the drive, and I answered every one of them with a smile.

"What's your favorite color?"

"Purple."

"Mine's blue. What's your favorite animal?"

"Hm, probably rabbits. Especially the ones with the floppy ears."

She perked up and placed hands on either side of her face. "Those are so cute! Uncle T, can I have a bunny?"

Townes glanced into the rearview mirror. "No."

"He always says no," she whispers to me. "He said he had alargies."

I snickered and whispered back. "It's allergies."

We settled into silence when she grabbed her purse and pulled out a small sketch pad and a few colored pencils. Scottie was busy on his phone, and Townes kept his eyes on the road. Soon enough, we were pulling into the parking lot of the bowling alley, and Hayley was more than excited to get out. Once the car was in park, she and Scottie got out first. He took her hand and walked with her across the parking lot toward the front doors.

Townes and I followed, and as I reached for the door, a hand stopped me by the shoulder. A tattooed hand reached past me and grabbed the handle. From behind, Townes let out a small noise, urging my feet forward as he held the door open. I looked at him with a raised brow once we were both inside.

"My parents raised a pessimist, not an asshole." Townes shook his head and started walking to the far side of the small bowling alley. Hayley already had her shoes on and was busy typing in everyone's names as Scottie watched. "What's your size?"

Once I told him, Townes walked toward the shoe counter and Hayley jumped in front of me before my eyes could dip down.

"Game time!"

"Okay, who's first?" I looked at the screen where she input everyone's names, and held in a laugh.

Sckoty

Unkle T.

Holes

Hayley

Scottie lined up his shot, and the ball went barreling down the lane more aggressively than necessary. Only to hit two pins. Hayley kicked her feet as he went again, only to hit four more before he walked back with his head held high.

"It's okay Uncle Scottie. You can get better." Hayley patted his arm when he sat next to her.

"I was just warming up." He smiled.

"Sure, sure."

Townes went next, the ball went significantly slower than Scottie's and hit all the pins. Hayley jumped from her seat and met Townes halfway to give him a high-five. He let a smile cross his face, a small one, but it was just big enough to send my heart spiraling. It wasn't fair what he was going through, and that fact only made my heart spiral further.

"Your turn." Hayley leaned in closer and dropped her voice to a loud whisper. "Don't get intimidated, you can totally kick Uncle T's butt." She then gave me a double thumbs up, and I was off. I picked up the pink ball I grabbed from a random rack, I was pretty sure it was too big. My arm hurt as I held it up, and I had to grip it right or it would fall off my fingers. Closing one eye, I did my best to aim, and took confident steps before I let the ball go.

I turned around before I saw how many pins it hit, because watching myself miss all of them would just be embarrassing. The pins echoed behind me, and I finally turned around to find that...I hit all of them.

As I looked at Hayley, a grin crossed my face and I moved toward her outstretched hands. "I told you!" She hugged me, and I ignored the eyes I knew were on me. "Now, my turn."

She steeled herself with determination as she walked to

grab her small, green ball, and then to line up her shot. We were all watching her...

Then collectively dropped our heads when her ball landed in the gutter.

Townes sighed and placed his hands on his thighs to stand. "I'll have them set up the bumpers."

* * *

We got back to the townhouse, and Hayley–coming down from a sugar rush and exhausted after spending hours in the arcade–had gone upstairs to take a nap.

I tried to leave as soon as we got back, deciding what I needed to say to Townes could wait another day, or never, I hadn't decided yet. Scottie though, had other plans, and requested a meeting in the living room. So, Townes and I were forced onto the sofa, where despite sitting on either end, Townes's legs still managed to nearly touch mine.

Stupid, giant hockey players with their stupid meaty thighs.

Glorious thighs.

No, focus.

"My dear, dear friends. Today we are gathered to talk about our problems, and work together to find a solution–"

"Is there a point to this?" Townes interlaced his fingers together as he rested his arms on his legs and leaned forward. I, on the other hand, was perfectly comfortable leaning into the couch, away from him.

Scottie placed his hands on his hips and raised an offended brow. "I had a whole speech planned, you know."

"Well make it short, I've got plans later."

Plans, like another date. Another chance for him to find a

wife so he could stay and take care of Hayley. I mulled over his admission more times than I should have, and landed on an insane–yet completely logical–answer. But maybe it was better if I minded my business, it wasn't like he was going to agree anyway.

"Well cancel them, cause buddy–" Townes shot Scottie a look that perfectly conveyed how much he didn't like that nickname. "I have a solution for you."

Scottie's eyes flickered to me, and a smile followed. It took half a second for it to click before Townes and I were standing, our words tripping over each other.

"Absolutely not."

"Are you crazy?"

Because I was, for even considering it. In my mind, I would bring up the idea to Townes. He'd grumble and cross his arms, but eventually he'd come around. We would get married and he'd be able to stay, and in return, maybe with enough asking, he could help me pay off my student loans. Or, at the very least, he could help me around the house with renovations. I bought a table saw, and even after reading the manual, had no clue how to use it.

"You're both being dramatic, and you haven't even heard what I was going to say."

"Then stop wasting our time and spit it out." Townes's fists were clenched together, but I didn't hear any trace of anger in his voice.

Scottie turned toward him, and his demeanor changed. Gone was the bubbly, joking redhead who had come to be one of my best friends. And in its place was the serious hockey player I'd seen on the ice countless times.

"Townes, I love ya man and there's nothing worse than

seeing you go on all these dates to find someone you'll pretend to like for who knows how long. You don't deserve that, and Hayley doesn't deserve that either. Do you think she'll be happy with you moping around until she's what? In middle school? High school?" Scottie pointed to me, and I did my best to keep my gaze anywhere that wasn't on Townes. His fists relaxed, then formed again as Scottie continued.

"There have been plenty of women you could have asked, but never did because you were more worried about Hayley's opinion than finding a solution to your problem. Well, your solution is standing right there."

I finally looked at Townes and felt my face heating. "I don–"

"Hayley loves Hollis, and she's already part of the group. So, the answer's simple right?"

When Townes stayed silent, and only his breathing filled the living room, we waited. Scottie's face softened, and he shook his head. "We love you T. And we hate seeing the lengths you're going to, to reach your goals. You guys should talk about it, and if it really isn't a good idea then I'll help as best I can."

Scottie walked out, leaving Townes and me alone. I was too worried what would happen if I approached him, so I turned on my heel and started for the door.

"Wait."

That one word had enough authority to stop an army. I stayed facing away from him as goosebumps tickled the back of my neck. Was he considering it?

He didn't say anything else though. No words of acknowledging how right Scottie was, and no questions to help him. So, when the goosebumps disappeared, and I felt him tear his gaze away, I left.

8

Townes

My hands hurt from how hard I was clenching them, and I did my best to take calming breaths. But they weren't doing shit to slow my heart and relax me as I walked up the concrete steps to Hollis's door. I was still pissed at Scottie for suggesting Hollis was the right person to fix my problem. He should have kept his mouth shut and let me deal with it instead of involving someone who had other things to worry about.

Not that I kept track of what was causing her stress, but I was reminded of it every time I caught a glimpse of her at the bar. Realistically, I knew I should have found a different place to go, because seeing her wasn't good for my blood pressure. But I liked the people, and the beer was decent–no reason to change up my routine.

I knocked twice on the dark wood door, hard and firm, and waited. There was a light shuffling before it opened, and I kept my expression blank despite the sight before me. Hollis wore loose fitting jeans and an oversized shirt, her hair thrown haphazardly on top of her head, and paint covered her body. Her arms were covered in different shades of yellows and blues, and she had a streak of red on her neck.

"What are you doing?"

She grinned, exposing those two snaggle canines, and opened the door the rest of the way before leaning against the frame. "The guest bathroom was looking a little dull, and I didn't see the small buckets of paint samples behind me. Wanna come in?" Without waiting for an answer, she turned on her heel and called over her shoulder. "All I have is coffee and flat soda."

"Why's it flat?" My eyes caught yellow splattering the dark hardwood floors as I passed the main hallway to walk into the kitchen.

"I dropped it putting it back in the fridge, but it still tastes fine." She pulled the drink out of the fridge and offered it to me.

I eyed the two-liter and shook my head. "I'm fine."

She shrugged and placed it back in the fridge as I sat at the oak table. My fingers ran over a small divot, and I focused on that spot while Hollis worked on making herself a cup of coffee. I hated how my chest grew tight and my stomach churned as I stared at her backside. I had gone over how I was going to approach this so much it followed me to practice. Nothing ever seemed right either. Even in my own mind I was too harsh, too selfish, and if I were Hollis, I'd turn myself down too.

I took a deep breath and nodded at myself. It was now or never.

"I think Scottie was right, and we should–you know–" I kept my focus on her despite how ragged my breathing had gone. I knew, logically, if I had something tangible to focus on I could get it under control. So, as my nail picked at the wood under my hand, my eyes identified all the colors on Hollis's ruined white shirt, and I listened to the sputtering of the old coffee maker. By the time the smell hit me, my heart had slowed, but my head felt like a tight rubber band was squeezing it.

It took me a while o recognize the headache was only the by-product of my elevated anxiety. By the time I was relatively back to normal, I noticed Hollis hadn't moved–or said anything.

"I didn't come here to beg, so just say no so I can get on with–"

She whirled around and crossed her arms. That fucking smirk on her face. "We should what?"

My scowl deepened.

"You said I knew, but I don't. What are you asking me Townes?" Hollis raised a brow and cocked her head to the side. A few blonde curls escaped and kissed her shoulder.

This was a bad idea, and I was never listening to anything Scottie said ever again. Hollis finished making her coffee and took the seat across from me. Her smirk morphed into a smile, but it wasn't the kind she gave to everyone else. The one that was full of joy and laughter. No, this was the kind she reserved for me.

Coy, mischievous, and unnervingly hot.

"If you forgot then that's fine. I already know, because it's the same thing I was going to ask you when we went bowling. But then of course, I didn't know that's what we were going to do that day. Honestly, I was hoping I could ambush you at home and have this conversation. And then Scottie mentioned it and of course I couldn't bring it up then, because how would that have look–"

"Has anyone ever told you, you talk too much?"

"An old coworker, my ex, and a police officer giving me a speeding ticket." She ticked off her fingers with each example, and we shared a moment of silence when she was done. Then, her voice dropped, but her eyes were still locked onto mine. "I ramble when I'm nervous."

I thought over her spewed words, and was relieved knowing she wanted to talk about this despite her nerves. That would make this conversation go a lot smoother. I tapped the hole in the table again and tossed my head back to look at the ceiling. "I'm sorry if I made you feel bad."

Her blue eyes widened when I looked back at her. "Am I hearing things, or did you just apologize?"

I leaned forward. "I want to make sure we start off on the right foot before I ask you this question." She went quiet, and her small fingers gripped the pink coffee mug. "Hollis, I've run out of time to find a wife. Someone decent enough who isn't just in it for my money, and who likes kids. And you're the only person who fits the bill."

"I find that hard to believe," she said with flushed cheeks.

"You shouldn't. I'm an honest man, Hollis, and I wouldn't lie about something like this just to benefit myself." I waited until her gaze locked with mine. "I'm willing to offer whatever it takes if it means you'll help me."

If Hollis said no…I was fucked.

I would resort to putting up an online ad, or asking Scottie to put me in contact with one of his cousins.

"Whatever it takes?" she asked, and I heard the hesitation in her voice.

"Anything."

Hollis continued staring into her mug, and bit her bottom lip in thought. I stayed quiet and tried to suppress the rising hope in my chest. I didn't like the sensation, because far too often that hope plummeted to my core and left me feeling worse than before. As she continued to think, my finger started tapping harder on the table. When she finally looked at me, I readied myself. There were plenty of things she could ask for; paying her student loans, maybe she wanted a new car, or help with fixing up her house. Whatever it was, I would do it.

"You shouldn't feel like you have to plead with me, Townes. I want to help you, and Hayley. So in exchange for my help"—she smirked and her eyes glimmered with something mischievous—"I want to see you get on one knee and pop the question."

Getting down to ask her to be my fake wife was a bit much, but I was desperate, and would ask her later what she really wanted out of this arrangement. Because I knew damn well she wasn't telling me for her own reasons. The wood chair scraped against the floor as I stood, and I ignored the flash of surprise on Hollis's face as I did as she asked.

I kept my bad knee off the floor as I knelt down. And just because she was being a little shit, I pretended to open a ring box. For the first time since I became Hayley's guardian, my heart pounded with something other than anxiety.

"Hollis—" Fuck, what was her last name?

She raised a brow and smirked. "Shay."

"Right." I cleared my throat. "Hollis Shay, will you marry me?"

Her hands reached out to the invisible box, and she picked up the ring that wasn't there and put it on her finger. She made a show of admiring it before winking.

"Oh, Townes, I thought you'd never ask. Yes, of course I'll marry you."

9

Hollis

I knew Townes needed to get married quick, but I wasn't expecting it to be this quick.

After I said yes two days ago, he went back home and I was emailed a first class plane ticket to Vegas a few hours later. And while I appreciated that he splurged, making the tiniest dent in his bank account, I would have been fine in economy. It wasn't like my fear of flying suddenly went away when I was sipping mimosas and chatting with whatever millionaire was sitting next to me.

I glanced at my phone as I walked through the airport, trying to find my gate before I went to hunt down a coffee. As I got closer, I noticed a crowd of people whispering and sneaking pictures with their phones. Someone important must be waiting for their flight. As I got closer, I started to wonder who it was; there weren't any concerts in the city that I knew of, so it likely wasn't a singer. Maybe it was an actor? There were plenty of beautiful places to film in Colorado–but who could it be to garner that much attention?

I fought my way through the crowd, and stopped when I

came face-to-face with the unexpected.

Half of the Denver Peaks team.

Townes was the only one I recognized, even with his hat covering half his face. He was the only one on the team with heavy tattoos on both arms, and legs long enough to walk across state lines in three steps. As people whispered behind me, I took the empty seat next to him.

"I didn't know you were going to be on this flight."

He didn't say anything, and it didn't look like he was breathing. I bent over to try and peek under the rim of his hat, and yup—he was sleeping. How could he sleep with all these people around? My eyes danced over the dark circles under his, and the way his jaw tensed despite his soft snores. I glanced at my phone; I still had almost two hours before boarding started, and I still needed caffeine. I removed my puffer jacket and placed it on the seat next to Townes, then I set down my carry-on.

The coffee shop wasn't far, but the line and wait time made me question whether the sugary drink I was going to get was worth it. I had moved a few inches when a figure stood behind me, a little too close for comfort. I was ready to whip around and tell the person to back up, but then I saw who it was. "You're awake."

"I was awake when you sat down."

"Then why didn't you say anything?"

Townes glanced up at the menu, and my gaze snagged on his perfect jaw line. I had to look away when he swallowed so I wouldn't follow his Adam's apple. "I was trying to get a few minutes of quiet, but you took too long to get coffee."

I gasped and took another step forward. "Who said I was going to get you anything?"

He raised a brow, unamused.

"Okay, I was going to get you something, you're right." I looked at the blueberry muffin in the display case as we got closer, and my stomach made itself known. I covered it with my hand and sighed. "What kind of coffee do you drink? So I know for next time."

We stepped up to the counter, and Townes surprised me when he ordered one of the sweetest drinks they offered. I got my coffee and the blueberry muffin, and as I went to pay, Townes stopped me. I peered up at him and mumbled, "I got it."

He bumped my shoulder to move me out of his way so he could insert his card. "You've got more important things to pay for than my coffee."

The words hurt more than they should have, and I was ready to say something sarcastic about making my financial obligations his responsibility. However, my mouth stayed shut as I stepped to the side. When he first asked me what I wanted out of this marriage of convenience, I was going to bring up my student loans. Between those and the home repairs I needed to do, I was struggling. But, I didn't want to seem like I was doing this for money. So I kept my mouth shut.

With our coffees and my muffin, we made our way back to the gate. The crowd of people had dissipated by the time we sat down. I bit into the muffin and stifled a small moan. "This is delicious."

Townes stayed quiet and pulled his hat over his eyes as he took another sip.

"So, since you were awake the whole time, you going to answer my question?"

He sighed. "We fly commercial for some games, so I got you a ticket on the same flight as us. It'll save time and confusion when we land."

Oh, that made sense.

"Why'd you get me an expensive seat? I don't know if you've seen my legs, but I don't need the extra leg room."

His eyes dipped toward me, then over my legs. "I've seen them plenty. And, I bought you the ticket because that's where I'll be. The thought of standing around and waiting for you to get off the plane didn't sound appealing. This way, we'll get off at the same time, and can head straight to the hotel to drop our stuff off."

Someone on the intercom spoke, calling people to start lining up and my heart decided to leap into a gallop.

I would be fine. People flew all the time and nothing ever happened.

Townes stood and grabbed his carry-on, then he grabbed mine and jerked his head to the line that was forming. I followed without question, and as the woman checked my ticket, I attempted to take calming breaths. When we got to the door of the plane, where a flight attendant was waiting, I reached out and grabbed the bag slung over Townes's shoulder. He peeked back, but it was too late to hide my panic.

He saw me breathing rapidly, face pale as I stared at the gigantic metal death tube I was about to walk into. We stepped off to the side, and he didn't say anything. Not that words would have made me feel any better, but something about his presence was calming. His eyes bored into my side as I fought to get my breathing under control.

"My Aunt hates flying too. She always knocks on the plane

before she enters because she thinks it's good luck."

I looked at him, and all he did was shrug. It was stupid, but his words helped, at least a little bit. I nodded and we turned back to the plane.

I knocked three times before I boarded.

* * *

After we checked into the hotel, we headed out. Townes had just two hours before he needed to be at the arena to start getting ready for his game. As we walked down the busy, bright streets of Vegas, I kept my eyes glued to the map directions on my phone. I found a small chapel a few days ago and made an appointment. We turned a corner and found the small, white building nestled between two different casinos.

Vegas right?

Townes opened the door, and I stalked right up to the desk where an older woman sat. "Hi, I made an online reservation. Name's under McCarthy."

The woman smiled as she chewed her gum and walked us through what our wedding package entailed. We opted out of the bridal suite, figuring what we wore when we walked in was fine, and finished signing the paperwork. The woman gestured to the double doors adorned with pink and white flowers.

"There's another couple in there right now, but when they're done, feel free to go on in."

We nodded and walked to the farthest corner to wait, and it suddenly dawned on me. We didn't have rings. I knew it wasn't realistic, since it would cause Hayley to ask questions; but I had imagined my wedding day since I was a little girl. Would it be the worst thing to ask for a little something to represent it? A necklace or something else I could wear?

"Are you having second thoughts?" Townes asked with a tight voice.

My stomach dropped at the thought of him thinking I wanted to back out. I met his eyes and smiled. "Not at all. I was just thinking about something silly."

"What was silly about it?"

My cheeks burned, and I dropped my gaze to the white floor. "Rings. I know it's not practical, because Hayley would notice. But—yeah, that was it."

The doors burst open, and out walked a newly married couple. The men wore matching blue tuxedos and were grinning at each other from ear to ear. Once they were out the door, Townes and I filed into the ceremony room. The benches were empty, and the man standing at the altar smiled as we approached.

"Are you both ready?" he asked.

Townes and I shared a nod, and listened as the man went through his rehearsed speech. When he got to the exchanging of rings portion, and we informed him we didn't have any, he kept going. Someone was standing in the middle of the aisle taking pictures. The rest of the ceremony went by in a blur...until the priest said, "You may kiss the bride."

Oh, of course. That was how these things ended, to solidify it or something. I looked at Townes and the way he scowled, as if working up the courage to move first. For someone who was covered in ink, and incredibly tall, you'd think a kiss would be nothing. I cupped his face and ignored the cameraman as he moved in. My fingers tickled over his beard, and my heart thundered as Townes placed his hands on my waist.

In high school, I was a huge theater kid. My sophomore year, I had a huge kiss scene with Joshua Muley, a senior, and I freaked out over it. That was, until I learned a classic trick.

I drew my thumb over Townes's lips as soon as I was close enough so it wouldn't show in any pictures. Then, I closed the distance to complete the perfect, fake kiss.

My new husband looked stunned when I pulled away, I grabbed his hand and pulled him down so I could whisper in his ear.

"You know, people usually smile right after they get married."

10

Hollis

"You're leaving me?" Scottie's eyes widened as if he didn't see this coming.

Hayley placed a small hand on his shoulder, a small attempt to soothe him. "I love you Uncle Scottie, but it's time for bigger and better things."

I held in a snort and turned around to cover my mouth. Once we got back from Vegas two nights ago, we headed straight to the immigration office to start filing paperwork, then we picked up Hayley. When we told her they were moving in with me, she squealed. Scottie had walked in the door an hour ago, and Hayley promptly told him the news.

I couldn't blame her for her excitement, either. She would be getting a bigger room and would have more room for her toys. When I bought the house, I initially had wondered when Ryan would decide to move in. Sell his condo in the city so we could finally live under the same roof like we'd talked about so many times. His excuse of wanting to be close to work, and his love of the city was the major reason we hadn't lived together. Well, that and because his family was incredibly old-fashioned and visited regularly. If his mother caught my toothbrush in the bathroom, we'd have been married faster than either of us could say *I do*.

Scottie dipped his chin to his chest and sighed. "So long as you're happy Haybug, I guess it's okay."

"I'll miss you," Hayley said, her voice sounding tight.

Townes walked past me, his muscles straining from whatever was in the box he was holding. His brows pulled together as he rolled his eyes. "Guys, it's not like we're moving states. You'll still see each other plenty."

Hayley whirled around and placed her hands on her small hips. "It's not the same Uncle T!"

"Yeah! Who am I going to make pancakes for?" Scottie asked, standing to his full height with the same expression as the sassy seven-year-old. Townes stared between them for a moment, blinked, and continued carrying the box outside to his truck.

I laughed and closed off the last box of kitchen supplies that were coming with them, then I walked over and knelt so I had Hayley's attention. "You wanna let Scottie make you some pancakes before you leave?"

She smiled and looked up at the red head. "Can we?"

I went back to grab the box and called over my shoulder, "Scottie, if you can just finish helping her pack her room when you're done? We're going to take some stuff to my place."

He nodded and moved to grab his apron from the pantry. With his hands clasped together, he raised a brow and smiled at Hayley, who was already gathering mixing bowls. "Do you want chocolate chips or blueberries?"

I didn't wait to hear her answer as I continued to the door. The sun was bright when I stepped outside, and it took a moment to recognize Townes waiting by the truck bed. His arms were crossed, and it was hard not to stare as I got closer. He took the box from my hands, and I watched as his muscles worked as he lifted it and set it against the other already loaded boxes.

"Is he going to help her pack?" he asked, inclining his head to the house.

I nodded. "Yup. After he makes pancakes, of course. That'll give us plenty of time to unload and unpack a few boxes.

He gave a curt nod before walking around to the driver's side. I followed suit, and soon enough we were driving to my place. The air was thick between us, and I couldn't decipher if it was because of the summer heat or something else. My fingers thrummed along my knee, until I couldn't take it anymore.

"Do you always drive in silence?"

"Usually."

"Why? That's so lame. Don't you have music or something?"

He shook his head and dropped one arm to rest on the center console. With one hand on the steering wheel, he glanced at me. "Most of the time driving is the only time I get silence for more than two minutes." His eyes dipped over me, and I suppressed a full body shiver. "So, if you don't mind, I'd like to keep that up."

"Okay." I tried to keep my voice level as I smiled. A quiet car, in my mind, was the worst place to be. Singing was how I relieved stress. I could drive forever with the windows down, and the music so loud I risked blowing out my speakers. I could respect Townes and his need for silence.

However, at some point, I started humming. It wasn't

anything specific, just something to fill the silence if only a little bit. The sound wasn't meant to carry to Townes, especially since he had opened the window, I thought he couldn't hear me. Eventually we pulled into my driveway, and he was out of the car before I even unbuckled.

I met him at the door with my own box and shifted it into one arm so I could open the door. I put in an air freshener before leaving this morning, so cinnamon welcomed us when we walked inside. Our plane had gotten in late, so when I came home I hadn't bothered to put any of my things away. My suitcase was still in the entryway, and the dishes hadn't been done. I crinkled my nose when Townes stiffened before placing a box on the coffee table. He took a quick look around before turning around to walk back outside.

"I'll unpack if you start cleaning. If Hayley see's that old cake package on the counter she'll ask for a slice, and you'll be goaded into going to the store for her."

When he was past the porch, I let out a soft laugh and picked up a cup on my way to the kitchen. How many times had he done just that? Gone to the store for the little girl who had him wrapped around her finger?

* * *

Hayley pointed to the bigger of the two guest rooms with a curious smile. "Can I have this room?"

I shook my head as I placed one of her boxes in the room down the hall from where she stood. "That's your uncle's, he already called dibs."

Aside from that particular room being almost the size of mine, and my new roommate being huge and needing the space, there was also a leak in the roof and water accumulated in that room. I had put a hold on contacting someone to come out and fix it, because it was incredibly expensive, and just hoped everything would be fine. Townes and I decided she wasn't sleeping in there until it was fixed. Then, if she wanted to fight Townes for the space they could.

Her mouth went slack jawed as she eyed Townes walking up to her with a box of his own. "You can't call dibs unless everyone is present! You know this Uncle T."

Townes looked at the room for a second, then back down to her. "Dibs."

I laughed as I made my way to the kitchen, ready to make dinner. I opened the fridge and glanced around, then paused when I realized...I knew nothing about Townes or Hayley's food preferences. A few years ago, after a terrible bout of food poisoning, I cut out meat. Which, had never been an issue with Ryan because he ate a plant-based diet. In a slight panic, I moved to the pantry to see if I had anything to make a quick and simple dinner.

Only to find a box of instant rice and a bag of expired lentils. I hadn't gone shopping before Vegas, and binged on takeout when we got back.

Hayley came up beside me and peered up. "Whatcha doin?"

"Trying to find something to feed you guys." I grabbed the rice and shook the box. Shit, it's not even completely full. "Or, we can go out? What do you wanna do on your first night in your new house?"

She brought her hand to her chin and thought for a moment. I watched her in silence and silently prayed she'd opt to get food from somewhere. "Can we get burgers?"

"No, you had burgers last night." Townes walked into the

kitchen, and I shoved the half empty rice box into the pantry. He walked between us and looked around, then moved to the fridge and did the same thing. "I'll run to the store and get stuff for dinner. Hollis, you don't eat meat, right?"

I thought of when he could have picked up on that information, and realized it was probably when we got burritos. I asked for a vegetarian option with mine, and didn't realize he paid any attention. "Right."

"Okay, I'll be back then. Hayley, are you staying here, or do you want to come?"

She took a step closer to me. "Stay."

Townes nodded and grabbed his eyes from the black bowl on the counter. Then, he walked out the door without a word. I sighed, relieved he offered to get dinner, and moved to the living room to sit on the couch. Hayley joined me, grabbing the remote to search for a movie. I wondered what she thought of this whole thing. Townes explained the move to her as Scottie needing his own space, and them needing more. As far as I knew, it was the first time she'd moved–was she really okay with being here? I knew big changes could result in behavior changes in children. Mood swings and defiance in even the sweetest kids. I didn't want to bring that on either of them.

I leaned forward as she kept scrolling through movies. "Can I ask you something Hayley?"

"Yup, I'm a book that's open. Ask away!" Her eyes remained on the television, and I laughed at her choice of words.

"I want to know your honest opinion, okay? Can you look at me for a second?" She set the remote in her lap and looked at me. "How do you feel about moving in? Because I want you to know you can tell me anything. Especially if you're upset, because I know this is a big change."

She blinked, then smiled. "I'm okay. Your house is way cooler than Uncle Scottie's." I nearly sagged in relief knowing she was going to be okay, but then she kept going. "Plus, I've always wanted Uncle Townes to have a pretty girlfriend. Because then we could live together and be a happy family."

All the blood in my face drained, and I was frozen as she clicked on a movie and leaned back into the couch. "Plus, then I can finally have a sister or a brother. But probably a sister cause boys are gross."

This was not how I imagined this night going.

11

Townes

The family room was quiet when Case and I walked in, everyone was hugging their significant others, who whispered uplifting words. Usually when we lost, it wasn't quite this solemn in the room. Because there was always *next game*, but when you lost a playoff game that determined whether your next game would be at the championships, well, it was tough.

Case made a beeline for Basil, who held out her arms and embraced him once he reached her.

"Uncle T!" I let out an "*oof*" when Hayley barreled into me, wrapping her arms around my legs as she squeezed me. "I'm sorry you didn't win, that sucks."

I placed a hand on her head. "It happens, Haybug. There's always next season."

Hollis walked up then, but she stopped short a few feet away with a nervous smile. I met her eyes and tried to search for the reason she was being so distant. It started when I came back from the grocery store. She had been so quiet, more reserved than I knew she could be, and at this point, I was starting to worry. Maybe she was coming down with an illness that affected how often she smiled and laughed. For her, that seemed like the worst kind of sickness.

"Let's get going," I said to Hayley. She nodded and grabbed my hand before she led the way out of the room. Hollis followed at a distance, staying quiet as we made it out to the truck. I threw my bag into the back with Hayley, and when I got into the car, Hollis was staring out the window. The car was quiet as I drove home, Hayley was falling asleep in the back, and Hollis still hadn't said anything.

I looked in the mirror when we came to a red light and saw Hayley with her head rolled onto her shoulder with her eyes closed. "You're oddly quiet."

Hollis turned her head, and double-checked Hayley was asleep. She blew a stray curl out of her face. "I had no choice. Hayley told me she thought we were dating, so I had to create some distance."

The car behind me honked when I stayed at the green light a moment too long. "She thought we were dating?"

She nodded, and my mind reeled with the information, but something didn't seem right. "Did she say anything else? Why didn't you tell her—well—not the truth. But that we were just your new roommates?"

Hollis cleared her throat and looked down at her lap. "She uh—she may have also asked if she was going to get a brother or a sister? Well, she prefers a sister because, according to her, boys are gross. And—I mean—you want to tell me how I should have approached that? I thought you told her you guys were just moving in so she could have more room for her things."

"I did." My hands gripped the steering wheel until my

74

knuckles turned white. Hayley had an active imagination, and I assumed that's what happened. Because I never told her Hollis and I were together, and I never would. So, the fact she told Hollis she wanted a sibling? I had to talk to her. "Look, I'm sorry she said that. I'll let her know tomorrow we're not–you know."

"I know." She thumped her head against the window and let out a small chuckle. "I know I should have told you sooner, but you were so busy with practice, I didn't want to bother you."

I wondered if it also had anything to do with her work schedule too. Because she insisted she didn't want anything out of our arrangement, she picked up extra shifts at the bar. Ever since Hayley and I moved in, one of us has been busy with work. Luckily, she went to work after I got home, so we didn't have to bother Marion about babysitting.

We pulled into the driveway, and I walked around to get Hayley out of the car. She didn't stir when I picked her up, and snored against my shoulder as I walked into the house. Hollis made herself a drink as I put Hayley to bed and got some pain medication. I was halfway to my room when something stopped me.

How Hollis feels isn't my responsibility, but for some reason I felt the need to make sure she was okay. It might not have been a big deal–what Hayley said–but if I knew anything about Hollis, it was that she was more sensitive than most. I dropped my head and walked back down the hallway. When I peaked around the corner, Hollis was stirring something in her mug, and a small smile played on her lips.

"Hollis?"

"Hm?" Her smile was still there as she looked at me, and for a second I reconsidered saying anything. Until she cocked her head and her hair fell over her shoulder. "What's up?"

This woman had given up a big part of her life to help me. So, whether she'd gotten over what Hayley said or not, she deserved an apology.

"I'm sorry again, for what Hayley said to you. I've been on the receiving end of her assumptions, and I know it kinda hits you in the stomach. I'll talk to her."

Hollis's smile widened, but it wasn't full of happiness like all the other ones. This was a soft smile, filled with a kindness I didn't deserve. "You don't need to apologize to me, Townes. At the end of the day, all Hayley wants is a family. I think, maybe, we should show her she already has that." She set her mug down and crossed the wood floors.

"I have this weekend off, let's go do something."

I looked her over, the words she said pressing down on me. All Hayley wants is a family. Had I not done enough? Was I failing at making her know how loved she was, not only by me, but the people I chose to be in her life? Did Case, Scottie, Basil...did they not mean anything to her?

"Townes?" I blinked away the blurry vision to Hollis, reaching out a hand. "Are you okay?"

No. The only thing I have left, that matters, doesn't think what she has is enough.

"Yeah. Goodnight." I turned around and walked to my room. The door shut harder than what the hinges could handle for an older home, but I couldn't bring myself to care.

* * *

"Uncle T, do you think Hollis would like these? They're yellow like her hair, aren't they pretty?" Hayley held up the daffodils and grinned. Hollis had gone to work a few hours ago, and I noticed her to-do list on the counter.

I wasn't being nosey on purpose, but when I saw "bathroom renovation" I got curious. The backyard was one of the things listed, and I figured it was something Hayley would enjoy helping with, especially now that the season was over and I would be home full-time with her.

The flowers were indeed yellow, but not like Hollis's hair, which was a golden hue. Totally different from the bright flowers Hayley put in the cart. She was the one who came up with the idea for a garden bed, so I was letting her pick everything she wanted to put in it. So far, we had three different types of flowers, a variety of vegetable seeds, and a birdhouse. The backyard already had a small, raised garden bed, so I didn't have to build anything.

"Can we get watermelon?" Hayley held up the packets.

"There isn't enough room Haybug."

She nodded and continued on, looking through the other foods she could plant. As she looked, I couldn't help but keep replaying last night over in my mind. I hadn't talked to her yet. We both woke up late, and despite laying awake almost all night, I didn't know how I wanted to bring up the conversation. That was the thing with kids–forming questions in ways that were easy for them to process.

I let her get a packet of strawberries before we headed to the checkout. When we got home, she headed straight to the backyard while I opened the gardening tools. Hayley had her pants rolled up, and the vegetable packets lined up when I met her outside.

"Start digging small holes on that side, and I'll work over here." I handed her the small shovel, and we each got to work.

The sun was beating down on us, and Hayley eventually went inside to get a drink. She brought me back a glass of lemonade and smiled. "Hollis and I made this yesterday. It's so good, like the best thing you'll ever have."

I took a sip, and I couldn't keep it in any longer. Words weren't my strong suit, and while I knew I should be gentle about the topic of family with Hayley, I didn't know how else to say it.

"Hollis told me what you said to her the other night, Haybug."

"Oh." Her smile dropped and her gaze found the ground.

I tapped her shoulder. "Hey, I'm not mad. But I'd like your help to understand what you meant. I told you we were moving in so you had more space, why'd you think Hollis and I were together?"

She took a deep breath and held my stare. "Because I never saw you talk to a girl before, and she smiles a lot when you're around."

"You know I can talk to women and not like them, right?"

"Nuh-uh. Cody Jones at school said boys only talk to girls they like."

I raised a brow. "So does that mean Cody likes you?"

"Oh my gosh. Uncle T, we have a problem cause that boy totally has cooties." She threw her arms at her sides and visibly shook with disgust, and I laughed. So that was where it came from. Well, the girlfriend thing.

"Hayley?"

"Yeah?" Her smile returned and the similarities hit me again. She looked just like her mom did at this age.

I pushed the image out of my mind and my brows grew closer together. "Do you feel like you have a family? With me, your nana, and your uncles?"

"And Hollis, you can't forget her."

I nodded. "Hollis too."

She brought her finger to her chin and tapped. "Hm, I do have a family." I dropped my head in relief. "But sometimes I think having a bigger one would be fun. Amanda in my class has one sister and a brother, and that sounds cool. Do you think maybe one day I can have one, Uncle T?"

The question hit me in the chest, knowing if her parents were still here, she'd probably have more than she could stand. Kennedy had always wanted a big family, and Hayley was the start. My throat constricted, and I coughed away the emotion clogging it.

"I don't have an answer, Haybug."

She blinked, then placed her hand on my shoulder. "That's okay, sometimes answers are hard to find." Her hand dropped, and she turned back to the garden bed. "Now let's go slowpoke, I want Hollis to be so surprised by the pretty garden."

We worked on the garden until Hollis came home, and I made a huge deal about all the work Hayley did. When they went inside to cook dinner, I stayed outside and watched the sunset with an aching heart.

There was nothing more I wanted than to give Hayley everything she wanted, and knowing I couldn't was almost unbearable.

12

Hollis

"I take it things are going well?" I eyed the assortment of flowers Finn sat on the bar top, and his polka dot bowtie. The old man was smitten.

"They sure are. I'll tell you what Holly, Abigail, I think she's the one." The fondness in his words seemed to sooth his wrinkles and brighten the blue in his eyes. I continued wiping the counter as he kept his eyes on the door. This was the happiest I'd seen him since we met. Ever since his wife passed more than twenty years ago, he'd closed himself off to dating. He claimed when she passed she took his heart with her.

I wondered what exactly changed.

Finn turned around and sipped his virgin bloody Mary. "What's new with you, huh? Franny said she and Meghan saw you talking to a rather handsome fellow a few weeks ago." He wiggled his brows, and I chuckled.

"Tell them they need to check their prescriptions. He's just a friend."

"A friend, sure." He smiled and glanced back at the door. I

shook my head and moved to take a couple's order. The word *friend* didn't fit what Townes and me were. To be honest, I didn't know where we stood half the time, despite the fact that we were husband and wife, at least on paper. Most of our interactions consisted of me getting under his skin to get a reaction that wasn't his usual scowl.

That hadn't changed either, just because we now lived under the same roof. Most mornings, we passed each other without a word and in the evenings Hayley was the one filling the silence with stories about her day.

He also hadn't brought up my offer to do something when I got off work this afternoon. I had a rare weekend off and intended to use it to get to know them both better. Because we were stuck together for the next five years.

I handed the couple their shots and started wiping down the counter until my phone buzzed.

Em: *You + Me = Lunch next week? I have a few days off, let me know your schedule? I miss my favorite sister!*

Me: *I'll let you know, I've got some stuff going on.*

Em: *Okay! <3*

Emma had been relentless about finding time to see me, but with everything going on, I hadn't found the time. I'd make plans with her soon, after I figured out how to get Townes and Hayley out of the house, so she wasn't suspicious. Emma was great at a lot of things, except keeping a secret and minding her business.

I kept scrolling through my phone behind the counter and had to do a double take when I came across an email. I scanned it, and attempted to contain my excitement. It was from White River Academy, extending an offer for an interview.

Right before Vegas, I sent in my resume, not expecting much. The requirements for the job were extensive, but I met at least half of them, so I figured *why not?*

My phone buzzed again, but this time, I didn't recognize the number.

Unknown: *Do you want to go ice skating?*
  Me: *With a stranger? No thanks.*
  Unknown: *It's me. You don't have my number?*
  Me: *Townes? How'd you get mine?*
Townes: *It was on your fridge under a list of emergency numbers.*
  Me: *And you expected me to have your number when you got mine from the fridge?*
  Townes: *...we're getting off topic. Ice skating, yes or no?*
  Me: *Meet you at the house when I get off.*

"You talking to your friend?" A gentle voice called from beside me. I glanced up and saw Abigail and Finn with their arms around each other.

I quickly put my phone back in my pocket and resumed wiping the spotless counter. "What's it to you who I'm texting, Abby?"

"Oh dear, I just want to know who it is that's making my favorite employee here smile like that."

I wasn't smiling any kind of way, but by the smirks on both their faces, I could have been wrong.

* * *

I would not fall on my ass.

My hand stayed along the plexiglass as I took a tentative step onto the ice, and almost fell when someone whizzed by me. Once my feet were sturdy again, I started slowly making my way toward Hayley who was using a plastic skate helper. It was nice seeing I wasn't the only one who needed help, regardless of age. I turned it down when Basil offered it to me because I was determined to figure this out without it.

Hayley met me halfway, her curls bouncing around her face under her knit hat. "Have you never ice skated before?"

"Is it that obvious?" Her answering nod was exactly what I expected, and I shifted my gaze forward. "Perfect."

"Maybe Uncle T or Uncle Casey can help. Let me get them for you."

Before I could assure her I was fine, and I'd figure it out on my own, she was off. Townes and Case were waiting by the sideboard for Basil to get her skates on. Scottie had taken a phone call from their coach, and stepped outside where it was quiet. I turned around, ready to try and show them, at least a tiny bit, that I didn't need help.

My left foot touched down, and I gently pushed off the wall and glided. I went back and forth like that, pushing myself with either foot until I was—albeit slowly—moving on my own. It was a lot like roller skating, just more slick.

"You're doing really good, Hol."

"You flatter me, B." I smiled but kept my eyes forward as Basil skated by my side. Townes and I agreed to tell our friends about our arrangement, simply because of Hayley. It would have made things too complicated if they didn't know, and considering Basil and I hadn't had that girls' day she mentioned...

"I have to tell you something, but you have to promise to

83

not freak out. Okay?"

She stopped and tugged on my sleeve. "Is everything okay?"

"You know how I had to cancel our day together last weekend? Because I said I had work?"

"Yeah?" Her brows pulled in.

I waited until Hayley skated past us and was out of earshot. "I didn't have work. I was in Vegas with Townes, and we got married at a little chapel thing. Which, by the way, did not have an Elvis impersonator. And I did it because he's not renewing his contract and needed a green card so he could stay Hayley's legal guardian."

I saw the hushed word vomit land on Basil, and her eyes shifted as she took everything in. She looked back to Case, who seemed to be getting the same information from Townes.

"Are you serious?"

"As serious as our marriage license."

She blinked. "But–ho–wh–why? Why on earth would you do that Hol? What happened to not needing a man, and finding yourself? And of all people, why Townes?"

"Is there a problem with him I don't know about?"

"What? No, Townes is great. But he's just so–him. I'm pretty sure his scowl reaches his brain, it's so deep."

We started skating again, this time in silence as the news sunk in. I knew she was going to react this way, out of love of course. As best friends, we wanted what was best for each other, and I knew deep down she was right. Townes wasn't someone I would have seen myself with romantically or platonically. But he needed help, and that was something I could offer.

"Hey Hol." Case skated up to Basil and placed his hand on her back. "Mind if I steal her?"

"Of course," I said with the brightest smile I could muster. Basil's eyes were full of confusion as she and Case skated away.

Townes quickly took their place. "Well, that went."

I started skating again, but on weaker knees. "What did Case say?"

"He understood, I think he was a little upset I didn't tell him beforehand though. But I didn't want him to keep it a secret from Basil, she deserved to hear it from you."

That made sense, considering last year Case kept his ex-girlfriend and public cheating scandal from her. I reamed him for not telling Basil what was going on, but I understood he wanted to protect her.

Townes and I skated together, neither of us saying anything as Hayley continued to make laps around us. I was just getting comfortable going a little bit faster when Scottie finally came up to us.

"Sorry that took so long. Now, who's ready for some fun?"

"What did Coach want?" Townes asked.

"Ah, he was oddly interested in my living situation since you moved out. He said something about someone needing a place to crash."

Hayley skated up to Scottie, her smile wide and full of excitement. "Uncle Scottie! Can we do super skate?"

Townes tensed beside me, but it went unnoticed by Scottie as he grinned at Hayley.

"What's super skate?" I asked.

Scottie peered up, and he winked. "Just watch."

He grabbed Hayley's hands and started skating backwards. It was slow at first, but as more people exited the rink, he went faster. Until he was whizzing past us, and Hayley's giggles echoed around us.

Ah, so that's super skate.

I peeked at Townes, who hadn't relaxed. His eyes were locked onto the two of them as she rounded a corner, and he tensed even further when Hayley's skate angled inward. My hand reached out before I thought better of it, this wasn't the first time I'd seen him like this, but I wanted to help in any way I could. My finger tapped the back of his hand, but he still didn't' look at me.

"Can you help me?"

"Hm?" he asked, eyes still forward.

Determined to pull him out of wherever his mind went to, I grabbed his hand. "I need help learning how to stop so I don't have to use the wall. Please?" Still no reaction. "Or are your skating skills not up to par with everyone else's? It makes sense, goalies don't really do anything. I think I'll go find Case–" I moved to pull away, but his hand tightened around mine and made me pause.

"You think goalies are out there to look pretty or something?"

"Well, you certainly do. I don't really pay attention to the other ones." My face burned as I tried to move on from the confession. "Now if you won't teach me, I'm sure I can ask someone." I smiled and turned away.

Townes gently pulled me to the side, and under his breath mumbled something I couldn't understand. He pulled me into a quiet spot and crossed his arms. "How much do you know about ice skating?"

"You watched me, right? I think that should answer your own question."

He sighed and rubbed a hand over his face. "I want you to

skate to me."

"You aren't going to move, are you?" He was standing closer to the center, so if I fell I'd have nothing to grab onto. He shook his head and held out his hands. I looked at him for another second before I pushed myself away from the wall. At this point I was pretty confident that I could move without problems and skated toward him on steady feet.

"Good, now to stop, I want you to crouch down and angle your feet outward."

I did as he instructed, but when I angled my feet nothing happened. "I'm still moving."

"Lean back a little bit, plant your skates into the ice."

I felt ridiculous. My skates cut into the ice, and I stopped right in front of Townes. I smiled, proud of myself for picking it up so quick. "I did it!"

"That's called a snowplow."

"Can you teach me how to spin?" I asked.

Townes blinked, and I could have sworn a smile tugged on his lips. "Let's get you comfortable with stopping and moving before we add anything else into the mix okay?"

Scottie skated toward us with Hayley, who was beaming. "Did you see how fast I was?"

"It was a little too fast if you ask me," Townes said. His attention was on Scottie who didn't seem aware of the daggered look aimed at him.

"Ah, it's fine. No one was hurt."

"But she could have been, go slower next time."

We all watched as Townes made his way to the sideboard, stepping up to exit the rink. Hayley, who wasn't aware of her uncle's quiet outburst, was on her way to grab the skate helper. Scottie, shook his head and the looked at me. I couldn't place the emotion on his face.

"Is he okay?" I asked, never taking my eyes off him.

"He can get really protective over Hayley sometimes. I don't completely understand it to be honest. He'll be fine."

Scottie skated off, but my eyes stayed on Townes. I wondered if his protectiveness over that little girl was connected to how he spaced out sometimes. If it was, I could help him.

That seemed to be the only thing I was good for when it came to our relationship.

13

Hollis

Emma showed up with a tray of gluten-free cookies. Neither of us had any allergies, but she swore they tasted better.

Yes, she was the weird one.

Townes left with Hayley twenty minutes ago, and I spent that time emotionally preparing for my sister. She kept hounding me for a day to meet up, so I settled on the last day she was free.

She spun into the house, throwing off her jacket and shoes without a care for where they landed. "Your house is so stinking cute!"

"Thanks Em," I said as I picked up her things and set them on the entry table. As she walked around, I felt myself stiffen. I spent all last night putting away any evidence I wasn't the only person living here. Hayley's toys went into her bedroom, Townes's journals were shoved into the hall closet, and even found all of Hayley's colored rubber bands off the floor and put them in my bathroom.

Now, the only things Emma could see were the torn-up

baseboards and paint swatches on the walls.

Emma turned, and despite her slightly darker hair and brown eyes, we looked identical. Sometimes I wondered if it made my shortcomings harder on my parents. How could two children, who looked so much alike, be so different? We were raised under the same circumstances; being thrown into every activity imaginable from sports to theater, and expected to play one instrument well before we started middle school. Yet, only one of us went on to do anything worth bragging about.

Then our brother came along, and they felt redeemed.

My sister's blue summer dress fluttered around as she sat on the couch and patted the space next to her. "Come. Sit."

I sat next to her and took the cookie she offered. "So? How have you been? I haven't seen you in months. What's up with that? Too cool to see your sister?"

"More like you're too cool for me, Em. Besides, you could have come to see me too. You're not the only one who's busy" I appreciated that I could be honest with her without risking hurting her feelings.

"Okay, okay we've both been busy and suck at making plans with each other. How's that?"

I smiled and leaned in to wrap my arms around her. "I missed you."

"I've missed you too. Now, fill me in on everything. But start with Ryan, last time you brought him up you guys were in a fight? How'd that end up?" Her nose scrunched with the question, and I chuckled. Emma never liked Ryan.

I wiggled my brows. "Actually, I broke up with him a few months ago."

"Fucking finally!" Emma pulled me into a tight hug, then

pushed me out and held my shoulders. "Now that you're single, I know the perfect guy. He's in the orchestra, but he's not snobby like everyone else."

"Hold on, hold on. I'm not looking to date right now."

Was I going to tell my sister it was because I was already married and would be off the market for the foreseeable future?

Absolutely not.

Emma raised a brow and looked me over. "Who are you and what have you done with Hollis?"

"I mean it Em. I broke up with Ryan so I could focus on myself and what I wanted. I need time to do that. Can we change the subject?"

Her brows furrowed, and she got off the couch to grab another cookie. I followed her into the kitchen and leaned my hip against the counter. She gestured with her free hand. "Continue."

"Well, I have an interview for a new teaching position in a few weeks. So, if all goes well, I can stop working at Al's."

"I can't believe you decided to work there full time when you got fired. You know Lionel or I would have helped out while you looked for a better job."

Emma was always pushing me to do my best, and in her mind, bartending wasn't it. "Okay, if you're going to be judgy we won't talk about me anymore. What's going on with you?"

Her shoulders tensed, it was so slight that if I hadn't grown up with her, I would have missed it. Emma wasn't great at keeping secrets, and I was determined to find out what hers was. "Em?"

"Weren't you planning on doing something with the spare bathroom? I wanna see what you've done so far." She brushed past me to head toward the hallway.

I rolled my eyes and followed after her. "I haven't done much excep–"

"What's this? Man soap! Hollis!" She darted into the small space and came back out holding a bottle of men's body wash. It definitely wasn't mine.

I opened my mouth and gaped. "I uh–I can't smell nice? The men's stuff last longer anyways." I tried to brush it off, but Emma wasn't having it.

"Oh my god! You little liar. Ms. Oh, I'm working on myself, you're totally seeing someone!"

I grabbed the bottle from her hands and stared at her with burning cheeks. "I can't smell like sandalwood?"

"Oh, you can. But that bottle says sea salt."

The burning in my cheeks traveled down my neck and crept across my chest. Emma leaned in, and smirked. "I bet your sheets smell so good, huh Hol?"

"Emma!" I turned and slammed the bottle on the counter. "I am not seeing anyone."

If she found out about Townes and Hayley, then she'd tell our parents. And it would add yet another reason why I was the family disappointment. Their daughter married, not because of love, or out of wedlock, but because she felt bad for someone she barely knew. They wouldn't understand, so they'd never find out.

Except maybe in five years, after they pestered me about giving them another grandchild.

I stared at my sister, who looked me over with an unbelieving eye. She threw her hands up and turned back to the kitchen. "Fine, fine. Keep your secrets."

"Thank you. Now, we've talked a lot about me today. We

can either put on a movie, or I can grill you about your life."

She plucked a cookie from the tray. "I get to pick the movie this time. Do you have any popcorn?"

"Yeah," I said as I watched her disappear around the corner. Emma was being, well, odd. On a normal day, she loved talking about work and the things she got to do. Like traveling, or meeting amazing musicians. So, the fact she kept dodging what was going on was different, but unlike her, I wasn't going to press. I made the popcorn and settled next to her before I pulled the blue throw blanket over my lap.

She laid her head on my shoulder as she pressed play and sighed. "We should do this more often."

I tried to sort through what my typical year would look like now that I had two other people to think about. How would we coordinate school pick-up and drop-off? What would our routine look like when the season started again, and Townes would travel? I didn't think I would have that much time to see my sister, but I'd make it work anyway.

"Yeah, we should."

* * *

"Okay, if you just–come–off–I won't throw you into the woodchipper." I tugged again on the baseboard, and in retrospect, it was probably because of my grunting that I didn't hear Townes walk through the front door.

"Ow!" My finger caught a stray nail on the backside, and I shook my hand to try and ease the pain. "Okay, that's it, you're going into the woodchipper, and I'm burning your remains afterward." I readjusted my grip on the wood and got ready to pull.

"Do you always talk to yourself like this?"

The wood snapped against the wall as I let go and whirled around. My heart thundered as I stared at the door frame Townes was leaning on, a bag in his hand. "You scared me!"

"I can see that. You hungry?" He lifted the bag and his eyes shifted to the bottle still on the counter. "Why's my body wash there?"

I moved and grabbed the bag from his large hands before starting for the kitchen. "Because my sister is nosey. She grabbed it and got super interested in my sex life, so I told her it was mine to get her off my back."

"Did it work?" Townes asked as he grabbed plates from the cabinet.

I shrugged. "I don't think so, but she didn't bring it up again."

Townes stayed quiet as I filled our plates with the rice and curry he picked up. Then, we moved to the table. "Where's Hayley?"

"She's staying with her nana for the week."

"Ah, gotcha."

I hadn't met the woman, and my stomach suddenly churned. How much did she know about what we were doing? Would she tell Hayley? I shoved food into my mouth to distract myself. There was one more month of summer vacation left, I'd have to meet her at some point.

"When she gets back, we're taking a trip."

"A-a trip? Like, all of us?"

Townes kept his eyes on his food, but nodded. "We take one every year right before school, and Hayley requested we make it a group thing this year."

I had a feeling if Hayley hadn't made that request, he never would have brought it up. It made me smile, seeing how much of a soft spot he had for her. She seemed to be the only person who he'd do anything for. "That sounds fun. Is it a camping trip or something?"

"Or something. There's a campsite that's exclusively treehouses, I already have them booked."

"Okay, yeah cool. I'll get the time off."

"Okay."

We fell back into silence, but this time it didn't bother me. For once it didn't seem like Townes was uncomfortable being in my presence. I smiled and found myself looking forward to this little trip.

14

Townes

I found one of Hollis's to-do lists sitting on the counter under a pile of junk mail; finish spare bathroom, find pest control stuff for garden, find a guy to fix leaky roof. Nothing had been checked off, and I was positive it was going to take her a long time to actually complete the tasks.

With Hayley at her nana's this week, and with Hollis picking up extra shifts so she can come on our camping trip, I was left at the house with nothing better to do. So, when Hollis left for her afternoon shift, I ran to the store and got the supplies I needed.

Growing up, Kennedy and I would spend hours with our dad every week working on the house. Our parents bought their fixer-upper when we were in elementary school, and by the time I left for college the place still wasn't finished.

When I got home, and placed the new tools in the garage, I got started. First with the baseboards in the bathroom that Hollis was working on last night. I knocked them loose with a hammer before prying them off, then I started removing the water damaged drywall. Hollis never mentioned what her vision was for the bathroom; if she simply wanted to fix the damage and restore everything, or completely gut it and do a full renovation. So, I stopped at the drywall.

Once I patched the holes, I took everything out to the garbage cans. I made a note to ask her what she wanted, so I could restore the bathroom as soon as possible. With the bathroom mostly done, I headed outside to start on the garden.

Insects had invaded and were eating away at the vegetables Hayley planted. I sprayed the pest control, then I installed a trellis where the strawberries had started to grow. When that was done, and my hands were covered in dirt, my body covered in sweat from the sun; it was time for a break.

I pulled out some leftovers and reheated them for lunch, then stared out the window.

One summer, Kennedy and I were supposed to be collecting food from our mom's garden. She was in charge of the berries, and I was supposed to get the vegetables. We ended up staying outside all day and ate all the berries. Looking back, I think she did it because she knew our parents were on the verge of divorce. They always fought when we were at school, and often times one of our parents would be missing from dinner. Due to work, or other obligations that didn't matter.

It was why Kennedy made sure to have family dinner every night when she got married. It didn't matter if her and her husband were fighting. They'd either talk it out before or after dinner.

I pulled myself from the memories as I ate lunch, then got into the shower. I eyed the body wash that sat on the counter, and my mind went to what Hollis said last night.

My sister grabbed it and got super interested in my sex life...

I supposed all sisters were the same. Kennedy would ask me constantly if someone I was seeing was serious or not. She wanted a sister, and I was her only chance at getting one.

The shower was quick, and the heat eased the ache in my knee from being on the ground most of the day. I wrapped the towel around my waist and opened the door–only to collide with Hollis.

With wide blue eyes, she peered up at me. Then flushed beat red when her eyes dipped down. She covered her eyes. "You're naked!"

"No I'm not." I moved her aside and continued on to my room.

But, Hollis being Hollis, fucking decided to follow me. "You can't just walk around like that Townes! Other people live here too!"

I grabbed the doorknob, then turned around to face her. Her eyes were still covered, and the redness had traveled to her chest. "And you weren't supposed to be home. I'm not indecent Hollis, I've got a towel on. Is this your way of telling me you've never seen a man shirtless? What about that boyfriend you had for so long?"

She dropped her hands, but her eyes remained firmly on mine. "Of course I've seen shirtless men. However, none of them have looked like"–she motioned to my body, and I raised a brow–"like that."

"Like what?" I quipped. Then, I paused. Was I flirting with her?

It had been so long since I had done it, that it seemed foreign. Hollis had a tendency to get under my skin with her bubbly persona, but this time, I wanted to get under her skin. It was kinda...fun.

Hollis's eyes dipped down, and I didn't know if they traveled intentionally. I knew what she was staring at, all the tattoos. I started getting them in high school. First on my torso where my parents couldn't see, then I moved outward. The designs weren't anything special, except for the moth on my hand that had my sister's birthday hidden in the left wing.

Hollis cleared her throat, and looked away, her cheeks still flushed. "Just—be more careful next time. I could have broken something walking into you, you know." She stalked past me on her way to her room, and I fought a chuckle as her door slammed shut.

I changed quickly, refreshed and ready to continue working on the list. When I walked back out into the main living area, on my way to the garage, Hollis was peering out the window. "Did—did you clean out the garden bed?"

"Yeah." I kept walking to grab the box knife I set back in the toolbox. A small corner of my room had started to discolor, and I wanted to see the extent of the damage. If I could fix it myself, I would.

Hollis started to follow me. "Why?"

"Because it needed to be done?"

Her nose scrunched as she followed me back to my room. "You didn't have to do that you know. I was going to get to it."

"Well pick something else on your list to work on then."

"I will if you stop picking stuff."

I whirled around to face her, she peered up at me, and the tint of pink still painted her cheeks. I didn't understand why she was being so difficult. "No."

"Why not?"

I sighed. "Why do you want me to stop?"

"Because it's not your responsibility to fix things around here." Hollis sucked in a breath as the last word left her lips, as if she just exposed a secret.

"What is my responsibility then?" I stepped closer. "You didn't want anything out of this arrangement, and now you're telling me to not work on the house Hayley and I will be living in for the next five years? That doesn't make any sense."

I watched as her nostrils flared, and focused on the light dusting of freckles that danced with the movement. "You're not going to explain your thought process are you?"

"No."

"Okay." I shut the door in her face and turned around to focus on the task at hand. As I cut away the drywall, revealing the damage underneath, I wracked my brain as to why Hollis was being so difficult.

The woman who rambled nonsense when she was nervous, was ready to bury a dead body for her friends, and marry a practical stranger just because she was being nice–why couldn't she tell me what was going on inside her mind.

Not that I cared, but it would make our camping trip a whole lot less awkward.

* * *

"Basil also wants you to know that if Hollis comes to her crying, she's going to put water in your gas tank."

Case was going over all the threats Basil had made if I fucked things up with Hollis. Which included: putting glitter glue in my beard, water in my gas tank, and hurling annoying Canadian jokes my way that only involved moose and maple syrup as the punchline.

"Tell Basil she has nothing to worry about, okay?"

"Oh, believe me, I have. But she's protective." He eyed me with a smirk. "Like someone else I know."

I made a noise under my breath and glanced toward the rear-view mirror. The girls took Case's car, and Scottie bailed at the last minute. Apparently, our coach wanted him to meet the guy that was going to room with him—for some odd reason.

"So, tell me, how have things been? Hayley been adjusting okay? Have you?"

"Everything's fine."

Except it wasn't. Hollis hadn't really talked to me since that small argument, so it had been a quiet week. I kept working on small projects, and when Hollis got home, she'd grab food and head to her room. It was the quietest that house had been since we moved in, and I didn't like it.

We got to the campsite just before dinner, and unloaded the cars.

Treetop Taverns was a luxury campground, but instead of lodges or small cabins, they had treehouses. When Hayley requested everyone came along, I went ahead and booked two of them. However, they were on opposite sides of the campground due to the limited availability.

Basil came to stand by Case as we looked at the first one. Nestled in a giant oak, its dark brown exterior matched the tree perfectly. A balcony sat over a carport, and a ladder led right to the front door. This was the bigger of the two, and I assumed Basil was going to claim it.

"So, what's the sleeping situation?" I asked, turning toward them.

I expected some kind of proclamation of "boys vs girls" but

she…surprised me with a smirk. "Case and I will take the other one, you guys can have this since it's bigger."

"You sure?"

"Totally. Hayley wanted to room with Hollis, but I wasn't going to give up time with Case." I rolled my eyes as her smirk grew. "So, I guess your options are to sleep outside, or make up with Hollis so you don't spend the night on the couch."

I wasn't going to tell her this treehouse had three beds.

"Fine. Go unpack and we'll meet at the lodge for dinner."

"Come on sunshine," Case said as he looped his arm through hers and dragged her away.

Hollis was fixing Hayley's hat when they drove off, and Hayley came running. "I want the big room!" She started climbing the ladder.

"And I want the room with the queen-sized bed. See you up there," Hollis said as she walked past me with her bag.

It was the most she'd said to me all week, but I was determined to get her to say more. Now that Hayley was back at the house, we weren't going to pretend to be anything but normal.

Otherwise she'd notice, and our disagreements weren't her problem.

15

Hollis

The listing totally lied to me.

Three beds, one king sized bed and two queens. That's what was listed. So, imagine my disappointment when I walked into the second bedroom, and there was nothing except an empty bedframe.

I walked around the treehouse to find the other bedrooms. The big one, in fact, did have a king-sized bed, but the other had a full. I didn't know who was in charge of creating the listings, but they needed to relearn what bed sizes were. Townes walked into the treehouse and headed toward the open door that led into the first bedroom.

"You've got to be fucking kidding."

"Uncle T you swore! That means you have to put a dollar in the swear jar." Hayley ran up to him and held out a small plastic jar. It still had remnants of a peanut butter label, but at least it looked clean.

Townes stared at her. "What are you talking about?"

"Well, I hit my head and accidently said a bad word. So, Nana made me make a swear jar. It doesn't have anymore

103

money, but you swear. A lot, kinda, so I knew I could get a lot of money." She jiggled the empty jar. "A dollar please."

"Haybug I'm not giving you money because I said a word."

"But it's a bad word, and Nana said you have to pay up." She tapped the jar again, and Townes looked at me.

I tried not to laugh at the exchange, I was still upset. With myself of course, for not being able to explain to him why exactly I was so upset earlier this week. I school my expression and raised a brow. "You heard the lady, put a dollar in."

"You're so helpful." Townes reached into his pocket and placed a bunch of coins into the jar. "Now, if you don't mind, I'm going to make a phone call."

As Townes walked outside, I went and helped Hayley move her things to the smaller bedroom. She threw her head back and dragged her feet. "But I called dibs."

"I know, but unfortunately, if your uncle sleeps on this tiny bed he's going to be grouchy all weekend."

"But he's always grouchy," she said, throwing her bag onto the mattress.

I raised a brow. "Do you want it to be worse."

"I guess not. When is dinner?"

I tapped against the door frame and smiled. "Let me see what your uncle's doing and then we'll probably get food after, okay? Go ahead and unpack your stuff."

I left the room to let Hayley get settled, and went to place my things at the end of the couch. I sat down and threw my head back to stare at the wood ceiling. This week had been horrible.

I got off early because business was slow, and I wasn't expecting Townes to be home. So when I ran into his tanned, very muscular and tattooed chest, I didn't know what to think. Sure, I had thought about Townes shirtless a few times, but my imagination didn't live up to reality.

But when I glanced outside, and looked at the garden, all delicious memories of the half-naked goalie emptied from my mind. I hadn't asked him for anything, because I didn't want to burden him. Yet, there he was doing housework, because...why?

The last thing I wanted was for him to feel obligated in some way. He and I needed to reevaluate what we expected of each other.

Townes walked back inside, shaking his head as he ran a hand through his hair. It had been a couple weeks since he last cut it, the dark brown hair was long enough to hold onto.

If, of course anyone needed to—not that I wanted to or thought too much how it would feel. Or wondered what kind of sounds that would elicit—

"Hol?"

"What?" I blinked, suddenly feeling ridiculous about the thoughts I was dragged away from.

He sighed. "They had to replace the old mattress, and I guess the delivery truck was delayed. It'll be here some time tomorrow, so we just have to figure out tonight."

I threw my legs onto the couch. "I've got the couch."

Townes didn't argue as he went to move his bags into the room with the king-sized bed.

Hayley came bolting out, changed into a yellow summer dress with sheer sleeves, and white tights. "I'm ready for dinner!"

"Okay, uh, Townes? Where are we eating?"

He came out of the room and put his phone into his back

pocket. I hadn't paid too much attention to what he was wearing earlier; but now that he was in front of me, and I was determined to not be upset over his overbearing actions—I looked him over. His dark blue jeans were relaxed against his muscular thighs, and his white shirt—still crisp despite the three-hour car ride—draped over his hips.

"The campsite has a communal lodge and a cafeteria. We can eat there, or go grab food from whatever's close by."

We both looked at Hayley. She tapped the point of her chin, then threw her finger into the air. "Cafeteria!"

Townes let us go first down the ladder, then it was a quick walk to the lodge. Inside, past the check-in counter, was a huge room filled with tables. It was evident the space had multiple uses, but for now, it was filled with people. From families with young children to couples of all ages. Hayley quickly found Basil sitting at a large round table, and ran to meet her. I smiled at her when she glanced over, then held in a giggle when she looked at Townes. Her brows furrowed and she stuck her tongue out, which only made Townes shake his head.

I told Basil about our argument the day after it happened, and initially she was upset with Townes for making me upset. However, when I explained I was upset due to my people pleasing tendencies, and refusal to ask for help for fear of being seen as incapable, she changed her tune. I went to her place that night after work, and we watched movies while we worked through my emotional reaction.

I was still working on how I felt, and how I could do better in the future.

Townes was right behind me as we walked around and grabbed our food. When we got to the table, Case was sitting there, trying to convince Hayley that broccoli wasn't actually a tiny tree.

"I know, but it just looks like it. It's not a tree."

"Mm I don't know Uncle Casey. Cause in school my friend has a tiny tree, it's called a uh–Bansi and it's so small."

He chuckled. "It's called a Bonsai, and yeah those are trees. But broccoli isn't one, I promise you."

Hayley narrowed her eyes, then held out her pinky. "Pinky promise it's not?"

"Pinky promise." Case interlocked their fingers, then slung his hand over the back of Basil's chair. "So, what are we doing this weekend? Just relaxing?"

Townes started. "Well, I–

"Uncle T signed us up for activities! I asked to zipline, but they didn't have it, so I get to climb rocks."

"They have rock climbing?" I asked.

The Great Tree Lodge had a variety of outdoor activities you could sign up for, for those who enjoyed being active on their getaway. However, I hadn't realized I'd be forced into physical activity.

"It's more of an outdoor wall, it's nothing big," Townes said.

"Anything else?" Basil asked.

"No, that was the only thing. But feel free to see what there is to do. I'm not doing anything more than that besides relaxing."

She narrowed her eyes and looked at me for a second. "Sounds like you just want to become a hermit to avoid someone."

"B," I said, tapping her forearm with my fork.

Townes stared at her, but remained quiet. Case and Hayley's conversation had moved to the different kinds of grapes, and what made certain ones taste like cotton candy. The chair rubbed against the floor as Townes pushed off the table, then walked out. I looked at Basil, who seemed remorseful.

"Why are you being mean?"

"Because you guys haven't been under the same roof for a month, and he's already made you upset."

I threw my hands out to the side. "That's not his fault."

"Yeah, but he could have talked to you by now. He hasn't though, and I don't like it."

"Basil, not everyone is open to talking about their feelings."

Case was great, fantastic even about being open about how he felt. IF he fucked up, he was the first person to apologize. I however, knew better. "You're right, but could you give him a little grace? For all you know, he's felt bad all week that we fought but doesn't know how to approach the topic."

She stared at me for a minute before leaning back in the chair. "Fine. I'll ease up. But if he's going to keep shutting doors in your face cause he's upset we're going to have a problem."

Case leaned in to place a kiss on her temple, then took Hayley's hand to head to the dessert bar.

I pushed back from the table. "I'm tired. You guys mind dropping her off when you're done?"

"Of course, Hol."

I nodded and pushed my chair in, then I headed back to the treehouse. When I got outside my face started to warm. The air was still as the sun started dipping below the tree line, and the only sounds were bugs and the dirt under my shoes. I followed the path until it split into a narrower one, and I walked until I came face to face with the ladder.

What was I going to say to Townes?

Hey buddy, sorry for being so weird about you working on my house. I just grew up having my wants pushed aside because my two siblings are over achievers and our parents' primary focus was on them. So, I hate asking for things because even if someone says yes, it makes me feel icky.

I stared at the splintered wood and sighed. "Maybe sorry will be enough."

"So, you talk to yourself now too?"

I jumped at the deep voice and turned to see Townes standing there. "Where did you come from?"

"The car. I left a bag in the trunk." We stared at each other for a moment. "Up, down? Either way, could you move?"

I huffed and climbed the ladder. Townes was right behind me, and brushed past me toward the room when I stopped him. "We should talk."

"I'm tired."

"Okay, well, you can go to sleep after."

He rolled his eyes and turned to face me. The bags under his eyes were dark, and a part of me felt bad for keeping him up. "About earlier this week."

"Look Hollis, this isn't something I want to discuss with you when I'm about to pass out. I'm tired, we can talk about this later."

"But I don–"

He scoffed. "You're so pushy you know that?"

My cheeks heated. "And you're an asshole, you know that?" I mocked.

The crease between his brows deepened before he hauled the bag over his shoulder and moved to walk to the room. I sprinted across the room before he could shut the door, and walked inside to the room. I whirled around to peer up at him.

"Hol–"

"I'm sorry I overreacted to what you were doing. It's stupid, but believe it or not, despite my flare for helping others I have a hard time accepting it. It's why I didn't want anything in exchange for helping you." He blinked and that crease softened a fraction. "I'm trying to be better about asking for help, so bear with me for a while okay? In the meantime, I don't care what you do around the house. Hell, I'll even show you my Pinterest board so you can go all out."

I sighed and smiled to myself. "That's all I wanted to say. Goodnight."

As I walked out of the room, Case was coming in with a sleeping Hayley in his arms. He smiled, and a dimple showed. "I'll put her down, is Townes already asleep?"

I thought of those dark circles, and how he swayed just before I left the room. If he wanted to talk, he could do it tomorrow. Or, never at all. I said all I needed to.

"Yeah, he is."

16

Townes

All I could see was Hayley's bright purple top, and I was about to burst a blood vessel. Logically, she was perfectly safe tethered to the man at the bottom, but with each slip of her foot all I saw was her falling and getting hurt.

It didn't matter that this was the third time she had gone up the damn thing, I was still anxious.

"Guess who got the job!" Hollis squealed as she came to stand next to me.

I kept my eyes forward and remained quiet. Her nervous ramble was still being thrown around in my mind, and I hadn't been able to come up with a response yet. I wasn't great with dealing with my own confusing emotions, let alone others, but I didn't want to say something prematurely and make her feel worse. So, I was glad for the distraction, it gave me more time to think.

"For that school, right?" I asked.

Hollis mentioned an interview before we left, and I knew it was at a school, I just didn't know which one. She nodded and peered up at me with a smile. "Yeah. White River Academy, it's a private school and I'm so excited!"

Of all the...

"That's where Hayley goes to school," I informed her, my eyes staying on my niece as she smacked the red bell at the top of the wall.

"Oh, I know. It was one of the first things Hayley told me one of the first nights I went over to grade papers with Scottie. According to her, the math is too hard and her English teacher is mean for not letting her eat fruit snacks in the middle of class."

I blinked and was stunned into silence. *So much for teaching Hayley about safety and keeping things to herself.*

It had been very important to me that Hayley kept certain things to herself like where she lived, went to school, and how often she went to her Nana's. I wasn't sure if I was upset that she gave the information freely to Hollis, or if because I hadn't realized Hollis knew more about Hayley than she let on.

Hollis's smile widened, and I wanted to look, it was an urge that came out of nowhere. I found myself seeking them out, and it needed to stop. My focus needed to be on Hayley, not on some pretty smile.

"Well, that's super convenient then huh? I was worried about how it would have worked out with Hayley. But, since we're going to the same place, it's just one less thing to worry about."

"Yeah," I said as my eyes remained on Hayley as she reached the ground.

She removed her helmet and harness before running up to us, her curls bouncing. "That was so much fun! Uncle T, you should do it!"

"I don't think so," I said, crossing my arms. I was a big guy, and frankly, I didn't trust anyone here enough to trust them with my life. Besides, this kind of stuff fell under the part of my contract to not do dangerous shit.

"You're no fun," Hollis said before kneeling to look at Hayley. "I'll do it."

"Okay! Come on, I'll show you the harness. They have a pink one."

Hollis laughed as she was dragged back to the wall. I watched as she approached a younger employee and went through the safety speech Hayley had gotten. This guy though, was younger and the hairs on my neck raised as Hollis got into the pink harness and went through checking the ropes.

"Okay, so the ropes course they have is a no-go," Case said as he came to my side. He and Basil had wandered off to try some of the other activities this place offered.

"What happened?" I asked as Hollis placed her hand on the first fake rock.

"Basil fell into some poison ivy, she's back at the treehouse googling cures. So we might need to head into town a day early."

I nodded and moved my gaze to Hayley, who was climbing again. "That sucks."

"Yeah," he said before we descended into silence to watch the girls. "So, how have things been?"

"What do you mean?"

"Well, Basil told me you and Hollis got into it."

I had to keep from rolling my eyes. "We always get into it."

He smirked and shook his head as I looked on. Hollis had

already reached the top, and had hit the red button. My eyes shifted to the bilayer, and my heart leapt when I noticed he only had one hand on the rope. He wasn't looking either, so when Hollis threw herself from the wall…

He scrambled and Hollis yelled as she plummeted toward the ground. The man tried to grab onto the rope, but he was too late and she was already more than halfway down. It wasn't enough. Even though he managed to slow her down, she was already too far down for it to matter. I watched as she hit the ground, then let out a pained yell.

Case and I were rushing toward her before the employee could register what had happened.

Hollis was sitting on her butt, and was bent over grabbing her ankle. I was at her side, my hands hovering over her, unsure exactly where all she was hurt.

"Fuck, fuck, fuckitty fuck," she mumbled through deep breaths.

Case was yelling something at the employee behind us as I reached for where Hollis was grabbing. She smacked my hand away, but kept her head down. "It's fine, just give me a minute."

"It might be broken. Let me look at it."

She kept shaking her head, and I could see she was still crying. Hayley ran up and was on the verge of tears. "Are you okay?"

"She's fine Haybug. We're going to get her back to the treehouse. I need you to stay with Case though, and you guys can meet us when he's done."

"Okay." She nodded. "Just hold on Hollis."

Hollis chuckled and wiped a tear before she looked at Hayley. "I'll be fine."

"Can you walk?" I asked.

She looked unsure, so I grabbed her hands and pulled her up. When she was upright, she gently placed weight on her foot, then winced. I glanced behind me and was grateful I could see the treehouse from where we were.

I didn't ask to carry Hollis, because I knew there was a good chance she'd fight me on it. We didn't have time for that, I needed to get her back so I could get a better look at her ankle. I turned around and placed her hands on my shoulders as I knelt down. "What are you doing?" Hollis asked.

"Get on."

"Townes, I'm too big for a piggyback ride."

"You don't think I'm too old to give one? Come on, we're getting you back so I can look at your ankle."

I felt her hesitate for a second before she gave in. She wrapped her arms around my chest and did her best to get settled on my back. I molded my hands to her thighs as I stood, and made sure she wasn't going to fall before I looked at Case. He gave me a reassuring nod, and we started walking. Hollis tapped her fingers on my chest as I led us down the dirt path, then sighed into my ear.

Goosebumps littered my skin, and I hoped she wasn't looking at my neck to see them. "Well, today took a turn, didn't it?"

"Obviously," I said.

She didn't say anything for the rest of the walk, and I focused on the rhythm of her heart against my back. When we got to the ladder, Hollis cleared her throat. "Are you sure you can climb that with me on your back?"

"Of course I'm sure," I said before I started climbing. Hollis's grip tightened around me, and she held in a gasp as she locked her ankles together as best she could. Once we were inside, I dropped her on the couch and went to the small kitchen for ice. She had pulled her jeans over her ankle by the time I returned.

"You need to elevate it to keep the swelling down. Does it feel weird?" I asked as I started grabbing pillows.

"Just hurts. Is it broken?" She propped her ankle up on the small pile of pillows and hissed when I set down the ice.

I shook my head. "I'm pretty sure it's a bad sprain. In a little bit we'll try and have you put weight on it again. If you can't then it's broken."

"Okay."

I walked to my room and got the pain medication I kept in my bag. Then, I got a glass of water and held them both out for Hollis. She stared at me before slowly taking the water and pills. "Thanks."

"You sound like you're unsure if I'm trying to poison you."

She finished gulping her water and peered up nervously. "After last night, I'm just—confused."

"About what?" I asked as I sat on the floor.

Hollis looked up at the ceiling, then after a moment, rubbed her palms into her eyes and groaned. "I can't read you Townes. I don't know if you're still upset with me, or what. You walk around with that scowl, and I don't know what's going through your mind."

I blinked and tried to see where she was coming from. Was this because I didn't seek her out to continue our conversation?

"Hollis." She looked at me, and I got lost for a second. In the pretty shades of blues in her eyes. I cleared my throat. "I'm not upset. You had—uh—fuck. I'm not good at this. Point

116

is, I'm not mad and we can move on."

Her shoulders relaxed and she looked back at the ceiling. She was doing a lot of apologizing, and I hadn't done any. While I was still trying to process how she felt, the least I could do was own up to my mistakes.

"I'm sorry."

"For what?" she asked with wide eyes.

"For slamming the door in your face. I could have handled that a lot better."

She smirked. "Oh, that's nothing. One time I shaved the hair off my sister's doll, and I woke up with a new haircut. A door in the face is nothing."

"I shouldn't have done it, plain and simple." I could be an asshole sometimes, but that was crossing the line. I still felt bad for it.

The door opened, and we turned to see Case, Basil, and Hayley walking in. Basil was covered in a thick white cream, and Hayley was running to Hollis's side. "Do you have to cut it off?" she asked.

"What?" Hollis laughed.

"Your foot. When I get hurt, Uncle Scottie sometimes says we might have to cut stuff off if it doesn't stop hurting."

Case snorted, and I pinched the bridge of my nose. I'd have to talk to Scottie about reasonable reactions to children getting hurt. Hollis laughed and shook her head. "It's just a sprain Hayley, we don't have to cut anything off."

"Okay, good. Oh! I have a doll that'll make you feel better. Let me get it!"

We watched as Hayley ran to her room, then I turned to Case. "What happened after we left?"

"They shut down the wall, and the employee went with his

manager. They were both apologetic and said they'd contact us for a refund or something."

Basil tapped her skin in various spots, like how I would do when a new tattoo was healing and itchy. "First the poison ivy, now a sprained ankle. I don't know about you guys, but I don't wanna stay here another night."

"Yeah, I think we're going to head home early," Case said.

I nodded, and as heartbroken Hayley would be about cutting our weekend short, we'd leave too. With Hollis having a sprained ankle, she'd be limited to the treehouse until she felt better to walk. "Us too."

"Ah, but I wanted to sleep on the new bed," Hollis said with a pout.

"You can sleep all you want in your own bed when we get back to the house, how about that?"

Hollis narrowed her eyes. "Fine."

"I found it!" Hayley said as she ran out of the room. She gave the doll to Hollis and took in all of our solemn faces. "What's wrong?"

"Haybug, we gotta go home early."

"But we still have another day," she said, tears already forming.

I knew she was going to be upset, so I had to think of something to make it worth it. Kids loved rewards and treats, and I knew exactly what kind of treat she'd like. "I know, but to make up for it, we can go shopping."

"Shopping?"

"Yeah, back to school shopping. Sound good?"

"Yes!" She jumped and ran back to her room.

Hollis stared at me and smiled. "I betcha I can guess what her favorite thing to do is."

I didn't say anything as I thought of yet another way Hayley was like her mom–then pushed away the happy memories. Because that was all they were, and I'd cherish them in private. Otherwise, Hollis might see me reminiscing and would start asking questions I wasn't ready to answer.

17

Hollis

I yawned as I creaked the front door open and walked inside to Townes and Hayley, still in their pajamas. My feet dragged along the cool floors as I made my way to the kitchen, and Hayley gave me a smile over her pancakes.

"Uncle T made you pancakes," she said before impaling her own stack.

I looked around the counter and my stomach grumbled at the sight. Townes hadn't just made pancakes, he made an entire buffet. Eggs, hash browns, and he even made the carrot bacon I kept in the fridge. I made a plate and got my coffee started before I sat between them. Townes had his arms crossed as he eyed me. "You were up early."

"I wanted to start getting my classroom set up, and I wanted to do it before we went out."

"Where are we going?" Hayley asked with a smear of peanut butter on the side of her mouth. Townes motioned to it, and Hayley promptly wiped her face.

"Shopping, remember?" He raised a brow and crossed his arms again.

Hayley's face lit up just like it did when we told her in the treehouse a few days ago. I laughed and moved to finish making my coffee. It was cute seeing how excited she got over the idea of shopping, because I was the same when I was younger. One of the nice things about living in my sister's shadow, was I got to tag along whenever she needed a costume for a show. Our mom usually got me something too, because then it would make for nice pictures. I didn't really care, because I got a pretty dress.

Hayley finished her food and grinned. "When can we go?"

Townes looked at me, as if expecting me to answer. I cleared my throat. "Let me finish eating and change, then we can go."

"Okay!" Hayley ran to place her plate in the sink, then disappeared to her room. Townes leaned back in the chair, and for a second I thought he was going to ask about my ankle again. It felt better the day after the accident, but he kept asking. His brows pulled tight and he opened his mouth just to close it. Then, he got up and walked away.

I finished eating and went to find something to change into. This morning, I threw on sweats and a T-shirt, but I knew we'd be outside most of the day and it had gotten hot. Without putting much thought into it, I grabbed the first dress I found, and styled my hair into a low bun to keep it off my neck. When I walked back out into the living room, Townes was standing there, waiting to leave.

"We match!" Hayley yelled as she came up beside me. She was right, we did match. Both of our dresses were blue, and had white flowers scattered over them. Though mine were bigger, and her straps were thicker. She looked to her uncle. "See? Aren't we pretty?"

When I looked at Townes, my smile dropped. His gaze was heavy on me, making my skin tight as my heart skipped. Those brown eyes of his, caressed my body, and I suddenly became overly aware of how short my dress was. Chills took over when his eyes met mine again, and I saw a hint of something I couldn't explain.

It was over quick though when Hayley ran past us and opened the door. "Can we get ice cream too?"

I cleared my throat and started toward the door. Townes stayed where he was, his gaze locked on me as I brushed past him. But I kept my focus on Hayley, because if I acknowledged the *something* in Townes's eyes, I would start to think he thought of me more than his fake wife.

We piled into the truck and headed to one of the outlet malls. Hayley was in the backseat, and was trying her best to convince Townes she needed a pet.

"You're not getting a pet, Hayley," Townes said as he parked the car.

"I'll take care of it! I promise." Hayley had her hands clasped under her chin, and batted those small brown eyes at her uncle. The plan was to take Hayley back-to-school shopping, and I found it hilarious she was trying to convince Townes to stop by the animal shelter when we were done. According to her, it would help her be more productive, but Townes wasn't buying it.

"We've talked about this before, we're too busy for a pet." Townes had gone around and opened her door.

She hopped out and crossed her arms. I gave her a kind smile and reached out to take her hand. Townes walked ahead of us as she slipped her hand in mind and huffed. We exited the parking garage, and a gust of wind blew in our direction.

I let her go so I could hold my dress down.

Of all the days to lose my damn shorts.

"Where to first?" I asked once the wind died down and we continued to the shops. Hayley skipped between us, humming an unfamiliar tune.

Townes shrugged. "I usually just follow Hayley."

So, that's what we did. Hayley led us into almost every store, and only got the things she needed. New clothes for school with accessories to match. Townes, for the most part, stayed outside under the shade and on his phone since I was more excited to shop with her. Each time we left the store, he'd hold out a hand and take whatever bags we had.

By the time we stopped for lunch, Hayley had enough bags for Townes to warrant a quick trip to the truck to drop them off. Hayley and I waited at an outdoor patio for an ice cream shop; she was enjoying a mint chocolate chip cone, and I had a milkshake.

"This is so much fun," she said around a bite.

I smiled. "Does your uncle usually let you get this much stuff?"

"Yeah, but I don't need a lot. Just the cool shoes that everyone is wearing and pants. Did you know all my pants last year had a hole in them?"

"I believe it, my pants never held up either."

Hayley nodded and continued eating, while I kept glancing to where Townes disappeared. After a few more minutes, he finally appeared, and had a bag in his hand. He pulled out the seat between Hayley and me, and placed the bag on the table.

"What's that?" Hayley asked, already trying to take a peek.

Townes's brows were creased as he pushed the bag toward her. "Just something I thought you'd like."

She squealed and finished the rest of her ice cream before wiping her hands and pulling the bag into her lap. Townes and I watched on as she pulled out a pastel purple dress. It was adorned with flowers at the bottom and had bow tie straps.

"It's so pretty!" Hayley threw herself at Townes and wrapped her arms around his neck. "Thank you, thank you, thank you!"

Townes hugged her back, and had the smallest smile when he pulled back to look at her. And all I could do was stare. I'd never seen him smile before and I just wanted to pull the memory from my mind and frame it in the most masculine picture frame I could find.

"I think it's about time we head home. Your Nana's going to meet us so she can get a long weekend in with you before school starts."

"Nana?" Hayley faced me, her smile was wide and infectious. "Hollis, you get to meet Nana! She's super nice."

My stomach twisted, but I kept my smile even. I didn't know anything about her nana, or if she was aware of what Townes and me were doing. Regardless, I wanted her to like me. Because I was sure Townes didn't need her nagging in his ear about the woman he kept around Hayley.

Townes didn't look at me as we finished our ice cream and headed back to the house. It wasn't until we parked in the driveway, and Hayley had bolted out to meet her nana, that he spoke. "Marion's aware of what's going on. So don't feel awkward about anything."

"Has she told Hayley?" I asked.

Townes looked at me, and I saw the way his jaw tensed. "No. And she won't. We all want what's best for her."

I nodded and opened the door. I walked up the driveway and came face-to-face with the woman. Her hair sat close to her head in tight curls, and her ears were decorated with jewelry. She smiled, a tight expression that had me questioning how genuine it was, and when I approached, she didn't advance for a hug. "You must be Hollis. Hayley has told me so much about you."

"Hi, it's nice to meet you."

She yelled to the space behind me. "Hayley girl, go get your stuff so we can go, okay?"

Marion and I then exchanged a quiet, tense goodbye before I walked up the steps and into the house. Townes was in the kitchen, and I could hear Hayley getting her things together. All the shopping bags were on the table, except for the one he brought to Hayley. She came running out of her room while I was filling a water bottle, and gave each of us a hug.

"I'll miss you! Bye!" she said before she ran out the door, leaving Townes and me alone in the kitchen.

Silence echoed around us for a few minutes, before I decided I had other things to do. I could work out in the garden, or finish painting the spare bathroom. I cleared my throat and smiled. "Well, I uh, have stuff to do."

Townes stopped me as I went to turn, and when I faced him again he seemed nervous. I didn't know that was possible. He held out the bag, and I took it with confused brows. "Need me to put this in her room? Give me her other bags and–"

"Look inside," he said.

"Okay?" I put down my water bottle and opened the bag. I expected to find the dress Hayley pulled out earlier, and wasn't sure what Townes was having me do. So, when I spotted a dress that was a shade darker than Hayley's, my skin tightened. Did–did he get me a dress? I pulled it out of the bag, and saw it had the same floral pattern as the smaller one. Townes held my gaze as I looked at him, and I was frozen.

"What's this?"

"I saw it on my way back, and Hayley was so excited you guys were matching today so–yeah. If you don't like it, take it back."

I smiled and placed the dress back in the bag. "That's super sweet of you."

"I did it to make her happy, that's it." His eyes dipped down, and for some reason, I didn't think her happiness was the only reason he bought it.

I took a step back. "Well, that's still really sweet Townes. Now, I'm going to change. I'm still at Al's til next week." I turned and started walking out of the kitchen, and as I walked to my room I couldn't shake the feeling I was being watched.

18

Townes

Hollis placed her hands on her hips, and tapped her foot as I contemplated the list in front of me. Her last night at the bar was two days ago, and she had two weeks before school started. Yesterday over lunch, she mentioned having a bonding day. Something about getting to know each other better, so things felt less awkward in the house. Which I didn't understand, she was short, liked to walk around in a purple robe, and thought everything was funny.

What else did I need to know about her?

I finished looking at the list, then raised a brow as I pushed it back toward her. "Literally none of this sounds enjoyable."

"Don't be a Debbie downer, you'll have a good time. I promise."

"How can you promise that?"

She smirked. "Cause you'll be with me. Duh."

I pinched the bridge of my nose and huffed out a breath. I had already planned to get more things done around the house today before Hayley came home this weekend. The drywall in my room wasn't looking any better and I had no clue where the damn leak was, not to mention the fact I needed to look at the hot water heater.

"Going bird watching and eating cheap, gross food doesn't sound fun, Hollis."

"Oh my god. We're going on a hike and getting pizza afterward. Why are you making it sound worse than it is?"

I held her blue eyes and tried to bring myself to explain all the reasons I didn't want to hang out with her. Not that there really were any. We were stuck together, and it was inevitable we'd learn more about each other. The main reason I wanted to stay home instead of doing things with her, was because of that damn sundress. There was something laced in the blue fabric that kept pulling my attention to her waist and tanned legs.

I wasn't blind. Hollis was beautiful, but it was just another reason I couldn't let myself get too close. Hayley was still my priority, I couldn't let myself get distracted with thoughts that made my pants a little too tight.

"I'm not giving you a choice, anyway." Hollis's smirk morphed into an innocent smile as she turned and walked into the kitchen to fill a water bottle.

"What's going to happen if I don't go?" I asked as I followed her. I should have kept my distance, but something was pulling me closer to her. When she turned around, she had to tilt her head back to peer up, but she didn't falter.

"I'm going to tell Hayley how mean you were when she was gone."

"You're using my niece to threaten me? Seriously?"

She raised a brow, surprised. "Are you telling me that seven-year-old doesn't terrify you?"

I was quiet for a moment and went through all the possible things Hayley would say to me if she found out I was refusing to hang out with Hollis. Then, I dropped my head and sighed. "I'll meet you at the truck."

"Okay!" Hollis skipped past me and went to grab her phone from the table. She paused for a second, and her brows pulled in tight as she looked at something on the screen. "For fucks sake," she mumbled before heading to the door.

I took my time getting my things before I followed her outside, when I locked the door and turned around, I heard something. A man's voice that was eerily familiar, and I had hoped it wasn't who I thought.

"How many times do I have to say I'm sorry? I love you, Hollis. Please."

"Ryan. I'm not having this conversation with you again, and you certainly can't just show up whenever you feel like it," Hollis said.

I could see her hands shaking slightly as I walked up, but she didn't see me first—Ryan did. He stood straighter and puffed out his chest as if to appear bigger. I didn't know the man, but when I met him that one time after a game, I knew I didn't like him. Then, he went and left Hollis at the after party—I ended up taking her home and that drive was painfully silent as she cried with frustration.

"What are you doing here?" he asked.

"I could ask you the same thing," I said as I walked to Hollis's side.

He glanced between us, then narrowed his eyes. "I came to talk to Hollis, so, do you mind leaving?"

I glanced at Hollis and saw the way her cheeks flushed. "Sure." If he wants me to leave I would, just not by myself.

Hollis and I had plans. I placed my hand on her back and led her to the truck, ignoring Ryan's protests. We got in, and he had already gone back to his car before I pulled out of the driveway. Then, Hollis surprised me by lightly smacking the dashboard.

"I can't believe he showed up like that." She turned to me. "I'm sorry you had to deal with him."

"Has he been bothering you lately?"

She shook her head. "It stopped for a while, but recently it's picked up again."

"How recent?" I asked.

Hollis smiled, and I wasn't sure why. What did I say? "You know, for someone who didn't want to spend time with me, you're asking a lot of questions." She leaned in. "Let's play a game."

"I don't like games."

"I think you'll like this one, cause it might make me less annoying," she teased. I knew she was joking, but hearing she believed I thought she was annoying stung a little. Sure, she talked a lot, but so did everyone else I knew. However, if I confessed that, she might not tell me about this game.

"What did you have in mind?" I asked.

"Twenty questions."

I raised a brow, but kept my attention on the road. "Aren't we a little old for that?"

"So what if we are? We can get to know each other, and maybe the questions can be a bit more meaningful since we only get twenty each."

I nodded in understanding. She had a point, and the sooner she used up her questions the sooner I could go back to pretending she got under my skin. The truth was, the past few months hadn't been at all what I expected. Hollis was an easy person to live with, and respected boundaries.

"Rules though," she started, holding up her fingers. "They have to be meaningful questions. The whole point of this game is to get to know each other. Second, you have to answer the question. It doesn't matter if it takes a day or two, it just has to be answered. And last, we each get one free pass to use on any question. Sound good?"

I nodded and made the final turn that led to the hiking trail. Everything she said made sense, and I could play along. We parked and started walking to the trail head. Hollis smiled and started walking ahead of me.

"First question for you then, when's your birthday?"

That question caught me off guard. Not because of its simplicity, but because it reminded me of the worst day of my life. "How is that a meaningful question?"

"Because I need to know when to celebrate."

"I don't celebrate my birthday."

She turned around and started walking backwards. "Well, I'm going to, so just tell me."

I glanced down and saw a huge dip in the path. Hollis was headed right toward it, but she was still facing me. I lunged and grabbed hold of her before she could trip over it and turned her around. She looked down and hummed. "That could have ended badly."

"You should be more careful. I don't feel like carrying you back to the car."

I walked past her, but not before I noticed the small smirk on her face. "Ah, but you give the best piggyback rides." She caught up to me and poked my side. "Now, birthday. Cough it up."

131

I contemplated telling her the truth, that I didn't celebrate my birthday because my sister died the day before. That I'd spent the last four years holed up dealing with crippling grief on my birthday, so there was no point in celebrating. As I stared at her though, a small kernel of anticipation buried into my chest. What if this year was different? Maybe I could pretend everything was okay. Maybe I'd give Hollis a chance to replace that terrible memory with a good one. But I should give her a chance, because I wasn't strong enough to do it myself.

I sighed and started walking again. "December 27th."

Hollis was satisfied with that answer and smiled in response. I took the opportunity to ask her something I'd been curious about the day she showed up alone to Case's proposal. "When did you break up with your boyfriend? And can I ask why?"

She almost tripped again, and I wanted to say something. To tell her to be careful, because my knee was acting up, and if I had to carry her to the car, it would just make it worse. A nervous laugh escaped her, and she continued forward. "Do you want the long version or the short version?"

"Whatever you want to give me," I said, surprised by her willingness to talk.

"It was a few months ago, actually, it was the night you found me and Scottie grading papers. He was mad I didn't go to some dinner that *he* planned, knowing I was busy that night. I basically got sick of coming in second to his work. He never made time for me, or even made me feel like a priority when we were together. So, I broke up with him. And I've been happier since, I've been learning what makes me happy."

I forced myself to continue walking, even though I didn't

like what I just heard. "How have you found time to figure that out?"

Had she been seeing someone? We had never had a discussion about seeing people outside of our arrangement, and I would never tell her she couldn't. Besides, it wasn't like I'd be able to make her happy, even if that was something I wanted to do.

Hollis shrugged and turned to face me. Stopping this time to make sure she didn't accidentally trip again. "I'm still working on it."

19

Hollis

We got home just after lunch, and I was only a tiny bit closer to understanding Townes.

I had technically only asked him three questions, and only got one straight answer. So far, I knew his birthday, how many long-term relationships he'd been in, and that he had an older sister. When I tried to ask more questions about her though, he changed the subject.

There was a reason he stayed quiet, and I was determined to find out what it was.

Townes placed the groceries we bought on the counter, then went through the mail. His brows pulled tight when he came across one piece in particular, but then changed his expression so fast I couldn't question it. I started putting the food away and eyed the small cheesecake I picked up. I was going to demolish it later.

"What's the plan for the rest of the day?" I looked over my shoulder and smiled. Townes had gotten an apple and was still looking at the mail when he shrugged.

"Re-do the garden. It needs a new watering system, and

Hayley asked me to plant a few more things."

I nodded and glanced out the window. Having a garden was nice, Hayley loved going outside and would spend hours looking at the vegetables she grew. Last week, we harvested a bunch of the food. I wasn't knowledgeable enough to can anything and preserve it, but I did know how to make stock. So that's what we did, and anything leftover went into the compost bin Townes built.

"Did you want to help?" he asked.

I turned to him, shocked by his offer. These past few months he insisted on doing things himself, or he'd let Hayley help for a few minutes. Whenever I asked, he'd grunt and would go about his business. So, I shouldn't be surprised when my heart expanded with his offer.

"Let me go change, these workout pants are suffocating." I whirled around and walked to my room where I changed into shorts and tossed on the first shirt I found. When I opened the back door, I took a deep breath. The clouds had covered the sun like a thick blanket; in the distance they were dark and promised rain.

I loved the summer storms Denver often had, and I knew it was only a matter of time before we had to head inside. The air was thick as I walked to meet Townes, who was cutting pieces off a black hose.

I knelt down, and noticed the hose seemed thicker than I was used to. "What's that?"

"A hose?" Townes said, keeping his focus on where he was cutting.

"Duh, I can see that. I mean–what kind is it? It looks weird."

He sighed and turned to me. I saw the words die on his lips as he looked at me, then dipped his eyes down. "Is that my shirt?"

I glanced down, and my cheeks heated. "Yes."

It likely got mixed up in the laundry, which he had to have known. I wasn't going around stealing his shirts when he wasn't looking. Townes kept his eyes on his shirt for another moment before he turned back to what he was doing. "This hose is meant to be used for irrigation. It has a bunch of small holes so it acts like a sprinkler system. We need to frame the garden, and then put this up."

He stood and pointed to the pile of wood behind me. "I need you to hold that up while I drill it in place."

I wondered what else he drilled *into place.*

I snorted, shocked by the sudden thought. Townes raised a brow. "You okay?"

"Totally fine. Go get your–uh–tools so we can get started." My cheeks were burning as we stared at each other, but instead of asking anymore questions, he walked away. I let out a breath and placed my hands on my thighs as I tried to gather my thoughts. It wasn't appropriate to think things like that, especially now that we were living together.

By the time he came back, I had gotten myself under control. No more dirty thoughts about my fake husband. I picked up the first piece of wood and held it as Townes drilled the bottom to the garden box. The longer we remained quiet however, the more I started to wonder…if I wasn't thinking dirty thoughts about Townes, surely someone else was. I hadn't seen any late-night visitors, and as far as I knew, Townes never went out. Well, he never took detours, as far as I knew. Not that his sex life was anything I needed to know about, but I was a curious person an–

"You look like you want to ask me something," Townes said

as he finished the first post.

"I don't think this is something I'm going to verbalize." We moved to the other side of the box, and I put the next post in place.

"I never thought this day would come," Townes mumbled as he lined up the first screw. "Hollis is speechless."

"Oh, you think it's funny? Fine, I was trying to save both of us some embarrassment." I popped my hip and looked down on him. "I was wondering how you found the time to get a little action. I never see anyone come over, which doesn't bother me if I have a heads up, by the way, and you like never leave the house. So, what's up?"

Townes blinked and set the drill on the ground. "You're oddly interested in my sex life."

I shrugged, ignoring the burning along the back of my neck. "Not interested per se, just curious. Cause between the two of us, you're more likely to get it in. I mean, I haven't seen a dick in–"

"Hollis."

"Yes?"

Townes still had his eyes locked with mine, but something swam in the warm shades of brown, and I wanted to swim after it. To pluck it and examine the emotion I couldn't name. His nostrils flared, and he let out a heavy breath before he finally looked away and finished drilling the last screw. "Stop talking."

I nodded, and I was going to listen. My mouth was going to stay shut until we went inside, and I was going to avoid him for the rest of the night. Of all the things to ramble about, why did it have to be about that. Townes stood, but he didn't move; now it was him looking down at me and my heart sped up. Just a beat.

"In the spirit of talking about things that might make us uncomfortable, I have a question for you." His eyes danced between mine as his brows furrowed. "Would you rather I pay off your student loans, or your house?"

My mouth dried, and I tried to step around him. "Ha, you're funny. But I'm good, pro–" He blocked me.

"I'm serious."

"Didn't we already talk about this? I'm fine, I don't need you to do anything more than help around the house." The truth was, ever since I had gotten my new teaching job, I felt guilty. Guilty for thinking I could use Townes to help myself financially, and guilty I hadn't told him sooner I didn't need anything from him.

At some point, my gaze drifted to the ground, and a wet spot hit the place between my shoulder blades. The air changed so quick. I looked at Townes, who didn't seem to care it was about to start pouring on us. "We should go inside."

"Not until you give me an answer." He blinked away a raindrop that landed on his lashes. My skin broke out in goosebumps, and I tried to move past him again. "Hollis, I'll admit that I was being selfish when I asked you to help me. I should have clarified that this is a mutually beneficial agreement, and me doing projects around the house isn't enough."

"Can we talk about this inside?" The rain fell heavier, and I was starting to get cold.

He just shook his head. "Not until you give me an answer."

Once more, I tried to get around him. Only this time, I ran, or tried to. I made it two feet before a strong arm was being wrapped around my midsection, and I was yanked back against a hard chest. Townes picked me up, and I tried to wriggle out of his grasp. However, I was tiny compared to him. "Answer the question and we'll go inside. I don't want to be out here either."

It was either the coldness of the rain, or the warmth of his chest to my back that made me stop fighting. I dropped my hand on his arm and did my best to look at him over my shoulder. "Student loans. You can pay for those. Now, let me go."

Once I was free, I ran inside, and Townes wasn't far behind. I grabbed the kitchen towel and started drying off my arms. "You really had to hold me hostage?"

"You weren't going to answer the question if I didn't," he said. I smiled, and when I noticed the whisper of a smile on his face, mine widened. When I was dry enough to not drag water all over the house, I sat at the table.

"Sorry we didn't get a lot done."

"Can't control the weather." His voice tapered off at the end of his sentence, and the promise of that smile was gone.

Today had been a good day between us, and I didn't want it to end. Not yet. I leaned over the table and bit my lip. "So, what other projects do you need to do?"

Townes looked at me. "You're the one with the list."

"Yeah, but you're the one who knows what they're doing." I stood and started for the garage. "Just tell me what tools to get!"

20

Townes

Hayley pulled away, and her hair slipped through my fingers.

"You have to stop moving," I said as I gathered the hair again and split it into three sections.

"Uncle T, you keep pulling and it hurts." Hayley's eyes were full of frustration, and I sighed. Yesterday she had asked me to do her hair for the first day of school, which I was happy to do. However, the style she showed me was beyond my comfort level. I could do simple braids, or a single French braid, anything more than that—well—it was why her nana took her to salons.

"Ow!" Hayley yanked her head away, and with tears in her eyes, rubbed it. "Too hard."

She ran out of the bathroom before I could apologize or try to make it right. I glanced at the oven clock and groaned. The girls were supposed to leave in twenty minutes, I had no clue where Hollis was, and I still needed to pack Hayley a lunch and make sure she had a snack.

Food first, hair later.

I opened the fridge and used the last of the lunchmeat to make her sandwich, then I grabbed whatever fruit I could find. I was halfway done cutting the strawberries when my phone dinged beside me. It was a notification from my bank, letting me know a payment was made to one of Hollis's student loans. She had given me the information yesterday after we finished painting Hayley's room, and I was shocked to find it wasn't as much as I thought.

Regardless, I was happy Hollis finally let me take care of it for her.

I finished making Hayley's lunch and put it in her backpack, along with a snack. Now it was time to find them. They had to leave in five minutes, and the last thing either of them needed was to be late. I walked past the bathroom again and paused when I saw Hollis helping Hayley with her hair.

"It didn't feel good at all, Hollis. Why does Uncle T have such big, meaty hands?"

Hollis laughed as she continued braiding. "Cause your uncle is a big guy. How silly would he look with tiny hands?"

"Hm, that's true. But he's not allowed to do my hair anymore, only you." Hayley put her nose up and crossed her arms. Her words landed on my chest and stung. I knew that, eventually, her and I would have disagreements—I just didn't think it would be so soon.

"As much as I love doing your hair Hayley, so does your uncle. Do you think that's fair to take that away from him?" Hollis asked in a calm tone.

"Hm, I guess not. But he has to learn to be gentle." Hayley put up a finger as she spoke.

I chuckled and they both looked at me with wide eyes. "Haybug, I promise to be more gentle."

She smiled. "Okay Uncle T. But you can do it next time, maybe this weekend you can practice."

Hollis finished tying off Hayley's braid and tilted her head to face me. The smile on her face was enough to ease the growing anxiety in my chest. It was stupid, the fact I was anxious at all. I didn't have a reason for it, which only made me angry. Hayley was going to be fine, Hollis was going to be fine. They would come home safe after school, we would eat dinner, and they'd tell me about their day before we went our separate ways. Just like every night the past three months.

Hayley brushed past me while Hollis stood hesitantly in front of me. She tilted her head up, and that smile was still there. "You okay?"

"Peachy," I said as my eyes roamed her face for a second. Hollis nodded then continued toward the living room, where Hayley stood with her backpack. As Hollis reached her, she turned to me and waved frantically.

"See you after school!"

I waved after them and was thrown into silence when the door clicked shut. I walked back into the kitchen and grabbed my coffee, then I stared out the window. My grandfather had done it growing up, and I used to look at him and think he was being cryptic. Was he thinking about the universe? Or maybe he was wondering how to convert plastic into oil.

I, on the other hand, thought of nothing except the garden, and how I needed to harvest the cucumbers. Also, I thought of the animal documentary Hayley made me watch a few nights ago–then proclaimed she believed I could fight an ostrich.

She was right, of course.

I had a week before pre-season started, which meant I had

to fit as many house projects as I could into that short amount of time. After I finished my coffee, I went to the garage to get my tools, then I got my list. The list had grown since I first started it, because a lot more needed to be done than Hollis originally thought. The lights in her bathroom were going out, and the kitchen fan wasn't working. Not to mention the patio needed to be repainted, and I had to organize the garage.

I had gotten halfway through changing the lights in the bathroom when my phone started ringing. I answered the video call and set my phone upright against the mirror.

"Hey man, we're right around the corner. Want us to pick you up anything?" Scottie asked.

"Why are you around the corner?" I asked as I finished screwing in the last lightbulb.

Case popped in, an iced coffee in his hands. "For the record, I told him not to. We were just supposed to get coffee."

"How can I tell you guys the tea when neither of you want to hang out with me?"

I pinched the bridge of my nose and went to put the tools away. There was no need for them if the guys were coming over. "Door will be open, just take your shoes off."

I hung up and waited so long I was sure they were lost. However, when I went to call Case, the door opened. Scottie waltzed in with a paper bag from Rhonda's and almost tripped taking off his shoes.

"You guys need to sit down for what I'm about to tell you," he said, pushing past me. Case and I exchanged the same confused look, but followed Scottie without question. We all sat down, and Scottie pulled some chocolate chip cookies from the bag. He handed me two and split the last one with

Case.

"Did you not want your own?" I asked, already tearing a piece off.

Scottie raised a brow. "Nah, we already ate breakfast." He slammed his hands on the table and looked between Case and me with excitement. "So, remember how Coach was trying to get me another roommate?"

"Yeah, what's up with that?" Case asked.

"I still don't know, maybe my mom is bribing him to keep an extra close eye on me or something–anyway." He waved his hand. "You'll never guess who's moving in."

Case and I looked at each other, but it was me who spoke. "I'm not guessing, so either you tell me or you leave. I've got shit to do."

Scottie narrowed his eyes. "You're no fun. Anyway, it's his daughter! She's been studying overseas for college, and I guess she's moving back after she graduates. Coach is sticking her with me, something about helping keep an eye on her. I guess it's a win-win situation for both our parents."

"Seriously?" Case asked as his eyes darted to mine.

I'd only met our coach's daughter a handful of times over the years, and she was a force to be reckoned with. I shrugged toward Case, and turned my attention abck to Scottie.

He raised a brow and hesitated. "Have you guys met her? Is she horrible or something?"

"No, not horrible. She's just, rough around the edges? I don't know, Townes, how would you describe her?" Case asked, rubbing a hand through his hair.

I looked at Scottie and leaned forward. "Tiny and angry."

He chuckled. "Well, I lived with a big and angry guy long enough to be fine with the opposite. Besides, I'm trying to

turn the townhouse into a bachelor pad til she moves in."
Scottie waved a hand. "Now, you want any help around the
house? We've got nothing else going on."

"Nah, it's fine. I already did what I wanted, so I was
planning on taking a nap."

Case stood. "Well that's that. Come on Scott, let's let the
old man be."

Scottie and Case gave a quick goodbye before they left, and
I finished my cookie before I got my tools again. I wasn't
going to ask for help, I had everything covered.

* * *

"Well shit," Hollis said as she walked toward the pile of wet
drywall on the floor. "What happened?"

I had been reorganizing the garage when I heard a wet
thump from inside. Initially, when I walked into the living
room and saw Hollis, I thought the front door had gotten
shut a little too hard. But then Hayley yelled from my room
and we both ran to see what caused the commotion.

The leak in the ceiling had drenched the drywall, and it all
came down. The ceiling had a new hole in it, and the wall
was no longer there. Hayley walked back into the room with
a handful of towels. "Uncle T, is my ceiling going to break
too?"

Hollis grabbed the towels and gave her a kind smile. "We'll
double check, but I'm positive you'll be fine."

Hayley nodded and walked back out. Hollis looked at the
towels and sighed. "This isn't going to work. I think I have a
shovel and a bucket." She tossed the towels onto the bed, then

faced me as her hands settled on her hips. "In the meantime, you need another place to sleep."

"I think your first priority should be giving me the home insurance company's number, so I can get this fixed." I stormed out of the room, hungry, annoyed, and tired. After Case and Scottie left, I had worked on the patio and finished painting the room. The plan was: say hi to the girls after they got home, eat, and go straight to bed.

After dinner, I got blankets from the linen closet and the only dry pillow on my bed, and set them on the couch.

Hollis however, had other plans. She stood there with her arms crossed, her brows pulled together. "No."

"No?"

She grabbed my pillow and held it close to her chest. "You're not sleeping out here. You're what—forty? Sleep on this old thing and you'll throw your back out and won't be able to play. Get up."

I stared at her and blinked. "How old do you think I am?" When did I start following her?

She looked over her shoulder with a raised brow. "I said forty, didn't I?"

I shook my head as she opened her bedroom door, and my eyes snagged on the air mattress on the floor. "First off, I'm thirty-two, second, what's this?"

"A bed. I figured this would make things less awkward when it came to sharing a room. I would offer my bed, but I kick in my sleep, and I don't want to hurt you." She shoved the pillow into my chest and smirked. "I'll let you get ready for bed before I come back in."

She shut the door behind her, and I looked at the air mattress again.

My room needed to get fixed ASAP.

21

Hollis

I fucked up.

Initially, when the roof caved in and I offered my cheap air mattress to Townes, I didn't think anything of it. We were adults who could put up with a temporary sleeping arrangement. He was safe on the floor, away from my restless legs and tendency to snuggle anything close by. It was fine.

Until it wasn't.

Every morning for the past month, Townes had woken me up with the shower. It wasn't a big deal, considering it forced me to get up instead of snoozing my alarm. The shower wasn't the problem though, no, the problem was that Townes–assuming I was still asleep–would open the door to let the steam out. Shirtless.

Every. Single. Morning.

The first morning it happened, I peeked through my covers like a creep. Not because I was expecting to see anything I wasn't supposed to, but because who does that? Who lets the steam out while their totally platonic, kind of friend, fake wife is still sleeping. He clearly didn't care that I needed my beauty rest.

It also didn't help that when I called to get someone out here to take a look at the damage, I was informed they were severely overbooked. And wouldn't get out here for a month. As much as I wanted Townes to have his space back and be comfortable, I knew I was going to miss sneaking a peek at his back muscles.

Townes and Hayley were finishing up their breakfast when I walked into the kitchen. I wasn't one to normally wake up late, but my throat was sore and I couldn't get out of bed. Hayley put her bowl in the sink and ran up to me with her hair already done.

"I see your uncle's been practicing," I said as I examined the large, neat braids.

She twirled and grinned. "Yeah! And it doesn't hurt anymore!"

I snuck a peek at Townes, and then winked when we locked eyes. He cleared his throat and looked away. I moved on and got my coffee ready, while Hayley sat at the table and chatted with Townes. I wasn't paying attention to her, not when my focus was on the coffee, and about the email I received from the principal yesterday. In it was a vague description of an annual fundraiser, and how the school was honored to put it on again. Being that this was my first year at the school, I was out of the loop and would have to ask what was going on.

When my coffee was done, I packed up my work bag and we said goodbye to Townes.

"Hey Hollis?"

"Hey, yeah?" Hayley worried her bottom lip in the mirror, and I asked in a gentler tone. "What's up girlie?"

She blew out a breath and met my gaze. "Some kids in school ask why I always come to school with you. And they don't believe me when I say you and my uncle live together."

"They don't? Why do they think that?"

Her brows furrowed, and I could tell she was struggling to find the right words. But I gave her the time to find them. Finally, she took a deep breath. "They said only moms and dads can live together. And because you're not my mom, I don't live with you."

Her words kicked me in the stomach, then tore out my insides. Why were some kids so...cruel? I always tried to give children the benefit of the doubt, because well, they're children. However, some ideals were taught at home, and it was hard to teach them anything different because of that home environment. I didn't want to fault whoever these kids were, but I did want to find out who their parents were and send them a glitter bomb.

This was a topic I had to tread lightly, especially since I still knew nothing about Hayley's parents. She needed to know I wasn't trying to replace anyone either.

"How did that make you feel?" There, that was a solid question.

She thought about it for a moment. "Kinda sad."

"Sad because–"

"Because I don't think they have enough people to love them." Her brown eyes met mine. "Uncle T said I'm surrounded by love and nothing's going to change that. So I feel sad for those kids."

Kids man.

"That's really insightful, Hayley," I said as I parked.

She shrugged. "I don't know what insightful means."

I laughed, then coughed to soothe my throat and got out of the car. Hayley followed me into my classroom like she did every morning, then got her favorite marker from the drawer and started drawing on the whiteboard. I was halfway through setting up for the day when Ms. Borders–the teacher across the hall–poked her head in.

"Good morning!" She walked into the room, her lanyard jingling with each step.

Hayley turned from the flower she was drawing. "Morning Ms. Borders!"

"Hi little lady–oh my gosh! That artwork deserves to be in a museum!" Ms. Borders was one of the oldest teachers at the school, and loved making the kids feel special.

Hayley looked at the picture and tilted her head to the side. "Yeah–yeah it does," she said before she went back to drawing.

My colleague walked up to my desk, then sat on the edge of it. "Did you get the email?"

"Yeah, I did! But do you know what it meant exactly? A fundraiser?"

She gasped and put a hand to her chest. "I can not believe they didn't tell you about the fundraiser. Well, every year–usually around spring–the school rents out the small amusement park downtown. The teachers each host a booth, and all the proceeds go back to the school and a charity the children choose."

I stared at her as I took in all that information. "That sounds like a lot."

"Oh it is, but believe me, it's a ton of fun! Anyway, I got another email this morning. They want to pair me up with Mr. Gonzalez."

The art teacher was one of my favorite co-workers, and no,

it didn't have anything to do with the treats he brought in on Fridays. He had a great sense of humor, and often come in during some of our planning periods to help out. I also knew he was single and had his eye on a certain redhead. I smiled and leaned forward. "Lucky."

She blushed. "Anyway! Keep an eye out for who you'll get partnered with. We're supposed to meet weekly after winter break to plan our booths."

"I'll keep an eye out, thanks for the info."

She walked past Hayley. "See you later, alligator."

Hayley slowly turned to face her and spoke in the most serious tone a child could muster. "I'm not a reptile, Ms. Borders."

"Of course not, how silly of me," she said as she walked out of the classroom.

Hayley stood and walked back to my desk, then set the marker in the top drawer where it would be safe and ready for tomorrow. "She's silly. How could she mistake a child for a reptile?"

I tried to smooth a wrinkle at the bottom of her shirt and smiled. "I have no idea, you're a lot prettier than an alligator."

* * *

Townes was gone when we got home, and initially I was upset. It wasn't like him to do his own thing without telling me, especially when I had Hayley.

But then I charged my phone and saw the text messages.

Townes: *Have to run in and do some promotional stuff*

Townes: *Idk when I'll be home. Probably late.*

Townes: *Either your phone died or something else happened since I haven't gotten an enthusiastic response.*

That last one made me giggle.

Me: *Phone died, just getting these. I can save you some dinner.*

Townes: 👍

While Hayley did her homework, I started making dinner. She finished just as I was ready to set the table and grabbed the plates before I could. "Uncle T said I have to do more chores."

"Setting the table isn't really a chore though," I said.

She blinked. "He didn't say what I had to do. And then said something about initiative."

"You know, I'm starting to realize we use big words around you. Go ahead and set the table then."

Hayley and I ate while we talked about our day. By the time we finished, and did the dishes, we were both pooped. My throat had also gotten worse, and I had to suppress a cough with every breath. I needed to pick up some medicine at the store over the weekend. After we cleaned up for the tonight, and Hayley went to bed, the front door opened. Townes walked in, and I went to grab the plate of dinner I had set aside for him.

"You better be hungry."

"Starving," he said as he dropped into the dining chair.

I sighed and brought the plate to him. He pinched the bridge of his nose. "Hol, I didn't mean for you to bring me my food. I just needed to sit for a second."

"Well, if serving you dinner one time makes your life easier, then I'll do it. But again, it's just this time. Got it?" The truth was...I really didn't mind it. Often times, Ryan wouldn't like my cooking, and would get takeout. Townes, on the other hand, would eat everything. So, serving him a plate was just my simple way of showing gratitude that he wasn't an asshole, at least not when it came to food.

"Thank you," he said as he dug in.

"Welcome. Now, it's late and I'm tired. Goodnight."

On any other night, I would have stayed up and talked with him more. But I was tired, and my bed was the only place I wanted to be.

22

Townes

I used to not have any pre-game rituals like the other guys on the team. Riley tied his skates a certain way to ensure they didn't come undone in the middle of a game, and Case always crawled into his mind—I never asked what he thought of or if it was worth it. If it helped him play his best then I was going to leave it alone.

Even Scottie had a ritual, but he usually excused himself to do whatever it was in secret.

The reason I went so long without any pre-game rituals was because I truly didn't believe it made a difference. That was until one day, when Hayley had just turned four, she gave me her small stuffed grey cat to keep in my duffle bag. According to her, if I had the cat, then I wouldn't miss her so much because we would be connected by Mr. Whiskers.

So it stayed in my bag, and one night before a game when I was missing home, I gave it the smallest touch on its stuffed paw. Later that night we won after losing the past three pre-season games.

Now I touched that paw before every game.

I zipped up my duffle bag and looked up in time to see Scottie stretch out his hand. I took it and we started for the arena. The cheering of the crowd reverberated through the walls and I fidgeted with my pads as we walked.

"How are you feeling?" Scottie asked.

"Like I want to go home," I said as my eyes darted across the crowd it came into view. I wasn't going to analyze the reason behind it, wasn't going to admit that I was hoping to see Hollis before the game started. She'd come to plenty before with Hayley, but Scottie's question knocked me off center a bit. Because somewhere between asking Hollis to be my fake wife and working together in the garden—my reasoning for wanting to go home had changed slightly.

I still looked forward to falling into my routine of spending time with Hayley, but now I got to share that with Hollis.

Case shared a few encouraging words before we all split up. I took my position at the net and focused on the players of the other team. My eyes were scanning the faces—some familiar and some new—when I heard it. I whipped my head around at Hayley's voice, and my eyes landed between her and the two women standing beside her.

Basil wore a jersey with Case's number ten plastered on both sides. Her hair was braided back, and our team colors were painted across her cheeks. Hayley's hair was braided out of her face, and ribbons were weaved through her pigtails. She waved enthusiastically and pointed to her shirt, then to Hollis's. As if I couldn't see that they both wore jersey's that had the number thirty-one plastered on them.

My eyes lingered on Hollis longer than I intended, but I wanted to take in the way her hair was braided similar to Hayley's and how she painted my number on both cheeks.

It distracted me.

"Townes!" Case yelled from my left.

When did the puck drop? Hell, how long had we been *playing*? I didn't have time to process where the puck was coming from and moved to block my right side.

The puck whizzed past my left side and I cursed under my breath.

Scottie skated by and furrowed his brows. "What was that?"

I wasn't going to admit that I wasn't paying attention, so I shrugged. Scottie looked me over for another moment before he turned away. Case however didn't leave my side right away, he stared at me for a moment and I watched as his eyes darted to where I knew the girls sat in the stands.

He looked back to me, and I was expecting some snort of remark or a reminder to focus on what was going on in front of me. Instead, he smirked and skated away to take his spot on the right side of the rink.

I shook my head and set up as the referee walked over with a new puck. Nothing was going to distract me the rest the game, I just had to keep my head forward.

* * *

Scottie threw an arm over my shoulders, and laid his head back as we started walking back to the locker room. "I don't know where your head was for that entire game, but I'm glad you were able to come back to us man."

I grumbled and attempted to shrug him off, but he just laughed it off. We had barely won tonight by one point, and it was all my fault. My focus kept wandering to the two girls in the stands who cheered the loudest for me. Coach threatened to swap me out if I didn't get my shit together. So for the remainder of the game, I pretended the girls weren't there—it made my mood worse but at least I played better.

"Are you coming to Riley's?" Scottie asked.

I shook my head. "Nah, not tonight. I gotta get Hayley home."

He dropped his arm as we entered the locker room, and his eyes narrowed as he pointed at me. "You're just using that as an excuse to spend the night with Hollis. You can't fool me McCarthy."

"What? No. God forbid I want to get Hayley home after being out so late."

"So does that mean you'll come to Riley's after?" he asked with a raised brow as he started to remove his gear.

I pinched the bridge of my nose. "No, because I'm tired and would rather be home than out drinking."

Case walked up to us, fresh out of the shower and with his bag already packed. "I feel you there Townes. Basil and I are heading home too."

Scottie gasped and smacked his hand against his chest. "What *happened* to you two? When I first joined the team, you were both eager to go to after parties."

"I wouldn't say I was *eager*. Hayley was just younger and was always at Marion's when we had games. Now that she's older, she needs me at home," I said.

"Basil wanted to stay in tonight." Case shrugged. "Anyway, I'll see you guys later."

I finished taking off my gear, and went to change. After I tossed my uniform into my duffle, I hauled it over my shoulder and gave Scottie a small wave as I walked out of the locker room. With every step I took down the hallway, my heart pounded behind my ribcage.

What is with me?

I rounded the corner, and hadn't fully looked up before something small was hurling into my legs.

"That was so good uncle T! I mean, you didn't play as good as normal, but you still won!" Hayley said as she looked up at me. I smiled and picked her up before I started walking to where Hollis, Basil, and Case stood.

"Your observation skills are outstanding for a kid your age you know that?" I asked.

She nodded. "Yup. Oh! Hollis let me have so much candy. It feels like I'm vibrating. Can I go run around until it's time to leave?"

I chuckled, and shook my head as I finally came to stand next to Hollis. She lowered her voice to a whisper, as if it would keep me from hearing her. "Haybug, that was supposed to be our secret. You know how you uncle gets when you have sweets after five."

Hollis's blue eyes met mine, and I had to keep them from glancing down to the numbers on her cheeks. They seemed like they'd faded, and the number on her left cheek was a little smeared.

I swallowed then cleared my throat. "Have fun?"

She nodded and started to smile but I had to look away. Otherwise, I might have looked at her longer than necessary. Hayley worked her way out of my arms, and started skipping around our small circle.

"So, I guess we'll see you guys later?" Basil asked.

"Yeah, we'll see you!" Hollis said.

We watched as they walked away, and then I reached down to stop Hayley. She didn't protest, and instead skipped forward as she held my hand. Hollis walked by my side, but remained quiet until we got into the car.

Hayley was fighting a sugar crash in the back seat when Hollis shifted toward me. "So, when do you guys start traveling?"

I didn't have to think too hard before I responded. "Next week. I'll be gone about a week, then I'll be home for a bit."

Hollis nodded, then turned her eyes to the road. It wasn't quiet for very long, but it was long enough for me to realize I wanted her to keep talking.

"Did you have fun?" I asked.

My question must have caught her off guard, because her head turned so fast I was worried she had given herself whiplash. Yet, she stayed quiet. I looked at her fully when I came to a stop, and raised a brow. "What?"

"Nothing it's just—I'm kind of surprised. You're making small talk with me." She placed a hand over her heart. "I'm touched."

"You're rubbing off on me is what's going on, and I haven't decided if it's a good thing or not." I grumbled.

She chuckled. "Trust me, it's a good thing. And yes, I had a lot of fun tonight."

We fell back into silence, and for the remainder of the ride home I had to keep from asking her anymore questions. Because it was true, it was a good thing she was rubbing off on me.

I just wasn't going to give her the satisfaction of being right.

23

Hollis

The house was spotless. Marion was going to be dropping Hayley off any moment, and I wanted everything perfect considering our first meeting hadn't gone as well as I'd hoped. It was tense, and she didn't seem like she had any interest in me. Which was fine, but considering the circumstances, I just expected something different.

Townes made it a point to coordinate all the pickups and drop offs because it made him feel better. But with him away for a game, it was my turn. I was probably overreacting—I was nervous. Hayley talked all the time about the things she does with her nana, from feeding the neighborhood squirrel to trips to the aquarium. Then, when they had a slow day, they'd bake together and watching movies or do crafts. I wanted to show Marion that not only was I responsible, but that Hayley also had fun here.

Granted, Townes and I weren't taking her out every single weekend to fill our time—but Hayley enjoyed being here. Enjoyed being with me.

I never asked Townes about what she thought of our situation, and I knew that, in the grand scheme of things it didn't matter–but I needed to know what to expect. Surely, she'd be grateful he was able to continue taking care of Hayley.

I was overthinking things, everything would be fine.

A green sedan pulled into the driveway, and I pushed down the nerves in my stomach before stepping outside. Hayley was grabbing her bag from the trunk when she saw me.

"Hollis!" She ran toward me and held up a drawing when she stopped at my feet. There were three stick figures. "It's us! You, me, and Uncle T! Do you like it?"

I smiled and leaned down. "It's amazing. Why don't you put it on the fridge? I'll meet you inside."

She nodded and turned to wave. "Bye Nana, love you!"

Marion blew Hayley a kiss, and I walked down the steps to meet her. She wore her braids wrapped into a bun on top of her head, and gold bracelets adorned her wrists. I smiled and gestured toward the door. "Would you like to come in?"

She dragged her eyes over me, her friendly expression gone now that Hayley was inside. "No, thank you. It's uh," her eyes dragged over the exterior before she raised a brow. "Charming."

I smiled, determined to clear whatever tension was between us. "Thank you! It's why I fell in love with it. I've done quiet a few renovations, so it's nicer on the inside, I promise."

"Well, I hope so since my granddaughter is sleeping here. How many bedrooms does it have?" she asked, staring at me as she crossed her hands together.

My brows creased. "Three. Why?"

She waved a hand. "Just making sure everyone has their own space. Don't want things to get *confusing* is all."

162

Did...did she think there was something going on between me and Townes? And, even if she did, why did she feel entitled to that information? I cleared my throat and placed my foot on the first step leading back to the porch.

"I can assure you, Marion, nothing is going on you need to be worried about. Okay?"

Her brown eyes met mine, and I could see something brewing in them. Protectiveness.

"I'll get going, but do me a favor? If you need anything while Townes is gone, don't hesitate to reach out."

Yeah right. Her attitude makes her the last person I'd ask for help from.

"Will do, Marion, get home safe!" I said before I turned and headed back inside. I'd have to ask Townes if she'd said anything about our arrangement. Was she mad that he chose me to be his fake wife, or was there something else going on I needed to know about?

* * *

If I didn't know any better, I'd have thought Hayley was going to jump over the coffee table.

"Get it, Uncle Casey!" She threw a fist in the air as she cheered him on to steal the puck from the opposing team. "Come on!"

This was the Peaks first away game since the season started, and Hayley begged to make a whole night out of it. So Basil came over and we loaded the coffee table up with drinks and snacks. I was warned by Townes before they left that Hayley could get...competitive. I just wasn't expecting her to have the same energy as a die-hard, middle-aged man.

163

Basil snickered as Hayley whooped and danced when one of the Peak's players made a goal.

"Hollis, can I please have some more chocolate milk?" Hayley held up her special cup to her chest and pouted.

I glanced at the clock and sighed. "It's your last cup, okay? Game's almost over then it's bedtime."

Instead of answering, she bolted past me toward the kitchen. Basil shifted on the couch and pulled her feet beneath her legs. She let her head lean against the back of the couch for a moment before she rolled it to look at me. "So how have things been? With Hayley, and the guys traveling, I mean."

I wasn't going to tell Basil that my sore throat had gotten worse, or that the past few days I had been plagued with a pounding headache. Because this was the first time I was solely responsible for Hayley, and I wasn't going to let Townes down.

"Oh, it's fine. I've been making sure she sticks to our routine, so nothing's wonky when he gets back."

Hayley walked back into the living room, her cup was filled to the brim. Her steps were shallow and soft as she made her way to the coffee table. "You're really making the most of that last cup huh?" I asked with a smile.

"Oh yeah," she said as her eyes stayed focused on not spilling her drink.

Basil glanced at me again. "How's uh–everything else been?"

I wasn't sure how to answer that question, at least without making things seem weird between Townes and me. Explaining to my best friend that I had the smallest, tiniest crush on my fake husband wasn't on my to-do list. For the simple reason that I knew the feelings weren't going to be reciprocated. I was well aware Hayley was his priority, and he didn't need to worry about his fake wife having feelings for him. It would threaten our dynamic, and I had to make sure this thing lasted the full five years. Once we split, then I could direct those feeling to someone else.

It was fine.

"Everything's good. Oh, aside from Townes sleeping in my room cause his is ruined. He snores."

Hayley glanced behind her and nodded. "He snores so much."

Basil waited until she turned away before she widened her eyes. "You're sleeping in the same room?" Her voice was a hushed whisper. "What the fuck happened?"

"Swear jar," Hayley said, pointing to the jar on the counter.

"I'll do it when I leave, I'm probably gonna say more," Basil responded as her eyes narrowed.

I held up my hands in defense. "It's not what you think, B. Remember how I told you about the leak in the roof? Well, it accumulated all over his room and everything's ruined. I've got an appointment for someone to come take a look, but in the meantime, Townes is sleeping on an air mattress."

"And—that's it? Nothing uh—interesting has happened you're not telling me?"

I knew Basil still wasn't completely onboard with what Townes and me were doing, she was just looking out for me, and I appreciated it. However, with it also came the overbearing questions. I rolled my eyes and let my smile slip. "No mom."

"Listen, I'm just saying that I know what happens when you're forced into a small space—

"What happens?" Hayley asked.

I threw my head back with laughter as Basil scrambled to come up with an excuse. "They-uh–well–"

"You play card games until someone cries," I said, tears forming in my eyes from laughing so hard. To my surprise, Hayley bought it. She nodded as if the logic made perfect sense, then she went back to the game.

I shook my head and hid a wince when the movement caused my head to pound. One thing I had gotten used to while being a teacher, was getting sick easily. Especially being in an elementary school, I'd have to schedule a flu shot and keep chugging medicine until I felt better. Which hopefully would be before Townes got back. I cleared my throat and resisted the urge to rub it.

"Enough about me, how are you guys?" I asked Basil.

She shrugged. "We're good. We decided a date for the wedding–it'll be next winter."

Giddy, I sat straighter and clasped my hands together. "When are we going dress shopping? And what's the venue so I can look at reviews? Also, do you need literally any help? I mean, as your maid of honor, I am here to help!"

"I appreciate you, Hol. I promise when I start making appointments I'll let you know. I'm just swamped at work right now."

I pulled her into a tight hug. "I understand, B. I'm just so excited for you."

And that was the simple truth, that I was excited for her. The hard truth, though? I was excited for her because she was getting the wedding she wanted, and was getting married to her person. A dream I gave up, and one that might never happen.

The buzzer rang, and I knew the Peaks won when Hayley jumped up and squealed. "Look at all the stuffies!"

This first away game was sponsored by a gigantic animal charity that aimed to place shelter dogs with their perfect families all over the country. I watched as people threw stuffed animals into the rink, piling high enough to cover almost half of the plexiglass. Some athletes skated right into the giant pile, while others took their time sorting through the items. I noticed Townes, one of the last ones to skate toward it, and I didn't wait to see if he was going to grab one. I turned off the television and crossed my arms when Hayley whirled to look at me.

"Bedtime. Let's pick all this up first though."

"I'll help," Basil said as she stood.

I shook my head and gave Hayley an empty bowl from the coffee table. "We got this, I know you've got a game early in the morning."

"You positive?"

I pulled her into a hug and gave her a gentle squeeze. "Yes, and don't forget about the swear jar. Hayley counts it every night before she goes to bed."

Hayley walked past us, her arms full of trash and dishes. "Uncle T said I'm a lizard at math."

Basil and I chuckled before she placed a dollar in the jar then finally walked out the door. I continued to help Hayley clean the living room, and as I did the dishes, she got ready for bed. The dishwasher shut, and she came to stand in the walkway with a brush in her hands as my phone lit up with a new text. I grabbed it from its spot on the counter and smiled when I opened it.

"Wanna see something cool?"

167

"Yes!" Hayley skipped to my side as I lowered my phone so she could see what Townes sent.

It was a picture of two stuffed animals sitting on the hotel nightstand. One was a purple dog, with long ears and a fluffy tail. It sat next to a brown lop-eared rabbit, and my heart soared with the message that came along with the picture.

Townes: Hope you like. Had to fight Scottie for them.

I sent Hayley to bed after she had her nightly phone call with Townes. Then I took more medicine before I went to bed myself. He would be coming home soon, I just had to suffer through a few more days.

My head–despite the pain medicine–pounded as I shut my eyes.

24

Hollis

The pounding in my temples wasn't this bad last night, where it was allocated right behind my right eye. Now, it radiated around my entire head, each pound felt like the snapping of a burning rubber band, and nothing was helping. Not the medicine, not the electrolyte water, and certainly not the cold and flu medicine I bought last minute two nights ago.

My fluffy socks gathered the fine dust on the floor– because sweeping was the last thing on my mind when I could barely move my body– as I made my way to the kitchen. I grabbed a cup and dumped a packet of vitamin C into it. Townes was coming home later today, and when he walked through the door, I would go see a doctor. Basil asked me multiple times over the past few days how I was feeling, if I had gotten any better, but I couldn't bring myself to be honest.

This was the first time Townes fully trusted me to be with Hayley long term, and I saw the worry in his eyes as he hugged her goodbye at the airport. I didn't want to let him down by abandoning her with Basil while I got checked out.

Was this how single parents felt?

Even with a community, leaving her felt...icky. And knowing Townes, I couldn't imagine how long it took for him to finally ask for help.

Hayley skipped into the kitchen, unaware that her footsteps echoed in my head. She grabbed the cereal from where I set it out, and her smile dropped when she looked at me.

"Um, you don't look good."

"Good morning to you too," I said, trying my best to sound normal. Shit, when did my throat start to burn? I hoped I still had cough drops hiding in a drawer somewhere. I took a long sip of my water in an attempt to soothe the feeling.

Hayley leaned over her bowl and married her eyes as she looked me over. "One time Uncle T ate a lot of food, and then he got sick. I heard him from my room. You look like that."

I sighed and rubbed my neck to try and get rid of the ache that formed there too. Thank goodness it was Friday, if I had to go another day teaching like this I'd probably collapse. "It's almost time for school, hurry up and eat please."

Hayley dropped the subject and finished her cereal. In the meantime, I walked into my bathroom and splashed water on my burning face and neck. Then, I took another cap full of medicine. I looked in the mirror, took in my pale face and chapped lips, then covered myself in makeup. I didn't look that much better, but at least I wouldn't scare the kids. As Hayley was putting on her shoes, I picked up my work bag. It took a huge amount of effort, and I had to catch myself from falling when it settled on my shoulder.

Was it always this heavy?

The ride to school was muffled, my ears pounded as Hayley read her library book in the backseat. The sun was brighter than usual as well, but my sunglasses did nothing to keep my eyes from burning. We got to school, and I was grateful none of the students had arrived yet, and wouldn't for another fifteen minutes. Which meant I still had time to pull myself together before the day started. Hayley hopped out of the car and frantically waved toward the other side of the parking lot.

"Hi Mr. Arnold!"

Her voice rang in my ears, despite her being on the other side of the car. I straightened my back and forced a smile as Joshua– the fourth grade Science teacher– walked up to us. His hair was a bit disheveled, and his glasses were crooked like he rolled out of bed in a panic.

He smiled. "Good morning Hayley." He looked at me. "Hollis."

"Morning, your-uh glasses are wonky," I said as I pointed to the tortoiseshell frame.

"Of course they are." He took them off and bent the middle and sides before placing them back on. "This better?"

Hayley snickered. "No."

"Ah well, it's a good thing I keep an extra pair at school. Our dog knocked them off the counter last night trying to get to dinner. I think he stepped on them too."

Hayley let out another laugh that made me wince. "Okay, okay, let's all get inside before everyone else starts arriving." I turned around and swayed.

"Are you okay?" Joshua asked.

"I'm fine," I said as I continued toward the door. I heard Hayley whispering to him, but I couldn't focus on her words as the pounding intensified in my head. Once we made it inside, and I promised Joshua I'd tell him if I needed anything,

I headed to my classroom. Hayley sat in a seat and pulled out a book as I sent an email to the principal. I didn't tell her I was sick, just that I felt a little run down and thought today was perfect for my classes to watch a movie. Educational of course, and it would come with a worksheet.

She, being the amazing person she was, approved the idea and even offered to bring me the school's television.

Hayley ran past her, and a few other students, right before the bell rang. And Layla, the principal, gave me a concerned look. "You should go home."

I smiled and helped her get the television into the room. "I will after school."

"Hollis, I'm serious." She raised a brow, and I held her stern gaze. Layla cared greatly for all the staff, and I knew she had good intentions. But, even if I did go home, I would have to come back for Hayley, and who knew what I'd be like then.

"How about this, if I pass out, you can call Hayley's uncle to get me?"

Her face turned a light shade of red, and it made my stomach twist. However, I didn't have the capacity to analyze my feelings. I just wanted to sit down and close my eyes. She smoothed out her dark pixie cut and cleared her throat as I finished plugging in the television. "Fine. But please don't pass out, do it in the nurses' room, okay?"

"You got it." I agreed and went to sit down as the last of my third graders entered the room.

"A movie? Which one?"

"Can we have popcorn?"

"Is it going to be scary?"

The kids continued asking questions despite my immediate explanations. Until finally, I turned off the lights and had them get out a slip of paper. "I want you guys to write down whatever you want about the movie. Names, places, jokes. And then take it home to study, because on Monday we're taking a quiz."

I sat at my desk, pressed play, and closed my eyes.

Each class showed their excitement at the movie choice, and fervently took notes as I dozed in my chair. The only times I opened my eyes was when the movie ended, and it was time for my next class. By the time school ended, I felt the tiniest bit better, and managed to get Hayley to the car without swaying on my feet. The pounding, however, had grown in intensity, and I had the chills. I'd put my sweater on just to take it off five minutes later, but Hayley didn't say anything when I kept changing the temperature in the car.

I glanced at her in the mirror and did my best to smile. My lips cracked, and I tried to dig out my ChapStick. "Excited to see your uncle?"

"Mhm." She looked down, then glanced out the dashboard mirror. Like she was looking for something. I shrugged it off and turned the street corner, only to see a very familiar car sitting in the driveway.

"Hayley? Do you know why Uncle Scottie is at the house?"

"I don't know."

I didn't believe her, but I let it go. I was sure I'd find out as soon as I parked. Scottie was waiting outside as I pulled up and Hayley leapt out of the car as soon as it stopped moving, and ran to him. I took my time grabbing my things, which seemed heavier than they did this morning. When I got to the steps, Scottie grabbed my things, his brows pulled tight.

"You look like shit," he said as he grabbed the keys.

I walked in behind him and laid on the couch. It didn't get

173

past me that he handed Hayley a dollar bill for her swear jar, but I couldn't even laugh. My throat and body burned, and keeping my eyes open took so much energy. Scottie sat on the couch and touched the exposed part of my neck. "Shit. How long have you been sick?"

"Since you guys left, I think." Thinking was hard, I just wanted to sleep.

"We left just over a week ago." He sounded...not angry, but concerned? With a hint of annoyance.

I made a noise and snuggled into the throw pillow. Now that he was here, I didn't feel the need to keep my eyes open. He could watch Hayley until Townes showed up, it was fine.

I heard Scottie talking on the phone a little while later, then a blanket fell over my shoulders. He said something, but I was too far gone to understand anything he was saying.

* * *

I felt like I was floating, but when I opened my eyes, the only thing I found was a clean, dark linen shirt. We were walking somewhere. Where were we going? The couch was just fine.

The door to my room creaked open, and I barely saw the deflated air mattress before I was set on the bed. I looked up through heavy lids and could only make out a dark silhouette. The blanket was pulled over me, and like a current, it pulled me under.

* * *

My hair was being tugged. I peeked my eyes open to find nothing, but the tugging was still happening. I tried to look behind myself, but was stopped by a gentle voice.

"I don't want your hair to get tangled, go back to sleep."

I recognized the voice and smiled to myself as Townes continued braiding my hair. I was drifting off into the deepest parts of sleep when the tugging stopped, and something pressed against my head.

* * *

The last thing I remembered was the smell of food. It filled my senses, and I pushed myself off the bed. My stomach grumbled, and I was surprised.

The pounding had turned into a small throb, and my body could regulate its own temperature. I lifted my hand to my forehead, and I was pleased when I couldn't detect a fever. I moved the covers and draped my legs over the side of the bed; I was ready to explore and see where the smell was coming from, when the door opened. My eyes saw the food first, then glanced up to the man holding it. Townes wore his usual scowl and shook his head.

"I don't think so. Lay down." He didn't give me the chance to listen before he was setting the food on the nightstand and moving my legs back to where they had been the past few–I didn't know how many days. He then moved the covers back to my waist and sat down. "You need to eat."

"What is it?" I asked as he grabbed the bowl.

"Soup. The good kind, too."

Things came back to me in small pieces. The braid in my hair, and how it got there. Being put into bed, and the soft mumbled words I didn't understand. What happened after I fell asleep? Where was Hayley? How long was I asleep?

175

"You're spiraling, stop it and eat," Townes commanded. He held out a spoonful of the dark liquid, and I shook my head. "Eat."

"You don't need to keep taking care of me, Townes. I'm sure you have more important things to do. Like, oh, I don't know, work?" I was sure he had practice, and games to get ready for, and I didn't want to keep him any longer than necessary.

Why was he even here with everything he had to do?

The spoon dropped an inch, and his scowl softened. He sighed and shook his head lightly as his eyes stayed on mine. "How about you let me determine what's important, okay? Now, open up baby girl, your soup isn't going to eat itself."

My mouth opened in protest, I didn't even want to focus on what he just said, but he stopped the words from coming. Gently, Townes moved the spoon into my mouth. "Close."

I did what he said and sighed against the flavors of the soup. It was divine, and just what I needed. "How–"

"Don't talk. Just eat," he said as he filled the spoon again.

I wanted to argue, tell him I was fine, and he could leave me alone. But something in his features softened that part of me that wanted to fight. So, we sat in silence until the bowl was empty and I was tired again. I closed my eyes, but never felt Townes leave the room.

25

Townes

The bench dipped under Scottie's weight as he sat next to me. "How's Hollis? Feeling any better?"

I made a noncommittal noise as I continued texting.

Me: *There's still soup in the fridge, make sure you take some to work.*

Hollis: *But then I won't have any for when I get home. I'm trying to make that shit last as long as I can.*

Me: *Take. The. Soup.*

The text bubbles appeared and disappeared a few times before they went away completely. I stared for an extra minute though, not because my heart beat a touch faster and I wanted to hear from her, but because I wanted an answer. I left for practice before she or Hollis woke up for the day, and this was the only way I knew she'd take care of herself. When I realized that I wasn't getting a response, I tossed my phone into my duffle and looked at Scottie.

Whatever he saw on my face made him raise a brow and smirk.

"What?"

"You're acting weird," he said. I rolled my eyes and made my way to the ice. Scottie was right behind me though, that smirk still on his face. "You still didn't answer my question, is Hollis any better?"

We started stretching, but I kept my eyes down as I answered. "Yes."

She wasn't though, not really. The doctor said she had the flu, and pushed herself while I was gone which made it worse. While her fever was gone, and she could get around, she wasn't at her best. I spent the first three days after we landed taking care of her. I missed two practices, but I didn't really care.

It was weird. How worried I was when Scottie called and told me she passed out on the couch. According to him, Hayley managed to sneak a phone call in when Hollis wasn't looking; he told me he'd check it out while I went to the immigration office. It was worse than either of us thought, and I headed straight home. My heart thrummed in my ears the entire drive to the house, and I ignored the reason for it.

The only reason I cared so much was because she was responsible for Hayley while I was gone. That was it.

Practice went by in a blur, and at the end of it, I was the first one off the ice. I took off my skates and grabbed my duffle. I could shower at home, then I'd make Hollis some more soup.

My phone rang, and when I glanced at who was calling, I groaned. "Hi, Marion."

"Townes? Goodness, you can't answer any of my calls? How are things? Is Hollis feeling better?"

Marion had initially been upset Hollis didn't ask for help

while I was gone, but I didn't blame her. Because I was the same way when I first took Hayley. "She's doing fine."

She clicked her tongue, and I could imagine the way she dropped her head into her free hand. I heard her bracelets jingle. "That's just dandy. Now, I hope you told her how irresponsible that was of her. She does know we're here to help, right? Honestly, I knew you had to get married, but you couldn't have picked a better–"

I hung up before she could finish that sentence. See, while Marion was okay with Hollis, she wasn't a fan. For the simple fact that she didn't know her, and thought I picked the woman with the biggest boobs to fake marry.

While her boob size wasn't a factor in my choice...I wasn't going to complain.

I needed to get them together, dinner or something, so Marion could see Hollis was the perfect person to fake marry.

I pulled into the driveway and was surprised to see her car. Then, I panicked. Had she gotten sick at work? I got out of the car and did my best not to sprint to the door. When I opened it and walked inside, there were voices coming from the kitchen. My duffle dropped to the floor as I followed the voices, then I paused in the doorway. Hollis and an unfamiliar man stood across from each other, he was smiling at her in a way that made the hair on my neck stand straight.

She saw me first, and the smile she was already wearing widened. I could still see how sick she was feeling from where I stood; pale skin and cracked lips. The man across from her stood straighter as I walked to stand by her side. He cleared his throat and held out his hand.

"I'm Donald. I'm here about the broken ceiling."

I didn't take his hand, and instead put my hand on Hollis's

lower back. "Babe, you didn't tell me he was coming today. I would have shown up sooner."

Hollis peered up, and those light blue eyes didn't shine as bright. She definitely needed some soup. The man, Donald, cleared his throat and pushed a piece of paper toward us. "As I was telling your girlfriend–"

"Wife."

Donald gave a quick nod. "As I was telling your wife, the damage is pretty extensive. You'll need to replace part of the roof with all the water damage, and then we can focus on the interior wall."

I took the paper and looked it over. Then, I came across the total. "Is this not covered by the homeowner's insurance?"

"Due to the age of the roof, it's not covered."

"That's ridiculous."

Donald held up his hands in defeat. "I don't make the rules. The estimate is what's on the paper. You're more than welcome to find someone else if it's cheaper to."

Hollis tried to grab the paper, but I moved it to the side. "We'll be in touch."

Donald nodded and gave Hollis a quick glance before he grabbed his binder and walked out the front door. When it clicked shut, and Hollis knew he was gone, she reached across for the paper. "Let me see."

"Don't worry about it. And why aren't you at school?"

Hollis huffed, overexerting herself from trying to snatch the paper. "I will worry about it because it's going to be expensive. And, I came home during my planning period." I held the paper back again, and her hand brushed my forearm. "Give it."

"No. Now, get some soup and eat it before you have to go

back."

She crossed her arms and seemed more tired than before. "I already had some," she said as a flush crossed her cheeks.

"Get some more."

"You're insufferable sometimes, you know that?" she asked, and I saw it. That spark I hadn't seen in almost a week.

I had to keep a smile from my face as I peered down at her. "I'm well aware. Get some soup, and I'll take care of this." I waved the paper. She bit her bottom lip and married her eyes.

"Fine. But only because I have to get going. I'm stealing that paper when I get home."

I was happy she wasn't looking when the smile I was fighting finally won. She packed up the soup and gave me a quick goodbye before she headed out the door. Then, because I was exhausted and my knee ached, I took a nap to pass the time until Hollis and Hayley came home.

Because lately, seeing them both walk through the door had become the best part of my day.

26

Hollis

At my old school, fall break meant getting caught up on grading, answering crazy parent emails, and trying to sleep in well past my alarm. Then, by the time the two weeks was over, I always felt horrible. What was the point of a break if I worked the entire time?

This year was different though; we were expected to leave all school related items at the school; were given gift cards for the local coffee shop; and no one stayed late on the day break started. I had woken up each day so far feeling better than the last, even before coffee—it was amazing.

Practice was in full swing for their pre-season, so Townes wasn't home as much, and Hayley was with her nana for a few more days. Which meant I spent most of my time catching up on shows, cleaning up the garden, and finishing up other things around the house. The spare bathroom was almost done thanks to Townes, and all it needed was new hardware and a curtain. Townes being gone also meant I hadn't been able to properly thank him for making sure I was taken care of when I was sick.

It was…jarring. The last time I had gotten this sick—it was Basil who helped me. Ryan had been too busy with work to do anything other than send a quick text asking if I was doing okay. When I asked if he could bring me soup, he brought me the wrong kind, then complained about how I was being *picky.*

The last time someone made an effort to check on me every hour, make sure my blanket was in it's optional position—tucked under my chin—and refilled my water bottle was my mom. I hadn't expected Townes to do it. Hell—even if I had been able too, I would have reassured him that he could have stopped. That kind of treatment should have been reserved for Hayley, not someone he tolerated because of what I was able to do for him.

With our schedules, I hadn't been able to talk to him about it, or about the fact he corrected the contractor who looked at the roof. We were only married on paper and neither of us had rings; what difference did it really make if the man thought I was single?

I was in the middle of hanging the curtain–standing on a step stool because the rod was higher than the last one–when the door opened. I recognized Townes's footsteps before I saw him walk through the door.

"That was a short practice," I said as I placed a hook on the rod.

"Yeah, well, Coach was feeling gracious and let us leave early. Scottie invited us out later."

I stepped down and admired my handiwork. "To do what?"

When I turned around, Townes was leaning against the door frame, and the skin on my neck broke out in tingles. My eyes skirted over his exposed tattoos, and my face heated knowing how much was hidden under the fabric of his shirt. He cleared his throat, pulling me out of my imagination.

"He got tickets for a haunted house or something."

Ah, right. Halloween was at the end of the month. I enjoyed horror movies for the theatrics and for being able to make fun of the characters when they did dumb shit. However, things like haunted houses and people scaring you while trick or treating? I couldn't handle it. But, I did want to see my friends since we hadn't all hung out at the same time in months. Sometimes it was hard to see everyone between all of our schedules.

I could be brave enough for one night.

Townes must have seen the hesitation flicker across my face, because his scowl deepened with concern. That look often was directed at Hayley, and it was strange to be on the receiving end of it for once. "Do you not want to go?"

"What? No, of course I want to go—it sounds fun." I tried to cover my worries with a smile, but I wasn't sure if Townes bought it. "Do you want to get something to eat first? Al's is having an extended happy hour. We could meet everyone there?"

He stared at me for a second before glancing at his phone. "Sure."

I nodded and turned. Townes followed behind me as we walked out to the truck. He started down the road, and like so many times before, I started humming. I glanced over after a few minutes, and noticed how he tightly gripped the steering wheel. My humming ceased, and I rested my head against the window. I focused on the passing trees, and fall colors as I reminded myself that silence was okay—and that Townes preferred it.

I was so entranced by the colors outside that Townes startled me when he spoke.

"You don't have to stop."

"Stop what?" I looked at him and saw the way his Adam's apple bobbed.

He cleared his throat, and rested a hand on his thigh when we came to a light. "Humming."

"But you said you preferred it quiet," I said, my voice getting caught in my own throat.

"Not anymore. Not really."

I looked back out the window as the light changed to hide my smile. "Are you turning soft on me?"

"Between you and Hayley I realized I'll never know peace again. But by all means, keep quiet if you want."

I turned in my seat, smiling wide as I poked Townes in the side. "You are going soft. You big old teddy bear."

Townes gripped the steering wheel until his knuckles turned white, then, feeling satisfied I faced forward and hummed a melody until we pulled into the bar's parking lot. Townes slammed his door before stalking inside.

With a smile, I followed right behind him. The music was blasting when we walked inside. Cheap cleaning supplies and stale chips invaded my senses as we walked to the bar. My old regulars said hello as we passed by, but it was Finn who swallowed me in a hug.

"You get a big girl job and can't stop by to say hi?"

"I've been too busy teaching our future leaders to find time to come in, sorry Finn."

He smiled, and it saddened me to see how much older he seemed. "Well, you're here now. And with your boyfriend no less, so it's a great night."

My cheeks heated as I glanced around to find Townes. When I realized he was already sitting at the bar, my heart slowed, but I was still warm. "He's not my boyfriend."

Abigail walked up to Finn's side and wiggled her brows. "I know love when I see it."

"Okay, okay. We came together to eat before we met with some friends. It's not love or a date. But feel free to speculate from afar," I said as I walked away. I could feel them already gossiping as they went back to their own table.

By the time I sat down next to Townes, he had already ordered food and drinks. He placed his phone down and took a sip of whatever dark beer he ordered. "Everyone'll be here soon. I ordered nachos."

"Oh, okay cool."

We stared at the game playing above the television while we waited, and it wasn't until he went to take another sip of his drink that I spoke up.

"I uh–I never thanked you for what you did. So, thank you."

"What are you talking about?"

I tapped the bar top. "When I was sick. You were there when you didn't have to be, so, thank you."

Townes kept his eyes forward, and I knew him well enough by now to know he was searching for the right words. I took a nacho and licked the cheese off my fingers. "You know, normal people say 'you're welcome.'"

He shook his head, and I saw the way he fought off a smirk. I held out my hand, ready to poke him again, when suddenly, an arm was thrown over my shoulders. "Who's ready to get the shit scared outta them?"

A chill went down my spine remembering why we had come out. I smiled anyway and peered up at him. "It better actually be scary or I'm going to be upset."

* * *

"You can uncover your eyes," Townes said.

I shook my head fervently and kept my eyes covered. "No."

When Scottie showed me the ad for the haunted house, I didn't think it would be that bad. On the outside, it looked rundown and quickly put together. So I walked in thinking it wasn't going to be that bad; but then the first scare actor popped out with a chainsaw and I about cried.

This haunted house wasn't like any of the other ones I'd been to. No, these scare actors were allowed to touch people. One grabbed my ankle, and I almost kicked the guy before Townes pulled me into a small closet off the path. Since then, he'd been trying to calm me down and get me to finish. "It's not that bad. Don't you watch horror movies? Why're you so scared?"

"Because those are movies, and I know nothing can hurt me."

"But this is all fake," he said, his voice a touch softer.

I shook my head. "I didn't see anyone touch you. It might be fake, but it feels too real."

He was silent for a minute. "You can't stay here, you know. We have to get out and then we can leave."

"The only way I'm leaving is when the thing ends, or if I'm carried out of here." I shook my head again and tightened my hands on my face. Townes was quiet for so long I thought he had left me to my fate. I was ready to peek through my fingers to at least find a place to sit down when I was interrupted by a soft. "Fuck it."

The next thing I knew, I was being lifted over a broad shoulder. Two hands found their place on the backs of my thighs, and we were moving fast.

"What are you doing?" I asked as he carried me. By the way my hair moved, I could tell he was walking pretty fast as I tried to block out people screaming around us.

"I'm not waiting till this place closes for you to come out."

I remained quiet, hands over my eyes, as Townes navigated our way out. Soon enough the screams turned to chatter and laughter as he walked out of the house. But he didn't stop, and I dropped my hands to realize he was walking toward the parking lot. "What are you doing?"

"We're leaving."

"Why? Shouldn't we wait for everyone else?"

I felt his head move against my hip, and knew he was shaking his head. "They're going to want to go again, and I'm not doing this again."

He placed me next to his truck, and his hands brushed over my hips as he pulled away. I sucked in a breath and looked at him. His cheeks were a touch red, likely from carrying me. Mine though, were warm for a different reason. The ghost of his hands were still on my legs, and I was so touch deprived I wanted to be close to him.

Or anyone.

Anyone who wasn't Townes because I knew that would never happen.

He moved around and slammed his door as he got in the car. I followed and kept my eyes forward as he started the drive home.

"Thank you," I mumbled, cheeks still warm.

He shook his head and sighed. "Stop thanking me for things I choose to do."

I furrowed my brows, and my mind spiraled. "For things you choose to do? Townes, when I was sick–that was–you. No, I don't know if you felt obligated or something cause I had Hayley. And if you did, then I'm sorry for–"

"You're rambling," he said.

"I'm trying to explain that, sure, you chose to help take care of me, but you did other things. Like, you kept my hair out of my face, and fed me soup, and went above and beyond and–"

He turned to look at me, and the intensity in his eyes kept me frozen. "If you don't just accept that I can do things simply because I want to, then we're turning around and I'm going to drop you off in the middle of that haunted house."

I closed my mouth, faced forward, and smiled to myself as I hummed the rest of the way home.

27

Hollis

Hayley pushed around the red and green cereal in her bowl and sighed heavily. She was bored, and to be honest, I was too. Townes wouldn't be back until the end of the week, then he had one more game before he was off for Christmas. Before he left a few days ago, he promised Hayley they would decorate gingerbread houses when he got back, and she didn't want to do anything else until then.

It was cold outside, so the park wasn't an option. I blew in my mug to cool the tea, and Hayley let out another heavy sigh as her head clunked on the table. "What's up?"

"I'm bored." She turned her head to face me. "I don't have nothing to do, and it's not fair. Rocky at school has two dogs. He's never bored!" She threw her hands out.

"What are you trying to say?" I asked with a raised brow. She had brought up getting a pet a few times, and I was tempted to say yes. Afterall, Townes's only excuse was that they didn't have the time, but now that I was here–well things were different.

Hayley huffed again as her arms dangled. "I mean, he has a friend like all the time! And he's never bored. I wanna never be bored too."

I walked over and knelt down to look at her. Then, I smiled. "You want a dog?"

"Or a chinchala like Lucy."

"It's chinchilla."

I raised a brow. "What about that craft kit you got for your birthday? Go play with that."

She shrugged. "I played with it too much so everything's almost gone. I made *so many* bracelets."

I stared at her for a moment before I let out a heavy sigh. I knew I should talk to Townes first about what I was thinking. Afterall, he did tell her no. This is my house though, and there's plenty of room for another family member. I stood and walked back to get my mug from the counter. "Go get your shoes on."

"Why?"

I grabbed my keys and moved to the door to put on my shoes. "Cause we're gonna get a pet."

I had never seen a child move so fast before, Hayley was up and rushed past me before I could blink. When I turned around, she was sitting by the door putting on her shoes. Then, she stood and was bouncing as I walked toward her. "Really? Are you for real?"

I unlocked the door and clicked the button to open the car. "Super for real."

* * *

We had been here for three hours, and the only dogs Hayley was interested in had already been adopted. We didn't know that when we asked to take them into a room, according to the front desk worker, they had run out of the pink adopted signs and were making more. Since then, we had been walking around, and Hayley had been analyzing each and every dog.

"He looks nice, but do you think he has manners?" she asked with her face pressed against the glass. She was referring to the white mutt in front of us, and it was clear she didn't read the part on his paper that said "will need extensive training."

"I don't think so," I said as I continued walking down the hall.

"Oh, okay." She dropped her head and walked to my side.

I placed my arm over her small shoulder and gave her a squeeze. "We can go to a different shelter another day. Or come back here later this week."

"But I wanna find a pet today."

Hayley wasn't one to complain, so the defeat in her voice was a punch to the gut. We walked past the glass cages as the dogs barked, and I was determined to get her a friend. Near the exit, another door caught my attention. I looked over, then started walking. "Where are we going?" Hayley asked.

"To look at the cats," I said with a shrug before I opened the door.

"But Uncle T's allergic."

I walked up to the first cage, where two tuxedo cats laid curled together. "No harm in looking."

Hayley seemed hesitant, but the more I walked around and looked, the more comfortable she became to do the same. Five minutes after we walked into the room, I was sticking my fingers in a cage with a small orange kitten when Hayley ran up.

"I found one!" I let her drag me to a single cage at the end of the room. She pointed to the corner, where a beautiful long-haired white cat was cleaning itself. "She's so pretty."

"You're right," I said as I tried to find the paper with her profile and adoption info.

"And her eyes are pretty too!"

The cat looked at me, and I was surprised by the striking blue eyes. I clicked my tongue and wiggled my fingers, but it just looked at me. I read somewhere, once, that blue eyed white cats had a high chance of being deaf. Was that the case here? An employee walked by, and Hayley jumped out with flailing arms.

"Scuse me!" The employee walked over with a smile, and Hayley pointed to the cage. "Can we get this one?"

The woman snickered. "That's up to your mom." She looked at me. "Would you like more information first about Bilbo?"

I glossed over the fact she assumed I was Hayley's mother, and how neither of us corrected her. "I'm sorry, Bilbo?" My eyes snagged on a paper at the bottom of the cage, and noticed right at the top, the cat was indeed named after office supplies. I scanned the paper, and she seemed a well-rounded cat. "Can I ask why she was given up?"

There were plenty of potential reasons: owners moved or had a child, maybe she had behavioral issues. I just needed to know if I had to prepare for anything. The woman shook her head. "She's deaf, and their household became unsafe due to other animals and children."

I looked at the cat and stared. I could have sworn I saw her ear flick when I clicked my tongue. Hayley tugged on my shirt, and when I looked down, she was pouting. "Please Hollis? Can we please get Bilbo?"

"What about your uncle's allergies?"

She scoffed and turned to face Bilbo. The cat walked up as Hayley stuck her fingers in the cage, and started purring. "He'll be okay, I think."

I turned to the woman, who was patiently waiting with a smile. "What do I need to sign?"

She grabbed Bilbo from the cage and put her and Hayley into a room where they could get to know each other better. Then, I was led to a desk right across the hallway, and I started filling out paperwork.

A short while later, Bilbo was put into a cardboard box, and we were given a list of things we needed for our new family member. We stopped and grabbed cat litter and a box, then Hayley decided to find everything else online. When we got home, we let out the cat–whose new name was still being decided–and sat on the couch. As I scrolled, Hayley let me know what to add to the cart and what things to pass on. We settled on cat toys that looked like mice, a pink food bowl, and enough treats to last for the next six months. I also ordered a cat tree online—one that looked like a giant cactus.

We did this until my phone started ringing from an incoming video call. From Townes. The cat was sitting at the far end of the couch, and I contemplated hiding her until I told him. I wasn't sure how he'd take it if she walked across the screen. Hayley hit the answer button and yelled.

"Uncle T! Guess what we got!"

"What's that Haybug?"

"We got you allergees and Hollis and I got a cat!" She disappeared to grab the surprisingly content cat, and held her up. "See? Isn't she so cute?"

Townes's voice was tight. "A cat? When was this decided?"

"When I was lonely, and Hollis wanted to make me feel better. Oh! It's dinner time." Hayley stood and carried the cat to the kitchen. "Come on Sparkles."

I laughed as I watched her walk away, but my laugh died when I faced Townes. He didn't seem happy. "So how was your game?"

"We won. Why did you let Hayley get a cat? I already told her no pets."

"To be fair, your reasoning didn't make sense."

His scowl deepened. "Explain."

I leaned back on the couch and listened as Hayley giggled from the other room. "You told her you didn't have time to take care of a pet. But since, you know, I'm in the picture, that didn't make sense. I'll always be home to make sure it's taken care of."

My reasoning was flawless, and he knew it despite the flared nostrils I was looking at. I wanted to ask him more questions, but kept my mouth shut as his eyes roamed over me. I wondered what he was thinking; about coming home, or about the night at the haunted house. His hands on me were still a phantom against my skin, and I wanted him to touch me again. So I knew those imprints weren't a figment of my imagination.

"Just make sure that when you name the damn thing, it's not stupid. I gotta go." He hung up, and I tossed my phone on the couch.

"No, Pickles! Not the counter!"

I hurried to the kitchen, to find the cat on the counter, innocently knocking things onto the floor. Hayley was trying

195

her best to grab the cat, but she kept moving away. I shook my head and promptly set the cat on the floor as Hayley picked things up. "Can't settle on a name?"

"No. I keep trying things, but they don't make sense. She's not a Sparkles, or Elsa, or Pickles. Naming things is hard."

I laughed and looked over at the cat, who was now eating her food. Townes wanted the cat to have a cool name? I could make that happen. "So, we clearly need some inspiration for names, don't you think?"

"Yeah, but I've seen all the kid movies on tv, and it hasn't helped."

I put some popcorn in the microwave and raised a brow. "You need different inspiration. Have you ever seen *The Lord The Rings*?"

28

Townes

The newest member of the family–Bilbo–wouldn't stop staring at me as I got ready in the bathroom. She sat right in the doorway and flicked her tail as her eyes narrowed. I turned around and knelt–ignoring the ache in my knee. "Do you have a problem?"

Bilbo blinked, then licked her front paw. She wasn't intimidated at all, and it pissed me off. How hard was it to get dressed and not be stared at–yes I knew Hollis did it. The only reason I knew that was because one morning, she didn't move the blanket in time and then proceeded to fake snore.

It wasn't enough to make me change my routine. She could watch me put a shirt on all she wanted. I wasn't bothered by it.

The cat though, that was odd to me. I sniffled, then glared at the cat again. When I came home after my game last week, Hollis showed me the medicine cabinet where she stocked up on allergy medicine for me. At this rate however, I'd have to get the shots because the small pills weren't doing much.

Hollis walked into the room, and I turned around so I wouldn't be tempted to look at her exposed legs. She insisted we go to Al's for country night–neither of us knew how to dance, but that wasn't going to stop her. Her shorts were too short for the winter weather outside, but the way she smiled and spun told me she didn't care.

"I can't wait! Ryan never wanted to go with me to these things," Hollis said, and I noticed the way she tried to keep her voice full of joy. Like the fact her ex not doing things with her didn't hurt as much as I knew it did.

I turned around and grabbed my jacket off the door hook. "Well, it better be worth it. I don't stay out past my bedtime for just anyone."

She smiled, and I had to remember to keep walking. Otherwise, I'd get caught staring. "Well, I appreciate you staying up for me. It doesn't go unnoticed, and I promise to make you breakfast in the morning."

I raised a brow toward her as she followed me to the door. "Will it have chocolate chips?"

"Hm, we might have to get some at the store. But I can definitely make them with chocolate chips, yeah." Her smile widened, and I was grateful I could busy myself with locking the door. "You know I spoil you, right?"

"Is that what you call it?" I asked as we made our way to the truck.

She didn't say anything and shook her head instead as she got in the car. I followed in soon after, and as I made my way to the main road–I waited. I waited for her to start humming like she usually did, because now, it was better than silence. I had gotten so used to her insistent talking, that being in complete silence around her felt wrong. Now, I needed those soft melodies to quiet my mind, to make me think of things other than her. I wasn't sure when it happened–when I started thinking about her.

At first, it was just at practice; how were she and Hayley doing? Had she made dinner yet? Then, it became anytime I went out. I constantly wondered what Hollis was doing and I couldn't wait to walk through the door and see her smile. It was all wrong though.

Those were things I didn't need, and questions I forced myself to ignore. Hayley came first–it didn't matter that I liked how Hollis smelled of rosemary and cherries, or that I liked how she got along so well with my favorite little girl. What mattered was she was good for Hayley–that was it.

"You're quiet," Hollis said. I glanced over and noticed how her hands were neatly folded in her lap as she stared at me.

I cleared my throat. "I'm always quiet."

"No–this quiet is different. Like you're thinking about something." She leaned in and narrowed her eyes. "What is it, huh?"

I wasn't going to give her anything, so I kept my eyes forward.

She kept staring though, then gasped. "Oh my god. Did you meet someone at a game? Was it this last one? Tell me everything! Is she pretty? Did she approach you after the game or did you see her on the jumbotron and just have to meet her? Did–"

"What makes you think I met anyone?" I asked, keeping the humor from my voice. When Hollis rambled, I tried not to interrupt because it was–endearing, and cute. I liked her voice and how her mind got away from her.

"What else was I supposed to think with you being all stoic?

199

For all I knew, you were thinking about the most amazing tits you ever saw."

I choked. "Your mind goes to some pretty incredible places. You know that, right?"

She turned her head away, and I hated how her voice lowered. "I know."

Fuck. Making her upset was the last thing I wanted. We sat in the quiet car for the rest of the drive. The parking lot was packed when I pulled in, but I managed to grab an empty spot close to the doors. Hollis still hadn't looked at me, so I got out first and walked around to open her door. She stared at me, those blue eyes wide.

"First, you're quiet, then you're opening doors? Odd."

"I'm trying to make up for putting my foot in my mouth. So, is this okay or are you going to make me grovel?"

She looked me up and down, then she smirked. "If you're offering."

I shut the door and started toward the bar. Hollis's giggle rang from behind me as she ran to catch up. I held the door open just enough for her to slip in under my arm, then we made our way through the crowd to the bar. It was either the Christmas decorations, or the holiday country music that stopped me in my tracks. Hollis had failed to mention Al's would be decorated for the holidays, and I sighed before I started walking again. Chairs and tables had been pushed to the side of the building, and people lined the middle to dance.

Garland hung from the bar, and I made sure not to touch it as we ordered drinks. Hollis spun in her chair to watch everyone.

"You gonna dance?" I asked.

She shook her head. "Don't know yet. Swing dancing isn't

200

really my thing."

"Why'd you want to come then?"

I watched as she bit her bottom lip for two seconds before I had to look away; but she ended up shrugging and grabbing her drink when the bartender laid it in front of her. "I like the atmosphere more than anything. But also, if someone asks me to dance, I'll tell them about my two left feet and hope they're fine with it."

"Did your ex never take you dancing?" I asked. That asshat didn't seem like the kind of man to dance, but if Hollis wanted to try something new, he should have done it with her.

She shook her head, and her smile became heavy. "No. I signed us up for classes once, and he called it a waste of time and worked that whole evening."

As I looked at her, I couldn't help but wonder how she allowed herself to put up with that behavior. Didn't she know she was deserving of everything she wanted? "Question for you." I spun her chair back around so she was facing me. "Why did you put up with that for so long? I mean, I only met the guy once before you two broke up, and I didn't like him even then." In an effort to make her laugh, because the sound was addicting, I leaned in closer and whispered. "Was it the sex? Was it too good to pass up?"

She snorted before promptly covering her mouth, her eyes wide. I saw the sparkle in them as she tried to contain her laughter. "No! I can't believe you said that!"

I couldn't either, but the words were already out there, and if I changed the subject Hollis would only pester me. Maybe she was rubbing off on me—and I was going to ignore how I didn't mind it.

"Just trying to understand you better," I said as I peered

down at her.

She took a second to calm down, then shifted her gaze to the crowd again. "When we met in college, he was different. We complimented each other really well, and it made sense. But then after graduation, he got a high-paying, stressful corporate job and I slowly fell to the wayside." She swallowed, thick and slow. "At first, I thought it was temporary, and he would always tell me that too. He'd promise me things too like nice dates, and would hint at getting me gifts if there was something I really wanted, but they never came. I was honestly so used to having my needs brushed aside, I didn't see anything wrong."

"But after that party…" She looked at me and I knew exactly which one she was talking about. "I'd had enough. We had a huge fight, and he promised to be better. It lasted for a little while, but things just didn't work out and I got tired of it."

I opened my mouth to speak, but then we were interrupted by a man wearing a gigantic belt buckle and a backwards cap. He smiled at Hollis as he held out his hand. "Care to dance?"

She glanced at me, as if looking for permission. I simply grabbed my drink and turned back toward the bar. The man left with Hollis, and I downed my drink. I told myself it was because of what she just told me, and had nothing to do with the pit forming in my stomach. The thought of someone–who was supposed to love her–putting her second was asinine. I wasn't the most well versed in relationships, but even I knew that wasn't okay.

I turned around when the song changed, and Hollis hadn't returned. The man she walked off with was holding her to him, with his arms around her waist as they spun. My eyes locked onto the way he pulled her close and whispered into her ear. All I could do was watch as jealousy landed between my shoulder blades. I sat up straighter to try and shake off the feeling.

Jealousy wasn't something I was familiar with, because I never needed it. I shouldn't be jealous of another man holding my fake wife. Hayley was my main priority, I needed to focus on her and make sure she was taken care of. It didn't matter that I could feel my responsibilities shifting—that I wanted to make sure Hollis was taken care of too.

It didn't matter that my skin tightened as I watched Hollis's dance partner lower his hand to the small of her back until it rested just above her waistband.

Fuck.

After another song, and another beer, Hollis reclaimed her seat. She was smiling as she smoothed her hair into a bun, releasing the hairs sticking to the back of her neck.

"Have fun?"

She whirled to face me, and I caught a glimpse of her dance partner. He was chatting with a couple other men, but his focus remained on Hollis. "Oh my gosh! Yes! I'd nev–"

"Was that guy flirting with you?"

"What? Oh, yeah he was. But don't worry I–"

I reached down and gripped the seat of her chair before tugging it closer to me. My eyes never left the man, and something like satisfaction ran through me when we locked eyes from across the room. He looked away, and I looked at Hollis. "I'm not worried. Now, what was that pretty mouth saying before I interrupted you?"

Hollis glanced to where I was looking, then smacked my chest with the back of her hand. "Stop acting all jealous and protective. I was saying, I told him we were together when he started flirting. That's why I came back."

"You told him that?" I asked, shocked.

Her cheeks turned pink, and she lowered her voice. "Well, yeah. If I'm going to uh—seek anyone out, it's not going to be in front of you."

I glanced down and realized my hand was still holding the seat between her thighs. I pulled away and grabbed my beer. "Do what you want, it doesn't matter to me."

She scoffed and downed her own drink. "If you say so."

We both looked back to the dance floor, and noticed how much more crowded it was than before. I knew I wasn't going to dance, and given what just happened, I didn't think Hollis was going to either. So, I nudged her knee with mine, and inclined my head to the door. "Wanna go home?"

She sighed and took one last longing look before nodding. As she walked in front of me, I was hit with disappointment. I made an ass of myself, and it ruined her night. I wasn't any better than her ex.

29

Townes

Christmas was never my favorite holiday for a lot of reasons; my parents always fought, every year, like clockwork. Mom and Kennedy would wake up in the morning and start making breakfast before Dad would come down and yell at them for making a mess.

There was never a mess, but he was always too hungover to notice.

Sure, we got presents, expensive ones from extended family–but our parents never gave us anything. Kennedy would tell me stories from before I was born, our parents buying her all the newest toys and gadgets. Then, when I was one, Dad lost his job and things only went downhill from there.

Then, it only got worse when Kennedy passed. I tried to be happy for Hayley, but it was the hardest thing I'd ever done. I had just celebrated my birthday with a beer when I got the call that Kennedy and her husband were gone.

The only thing that made the holidays tolerable was Hayley, and seeing how happy she was to wake up and find gifts under the tree. If it wasn't for her, I wouldn't get out of bed.

I watched as Hayley placed yet *another* gumdrop on the edge of the roof, and kept my mouth shut as I waited for it to fall off.

What did they put in that icing to make it so strong?

"There! Now, where did I put those peppermints?" she asked, placing her hands on the table.

Christmas music played from the speaker in the kitchen, and the smell of sugar cookies filled the air. We had spent most of the day out of the house, driving around to look at Christmas lights on houses and we even stopped for ice cream despite the few inches of snow that covered the ground. All day Hayley had asked about building her gingerbread house, so after Hollis threw the cookies into the oven, Hayley got to work.

Hollis reached over the table, the red table runner bunching under her chest, and held out a small bag between her fingers. "Here you go."

"Thanks! Hm, where should I put it?" Hayley asked as she shoved her hand into the bag. Hollis and I exchanged a knowing glance—there was no room for any more candy. It looked like a reindeer had thrown up all over the place, leaving nothing uncovered.

"You know Haybug, we can take a break. I think your house is going to crumble if you put anything else on it," Hollis said.

"Hm." Hayley's eyes scanned her creation before she nodded. "I think you're right. Will the cookies be done soon?"

Hollis flipped her phone over to look at the timer she set. "Five minutes."

"Okay! Don't decorate them yet! I wanna put on my pajamas," Hayley said a second before she bolted to her room.

Hollis and I moved at the same time, both of us reaching for the empty wrappers that littered the table. She cocked her head to the finished gingerbread house. "Do you think it's going to hold?"

I shrugged and held out my hand toward Hollis so I could take the trash she had gathered. "If it doesn't I'll glue it back on, she won't notice the difference."

She laughed, and the sound sent a shover down my back. Then she was silent for a long moment, her eyes darting between me and my hand before she finally handed me her trash. "Question?"

I nodded and stayed right where I was, her hand still resting in mine.

"Did you ever want kids? Before Hayley I mean?"

"Yes," I said without missing a beat. I hadn't thought about having kids until after Hayley was born and I saw how much she was loved by her parents. If Kennedy was able to be an amazing mother despite our upbringing—then I could do it too. I cleared my throat and dropped my hand with the trash in it. "Even after Hayley, I wouldn't mind more."

Hollis blushed before she looked away, and I knew—I knew that wouldn't happen until after she was gone. So why did that make my chest ache?

"Do you?" I asked.

She nodded. "One day."

I wondered what her timeline was for starting a family, then wondered how long I was derailing those plans.

Hayley barreled into the kitchen and her Christmas themed nightgown that was two sizes too big hung on the floor. Her smiled fell as she tilted her head up, and sniffed.

"What's that smell?" she asked.

Fuck. The cookies.

* * *

The cookies were brunt, but thankfully we had extra in the pantry. However they didn't last the first ten minutes of the movie, and Hayley didn't last thirty. Her head rested against Hollis's lap as *Elf* played on the television. I had one arm sprawled across the back of the couch, and a beer in the other.

An ache spread in my chest with each minute that passed, but I had to keep myself together. At least for now.

"You know, she wouldn't stop talking about the gift you got her," Hollis said as she continued to brush back Hayley's hair.

My eyes flickered forward, and I cleared my throat. "That's good."

I had gotten her new dancing shoes and a keyboard with some piano books. I had already signed her up for lessons as well. Whatever Hayley wanted, I usually got her. Only because denying that little girl anything just wasn't possible. My head rolled to the side so I could see Hollis. "Did you grab your gift?"

She blinked. "My gift? From who?"

How hadn't she realized...

I stood and walked toward the fridge. The wrapped box had been sitting there since before I left, I was surprised she didn't see it.

Hollis's eyes widened as she took the box. "What's this?"

"Open it," I said as I sat back down.

She eyed it, then started to unwrap the box. When the floor was covered in wrapping paper, she opened the box and let out a small gasp. "Wha—"

"Hayley picked it out, said she thought playing tea with you would be fun." We were at the store, and Hayley noticed the expensive tea set. She begged me to get it and as soon as we got home, she wrapped it.

Part of me had wondered if she had an ulterior reason for wanting the tea set. Did she want to play with Hollis because it would be the closest she got to playing with her mom she barely remembered? Or, was this going to be a new thing that belonged to the two of them?

The ache in my chest came back, and this time when I glanced at my phone, I knew it was time to turn in for the night. Otherwise, I was going to wallow on the couch, and I didn't want that to be the first thing Hayley saw when she woke up. "Well, goodnight."

I moved to grab Hayley, but Hollis stopped me. "I've got her."

"She's heavy," I reasoned, trying to grab her again.

This time, Hollis grabbed my wrist, causing me to meet her gaze. She smiled, and it was so warm, so kind, I wanted to find a way to wrap myself in it. "I've got her Townes. Go get some sleep. We'll see you in the morning."

I nodded and walked to the bedroom. Unable to confess what tomorrow was going to entail, because almost five years later, it was still too hard to voice.

30

Hollis

Something was wrong with Townes, and it killed me that I didn't know what. I peeked my head into the dark bedroom, with a breakfast tray in my hands. Then, let out a quiet, worried sigh when I noticed how he was still laying on the air mattress. A quiet hiss echoed around the room, but it didn't seem like he cared as his body slowly sunk to the ground.

I took the tray back to the kitchen and stared at the pancakes as I thought of all the birthday plans that had been derailed. I was going to take him and Hayley out for the day, and we would have gone wherever Townes wanted. Then we were going to relax at home while I tried to recreate his banana bread. He'd only made it once before, but I was confident I could make it without a recipe.

Then Hayley and I were going to bake him a cake and have him blow out exactly thirty-three candles. Today wasn't supposed to start off like this.

Bilbo hopped onto the counter, and I scratched the area behind her ear. She purred under my hand, and I sighed. "I'm worried about him."

"Hollis, can I have some pancakes?" Hayley asked, startling me.

I jumped, and turned my head, only to find her eyes full of unshed tears. I knelt down and rubbed my hands over her shoulders. "What's wrong?"

"Uncle T is sad today. He's always sad and I want him to be happy." She sniffled.

Instantly, I pulled her into a hug and held her tight. I ran one hand over her hair, her soft curls tickling my hand. "Is that why you're sad? Because he is."

She took a step back and nodded as she wiped away a tear. "I don't like it when he's sad. And I can never make him happy."

"That's not your job, sweetie. Come on, he didn't want his pancakes. Why don't you take them and put on a movie or something. Let me clean up, and I'll be there in a few minutes." I gave Hayley the tray and watched her walk into the living room. Then, I busied myself cleaning and trying to think of what could be causing Townes to be so sullen.

The last mug went into the dishwasher, and I turned around only to pause at the sight of Townes in the hallway. His hair was a mess, and I saw the redness in his eyes as he stalked toward me. I backed up against the counter and looked up.

He was tired.

"I uh–I gave Hayley your food. But I can make you something if you want? Just let me know wh–"

"You're blocking the coffee maker," he said with a rough voice.

"Right." I moved to the side and eyed him as he turned on the machine. My gaze danced over the wrinkles in his shirt, and the pale color to his skin. As I was trying to decipher the cause of the bags under his eyes, a head of brown curls caught my attention. Hayley was poking her head around the corner, and I saw the crease in her brows from where I stood.

Townes didn't look at me as I made my way toward Hayley, and he didn't shoo Bilbo away as she walked in front of him. I grabbed Hayley gently by the shoulders and turned her away. "Do you wanna get out of here for a little bit?"

Her eyes darted back to the kitchen. "I don't want him to be alone."

"I think he wants to be alone sweetie, at least for a little bit. How about we get something to try to cheer him up? Hm?"

She smiled and slowly nodded her head. I grabbed her hand and shot Townes a quick text explaining we'd be out for a few hours.

He never responded.

So, I took Hayley to get hot chocolate before we went to the store. Her hands wrapped around the small cup, and her smile was back as she looked at the cut flowers. "These are so pretty! Do you think these will make Uncle T feel better?" she asked as she held up the yellow roses.

"I think any of them will work. But there's a lot more, go ahead and take a look."

She nodded her head and walked to the other side of the floral counter. I was watching her examine two different bouquets when my phone buzzed.

Case: *How's Townes?*

Me: *You know why he's acting all moody?!*

Case: *...he hasn't told you?*

Me: *Told me what?*

Case: *It's not my place, Hol...*

Me: *Please? Hayley's heartbroken seeing how upset he is, and idk what to do either.*

He didn't respond right away, and I thought that was the end of the conversation. Townes would be sad forever, and I was going to have to either deal with it, or piss him off trying to cheer him up.

Hayley set a bouquet on the belt and was busy picking out a snack when my phone rang. I quickly fished it out, worried it was Townes, and he needed something.

"Hello?"

"Hey, uh, can you come by when you're done?" Case asked.

Hayley placed her snack on the belt and smiled up at me. I placed my hand on her head and sighed. "Yeah, we'll be there."

Case hung up, and I finished checking out. When we got outside, Hayley had covered the flowers with her jacket as we walked to the car. I smoothed my hair when we got in the car, and I looked back at Hayley doing the same. "Are we going home?" she asked.

I started pulling out of the parking lot and glanced at her in the rearview mirror. "Not yet. Uncle Case wants us to come over."

"Oh! Maybe he can tell us what'll make Uncle T feel better. Cause, did you know they're best friends?"

"Yeah, I did know," I said as I kept my eyes forward.

The rest of the car ride was quiet as Hayley admired the flowers, and my mind ran wild. Townes was so strong, what was it about today that stripped him of that strength? Soon enough, we were pulling up to the large, white house and

Case was already on the front porch. Hayley bolted out of the car and barreled into his legs. Case effortlessly picked her up and waved to me as I walked up.

"Is B here?" I asked as I followed him inside.

"Nah, she's got a game today. Hayley, I've got to talk to Hollis. I put some brownies and some books in the living room. Can you hang out there for a little bit?"

Hayley practically flew out of his arms. "I'll do anything for brownies, Uncle Casey!"

When she was gone, Case led me to the island. His face was tight as we sat down, and it did nothing to soothe my worries. He folded his hands together, and I remained quiet as he sorted through his words.

"What do you know about Townes's sister?"

I blinked at the unexpected question. I tried to sort through all the conversations he and I had, but I couldn't find his sister in any of them. "Nothing."

Case's brows pulled tighter, and he dropped his head. "Of course," he mumbled. His eyes met mine, and I could see the sorrow in them for his friend. "I'm not going to get into too much detail, but ultimately–uh–she and her husband passed away, and that's why Hayley's with Townes."

My stomach plummeted, for both of them. As much as my family could get on my nerves, I knew I would be gutted if I lost any of them. Townes though, he lost a sister and jumped into taking care of a child. Did he even have time to process?

"And today, is the anniversary of her death. It's always been tough this time of year."

I glanced to the living room, where Hayley was reading and eating too much sugar. "Does she know? She doesn't seem as affected." Now that I thought of it, how old was she when this happened? Two or three at least.

Case shook his head. "She knows, but she was so young. The first year was hard on everyone, because she kept asking for her parents. As she's gotten older though"—he shrugged—"I don't know."

I bit my bottom lip and considered the information. Then, Case placed a gentle hand on mine, earning my focus. "He just needs someone right now. Go. Hayley can stay here until he feels better."

His tone left no room for arguments, so, I said my goodbyes and promised to pick her up later. Then, I headed home.

The door creaked open, and I shivered. It was dark and the only sounds were from the wind blowing on the house. I set down my purse and slowly made me way to my room. The air mattress was completely deflated when I opened the door, and panic surged in my chest. But it died just as fast when I realized Townes was under the huge mound of blankets on my bed. I couldn't tell if he was sleeping, or simply letting his grief suffocate him.

I rounded my side and found him staring aimlessly at the ceiling. He looked lost, and I didn't know how to help him find his way back. Or even if he wanted my help at all, we'd grown closer over the past few months, but I didn't think that granted me any special privileges. After a minute however, I moved the covers and got in the bed. Townes didn't have to acknowledge me; I was comfortable sitting in silence until this passed or he got sick of me and decided to suffer elsewhere.

So, I was surprised when he rolled over—and placed his head in my lap. I could feel his grief through his heavy exhale, and I went to run my fingers through his hair. My eyes traced over his exposed tattoos, until they landed on the hand that rested next to my hip. Nestled in the left wing of the moth I had committed to memory, was a date.

Today. Five years ago.

My fingers stopped moving as my heart cleaved in two.

"It's not usually this bad," Townes started. "It was worse that first year. I couldn't get out of bed and my body hurt so bad it wouldn't move. Case had to come get Hayley because she'd been crying, and I was useless."

"You were grieving someone you loved. You weren't useless."

He shook his head and moved his hand to grip my hip. "I told myself that Hayley needed me more than I needed to mourn. But, I think seeing you with her–seeing how Hayley looks at you it just–"

"Shh." I dragged my fingers over his scalp again, and he shuttered behind my touch. We plummeted into silence, and as my fingers moved across his scalp, his fingers drew small circles against my hip. The movement was the only thing that told me he was still awake. "Do you need anything? Want me to leave? I'll understand."

If he needed to be alone, I'd give him all the space he needed. But his fingers stilled, then his hand gripped my hip. "Stay. Please."

So I did, and as my eyes drew heavy, I whispered. "Happy birthday."

He didn't respond, instead we simply held onto each other even as our eyes drifted shut.

31

Hollis

"If you'd rather stay home, I can come up with an excuse. I don't want you pushing yourself," I said as Townes adjusted his tie in the bathroom mirror. It had been two days since we fell asleep in my bed, but I wasn't sure how comfortable he was going to a busy event.

He glanced at me through the mirror, and as his eyes roamed over my shimmering gold dress as I suppressed a shiver. "How many times do I have to tell you I'm fine?"

He turned and grabbed my bracelet from the counter before walking toward me. With gentle hands, Townes grabbed my wrist, and twisted it until my palm was face up. His fingers traced over the shallow veins, and I was helpless to do anything but watch. Ever since we woke up two days ago, his head still in my lap, something had shifted. It wasn't something I could pinpoint. Townes just seemed...softer.

I searched his face as he clasped the bracelet, but couldn't find anything. Not that I knew what I was looking for, anyway. He finally looked up and gave my wrist a gentle squeeze.

"Ready?"

I nodded and let out a heavy exhale. My mind shifted to what this night was going to entail. As we walked out to the car, and started driving to the concert hall, I started spiraling. Townes must have noticed, because he tapped my thigh when we came to a light. "You okay?"

"Yeah, it's just, I'm–anxious. About tonight."

"Why?"

He asked it like he wasn't worried about putting on a show for my family. As far as they knew, Townes and I had been dating for a few months, and were madly in love. The thing though, was I didn't know how to act with him. With Ryan, at least I knew what to expect. We'd hold hands, maybe he'd place a hand on my waist as he laughed at my parents' horrible jokes. I knew what was expected of me, and that was to be a decoration on his arm.

Would Townes expect the same?

"Come on baby, tell me what's wrong."

That nickname was another thing that kept coming up. He called me that when I was sick, and a few times after–like at Al's. I thought I was imagining things, because he said the word so soft before, I wasn't completely sure I heard him correctly. I blew out a breath, I could over-analyze the nickname later.

"How do you want to do this thing? I mean, my parents are going to hound us about our supposed relationship, so we need to get our stories straight. We should probably rapid-fire questions too, make sure we know enough about the other so it's not awkward. Quick, what's my weakness?"

"Directions," he said it with no hesitation, and I was surprised.

218

"Okay, uh what instrument can I play?"

"Piano, but growing up you wanted to learn the violin like your sister."

I turned in my seat and narrowed my eyes. "How do you know so much?"

Townes, Mr. I only know how to scowl McCarthy, *smiled.* He *smiled,* and it nearly sent me into orbit. I had only gotten the view from the side, but I needed to see the whole thing.

"You might not think it Hol, but I do listen. Now, are you going to ask anything else?"

I was still looking at his mouth, but smiled as I leaned back. "Nah, I think you've got it."

We pulled up to the valet shortly after, and Townes gave the man his keys before grabbing my hand to place it on his arm. I glanced at him with raised brows. We didn't have to act like this until we were around my parents. I let him lead me into the concert hall and directed him to the booth that was reserved for us and my parents. People all around us were dressed beautifully, women in dark glittery dresses, and men in black suits and ties.

I walked closer to Townes, suddenly feeling underdressed. My dress was nice, but it hadn't cost hundreds of dollars like the others I saw. As if sensing my discomfort, Townes leaned down as we walked to the door.

"I didn't tell you earlier, but you look beautiful, Hollis."

I peered up and noticed the faint pink dancing across his cheeks. "Thank you. And you look very handsome." I smiled to myself, turning my head away as Townes stopped walking, pulling me to a stop.

When I glanced up at him, he was staring and his breath caught in his throat when he spoke. "Do that again."

I blinked. "Do what?"

"Smile. You're fucking stunning when you smile." His words were a plea, and they caught me off guard. He'd seen me smile before—why was now any different?

I smiled anyway and a flutter erupted in my stomach at the way he took in a shaky breath. Then, because I didn't trust myself to stand there any longer, we entered the booth. My parents were conversing with Lionel and his wife Carly. Michael babbled in her lap as she tried to keep the two-year-old busy. He saw me first and threw out his chubby fingers.

"Hey monster," I said as I lightly pinched his cheeks.

"Hollis!" My mother walked up and placed a kiss on my cheek as Dad and Lionel continued their conversation. She looked me over, and it hit me—just how much older she seemed than the last time I saw her. The wrinkles around her eyes were a shadow deeper, and the grays in her hair had taken over. I was too caught up in looking into my future to notice she had started talking to Townes. "And I'm sorry, we haven't met." She held out her hand.

I cleared my throat. "Mom, this is Townes."

He reached out and took her hand. I saw her eyes widen at the tattoos, but if Townes noticed he didn't show it. "Nice to meet you."

"You too, hon. Now, we have a little while before the show starts. I'd love to hear about how you two met." Mom turned and headed back to her seat. "Hollis has kept you a secret." She winked.

I took the plush seat next to Townes, and he grabbed my hand, interlocking our fingers as my mom looked at us. "We met a year ago actually. I gave her a ride home when her ex abandoned her at a party."

My free hand connected with his chest as my mom watched us in shock. Her brows pulled close. "Ryan left you alone at a party?"

"That's beside the point, Mom. Townes and I hadn't really talked since then, until this past summer. I was working at the bar, he came up, and we just hit it off."

"And was there any reason we're just finding out about this? Huh? You keeping me from my future son-in-law?" Mom laughed.

My cheeks burned, and nerves lodged their way into my throat. If only you knew. Townes squeezed my hand, and while it wasn't enough to put me at ease completely, it did help. "Mom, that's a big accusation."

"Is it? You know, I had the same feeling about your father. And I knew your brother was going to snatch up Carly the first time they came home for dinner. A mother knows these things."

I cleared my throat, unsure of how to convince her she was wrong. This thing with Townes, it was temporary.

Even if my feelings were begging for it not to be. I'd come to look forward to his scowl over morning coffee. The way he'd shake his head when I did something wrong, but would move me aside and take over. All the small things no one had ever done for me before, it was addicting, and my withdrawals were going to be devastating.

The lights dimmed, saving us from forming a response. Mom turned in her seat and Michael babbled from behind us where Lionel moved to sit. The show started, and even in the darkness of the concert hall, Townes kept my hand locked in his.

* * *

Lionel and Carly left right as the show ended. Michael had fallen asleep, and they needed to race home before he woke up.

Townes and I stood along a far wall while my parents boasted about Emma to anyone who would listen. The show was beautiful. My bones still reverberated from the echoes of the music along the walls. We were only supposed to wait until Emma showed up, then we'd give our congratulations on a good show, and head home.

But she was nowhere to be seen, and I was trying my best not to fall asleep. I tilted my head to peer at Townes, who seemed equally as tired. "We can leave."

"I thought the whole point of coming was to meet your family," he said.

I sighed. "Well, considering half of them left already, I don't think it'll matter too much."

"What do you want to do?" he asked.

The question took me by surprise. I wasn't used to being asked that–so I took my time coming up with a response. "Let's wait another few minutes. If she hasn't shown up, then we'll leave." He nodded, and my stomach growled. "Can we get food on the way home too? I'm starving."

Something shifted in his gaze, and I think it was surprise. "Yeah, we can do that."

We fell into silence as people around us mingled, and I itched to reach for him. Townes let my hand go when my parents went to do their own thing, but I missed it. After a few minutes, I was about to signal our departure, but then I saw her. Emma's blue dress shimmered more than anyone else's, and her hair cascaded down her back.

She pulled me into a tight hug. "I am so glad you came!" She turned to Townes and gave me a knowing look. "You must be the secret boyfriend."

"Townes," he said, shaking her hand.

"I wasn't keeping him a secret Em, I just didn't tell you about him. There's a difference."

Her mouth opened in mock surprise. "What about when I found his body wash, huh? You were being secretive then."

I groaned and pinched the bridge of my nose. "It was mine, Em."

"Yeah, okay. Whatever you say." She turned to face Townes. "It was nice to meet you, but sadly I have to find our parents before they think I snuck out the back." Emma ran off, leaving Townes and me standing there.

I was busy watching Emma talk to our parents, and seeing how proud they were made my stomach sour. Why couldn't they be like that with me? Townes leaned down, his hands finding a spot on either side of my waist. "Still want some food?"

The whispered words kissed the shell of my ear and sent shivers down my spine. I turned, and the tips of our noses brushed against each other. What was happening?

"Yeah."

Townes lifted one hand to pat my waist and pulled away. I followed him out of the concert hall and waited in silence for the valet to bring the car. Once inside, Townes started driving back home.

"Aren't we getting food?" I asked.

"I already ordered something for delivery. I don't know about you, but I need to get out of this suit." He undid the top two buttons of his shirt, and it was just enough for me to catch a glimpse at the top of another tattoo. My mouth watered.

"S–sounds good."

Townes raised a brow but kept his focus on the road. When we got home, I grabbed comfortable clothes, and went straight to the bathroom. Bilbo followed me inside and settled on the pile of dirty clothes in the corner. I placed my hands on the counter and looked in the mirror. My cheeks were flushed, and my hair was falling out of the updo that took me an hour. I removed my makeup and took out my hair before I moved onto the dress.

When I opened the door, the smell of cheap pizza hit me. Bilbo bolted out, and I followed her into the living room. Townes was on the couch, scrolling through movie options. "One of them's for you," he said without looking away.

I opened the box and grabbed a slice before I sat next to him. He clicked play on a movie and leaned back. As I ate, I glanced down to the space between our knees and reminded myself that all the small touches, the hand holding, the brushing of our noses were all a show.

We were back to how we were before, and I wasn't sure how I felt about it.

32

Townes

Keeping my distance from Hollis was becoming harder and harder. Especially when she was sitting across from Basil in her cute pajama set. The fabric hung off her curves, and it made me want to peel the fabric away to see what was hiding underneath.

Ever since her sister's show, my self-control had been pulled taught, and anything could snap it. Each time she smiled, I looked away. When she laughed, I thought of something sad and upsetting so I wouldn't be drawn into the beautiful sound. When she asked me to go with her and pretend to be her boyfriend for the night, I didn't think anything of it.

Until I saw her–stunning–in that gold shimmer dress. There was only one thought I had as I looked her over and felt heat fill my chest.

Mine.

We had to put on a show though, so I made sure to soak everything in. The way I held her hand, or touched her lower back. Or how sweet she smelled when her hair was tossed gently over her shoulder; like cherries and rosemary.

Bilbo hopped into my lap, and I absentmindedly stroked her fur. Maybe I'd have an allergic reaction and could excuse myself for the rest of the evening. Hayley had already gone to bed after we played a re-recorded ball drop for her, because I wasn't having her stay up past midnight and risk being a grouch at her nana's tomorrow.

Everyone was gathered around the coffee table, sipping their drinks as they played a board game, when Scottie smacked his hands on the table. "What do you mean you've never had a New Year's kiss?"

To my surprise, Hollis shrugged and rolled some dice. "It just hasn't ever happened. Ryan was always at work, and I didn't go to parties in college. It's not that big a deal."

"You've had part of your adulthood stripped away, and I can't be okay with that." Scottie made a big deal of throwing his arm over his head as he leaned back. I rolled my eyes and kept petting Bilbo. While he was being dramatic, I couldn't disagree with him. Even I had my fair share of late light, drunken kisses to bring in the New Year.

Basil, who was sitting on Case's lap, leaned forward to move her piece on the board. "It is what it is, Scottie, leave it be."

"No." He stood and reached to take Hollis's hand. "I will break her from this horrible curse. Hollis, I will break in the New Year with you. It's what friends are for," he said.

She giggled and pulled her hand away. "Scottie, you know as well as I do that the last time we kissed, it didn't end well. I'll break in the year just fine by myself."

Everyone's mouths dropped as we stared at Hollis, and I felt a surge of jealousy zip through my veins. When the fuck did they kiss? And why did that make me so upset?

"Back up! You two what? When? Why didn't either of you

tell us?" Basil asked.

Scottie clicked his tongue and sat down with his arms crossed. "It was right after your engagement. Hollis was still moping over her break-up an–"

"I wasn't moping," Hollis said with a scowl.

He waved his hand. "And we decided to just give it a try. We didn't tell you guys cause we knew you'd freak out, and nothing came of it."

When I looked at Hollis, she had her head buried in her hands. Case was looking at Basil as if he was waiting for her to do something drastic. Scottie on the other hand, shrugged and continued playing the game as if nothing happened.

Basil placed her hand on Hollis's shoulder. "Hol?"

"We're never talking about this again. Understand?" She looked between us, and her gaze lingered on mine for a second. I didn't want to move on like nothing happened. I wanted to know more; like why things didn't work out. Scottie, while young, was a good guy, and they got along so well. Did something else happen that made them decide things wouldn't work out? I wasn't curious because I wanted them together–far from it–but because if she wasn't interested in him, then I didn't stand a chance. If I wanted one that is–not that I did.

Hollis leaned back against the couch, and her head fell back to peer up at me. She smiled, and I couldn't help but stare. I was obsessed with that smile–with her. She had this way of tethering people to her, and I was dumb to think I was immune to her charm. I pulled my gaze away, and stroked Bilbo one last time before I stood and headed toward the kitchen. This night needed to end, so I could sleep off whatever this woman was doing to me.

I finished off my beer, and waited until I heard the count-down celebration on the television before I walked back into the living room. They had stopped playing their game to watch the timer countdown from sixty to zero. Case rubbed Basil's arm as Scottie whispered something to Hollis that made her laugh. She gave those laughs so freely–I just wanted them for myself.

Bilbo met me on the couch and curled into my lap. I noticed how her ear twitched, and wondered if she was as deaf as Hollis was told. I kept petting her as everyone started counting down the seconds. I kept my eyes down as the timer reached zero, and the date changed on the screen. Case pulled Basil closer to him, and I looked up in time to see Scottie lean in to place a chaste kiss on Hollis's cheek.

There was a ringing in my ears as he pulled away, and I had to keep myself composed as he stood and stretched. "Well, this has been fun. But I am tired. Need any help cleaning before I leave?"

"No, we got it. You guys get home safe, okay?" Hollis said as she went around to give him a hug.

Scottie nodded and grabbed a few beer bottles anyways to throw away as he left. Case and Basil started gathering trash when Hollis moved to stop them. "You guys, go home. Really, I got it."

Basil sighed. "You know that we don't mind helping right?"

"I know, but you guys still have to drive home, and I don't want to keep you any later."

The two women stared at each other as Case continued to pile trash into a bag. When it was full, he cupped Basil's shoulder. "You're right Hol, we are pretty tired. See you guys soon?"

Hollis's eyes dipped to the bag, but didn't say anything about it. "Yeah, we'll see you."

Case gave me a nod before he led Basil toward the door. When it clicked shut, I moved to take the paper plates from Hollis's hands. Her brows creased and she tilted her head in confusion.

"You're exhausted, go to bed," I said as I took the plates and brushed past her toward the kitchen.

She followed and moved to block my path. When she took the plates back, her fingers brushed mine, and a shiver went down my spine. She peered up at me and batted her lashes. "I've got it, Townes."

"I'll do the dishes then," I said before I continued walking.

As I scrubbed the dishes and placed them into the dishwasher, Hollis continued putting things away and picking up trash. The sense of domesticity eased something in me, but I was afraid of it. This routine with Hollis had always been easy, and I was afraid of what might happen if things changed. When things changed.

When I was done, I turned around and found Hollis waiting for me with a tired smile. I walked until I was standing in front of her and peered down. There was a soft pink kissing her cheeks as we stared at each other, and I wanted to run my fingers over the color.

"Did you have a good night?"

I worked through the tightness in my throat. "Yeah."

"Good, I did too," she said before she spun on her heels and started for the bedroom. I followed after her, silently cursing that god forsaken air mattress. My back had been aching constantly, and I could never get comfortable. I looked forward to the day when I could have my own room again.

That was what I told myself, anyway. I'd miss listening to the way Hollis talked nonsense in her sleep and seeing her first thing in the morning.

We were almost to the door when she whirled back around and cocked her head. "Question."

"Shoot," I said. My stomach became uneasy as I waited.

"Have you ever had a New Year's kiss? Everyone was bagging on me, and, well, I was just curious."

I stared at her and clenched my jaw. "Do I not look like I have?"

"You're so—grumpy. And don't get me wrong, I can totally see the appeal." Her blush deepened. "But you also don't seem to like parties and stuff so that's why I was asking. I meant to ask you earlier, but I couldn't get a second away because if your answer would have been no, then—"

I leaned down until our noses were inches away. "Then what, Hollis?"

She worked a thick swallow, and her eyes darted between mine. Her mouth opened and closed a few times before she cleared her throat. "You don't care about me rambling, I know. So, I'm going to just—"

"Then what? What would you have done if my answer had been no?"

She kept her mouth shut, and I locked my eyes on hers so they wouldn't dip down to see the way her breasts moved with each ragged inhale. I could only put up with the silence for so long before I brushed past her and continued to the room.

By the time I came out of our shared bathroom, she was already laying in bed. The purple covers were pulled to her chin, and I didn't stick around to see if she was still awake. I sunk into the air mattress and closed my eyes.

And just as I drifted to sleep, I heard Hollis. She spoke like she was telling a secret as she said, "Then I would have asked to kiss you, Townes."

33

Hollis

I wasn't sure if Townes heard me last night or not. The man had a tendency to fall asleep as soon as his head hit the pillow, but the way he avoided me as I walked into the kitchen created that sense of doubt.

Butter and blueberries were the only things I smelled as I walked toward the coffee machine, only to find a mug already waiting for me. Townes placed another pancake on the ones already on the plate.

"Do you want eggs?" he asked.

I sipped my coffee. "Yes please."

When he nodded, Hayley came barreling into the kitchen. Her fuzzy socks caused her to slide on the floor, and almost run into the cabinets. Townes turned to her and pointed at her with the spatula.

"We talked about this yesterday, didn't we? Stop doing that inside."

Hayley walked past me and stole a pancake. "He's just upset cause I'm faster than him when he skates."

"Hey–"

I laughed and shook my head before leading Hayley to the table. "I have to agree with him, it's too early for dangerous activities. Can you wait until lunch? Maybe we can go to the rink or something and you two can race."

Hayley dropped her shoulders and nodded as she took a bite of her food. Townes, with his back toward us, poured some premixed eggs into the pan. "That's going to have to happen another weekend. You're going to your nana's Haybug, for the rest of break."

"He just knows I'll win. I'm more fast than him," she whispered.

I giggled and made to grab the plate of pancakes when my phone rang. Emma's picture filled the screen, and I wasted no time answering the call. "Hey, everything okay?"

My siblings and I rarely called each other, we talked and planned things solely through text, like normal adults. I tried to not let panic overwhelm me as I slid the button. "Em? What's wrong?"

Townes turned around, his scowl filled with concern, but I waved him off.

"You, me, and Lionel need to have an emergency meeting." Emma's voice was calm, which meant shit was about to hit the fan.

"Oh okay, yeah. Where?" I asked, already heading to my room to change into something more decent. What if we had to visit someone in the hospital? I didn't think the hospital staff would appreciate my taco patterned pajamas.

"Your place. I already called Lial and I'm almost there, anyway. So, see you soon." She hung up and left me staring at the wall. I had at least thirty minutes to get Townes and Hayley out of the house.

I walked back to the kitchen, and Townes spoke first. "Is everything okay?"

He pulled the unfinished eggs off the stove, as if he was waiting for something to happen. I stared at them, and something expanded in my chest. The man was willing to forget about his eggs for me; anyone else would have kept cooking. My vision turned blurry, and the next thing I knew Townes was at my side. Hayley stood and hesitated, unsure of what to do.

Townes wiped away a tear and spoke low, "What's wrong baby? What do you need?"

I sniffled. "You were willing to forget about your eggs for me."

"The–eggs?" he asked, confusion filling his voice as he wiped away another tear. I wondered, in that moment, what it would feel like to be in his arms. I bet that, despite his rough exterior, he gave the best hugs.

I shook my head and pulled away, wiping away the water in my eyes. "Forget about it–uh–everything is okay." I looked at Hayley and gave her a reassuring smile. "My siblings just need to stop by for a little bit. Nothing bad's happening."

Hayley blew out a breath and dropped back into her chair. "Thank goodness! You almost gave me a aneurysm."

"Uh–"

Townes stood straighter and walked back to the stove. "Her Papa has a condition, and he tells her that so she won't do dangerous things." He placed a few pancakes on a clean plate and handed it to me before he placed the dishes into the sink. "Go get your stuff, Haybug. We gotta go see Nana."

"Can I bring my new toy?" she asked, excitement sparkling in her eyes.

He nodded. "So long as you hurry, we don't want to intrude when Hollis's siblings get here."

Hayley bolted from the table, then paused at the edge of the kitchen. She thought for a moment, then started walking to her room. With the plate in hand, I turned to Townes and gave him a soft smile. "Thanks, I promise it won't take long."

"Take as long as you need. Just let me know if you need anything."

We stared at each other, and I was so tempted to bring up last night. To ask if he heard what I said, but I could do that another time. Maybe after he got back. After Emma and Lionel left. Because part of me wanted to know–needed to know–if he heard the quiet confession. I wanted to know what would have happened if we did kiss.

Because fake husbands don't kiss their fake wives unless there's a reason; and I wanted to give him one.

Townes continued past me, and I spent my time eating the delicious food he made before I went to change. By the time I came out of the room, they were already gone, and it wasn't much longer before there was a knock at the door. I hadn't even touched the doorknob before Emma was pushing the door in and walking inside in a panic. Her hair was a mess, and she seemed so–not her. She was still in her pajamas, and there looked to be peanut butter on the bottoms.

"What's going on?" I asked as I followed her to the couch.

She opened her mouth, but the door swung open again, and Lionel was stalking toward us. His brown hair was a mess, and his shirt wasn't tucked all the way in. "Tell me everything! Who's hurt? Where do we have to go? All of it."

"Oh my god no one is dying or dead!" Emma snapped.

Lionel and I looked at each other with raised brows. Our

sister never snapped. Not even when her violin got smashed in middle school and we had two days to replace it before a show.

"Then why the emergency meeting? I've got shit to do," Lionel said as he sat between us. We both knew he was swamped with homework and studying for exams. The life of a medical school student wasn't to be taken lightly. I caught a whiff of something strong, and vaguely familiar. I leaned in closer, and Lionel pulled away. "What are you doing?"

Another whiff. "Is that–why are you wearing that gross body spray from middle school?"

Emma leaned in, and her nose scrunched. "Ew. You smell like a locker room."

"Can I do anything without either of you attacking me?" Lionel sighed, running a hand through his hair. "Why are we here, Em? Cause if you're not going to tell us, then I'm leaving."

She groaned and sunk into the couch. Her hands went up to push into her eyes. "I'm having a crisis."

"Why? What happened?" I asked.

Emma sat straighter and pointed a finger toward us. "What I'm about to say stays between us. Got it?" We nodded and waited for her to start explaining.

She told us about the man she met after a performance this past summer, and how she'd been seeing him regularly since. It was a whirlwind romance that no one knew about, because it was supposed to be temporary. Well, according to her, he asked Emma to go back to Europe with him. She wanted to travel with him and build a life together. The reason she was in a crisis though, was because he needed an answer by next week and she was freaking out.

By the time she was done talking, she was shaking slightly, and her anxieties were taking over. "I don't know what to do," she said.

I moved to the other side of Lionel, who seemed to still be processing the information. I felt for my sister and couldn't imagine how much stress she had on her shoulders. Our parents put all their time and money into my siblings, and one of them was willing to throw it all away for love. It was a freedom I had taken for granted, being able to date and do what I wanted because my parents were focused on everyone else.

Even Lionel wasn't safe from their expectations. When he met his wife Carly, his freshman year of college, our parents were happy, sure, but they still expected so much from him. Then, Carly got pregnant their junior year and our parents–they couldn't hide their disappointment. All their hard work, in their minds, had gone down the drain. They were also young parents. They had Emma right after high school, and they were worried Lionel was going to struggle as much as they did.

It couldn't be further from the truth, though. Carly is a therapist, and Lionel got into medical school at the top of his undergrad class.

Seeing my siblings go through what I felt my entire life, feeling like a disappointment, hurt my heart.

"I think you should go Em," I said as I rubbed her arm.

"You do? Really?"

I nodded and thought about the opportunity she had in front of her. Maybe it was just me being selfish, or my form of self-loathing, but I hoped she could do what I was scared to. To take a risk and be with the person she loved.

Not that I was in love, but it felt close to it.

Emma looked to Lionel, who was staring down at his lap. "What do you think Lial?"

He worked down a thick swallow and met our curious gazes. "I'm thinking about dropping out of medical school."

This day was not going how I expected. Emma and I sat on our knees as we gasped. "You're what? Why?" she asked.

He sighed and dropped his head again. "I have a buddy who's staring a non-profit, it's for a good cause and I want to join in. Also, I'm so busy and so is Carly–but she's the one that ends up taking time off work if something comes up and it's not fair. We talked about it a while ago, and I want something more flexible so I can be with Michael more. A doctor isn't exactly the best thing for that."

Emma smiled. "I guess that settles it, I'm going to Europe."

Silence hung in the room as the news sunk in. My siblings, two people I loved most in the world, were finally deciding what made them happy, and were willing to do whatever it took to ensure that happiness.

So why was I so scared to do the same?

I groaned and threw my head back. "Well, since we're all confessing our deep dark secrets." My head rolled forward so I could look at them both. "I got married to a hockey goalie so he could get his green card, and so he could pay off my student loans."

Their eyes widened, and Emma smacked my arm. "I knew something was going on between you and tattoo guy! I fucking knew it!"

I hadn't heard the door open and rubbed my stinging arm. "First, ow. Second, he has a name."

Lionel's eyes shifted behind us, and soon Emma's did the

same. I was about to turn and see what made them go silent, when a familiar black and white moth came into my side vision.

"Townes. Since you seemed to have forgotten."

34

Townes

The only thing I wanted to do was sleep. Maybe then, when I woke up in the morning, my heart wouldn't be racing and my skin wouldn't feel tight. I wanted to peel it off, just so I could breathe normally again.

Everything was fine earlier, when I went to drop off Hayley. But then, Marion insisted I stay for lunch where she proceeded to lay out all of the things she thought Hollis and I were doing wrong. Ever since Hollis got sick, Marion had so many opinions. She was upset Hollis didn't reach out for help, then questioned her willingness to put Hayley in a dangerous situation. Which was fair, but I did the same thing many years ago and I didn't get that conversation. Marion was also concerned about Hollis bringing unknown men into the house. I told her that wasn't any of her business.

I walked into that house in a good mood, and left second guessing myself. I knew Hollis was the perfect person to have a fake marriage with. She was kind and always made Hayley feel loved. So why was it, that even when I knew the facts, I still felt like I wasn't doing enough? Hollis and I were stuck together for a few years—would Marion ever come around?

When I walked inside and came face to face with Hollis's siblings' surprised expressions—I wanted them out.

"First, ow. Second, he has a name," Hollis said as she rubbed her arm.

It didn't take a genius to realize they had been talking about me, so, since their memories failed them, I took it upon myself to refresh it. I walked up behind Hollis and reached past her toward her sister. "Townes. Since you seem to have forgotten."

Hollis tilted her head and smiled nervously. "I didn't know you'd be home so soon."

"It's been a few hours. I didn't know they'd still be here," I said as I let my hand drop. It landed on the couch behind Hollis's neck and I was tempted to reach out and touch her. Because I knew how her touch made me feel, it grounded me, and I needed that—not that I'd ever ask.

Her sister grabbed their brother by the collar and stood. "We were just leaving!"

She dragged their brother out the door without another word.

Hollis stood, but when she turned around, I was already moving. My hands tingled, and chills broke out all over my body. I hadn't found a way yet to regulate my nervous system, something I found out was the best way to get control of overgrowing anxiety. I tried the ice packs, the deep pressure, but nothing worked. Hollis stared at me as I moved, and I could see the concern in her eyes. It was similar to how she looked at me a few days ago. When she found me crumbled by grief and didn't know how to get me out of it. I hated that look.

Hollis deserved someone who could make her feel appreciated and taken care of, not the other way around. It was why a real relationship between us would never work. She was sunshine peeking through dark clouds, and I was the one driving more clouds her way. I selfishly wanted that sunshine to myself, to soak in its warmth.

I shut the door behind me. I knew I did, but it never clicked shut. Hollis was immediately behind me, and I started shaking. Usually, these anxiety attacks never lasted long, so why of all days–did it have to happen now? In front of a woman who I knew was going to want to help, it was embarrassing.

"What's wrong?"

I ignored her and tugged on the collar of my shirt. "You need to leave."

"But–"

The fabric of my shirt clung to my skin, suffocating me. I reached over my head and gripped the collar before pulling it over my head. Hollis had stopped talking, and I only felt a fraction better. She was staring as I moved around her to grab the extra blanket hanging off her bed. When I went to spread it on the deflated air mattress–I'd blow it up later–she gripped my wrist. Her touch radiated heat, and it sent a shiver down my spine.

I looked at her, and while there was still concern in her gaze, there was something else there too. It was warmer, softening those blue eyes. "You're not okay, let me help."

"There's nothing you can do, I've tried," I said. I tugged on the blanket, but Hollis just tugged back.

"What have you tried?"

"Ice, deep pressure therapy, exercise, almost anything you

242

can think of. Let go."

She tugged the blanket harder, and I took a step forward. Not because she was physically stronger than me, but because I was too weak to stay away.

She blinked but didn't falter. "It's anxiety, right? I used to struggle too, when I was younger. Sometimes now, but–I can manage it. Can I try something?"

I nodded. Hollis pulled the blanket from my grasp and tossed it back on her bed. Then, she took my hands and held them in hers. "Close your eyes."

My heart was still pounding, and the tingling from my hands had traveled up my arms. I felt like I was vibrating. Hollis moved my hands and placed them on her hips. I sucked in a shaky breath and gripped her tighter. I didn't want her to go. Her hands interlocked around the back of my neck, then, we were moving. Slow, side-by-side motions.

Dancing.

"What are you–"

"When I was younger, I broke my wrist falling off a bike." Her fingers tapped rhythmically on my neck, distracting me from how my heart beat rapidly for another reason. "And in third grade, I punched a little boy in the face because he pulled my hair."

"I love the summer because growing up, I would sit outside with my grandmother and peel peanuts before we fed them to the squirrels. She wanted to lessen the work they'd have to do, because she had the time."

I pulled her in closer and took in a shaky breath as my forehead dropped to hers. With my eyes still closed, I breathed her in. Clean, cherries and rosemary. "What are you doing?"

243

"I'm trying to distract you," she said, and even with my eyes closed, I could see her smile.

"Why?"

She was quiet for a long while, but we never stopped moving. I was ready to pull away when my heart steadied and my skin felt normal again, but Hollis held on. "There was one day, I came home and saw you and Hayley in the garden. It was a few days after the whole she thought we were dating thing. And I remember watching you with her. It was in that moment that I–I wanted to give you what you give her. Unconditional love and support, and not because I felt an obligation to do it. But because you've spent so long taking care of her, I realized no one's been taking care of you."

I opened my eyes and saw the sincerity in hers. There was no sadness, or pity behind her words. We were closer now, our noses an inch away as we continued to sway in the dark bedroom. When she opened her mouth, my eyes shot to the sight. Longing ached through my body, and my hand moved lower to rest just above her ass.

I couldn't. Not yet anyway. Hollis deserved everything good, and kind, and I had been nothing but a jerk to her for almost a year.

"I don't need anyone to take care of me," I said the words in hopes she would back away. That she'd finally realize it was useless.

But instead, she leaned in closer, and my arms wrapped around her waist to keep her steady. My mind and body were fighting each other, and I didn't know who I wanted to win.

"What do you want then, Townes?"

I couldn't remember the last time someone asked me that question, and I didn't know how to answer it. My mind wanted me to pull away and put this night behind us, we'd never speak of it again and would keep our distance. My body though...

"You don't want to know what I want, Hollis."

She looked up, and her lips were so close to mine. "Tell me? Please?"

I stopped moving and pulled Hollis toward the bed. I sat down and pulled her close until she was between my thighs. My hands moved over her, as if I could commit her to memory that way. It was useless though, I'd need to see her—wet and begging before I solidified her body to my mind.

"The thing I want, Hollis," I looked up at her, and gripped her waist harder. "Isn't something I'm going to get right now."

"Why not? I mean yo-you can have anything you want, I can help." She was breathless, and it was taking everything I had to keep her where she was.

I swallowed, and her eyes—filled with lust—darted to my throat. I groaned and leaned forward. My head rested between her full breasts, and I could hear her pounding heart.

It was too much.

We were too close.

I pulled back and placed a chaste kiss on her chest before I stood and walked toward the door. When I glanced back, Hollis's chest was heaving as she attempted to catch her breath. I didn't want to leave, but I also couldn't stay. Not if I wanted to regain whatever control I had left.

"I can help you Townes," Hollis said, her voice tight with frustration.

I shook my head and gripped the door frame. "No."

"Why the hell no-"

"Because. Hollis." I stalked back to her until she had to

look up. I gripped her chin so she couldn't look away, and so maybe she'd understand the severity in my words. "You saw me when I was vulnerable and asked me what I wanted, and what I want…" I tilted her chin up more until she let out a small groan. She was almost on her toes, but I didn't care. I leaned in until my breath tickled her ear, I breathed gently, waiting for the words to come.

What I want, is to spread your legs on that bed, and fuck you until you can't take it.

I couldn't say the words though, expose that small truth to either of us. So, I let her go, turned around, and walked out of the room before I did something I'd regret in the morning.

35

Hollis

I'd spent the past month pretending everything was normal between Townes and I, like nothing had ever happened.

At least until he started pissing me off.

He wasn't very good at hiding when he was in pain—I'd known about his knee for months—but he was walking around with a limp, and I knew it had to do with him sleeping on the couch. Something he insisted on doing ever since he walked out of my room that night, taking with him words I wasn't sure he'd ever say, he'd been avoiding me.

Every time I walked into a room, he left.

When I asked him a question, I'd get a grunt in response and nothing else.

Even Hayley noticed the shift, and he wasn't doing anything to keep his feelings hidden. She was sitting at the table, eating her colorful cereal and shifting her eyes between Townes and me.

I sipped my coffee and cleared my throat. "So, what's the plan for today?"

Over the past few months, Townes and I had gotten most of the house projects done. No more leaky pipes, the bathroom was renovated, and his room was almost finished. The contractors came by a couple weeks ago to get things started, now we were just waiting on them to install the new drywall and paint. Then, Townes would be back to his own room. This was the first weekend in a long time where we were free, and I was itching to get out.

"Can we go bowling?" Hayley asked.

"No," Townes said without glancing up from his food.

Hayley doubled down and turned in her seat to face him. "The zoo?"

"No."

"Ice skating?"

"No."

"Well, what can we do, Uncle T?"

He finally looked at her, and his deep scowl was answer enough that he was tired of the conversation. "We can relax today, we're not going anywhere." His gaze shifted to mine, and I saw the storm darkening them.

Maybe if he hadn't been sleeping on the couch he'd be in a better mood. I shifted to Hayley and tapped her arm. "How about you and I get some shopping done. Your uncle can stay here and mope."

"What does mope mean?" she asked before shoving her last spoonful of cereal into her mouth.

"It means he's going to be in a bad mood by himself." I ignored the heated gaze searing into my side and smiled. "Come on, let's get ready and we'll head out."

"Okay!" Hayley ran and placed her bowl into the sink before she ran and disappeared down the hall. I went to stand, my empty mug in hand, when Townes spoke up.

"I'll drive," he said, already moving and rinsing his plate.

I traced over the angles of his face, and over the full beard that had finally grown in. When he turned, he winced, it was such a small reaction I knew he thought I hadn't seen it. And it pissed me off even more. "No, you're staying here."

When I turned and walked toward my room, he followed, fighting a wince with every step. "I'm coming, Hollis."

We reached my door just as Hayley's opened, and I dragged Townes into the room. I wasn't going to have an argument with him in front of her. When I was sure the door was closed, and our voices would be muffled, I whirled on Townes and backed him against the wall. I craned my neck to look at him and crossed my arms.

"You've had a stick up your ass for a month, and just now you weren't very kind to your niece. So, excuse me for not wanting to hang out with you when you haven't said more than fifteen words to me since you walked out of my room *a month ago* without any sort of explanation." His nostrils flared, and suddenly I felt cornered. It didn't matter I was still staring up at him, the energy had shifted, and I no longer felt in charge. Townes took a step forward, but I didn't back away.

His eyes held mine, dark and stormy with whatever was going through his head. But he blinked, and just like that, it was gone. In its place were the light golden colors I had become so familiar with. "Let me ask you something," he said.

A chill ran down my spine. "Shoot."

"Have you thought about what I was going to say? Before I left? And did it ever occur to you that maybe that's why I've been avoiding you?"

I suppressed another shiver. Of course I'd thought about it–more times than I could count. The way he held my chin, his breath against my ear, there were so many possibilities. But I was deprived of them all when he walked out. However, I wasn't sure what that had to do with how he'd been acting. Whatever happened with a *heat of the moment* kind of thing.

It didn't mean anything.

"Are you going to answer?" he asked, his voice low.

I stood straighter. "No. I haven't thought about it. And I don't see what it has to do with anything." His eyes dropped to my mouth, but I snuffed out the fire in my belly and walked away. "I don't care if you come, but if you do, you're on your best behavior. Understand?"

He nodded.

"Good. Take some medicine before we leave too. I don't want you slowing us down." I turned around and didn't wait for him to leave before I walked into the bathroom. I didn't need to do anything, I was ready for the day, but I had to hide and catch my breath. Away from prying eyes.

By the time I collected myself and emerged from the bathroom, Townes was gone. When I made my way into the living room, he looked marginally better, but Hayley was eyeing him with suspicion. She poked his side. "Why are you happy?"

He swatted her hand away when she moved to poke him again. "Because Hollis said I could come."

"But you didn't want to do anything." She turned to face me with wide eyes. "Does this mean we can go to the zoo?"

I knew Townes was going to say no, that we had already planned on going shopping instead. However, if he thought he was going to get his way just because I let him tag along, he was mistaken.

"We can spend all day at the zoo Hay-girl," I said as I grabbed my bag from where it sat on the couch. I grabbed her hand before we walked out the door, leaving Townes staring after us–regretting his decision.

When we got to the zoo, I knew he wasn't feeling any better, but he was doing a great job at hiding it. I walked behind him as Hayley sat on his shoulders, pointing to every little thing she saw.

"Uncle T! The elephants are that way!" She tried to redirect his path by tugging on his face, but he didn't fight her and changed directions. We walked through the crowds of people until we made it to the metal gate, blocking us from the gigantic animals. Hayley giggled as one of them lifted its trunk and seemed to wave. I pulled out my phone when I noticed the smallest smile tugging on Townes's lips and snapped a picture.

"Well, aren't you just a beautiful family!"

I startled and whirled around to find myself face-to-face with an older woman. Her gray hair was braided down her back, and her wrinkles were blocked by her wide brim hat and slather of sunscreen across her nose.

I held up my hands and tried to contain my embarrassment. "Oh no, we're not–like together, you know? We're roommates. Just on a fun outing for the day!" My words were jumbled and tripped out of my mouth. I could feel Townes assessing me. I still hadn't told him about the incident at the shelter, where a woman assumed I was Hayley's mother. Not because I was scared of his reaction, but because I was afraid it would blur the lines between us, and he wouldn't want to continue with our fake marriage. If that happened, if he changed his mind, then it could affect his chance to get his green card.

It was more trouble than it was worth, so I kept my mouth shut. The woman cocked her head, and her kind smile told me she didn't believe me. A small hand laced with mine, and Hayley bounced next to me.

"Can we go find the hippos?" she asked, oblivious of the woman standing in front of us.

"Of course, just a sec–" When I glanced up, the woman was gone. Her oversized white flannel danced in the wind as she walked away with an older gentleman. Her arm was looped through his, and I could see her smile from here. Something twisted in my chest: longing. I wanted that.

One day.

Hayley tugged on my hand, and Townes stood there with his arms crossed, his eyes on the woman. Had he heard that short conversation? Was he upset by the assumption? I wondered, if we were alone, if he'd wrap his arm around me like he did at Emma's show.

As if he heard my thoughts, his eyes shifted to mine, and I could have sworn I saw a gentle yes there.

"Come onnnnnn, I wanna see the hippos!" Hayley said as she started tugging me toward the walkway. This time, Townes followed behind us, and I felt his eyes on me the rest of the day.

* * *

"Did you know a zebra can camouflage from predators?" Hayley asked from the couch while Townes and I finished cleaning the table. Before we left the zoo, we stopped by the gift shop, and Townes bought her a book on animal facts. She'd been telling us facts since we finished eating.

"And they can run super fast. Kinda like regular horses."

Townes put a cup into the dishwasher, and went to peer at her from the doorway. "As much as I'd love to stay up and hear more zebra facts, it's bedtime."

Hayley closed the book and carried it to her room with her nose held high. "Fine, but I'm gonna keep reading and not tell you anything."

"Oh. How will I ever live with myself without all this information I can find on google?" he muttered as he followed after her.

My gaze didn't linger to watch him disappear around the corner, instead they were focused on the backyard, where the garden was still covered with light plastic to keep out the winter cold. It would stay up another month or so, then we'd take it down and finally clean up the fallen leaves. Hayley could help haul them into the compost, and I was sure Townes would assess the garden boxes to make sure the wood was still sturdy.

It was all so domestic. The yard work, taking Hayley on a weekend outing, coming home and finding them reading a book together. When I agreed to this, I wasn't expecting how easy we'd fall into this routine. I thought we'd fumble for a few months before we found something that kind of worked. One of us surely would feel out of place in the other's life.

But that didn't happen, and the reality wasn't doing my heart any favors. It was how I imagined my future family, whoever they were; but Townes and Hayley brought that to me, and I was scared to let it go.

"You keep washing what cup you're going to go through

it," Townes said as he took the mug from my hands. I hadn't realized I was still washing it.

"It's ceramic, it'll be fine," I said, turning to face him.

Silence stretched between us like a rubber band, and I knew it was going to snap. So I might as well be the first one to break it. "Did you hear that lady? At the zoo?"

He nodded as he continued to put soap into the dishwasher. "I did."

"And?" I asked.

Townes stood to his full height, and part of me liked how I had to crane my neck to look at him. He raised a brow and crossed his arms. "And what? Am I supposed to have any particular thoughts on the matter?"

I blinked. "I thought you would. Do–do those comments not bother you?"

He leaned against the counter. "I've taught Hayley that a family is more than a mom and dad. It's the people that care about her, regardless of if they're related by blood. So, no, it doesn't bother me. Why? Did it bother you?"

No. It didn't.

I was more concerned about what Townes would think; worried it would make him and Hayley uncomfortable if they overheard. I shook my head, which threw us back into silence. At some point, Townes cleared his throat, which drew my attention in time to see how he rubbed the back of his neck.

"Mind if I borrow your room again? The couch is uncomfortable."

I smiled, and it didn't get past me how his eyes seemed to light up. "I'll get out the air mattress."

I went to walk past him, but he reached out and gently grabbed my wrist, stopping me in my tracks. My eyes met his, soft and warm. He licked his bottom lip as he took in a soft breath. "For what it's worth, I'm happy you're family. To Hayley I mean–she really loves you. I know she hasn't told you, and she might not, but you should know." Then, he dropped my wrist, and walked out of the kitchen. "I'm going out for a new bed, the one you have sucks."

36

Townes

Everyone in the crowd was booing–but there was nothing going on in front of me. Case was flying down the rink, dribbling the puck as he looked for an opening.

The booing continued as a defense man from the opposing team moved to block him. And he shot the puck at Riley at the last second. He wasted no time–the smack of his stick against the puck echoed around us before it hit the back of the net. It wasn't until the shot was made, that I finally glanced up to see what the fuck was going on. Had a fight broken out in the crowd?

My eyes scanned the unidentifiable bodies that sat in those uncomfortable plastic chairs, but nothing seemed amiss. Scottie skated by, and I noticed him just in time to catch him pointing up to the jumbotron. There was nothing unusual on the screen, besides the pink banner for the Kiss Cam. It darted between a few couples, who happily joined in on the fun. I was about to turn my attention back to the game, because that was more important. But I froze when Hollis appeared, with a man next to her.

Blood rushed to my ears as I watched them both hold up hands. It was obvious neither of them wanted to partake, yet people around them booed.

It was ridiculous. If she didn't want to kiss a stranger she didn't have to, for a second though, I wondered if she was going to. She looked at the man; decent hair, dressed well, and seemed like someone Hollis would be attracted to. My stomach churned as they spoke, still on the screen. I shouldn't care, I didn't actually. I was more concerned what Hayley would think if she was watching with her nana. Would she start asking Hollis about this mysterious man?

Family.

That was what the old woman called us at the zoo the other day, and it had been stuck in my head ever since. Was that what we were, in our own messed up way?

I couldn't look away as Hollis leaned into the man, and I couldn't explain the heat in my body as his hand rested against her cheek. It didn't matter. Hollis wasn't mine, she couldn't be.

So why was I clenching my jaw hard enough to hurt?

* * *

"So, why don't you want to go celebrate again? It's not too far past your bedtime," Hollis teased as she rolled her head to face me.

"Because we're leaving in a few days, and I want to rest up as much as I can," I said. It wasn't a complete lie. We were leaving in a few days, and I selfishly wanted Hollis's attention all to myself. Besides, what if the guy she kissed showed up?

257

What if he wanted to ask her on a date, and it complicated things between us? Those were things I didn't want to deal with, hence why we left right after the game without any formal goodbyes.

"Okay, but why are you dragging me home? I could have gotten a ride."

I kept my mouth shut, hopeful that for once, she wouldn't press.

Hollis drummed her fingers along her thigh for a moment, then, they stilled. "You know, I thought they didn't do the Kiss Cam thing anymore." My grip tightened on the steering wheel as she adjusted herself to face me better. "Or I thought it only happened in movies, but anyway–did you see me?"

The quietness in the car was suffocating.

"Of course not, you were busy working. Anyway, it kept swiveling back to me and this guy I was sitting next to. And we tried to tell the camera no, but the people did not like that." She laughed, and any other time I'd appreciate the sound, but right now I was ready to turn around and find whoever aimed that damn camera at her. "So, I ended up kissing the guy."

I could feel her staring at me, but I was too focused on getting home to respond. This...sensation. The heat running through my veins and the swelling in my chest–it was almost like the night we went dancing and I saw her talking to her dance partner. It was jealousy, and I didn't want it there.

I couldn't deny that I had developed feelings for Hollis, but I could still try to ignore the sensations in my chest anytime I thought about her. I was stuck between thinking Hollis needed someone who put her first, and knowing I was the only person who could do that if I had the chance.

A chance I wanted but didn't deserve.

Hollis narrowed her eyes for a moment, before she faced forward again and continued drumming her fingers. "I got his number too. Maybe we'll go on a date or something."

We pulled into the driveway, and I wasted no time shutting off the car before I rushed to the front door—desperate to escape the suffocating jealousy that hovered over me. Hollis followed behind me, and I swore I could hear something akin to humor lacing her words. "Do you think he would have been at the party?"

"Maybe," I said as I continued to my room.

"Oh." Her voice was soft and made me pause. "Okay, then."

"What?" I turned around and crossed my arms, surprised to see how upset she seemed.

She smiled and started walking toward her own room. "It's nothing."

I grabbed onto her arm and held her eyes. "It's not, what's wrong?"

Her face flushed deep red, and she was speechless for once. "I—uh—you had a different reaction than I was expecting."

"What were you expecting exactly?"

She shook her head and pulled away. "It's not important."

The way she darted her eyes away said otherwise, and it dawned on me. "Were you trying to make me jealous?"

"So what if I was?"

I was treading into dangerous territory. It wouldn't take much to get me to confess that, yes, I was jealous. If Hollis was going to be kissing anyone, it should be me, and not because she's my fake wife—but because I l—

Had feelings—strong feelings—for her.

I felt stuck, because even though I wanted her, I was still worried about the implications it would have on Hayley. If things didn't work out, we'd still be stuck until we could divorce. And that would cause too much contention in the house, which wasn't good for anybody. I rubbed a hand over my face and sighed. "You don't need to do that."

Hollis lifted her chin. "And why not? I can't be the only one who thinks things are–tense–between us."

I wondered if she knew how right she was–too often it felt like I was being pulled closer to her. When we walked together, I itched to reach out my hand and interlace our fingers; or at home cooking, I wanted to move her hair off her neck so she didn't get so hot over the stove.

So many times, I stayed up in my hotel bed and stared at the ceiling. I was still kicking myself for almost admitting to Hollis those dark secrets I never intended on telling her. Now, I had to tell her whatever she thought was there–wasn't.

Because the truth wasn't worth risking everything falling apart.

That was what I told myself, anyway.

I grit my teeth. "It's just you."

Her eyes narrowed before she huffed and walked toward her room. When the door shut, I sighed and walked to my room. I examined the wall where the giant hole used to be and was surprised with how good a job the contractors did–considering it took so long to get the job done I was expecting worse. I changed into more comfortable clothes, then headed to grab a drink.

However, I stopped when I rounded the corner and saw Hollis standing there in nothing but a T-shirt.

My T-shirt.

I'd be lying if I said I tried to keep my eyes above her waist. "Why are you wearing my clothes?"

Hollis grabbed some ice cream, then a spoon, and hopped up onto the counter. "Cause I'm doing laundry and wasn't about to parade around in my underwear. You don't want to see that, do you roomie?"

She wasn't wrong–I'd rather see her not wearing anything. *No. Don't got there.*

"You're right. Although, I'd prefer if you were on top of things like laundry, so you weren't wearing my clothes either."

"Do you want them back?" she asked.

Before I could respond, her feet landed on the floor. Then, she moved to lift the shirt. I caught a glimpse of purple underwear before I reached for her. My hands wrapped around her wrists and held them still. She was still gripping the shirt and was looking at me with a determination I hadn't seen before. I could feel my blood rushing south and making my pants tighter.

"What are you doing?"

"Taking off your clothes. Mine still have about twenty minutes before they're done so I'll head back to my room until then." She went to try and move the shirt up again, but my firm grip kept her in place.

"No, it's fine for now ju–just next time don't do it."

She raised a brow and took a step closer into my space. I looked down at her, and when she smirked…

I wanted to close the distance and bite her bottom lip to keep that fucking smirk from her pretty face.

"If I don't take this shirt off now then consider it mine. You won't get it back," she said, her tone challenging.

I clenched my jaw hard enough to crack a tooth, but I couldn't do anything but stare at her. Her eyes roamed my face as I contemplated my next words. My grip tightened, just enough to make her let out a small gasp. "There's something you need to know," I started, still holding onto those baby blues like my life depended on it. "Whatever this is–that we're doing. It has to stop."

Her brows creased, and she cocked her head to the side. "What are you talking about? I was under the impression you didn't care. So, what's a bit of harmless flirting between friends?"

"Just because I don't care doesn't mean I appreciate the flirting."

Her bottom lip quivered, and I felt like an asshole. Which, I knew I was, but right now wasn't the time to try and explain my complex feelings to her. So, I let her wrist go, grabbed my drink, and walked back to my room.

Two weeks away would be good for me to get my thoughts and feelings sorted. I just wished I left sooner.

37

Hollis

The thing about being paired up with a man named Kyle...I knew he was going to be an asshole. We hadn't been at the carnival for an hour, and he'd already pawned all the work onto me. Sure, he showed up with the stuffed animals we needed for prizes, but then he disappeared. Eager to grab a couple beers before the families and kids started to show up.

Arnold, thankfully, had gotten his booth done early and offered to help me. We had just finished setting up the last of the bottles for ring toss when a man walked up to us; his hair was combed to the side and he wore a plaid button up with gray slacks. A bit much for a carnival, but who was I to judge?

He embraced Arnold and gave him a kiss on the cheek. "You were supposed to be back fifteen minutes ago," he said. There was no disappointment in his voice, he was simply reiterating what Arnold had clearly told him.

"Sorry, I got caught up. Hollis, this is my husband, Taylor."

I held out my hand, and Taylor took it with a wide smile.

"Ah, so you're my husband's favorite co-worker. It's nice to meet you."

I hadn't realized I garnered so much favoritism over shared planning periods these past few months. "Likewise. Thanks for letting me borrow him."

"Not a problem, especially since your partner left you high and dry," he said, wrapping an arm around his husband.

I wasn't going to say anything bad about Kyle in front of anyone. Not because he didn't deserve it, but because it wouldn't change anything. Besides, they already knew what I was working with–nothing was going to change that. I cleared my throat and smoothed my dress. The weather was uncharacteristically warm for mid-March, so I jumped at the chance to wear the purple dress Townes bought me a while ago. The cuff sleeves sat low on my shoulders, leaving my collarbones exposed, save for the curls that fell over them.

I shrugged. "It's not an issue. To be honest, I'd rather him be gone, it'll make my night easier."

"If you say so," Arnold said, sparing a quick glance to Taylor. "Where's Hayley? I haven't seen her yet, is her uncle bringing her?"

I was relieved to know that all the teachers and admin at the school knew about her living situation. It saved me from explaining Townes wasn't her dad, and any questions that could have followed. "Her grandmother is bringing her, Townes isn't getting back until later tonight."

To say I was disappointed was an understatement. The plan was for Hayley to come with everyone, that way she'd be able to stay until the carnival closed. Marion however, wasn't going to let her stay out past nine, and they wouldn't even get here until an hour after opening. Whether Hayley knew that or not, I didn't know, but I wasn't going to be the one to break it to her. Arnold dropped his hand to lace his fingers with Taylor's and a longing tightened my chest.

I had been wrong about Townes, and how he felt, and it left a gaping hole in my chest. How could I have been so clueless?

"Well, the gates are about to open. If you need help with anything, feel free to steal me, or Taylor. Since I doubt Kyle's going to be back anytime soon."

"What are we talking about?"

We all turned, and found Kyle walking toward us, with a can of beer in his hands. "Just that we missed you," I said, keeping my voice free of sarcasm. Maybe I could convince him to stay, and I'd be able to take Hayley to some of the booths. Arnold, Taylor, and I shared parting glances as they walked back to their booth on the other side of the carnival. Kyle pulled out a chair and sat down.

"Are we allowed to drink? Around all the kids at a school function, I mean," I said as he put his head back and drank.

He shrugged. "Don't worry princess, I'm not drinking around the kids. I just wanted to grab one before it was all gone."

That word, princess, grated against my nerves. I smiled anyway and smoothed the wrinkles in my dress. Kyle then put the beer away, just as the first wave of laughter sounded from the gates.

The children and their families came in waves. With the adults splitting off to the concession stands, and the kids spending coins at the booths. Laughter filled the air, along with music and the sounds of prizes being won. Our booth was a hit too, most of the small prizes were almost gone after an hour, but I was silently hoping no one would get the giant, pink unicorn. That was for Hayley.

If she ever showed up.

Marion had ignored all my text messages, and Townes was still on a plane so I couldn't ask him for help. Was she still so upset with me she'd deny bringing Hayley tonight? My palms sweat with each child that won a prize, and my eyes kept darting around the crowd.

"Who're you looking for? A boyfriend?" Kyle asked as he restacked a few fallen bottles.

I shook my head. "Hayley, she's supposed to be here."

He raised a brow. "What's the deal with that anyway? Are you dating her uncle or something?"

"What? No, we're not dating," I said with heated cheeks. I busied myself with adjusting the prizes when Kyle stood.

He faced me, and I didn't like the way his eyes roamed over me. "Are you looking to date? Cause I gotta be honest, I've had a thing for you since you started."

"We barely know each other," I said.

"One date then? We can get to know each other that way. If we don't click, then we'll go our separate ways," he offered.

Kyle was a lot like Ryan. He put himself first and didn't seem to care if he hurt others in the process. If I were younger, and new to love, I'd jump on the chance to be with him. I knew better though, and even though I messed up and misread Townes's feelings–I wasn't going to be with anyone until this thing between us was over.

I cleared my throat of the uneasiness that settled there and did my best to smile. "I'm not interested, Kyle."

His proud smile fell, and initially I was worried it was because he was mad. It wouldn't be the first time I upset a man for rejecting him, so I braced myself. I was ready to tell him off or go find Arnold if I really needed help.

"I understand," he said before he turned around and busied himself with his phone. I was about to excuse myself to grab a drink when a loud voice called from somewhere in the crowd.

"Hollis!"

I whirled around just in time for a small, curly haired little girl to barrel into my legs. "Oof–"

My arms wrapped around her as she peered up and smiled. She wore a glow stick crown, and a few cheap beaded necklaces. "When did you get here? And where's your Nana?" I asked as I scanned the crowd again.

I vaguely heard her explain Marion was still at home because Townes came home early and surprised her. My eyes remained on Townes as he walked toward us, Scottie was at his side carrying prized stuffed animals, and Case walked with Basil as they shared cotton candy. I could feel the intensity in his stare as he walked, it's what kept me grounded instead of bouncing for joy to see him–though that would have been a bit much. I kept calm as they made their way to the booth.

Hayley ran to Scottie's side and tugged on his full arms. "You see all the stuff I got?"

"You won all that?" I asked, eyes darting around the group.

Scottie nodded. "She's a wiz at these games, I don't know how, but she's beaten all of us."

"Townes got really upset when he couldn't win the balloon darts, Hayley won the giant frog right there," Case said as he pointed to the stuffed animal, buried beneath the others in Scottie's arms.

Finally, I looked at Townes and smirked. "You let an eight-year-old kick your butt at darts?"

His eyes, dark and heated, dragged over my body, and I felt their touch like a whisper against my skin. Over my neck, my collarbones, and they widened when they landed on the dress. His nostrils flared, and his eyes flicked back up. Heat bubbled in my lower stomach—but it was too much. The reaction I was feeling wasn't warranted, so, I turned away and faced Basil.

"How come you didn't tell me they were coming early?"

She pinched off a tuft of cotton candy. "Hey, I didn't know until Case came home. I was planning on watching movies until I fell asleep."

"Townes mentioned the carnival, so we met up outside after he got Hayley," Scottie said. "And now if you'll excuse me, I need to put some of this in your car. Otherwise, you'll have to keep her from playing anymore games."

"We'll go with you. I want some funnel cake. Hayley, you coming too? We can find more games on the way back to the car," Case said, already walking away.

Hayley nodded and waved. "See you later!"

She ran past the line of children who gathered for the ring toss. I hadn't realized it had gotten so busy, but Kyle didn't seem to have any problems. I rocked back on my heels and looked around a moment before looking at Townes again. His eyes seemed darker—which had to be a trick of the light. "You wanna get some food?"

He didn't respond, which made the tension between us that much thicker. It didn't make sense, we knew where we stood, so why was he being all moody? I sighed and walked back to grab my bag from inside the booth. I faced Kyle and smiled. "I'll be right back, do you want me to grab you anything?"

Kyle looked between Townes and me, then shook his head. "I'm fine."

I nodded and slung my bag over my shoulder. Then, I headed toward the concession stands that lined the Ferris wheel. Townes trailed behind me the entire way, and I itched to break the silence. I ordered a funnel cake and waited patiently by Townes side. He held himself straight as a rod while his scowl scanned the crowd. I caved and poked his side.

"What?"

I blinked. "What do you mean, what? You're the one being all stoic. What's up your ass?"

"Nothing."

There was something about that word that snapped my patience. It never bothered me if Townes wasn't in a good mood, but after everything; the denial of any feelings I thought he had, not texting me back when I was panicking about Hayley, and how he acted when he showed up.

I was pissed.

The man called my name, and I marched to grab my food. Then, without a word, I stormed past Townes and made my way around the carnival grounds. Like last time, he trailed behind me, and it just made my mood worse. I passed laughing children, happy couples, and tired parents as I walked and envied their joy. My night started fine, but now it had soured, and it only got worse with the fact that Townes wasn't going to talk to me. I could push as much as I wanted, but he wasn't going to give.

The only thing I could do was calm down, then try talking to him.

I threw my plate into the trash next to a photo booth, and

sighed, preparing myself to face Townes. When I turned around, his eyes were still full of something dark, but I pushed away the chills it sent over my body. "What's your fucking problem?"

He walked closer, slow and deliberate.

"You show up without a heads up, had me anxious about where Hayley was, and then you don't say anything? I don't know why you even stayed Townes, you should have just gone off with everyone else if you weren't going to say anything. But no, instead you're following after me, and honestly, you're sending mixed signals. I get it, my feelings were misplaced, but that does–oof–"

Townes grabbed my wrist and pulled me into the photo booth. The black curtain shut, and I was hauled into his lap. His hands gripped the back of my thighs as he peered up at me. Heat rushed to all parts of my body, and I knew how red my face must have been.

What was he doing?

His hands tightened, and he pulled me closer until his chin grazed my breasts. My knees bit into the metal of the bench, but I was too focused on his touch to care. I placed my hands on his shoulders to keep myself steady as I tried to take in what was happening. His tongue ran along his bottom lip before he took a shuddering breath.

"The plan was to surprise you, have some fun before we went home and I could talk to you. But then I showed up and saw you wearing this fucking dress." His hands inched higher, and his voice lowered. "My plan went out the window."

My breath hitched with each inch of skin he discovered. "Wh–what were you going to talk to me about?" I had to keep my eyes from fluttering shut at the sensation of his calloused skin on mine.

He leaned in, and a hand moved to cup my face. "Do you really feel like talking right now?"

No. Not with how his thumb ran over my bottom lip, and the hand on my thigh worked to pull me closer to him. Talking was the last thing on my mind.

He was so close my breath caressed his lips as he moved closer. "I need an answer, baby," he whispered as his hand moved to the nape of my neck. I held in a moan as he gripped my hair and tugged.

"No, no talking." I breathed.

Nothing else mattered in that moment. Not the fact I left my co-worker high and dry, not the people bustling just outside that flimsy curtain. The only thing I could think about was his mouth on mine, and what would come after.

His grip tightened, both on my hair and on my thigh. Then, he pushed my head forward, closer to his lips before he whispered. "Thank fuck."

38

Townes

My hand gripped tighter in Hollis's hair as my lips met hers, and I swallowed the quiet, sweet moan that followed.

I had every intention of talking to her about the feelings that awoke in my chest every time I saw her. Everything was going great; our flight got in early, I surprised Hayley when I picked her up, and our friends came to help keep her busy while I was supposed to be telling Hollis my feelings on the Ferris wheel. Like in those summer romance movies she likes to watch, our passenger car would have stopped at the top, and I would have told her my feelings. They were still new, and I had hoped she would have been patient with me while I navigated them with her.

But then I showed up and saw her in that damn sun dress.

I wasn't going to lie to myself, and say I bought it just because I knew Hayley would have loved to match with her. I wanted to see Hollis wear it, because I let my dick do the thinking for once.

Hollis pulled back to catch her breath, but I wasn't ready

to let her go.

"Towne-"

"I thought we agreed. No talking," I said before my lips met hers again. I swept my tongue over her bottom lip, and she opened with another moan. I took my time; exploring her mouth, running my tongue over hers as she made no attempt to take the lead. My hand traveled up her exposed thigh until it rested on the curve of her ass. Then, I squeezed as I tried once again to pull her closer, it wasn't enough though. I needed more.

Hollis broke away, and while she started peppering kisses down my neck, I began loosening the floral fabric on her breasts. I wrestled it down, then worked on moving her bra aside, and when there was nothing separating her perky nipples against the air, I moved. She sucked in breath through her teeth when mine wrapped around her nipple, then she began to rock against me.

I squeezed her ass again, because if I smacked it here–where anyone could walk by any moment–this would have to end sooner than I wanted.

I took my time, sucking and biting her breast until Hollis was gasping against me. When I pulled away, Hollis's hands grasped my face, and her mouth was on mine again. I moved a hand from her ass, and grabbed her exposed breast before I pinched her nipple. As I kissed her neck, Hollis moaned and gasped against my ear. I was so overwhelmed with her; how she felt writhing under me, that sweet cherry smell, and how she sounded, that I hadn't realized the pounding coming from outside.

It wasn't until Hollis pushed away and adjusted her dress that I realized what was going on.

"Hey! This is a family friendly function! Go do that shit somewhere else!" a voice said from outside.

Hollis was trying to get off my lap, but I wasn't ready to let her go yet. "Hey, it's okay," I said.

Her face was flushed the most beautiful shade of pink, and I wanted to kiss her again. Trace the color with my lips and see how far down it went. She took slow breaths to calm down. "It's jus–I've neve–we're in *public*, Townes."

I moved a stray curl out of her face. "No one saw anything, it's fine."

Her eyes watched as my hand dropped back to her leg, and the pink along her cheeks deepened to a red. "I uh–I don't know what to do now," she said, her voice barely a whisper.

"Well, what do you want to do?" I asked, my hand moved along her thigh in slow strokes. I knew what I wanted, but Hollis was still technically working. Kind of. And while I was more than happy to continue this at home, I wasn't sure what she wanted. We still had to talk, clear the air before we went any farther.

I watched as she worked her bottom lip between her teeth and thought it over. My hand continued moving up and down her leg, as if I was working on memorizing this one part of her. Hollis smiled, but it wasn't bright and kind like all the other ones. This one seemed sad and vaguely annoyed. "I suppose I have to get back and help with the booth." She grabbed my hand and interlaced our fingers. She kept her focus on our hands and lowered her voice. "Do you want to come with me?"

With my other hand, I placed my thumb under her chin, and lifted her face so she could see me. "I need to make sure Hayley hasn't drained Scottie and Case of all their pride and money. When I know their egos are intact, I'll come get you."

She nodded, and I hesitated. It wasn't fair; when all I wanted to do was keep touching her, to feel her again, but I had to let her go. I kissed her fingers before I peered up at her, soaking in the softness of her face so it would tide me over until later tonight.

"Oh, let's take some pictures first!" Hollis reached for my pocket, and grabbed my wallet before she maneuvered herself so she was sitting in my lap, now facing the camera in front of us. She pressed a few buttons I hadn't paid attention to, because I was so focused on her. She faced me and smiled. "Say cheese, you big oaf."

As Hollis turned away, and as the camera clicked, I kept my gaze on her. It was impossible to look away, and now that I had crossed that invisible line between us, I never wanted to let her out of my sight again.

When the pictures were done, Hollis leapt off my lap and out of the photo booth. I took a moment to rub my knee before I met her outside. Her hair was wild, and she was frowning at the photos in her hands. "You're smiling," she said.

"You told me to. What's with the face?" I asked.

Her cheeks flushed again, but she just shook her head and handed me the pictures. "You take them since you have pockets. I've got to go. Can you bring Hayley by? There's a giant pink unicorn with her name on it that I've been hoarding from the other kids."

She turned, and I was too busy looking at the photos to realize she had paused. Hollis whirled back around and tugged on my arm so I was at her level before she placed a kiss on my cheek. "I'll see you in a bit."

I wanted to wrap my arm around her waist and keep her next to me. But she was too fast and was running back toward her booth. When she was out of sight, I put the pictures into my back pocket and started back toward the crowd. The carnival lights flashed across my vision as I walked, the sounds of laughter and music filled my ears and made it hard to concentrate on finding everyone. Eventually I found them–filling up a balloon by shooting water in a plastic clown's mouth. Hayley had more plastic beads on her neck than before, and a glow stick was wrapped around her head.

Scottie shot up and threw his arms in the air when his balloon popped first. "Ha! Take that loser!" He pointed to Hayley with a giant grin. People around us glared and whispered their disapproval of him mocking a child. Scottie's eyes widened as he tried to explain himself. "You don't get it! She's a menace! Wait, that's the wrong word. Hm, a cheat maybe?"

Hayley jumped off the stool, and patted Scottie's arm. "It's okay. Sometimes it's nice to let others win."

"What are you talking about? I won fair and square!"

She smiled, the expression was filled with mocking humor. "Sure, Uncle Scottie. If you say so."

His head snapped up at me, and he shook his head as he grabbed the stuffed monkey from the attendant. "How did you manage to raise such a smart ass?"

"Jar!" Hayley proclaimed as she skipped past him, and toward Case and Basil, who were walking up.

"I know!" He called after her. "Really though, how'd you do it, T?"

I shrugged. "I guess my attitude rubbed off on her, the only difference is she's happier."

I watched as Hayley grabbed Case's hand, and walked away, toward the carousel. We'd have to leave soon, it was well past her bedtime and she was going to crash from all the candy she ate. I noticed Scottie staring, and the small, teasing grin crossing his face. "What?"

"Oh, nothing. Something's just–different. Did you talk to Hollis?"

My non-answer was enough for him, because his grin widened. His hand connected with my upper back. "I'm happy for you man, really happy."

"Don't get sappy on me. No, she and I haven't talked yet."

"Well then what di–Oh! No way!"

I walked away as Scottie grabbed his head in dramatics. He didn't follow as I walked toward Case, who was watching Basil and Hayley whirl around while sitting on plastic horses. I rested against the metal gate separating the dwindling crowd from the machine and sighed.

Case raised a brow. "What're you doing here?"

"Hollis asked me to bring Hayley to the ring toss," I said.

Hayley giggled as the machine started to slow, and part of me wished I kept Hollis to myself. She'd have loved to be up there with Hayley.

Case nodded, and we both watched as Basil helped Hayley off the plastic horse, then down the steps so they could exit the area. When Hayley stood in front of me, she rubbed her eyes and stifled a yawn. Now, the smart thing to do would be to take Hayley home, and text Hollis an apology.

I wasn't smart though, not tonight.

"You want to go play one more game?" I asked.

Hayley nodded and yawned again. "Who's butt am I kicking this time?"

I chuckled and shook my head. "Mine, now come on. We need to go before they start tearing everything down."

We said our goodbyes to Case, Basil, and Scottie before we started for the ring toss.

The crowd thinned as we walked; parents carried sleeping children and couples walked leisurely back to the gates. Booths were also being torn down, and at some point, the music had shut off. Hayley was dragging her feet, and I had to grab her hand to make sure she didn't get lost.

Soon enough, the booth came into view, and Hollis stood there with a smile. We walked up, and I noticed it was just Hollis, the other man was nowhere to be seen. Hollis knelt and smoothed Hayley's hair. "You ready to kick your uncle's butt?"

"Always," Hayley said with a slow, tired nod.

Hollis explained the rules before she handed us both colorful, plastic rings. Hayley threw the first one, and it landed over a blue bottle. I threw the rings without any strategy or care for winning. My focus was on Hollis and how she still beamed under the dim lights. I traced over her body, ready to see how she looked bare beneath me.

"Ah, good try Uncle T." Hayley patted my arm, then rested her head against my side. "I'm tired."

I picked her up, and her head laid against my shoulder as I turned to Hollis. She already had that giant pink unicorn in her hands.

She was beautiful.

"Don't you need to tear down the booth? I can wait in the car," I said.

Hollis shook her head. "Kyle's got it." She stepped forward and wrapped her hand around my arm. "Let's go home."

39

Hollis

My eyes darted from Townes, and his white knuckles around the steering wheel, to Hayley who snored softly in the backseat. I hummed to try and calm my nerves, which were attempting to chew their way out of my body.

The way his hands felt, gripping my hair, on my ass, his fucking *mouth*–

A hand landed on my thigh, pulling me from my thoughts. I looked at Townes and tried to contain the heat building in my lower stomach. He kept his focus on the road though, and gave my leg a possessive squeeze. The tension in the car was heavy and didn't let up even as we parked in the driveway and headed inside. Townes had Hayley in his arms as I opened the door. I watched them disappear around the corner before I went to grab a drink of water.

I needed something to try and cool myself down.

The wind whispered against the window overlooking the garden, where the flowers danced above the soil. As I watched them, a chill ran down my spine at the sound of footsteps.

They were slow, deliberate, as if the person they belonged to wanted to preserve the sight in front of them.

A hand swept my hair off my neck, and my skin peppered at the coolness before a gentle kiss was placed over them. I sighed and rolled my head to the side.

Another kiss landed just below my ear.

"Do you know how many times I've thought about doing this?" Townes asked, his voice a touch above a whisper. One hand came to grip my waist before he pulled me back, and I gasped when I found him hard against me. "Shh, you've got to be quiet."

I rolled my hips back, and he let out a hiss. I did it again, which caused his grip to tighten. Looking back over my shoulder, I was stunned to see how disheveled he seemed. His hair was a mess, and his eyes were so dark, overflowing with lust and dark thoughts, I was drowning in them. Townes wrapped his free hand around my jaw, his fingers spread over my cheek, then he kissed me.

A moan escaped me as his tongue licked my bottom lip, a plead. My mouth opened without restraint, and I turned in his arms. His hands traveled down my back until they caressed my ass.

I bit his lip, and he groaned as he pulled me toward him, his kisses turning frantic. We were a mess—he pulled my hair as I yanked on the collar of his shirt, needing to be closer. I dropped a hand and grabbed him through his jeans.

"Fuck," he growled, thrusting into my hand.

I pulled back, breathing heavy as I smirked. "What happened to being quiet?"

Townes stared at me in defiance, and the look in his eyes sent flutters to my stomach. I was already hot and aching for him–I couldn't hold on much longer before I'd start begging.

"Oh, I can be quiet."

"Wait, what are yo–"

Townes placed me on the counter and pulled my hips forward until my ass rested on the edge. Then, he was lifting the skirt of my dress, and throwing it over my legs before he started working on tugging down my underwear. He moved back up to kiss me again and his fingers ran up my thigh.

"I've thought about this too," he whispered, his hand inching closer to where I was wet for him. "Wondered how much it took to get your cunt soaking wet, turns out, it isn't much."

I bucked my hips against his hand, and whimpered when he removed it from my skin. Townes pulled back a fraction to stare at me, his brows pulled in. "What do you want, Hollis?"

My tongue was like lead in my mouth as I opened it to speak. Nothing came out, and my mind went dizzy as Townes put his hand back and started those teasing movements again. He had one hand on my hip as he peered down. "God, look at you."

I went to buck my hips again when his fingers grazed my clit, but he kept me pinned down. "Townes–"

"Yes, baby?"

"Touch me." I held in a moan when his fingers hovered above my entrance. "Please."

"Touch?" Townes inserted one finger, and I had to bite his shoulder to keep from moaning out. He leaned in to whisper in my ear, "I'd rather taste."

He peppered kisses over my skin as he lowered to his knees, then he gave me a quick, glance when he paused an inch from where I wanted him most. It didn't take a lot to know what he was doing–he was asking for permission. My heart swelled at the gesture. I nodded, and he wasted no time running his tongue up my slit.

My head rolled back in pleasure as Townes took his time licking and sucking. The only sounds were my breathing, and the wet noises he made between my legs. As his beard tickled my thighs, I grabbed his hair and started moving my hips against him. I felt something thick brush along my entrance before I was filled, and I arched against him. Townes was fucking me with his finger as he sucked on my clit, and I was helpless to do anything besides *try* and stay quiet.

Townes continued to work me until the heat in my belly simmered, and everything started to pull tight. He moaned before his fingers started pumping faster, and his tongue flicked over my clit in a blinding rhythm. I yanked on his hair as I came and bit the back of my hand so I could contain the moan that was ripped out of my throat. I sat on the counter, legs shaking and chest heaving as Townes stood to his full height and wiped his chin.

Then, he helped me to my feet, and caged my head between his strong hands before he bent down to kiss me again. My head swam and my body felt limp, the only thing keeping me upright was the way he held me. He kissed me again, slow but still full of an ache that hadn't been satisfied. I reached down again and palmed his still hard cock.

He groaned and threw his head back. "Fuck, no—not here."

In one swoop, Townes was placed his hands on the back of my thighs and lifted me. His lips met mine as he started walking down the hallway. I wasn't sure where he was going, nor did I care, so long as he continued to touch me—I was happy.

A door clicked shut, and I wasn't sure if we were in his

room or mine, not that it really mattered. I was satisfied with any surface Townes decided to fuck me into. Townes knelt and leaned me back into the mattress, but his lips never left mine. Not even as his hands traveled down my body, or as his belt buckle being undone echoed in the room. He kicked his jeans off and removed my dress as his hands trailed back up. As I sat up to remove the fabric the rest of the way I could feel those brown eyes burning over my body.

Townes was taking shallow breaths as he looked at me, bare before him. A tingle of self-doubt crawled its way into my mind, and I moved to cover myself. Past insecurities–however much unwelcomed–had a way of rearing their ugly head. I'd been told before my stomach wasn't flat enough, as if keeping my body healthy was a bad thing.

"Don't do that," Townes said as he reached for my hands. He pulled them down and placed a kiss on my collarbone. "Not with me, please. I love looking at you."

I grabbed onto his hair and scratched my fingers against his scalp, earning me another deep groan and a small bite on my skin. Townes kissed down my chest, then stopped to flick a perk nipple with his tongue. I arched against him and realized two things; he had taken off his shirt, revealing tattoos usually hidden under his shirts, and he was touching himself as he touched me.

I watched as he fucked his fist, and whimpered when he bit the sensitive skin of my breast. Then, he traveled back up, and placed a kiss on my forehead before he pulled back. He reached over to his forgotten pants and pulled out a shiny wrapper.

Heat bubbled in my stomach as he unwrapped the condom and put it on.

"You always keep a condom in your pocket?" I asked with a smile.

Townes caged my head between his forearms before he lined himself against my entrance. "I picked them up after we landed."

"Oh, so you're cocky," I said.

He leaned in close to my ear and pushed forward, earning a gasp from me as I stretched around him. "So cocky."

Townes took his time, kissing my face as I adjusted to his size. It was too slow though, whether he thought I was fragile or because he was a masochist and he was delaying the inevitable. When he was fully seated, he buried his face in my hair to muffle his groan.

"Feel s–so fucking good baby girl," he said as he pulled out, only to pound back in. I gasped, and my mouth was promptly covered with his tattooed hand. "You've got to stay quiet."

I moaned against his hand as his thrusts turned faster. Then, my eyes shut as he hit a spot that made me grab onto his arm. My nails dug into his skin as he did it again. Townes kissed my neck, his movements unrelenting as I turned into a mess under him. He stopped and bit the skin just below my ear.

When I groaned, his hand tightened.

"You're doing so good for me baby, just stay quiet a little longer, okay?" I shook my head, I wanted to scream as he continued thrusting without abandon. Townes moved so his eyes were on mine, and he moved his hand so my face was level with his. "You can take it."

I grabbed his hand–needing something to hold onto as he fucked me–and closed my eyes with the overwhelming pleasure.

"Look at me, baby." His voice was a plea I couldn't ignore.

So, I opened my eyes, and held his stare. "Yes, look at me while I fuck your perfect pussy."

Through muffled moans and slaps of skin, Townes continued his words of praise, until I was a writhing mess and everything in me surged tight. He removed his hand and held my hips down as his thrusts picked up in intensity. I reached up and grabbed onto his headboard, making sure to keep my voice down as I told him. "Go—gonna come—"

Townes's grip tightened, and his mouth hung open. "Let me feel you baby."

Molten liquid spread throughout my body as I came undone, and I slapped a hand over my mouth as Townes fucked me through it. Only to tip over the edge himself a moment later.

He kissed me as he continued thrusting into me, his movements becoming as tired, and lazy as the kisses he gave me. Tired, I stared at the ceiling as Townes pulled out and threw the condom into the small trash can by his door. I took the time to sneak into the hallway bathroom while he finished cleaning up. When I got back into the room, and crawled into bed, I stared at him, naked and amazing as he walked back toward me. The tattoo on his chest was on full display.

It was two hands, reaching out for each other, with the pointer fingers barely touching. I'd seen it before, in a painting somewhere. It was adorned by other various geometric shapes that were full of dotted lines and mathematical looking equations I wasn't aware enough to contemplate. The ink stretched down his right side and stopped just above his waist.

Townes climbed into the bed beside me, and turned on his side to adjust the blanket over us both. Then he wrapped a tattooed arm around my waist, and pulled me against him so my back was against his front. He then placed a kiss on the back of my neck as my eyes drew heavy.

I knew we had a lot to talk about, but that could come another day. Because in this moment, being held in his arms was the only thing that mattered.

40

Townes

On a normal Sunday, I would wake up before everyone else. I had grown used to getting off that uncomfortable air mattress without making any sound. Bilbo would stretch from where she slept on Hollis's bed before jumping down and following me out of the room. She'd meet me in the kitchen, where I'd feed her overpriced wet food before I started making breakfast. Pancakes, eggs for Hollis, and some bacon for Hayley.

Today however, I was still in bed. Tracing the soft lines and contours of Hollis's face as she slept beside me. Her shoulders, bare and soft, moved as she breathed. The comforter was tucked under her arms, and I took advantage of the exposed skin, and traced the few freckles that adorned her body. She only stirred when I moved a curl behind her ear and placed a kiss on her forehead.

Her blue eyes opened, and found mine, as if they were the first thing she wanted to see. Hollis smiled, slow and tired. "G'morning."

I cupped her face and caressed her cheek with my thumb.

"You sleep okay?"

Her nose scrunched as her eyes narrowed. "Do you feel okay? Cause the Townes I know wouldn't be so curious about how I slept."

I smiled, and the surprise that flashed across Hollis's face didn't escape me. I dropped my head as I removed my hand from her face, wrapping it around her waist and pulling her closer. She gasped when I placed a kiss on her neck.

"The Townes you knew before hadn't fucked you into the mattress. So please forgive me for wanting to make sure you slept okay."

When I pulled back, her face was bright red, and the color traveled down her chest and hid under the covers. I wanted to pull them back and see just how far down it went. There were so many things I wanted to do actually, but something I needed to do first.

My brows pulled in, and I kept my gaze down on where I had interlaced our fingers on the bed.

"Hollis, if I misread anything–"

She placed her thumb under my, lifting my chin. "You didn't, I promise."

Thank god. If I had misjudged her feelings, got them mixed up with mine, then I'd be forced to avoid her until we eventually divorced.

Because that's still happening.

Right.

As Hollis looked at me, eyes so blue in the morning, soft and clear–I was hard. And by the way her face flushed again, she knew it too. I grabbed her waist, and rolled us until I was on top, and started kissing her neck. Careful, quiet moans escaped her lips as I started trailing those kisses down her stomach. I took my time worshiping her with my mouth, over her already perk nipples, her soft stomach. I traveled down and bit her hip, which earned me a squeal.

Her hands dropped and grabbed my hair, making me pause. I realized that last night wasn't enough, I would never get enough. But if she wanted me to stop, I'd give her another kiss and go make some food.

Whatever she wanted, I'd give it to her.

Hollis started to pull my head toward her, and I breathed a sigh of relief. I took one hand and spread her lips to find her already wet. Her clit swollen as I brushed a finger over it. She bucked her hips, reaching for more. I wasn't strong enough to deny her any pleasure, so I flicked my tongue over her clit and started eating. Hollis's moan was muffled, as if she had gotten a hold of a pillow, and her noises didn't stop.

"More," she breathed.

I pulled away for a second and wet my first two fingers before sticking them into her wet cunt. She stretched around me, and I was jealous of my own fucking fingers. It should be my cock fucking into her, but it was too risky.

I felt her start to tighten as I continued flicking her clit, and only pulled away at the very last second to swallow her moans with a deep kiss as she came undone. My fingers kept moving though, until Hollis was shaking from overstimulation, and she had to reach down to still my teasing hand. I continued to kiss down her face and neck until her breathing returned to normal. She grabbed my face between her hands and kissed my nose before pulling back to stare at me.

We didn't need words between us to know how the other one was feeling. In this moment, we were both happy. Stuck in our own little world where–

A knock.

"Uncle T? Do we have cereal?"

Hollis and I stared at each other in panic before she moved to roll off the bed, and I grabbed a pillow to place over my lap. The door opened just as Hollis landed on the wooden floor, and Hayley stood in the doorway with Bilbo in her arms. I cleared my throat. "Do you see any cereal?"

Hayley's eyes narrowed. "I can't see above the fourth shelf."

"Guess you'll never know then," I said.

"I'll ask Hollis. She's nice in the mornings." Hayley moved to walk away, but I removed the blanket and started for the kitchen.

"All this attitude for some cereal," I mumbled as I walked toward the door. I made sure Hayley rounded the corner to the kitchen before glancing back at Hollis. She stood there, putting on her dress from last night, and it was impossible to look away. I hated last night when she tried to cover herself, and it made me want to throttle whoever put any doubt in her mind that she was anything less than perfect.

"Uncle T?" Hayley called, her footsteps echoing back down the hallway.

Hollis cocked her head and smiled. "Go help her find cereal, I'll be out there soon."

God, I wanted to kiss her—but she was right. So, I left the room, and grabbed Hayley by her shoulders before I spun her around and led her back to the kitchen. She sat at the table, and I could feel her eyes on me as I grabbed the cereal from the top shelf in the pantry. I placed a bowl on the counter, and the sound of cornflakes hitting the ceramic filled the empty space. It was weird, Hayley being so quiet.

I placed the bowl and milk in front of her, and found her

eyes narrowed as she stared at me.

"What?"

"You're acting weird," she said, grabbing the milk and pouring it into the bowl.

I scoffed. "How?"

Her eyes darted between mine for a moment. "You're happy."

"So that means I'm acting weird?"

She shoved her spoon into her food and laughed. "Yes! It's like your scowl moved to your lips. You were smiling when you made my food."

Hollis walked into the kitchen, in jeans and a long sleeve shirt, as if her being covered would do anything to deter my thoughts of imagining her naked. Being bent over the counter an–

"Your uncle was smiling? Townes are you okay? Need me to make you a doctor's appointment?"

"I just got a checkup actually, and you might be surprised to know I'm in tip. Top. Shape."

Hollis bit her lip, and I was grateful that Hayley was too busy eating to call me out for the way I smiled. First, I was outwardly happy making her food, now I was smiling.

"I believe it," Hollis said as she walked past me.

"Uncle T, can we do something today?"

I crossed my arms and leaned back against the counter. "Something like what? You had a long night, don't you want to just stay inside today?"

She laughed. "Of course not. Can we meet Uncle Casey and Uncle Scottie at the park?"

"Probably not the park. But I'll call them and see what we can do."

Hayley skipped to place her bowl in the sink, then turned to give Hollis a hug. "I knocked on your door, but you didn't answer."

Hollis blushed, and I could see her scramble for an excuse. It wasn't like her to sleep in, so it wasn't surprising that Hayley was curious. I continued leaning against the counter as Hollis stumbled for words. "I was sleeping."

"But I didn't hear any snoring," Hayley said.

"I don't snore."

I coughed. "Yes you do."

Hollis aimed her glare at me and pointed a finger. "You stay out of this. Hayley, I promise, I was sleeping in this morning. Last night was–it took a lot out of me."

Hayley shrugged. "That's okay. So, can we–oh! Can we go to the trampoline park?"

I sighed when Hayley ran up to me, her hands placed under her chin in a plea.

"Let me call your uncles. You go get dressed."

Before I even finished talking, she was running back to her room. I crossed the kitchen to stand in front of Hollis, who was still glaring. "How dare you throw me under the bus like that. I don't snore, I am a lady."

I grabbed her waist and pulled her close. "A pretty lady, if I might add." I gave her a quick kiss, because if I didn't show an ounce of self-restraint, I'd have to make up an excuse to stay home, send Hayley with her uncles, and keep Hollis in bed all day. I reached down and gave Hollis a solid pat on her ass.

"Go get ready, we're leaving soon."

41

Hollis

"You've got the man whipped, Hol," Scottie said as he downed his water.

He was the only one who was able to meet us at the trampoline park. Case and Basil were busy with wedding planning–meeting vendors and taste-testing cake. Townes and I had tried to play it cool all morning; no touching, no smiling, and absolutely no glances between us that someone might identify as longing.

So, either Scottie was some kind of wizard, or we weren't subtle enough.

"What on earth makes you think that?" I asked.

Townes was jumping with Hayley, helping her learn how to do a backflip. I could see the tension in his face from where I sat on the bench. His hands hovered over her as if he was expecting her to break any moment, despite the fact she was simply jumping.

Scottie placed his water on the ground, then grabbed my shoulders and spun me so I was facing him. "You don't think I've noticed how his scowl disappears when he looks at you?

He's whipped. So, either you made him some bomb ass cookies, or you sucked hi–"

"Stop! No, we're not going there," I said as I shoved him away. My face burned when I noticed Townes had turned our way. I could feel his eyes assessing me, and it only made my body burn hotter.

Scottie leaned back, and when I looked at him, I was surprised to see him so–serious. He'd always been happy-go-lucky and the only time I'd seen him anything less than happy was when we met. I was at a stoplight when I got rear-ended–no thanks to a random October snowstorm–and Scottie was flustered. Stumbling over his words and making sure I was okay as he tried–and failed–to keep calm.

I cleared my throat and poked his side. "What's wrong?"

He rolled his head, and a red curl dusted his brow. "I know I haven't known Townes that long, but it makes me happy seeing him like this."

"Like what?" I felt my breath catch in my throat in anticipation. What did he see between Townes and me? Was it that obvious or was Scottie looking at us from a different angle?

"Happy. Relaxed? I don't know if those are the same thing to him, but whatever you did, it worked." I finished his water and smacked his thighs. "Now come on, if Hayley can learn to do a backflip, then so can you."

"I am not doing that!" I called after him, but he was already back on the trampoline, grabbing a foam ball and throwing it at Hayley. She giggled and sprinted toward the balls that were gathered by the wall. Townes and I watched on as she started pelting Scottie, who fell on his back in dramatics when a yellow ball landed on his chest. I laughed and picked up a red ball that rolled to my feet.

"You having fun?" I asked Townes, who hadn't looked at me since I walked over.

"As much fun as I can knowing that statistically, we're going to run Hayley to the hospital with a broken limb."

I shuffled the ball between my hands as I watched Hayley climb to the top of a foam fixture. Townes stiffened beside me. "Does a lot of your anxiety revolve around her?"

"Yes." His jaw clenched.

"Why?"

Townes kept his eyes forward, but I could feel the tension in his body as he stayed silent. As if he was struggling to determine whether to open up to me or not. I wasn't going to force him to open up if he didn't want to, even though I hoped he would, considering how...close we'd gotten.

He sighed and dropped his arms before turning to me. Brown eyes–light like warm caramel looked me over, and I smiled.

"Hol–"

"Got you!" Hayley yelled as a blue foam ball hit Townes on the side of his head.

He turned to face his niece, and her smile dropped at whatever she saw on his face. "Uh oh," she said before picking up an extra ball and running back to where Scottie waited.

As they whispered, Townes bent down, and grabbed the ball. "Did you play dodge ball in school?" he asked.

"Uh–yeah but I wasn't the best at it."

Townes cocked his head to the side, and the promise of a smile tugged at the corner of his mouth. "Lucky for you, I was. Come on, you get Hayley and I'll deal with Scottie."

I looked back to our opponents and saw the way Hayley

was sizing up her uncle. The large orange ball in her hands, and while Scottie looked enthusiastic, he was missing that murderous gleam in his eyes.

"Change of plans. You deal with Hayley, I'll take the redhead."

He balked. "W-what? No, you and Hayley are equal in strength and stuff. You got her."

The way he said it–how his brows raised and he got defensive...

"No way. You're scared of her?"

"I am not scared," he said as his scowl returned.

I smirked and delighted in the way his nostrils flared. "If you say so."

Hayley cupped her mouth and yelled. "Are we doing this or what Uncle T? It's okay if you're scared, Uncle Scottie said you would be!"

Townes sighed and gave me one last look before he stole my ball. "I've got her."

* * *

So, note to self: next time Townes and Hayley are going to duke it out, bring safety equipment. Because not only did I get hit in the head with a dodgeball, but it was so unexpected I fell sideways onto the trampoline. My head hit the hard mat, and well, the bruise was small.

But Townes was confident I'd gotten a concussion and was nursing me back to health.

I pulled the ice pack off my forehead as he walked into the living room with a fresh bag of frozen peas. Hayley was between my legs, looking through an old photo album from her nana.

Townes's eyes flickered to the old pictures before he walked back out of the room. Curious—I leaned over to peek at the photos, and my breath hitched. They were Hayley's baby pictures. Most of them seemed like they were taken with an older camera, the yellow ones you used to be able to get from the drugstore and had to buy film for. I used to wait with my parents at the store while our films were developed.

Some of the pictures were just Hayley as a baby, and some were of her parents. There was one in particular I studied; her parents were sitting on a bench, with a baby in their arms. Hayley looked so much like her mother; the same straight nose with a slight bump at the end, the same round, kind face. Then there was her dad, with a beautiful smile and locs well past his shoulders. He passed on his darker complexion and curls to his daughter.

Hayley ran a hand over the picture. "Nana said Dad was funny," she said. Her voice however, didn't hold any emotion, she was simply reciting a fact.

I wondered how much she remembered. She lost them when she was three, and sure the emotional connection was, there but were there any memories? Or was everything she knew about them stories told through others? I might not ever get an answer, but that wouldn't stop me from helping create new memories she could tuck in next to the old ones.

Townes returned, and sat next to me on the couch, his knee brushing mine. He moved my hand to get a better look at the bruise.

"I'm okay," I said, brushing his hand away.

"Just making sure," he said, lacing our fingers together. It was risky, the physical contact with Hayley right in front of us. We had so much to talk about, and I didn't like the feeling we were going behind her back. So I removed my hand and tucked it between my thighs just as Hayley turned around.

"Uncle T? Can I have a story about mom?"

He blinked, then cleared his throat. "What kind of story Haybug?"

"A happy one," she said with a smile.

Townes threw his arm over the couch, and goosebumps broke out when his hand touched my shoulder.

"Hm, a happy one." Townes thought for a long moment before he offered a rare smile. "When we were kids, we lived between a library and a farm. So, during the summers your mom and I would spend hours picking out books before going to the farm. It belonged to our parents' friend, Eric, a big guy with a long white beard who always wore overalls."

Hayley giggled while I watched his face light up as he spoke.

"Anyway, we'd check out books, then would spend hours along the hedges. He grew raspberries and blackberries. We'd eat them while we read, but we always made sure to not get the books dirty."

"Why wouldn't you just go home Uncle T?" Hayley asked, and it pained me when his smile faltered.

He rubbed his free hand on his thigh. "Cause at the time, under the berry bush was the best place to be."

Satisfied with that answer, Hayley turned around and continued to look through the pictures. Meanwhile, I kept my eyes on Townes. Aware that we didn't know much about each other's childhoods, and determined to get him to talk about it.

A little while longer, Townes picked Hayley up from the spot she fell asleep in, and took her to her room. I fed

Bilbo and tidied up the kitchen, then came face-to-face with Townes in the hallway. My eyes roamed over him, and a spark ignited in my body. My throat became dry so I worked a swallow, a monument Townes made sure to follow.

"So, uh–bed?"

"Bed?" He smirked.

Shit, did I want him to come to bed? Well, that was obvious, of course I did, but did he just want to go to his own bed?

A hand brushed aside a stray curl. "Baby?"

"Bed. Like us two sharing one–again. I–if you want, I mean."

His hand wrapped around the back of my neck before he pulled me in for a searing kiss. I held in a moan as I opened for him and ran my hands up his sides. It was over too soon though.

Townes rested his forehead on mine and cupped my face before whispering. "I'd like to take you on a date before I disrespect you in my bed again."

He gave me one more kiss before disappearing, leaving me aching for more.

42

Townes

It'd been a week of pretending things were normal between Hollis and me, all thanks to the little eight-year-old running around. Hayley had the ability to show up whenever I'd even try to get close to Hollis; asking for a snack, or just wanting to tell us a joke.

Why did the chicken cross the road? Because he was late for his job at the pizza place!

Kid humor. Something I didn't think I'd ever understand.

Today however, was different. Hayley was going over to Marion's for the weekend, and I had planned to spend the day with Hollis. Not a date though, just hanging out while we got some food and maybe went to the store to buy more plants.

I pulled up to Marion's house, and Hayley grabbed her bag from the seat. "Bye Uncle T! Bye Hollis!"

"Have fun, Hayley," Hollis said as she turned in her seat.

Hayley nodded and left the car, then she ran up to where Marion was waiting in the doorway. She smiled and ushered her granddaughter in before giving us a small wave, well, she gave me a wave–she ignored Hollis.

"I am starving. Do you want to try that new brunch spot that opened up?" Hollis leaned forward in her seat and rested her head on the dashboard as she smiled at me.

"Sure. But pick your head up, that's not safe."

She blew a raspberry and sat straighter. She pulled her legs to her chest and threw her head against the headrest. It was quiet for a long time as we drove down the highway, and I'd had it when she sighed and I heard her head thunk against the window.

"What?" I asked as I exited onto a side street.

Hollis lifted her head and shrugged her shoulders. Her head was cocked to the side as if she was trying to find words–or muster up the courage to let them out. Either way, I waited patiently until the restaurant came into view. The rustic building used to be a bakery and catering business, but was bought out two years ago by a huge restaurant chain. It didn't do well, and was sold earlier this year. Now, it's owned by some recent culinary school graduates and the parking lot is fuller than ever before.

When we parked and Hollis still hadn't said anything, I sat and laid my hand on her thigh. She was warm under my touch, and it made me happy that she didn't shy away from me. Instead, she put her head on my shoulder.

"What are we doing, Townes?"

"Well, you're starving, and I'm trying to feed you."

I felt her body move as she laughed. "No, I mean what are we doing?" She moved to look at me, and I forgot for a moment what we were talking about as I got lost in those blue eyes. "Townes?"

I cleared my throat and gave her leg a squeeze. "Let's get

some food in front of us first."

Hollis followed me out of the car, and I took her hand as we walked to the door. Growing up I had never been on the receiving end of physical affection–aside from an occasional hug from Kennedy–so it wasn't ever something I was used to dishing out. A pat on the back was enough to make me tense up. With Hollis though, it felt natural. Like, reaching for her wasn't something I could control. She had control over my body, and I didn't think she even knew it.

When we walked into the building, we were greeted by our hostess, who quickly got us a table. People talked and laughed as we made our way to the open booth, and Hollis scanned the menu while we waited. My eyes roamed over her, and I knew it would never be enough. Her beauty was too much for me to comprehend, but I was willing to take forever examining it and coming to terms that I'd never be enough for her. So maybe right now, she'd let me try, and I could prove to myself that whatever was between us could work for a while.

After our server took our drink orders, I leaned back and watched as Hollis drummed her fingers on the table. She was anxious, and for once I wasn't going to let my anxiety fuck things up.

"So," I nudged her foot under the table. "Penny for your thoughts?"

Her cheeks flushed, and she licked her lips–something I couldn't look away from. I'd been thinking about our night together all week, and it wasn't good for my self-control, which would snap at any moment.

"Well–we uh–slept together."

"We did," I said.

Our server brought our drinks, and I waited until he was far enough away with our food order to continue talking.

Hollis licked her lips again and huffed. "Where does that put us? Because I think things would get too complicated if things were casual. And to be honest, I don't want casual, not with you anyway. You don't seem like someone I could booty call even though we live in the same house–hell, even if we didn't, I still can't imagine it. But also, if you can't do serious, then that's fine too. We can just avoid each other until our deal is up and the–"

"Have I ever told you that I think it's cute when you do that? Ramble?"

Her cheeks burned a deep red before she shoved her face into her hands. "Shut up."

I stared at her and chewed on every word that spewed out of her mouth. I knew what I wanted, and while I had an idea she wanted the same–I had to make sure. Hollis still had her head buried when I reached across the table and pulled a hand away. She lifted her gaze, and I ignored the way her flush deepened.

"What do you want, Hollis? Because if I'm being honest, I've never wanted to be with someone more than I want to be with you." Her breath hitched, but I had to keep going. "I know I haven't been the best at showing it, but I'm still figuring out how to do that. Show you, I mean."

"Townes–"

I squeezed her hand. "Look, I know I have flaws; I'm not the friendliest person, I'm still trying to manage my anxiety issues, and I have Hayley to take care of. She's been my priority ever since I took her into my home, but I'd like to make you a priority too. If you'd let me."

I waited for a response by tapping my thumb against her soft skin and avoided looking at her. This was too new, all these feelings, but I owed it to Hollis to be honest. She tugged on my hand, and it felt like a punch to the gut when I glanced up to see her smiling.

"So does this count as our first date, then?"

My chest puffed with joy, and the only thing that broke my contact with Hollis was our food being placed on the table. I watched as she unraveled her utensils and placed the cloth napkin into her lap. She eyed me expectantly as she started sorting out the cranberries in her salad.

"Yeah. If that's what you'd like," I said.

Hollis lowered her fork and furrowed her brows. "What would you like, Townes?"

I didn't need time to think anything over, I wanted this date just as much as she did, I was just trying to be considerate. I lifted my water and held it out to her.

"To first dates."

She smiled and raised her own glass. "To the first of many."

* * *

"Wait, wait, wait. You mean to tell me you used to actually be fun, a–and happy?" Hollis stared at me with wide eyes while she took another bite of her churro. After breakfast this morning, we went to the plant nursery and bought a few things for the house. Then, Hollis insisted we go out dancing again, but I had something better in mind.

I brought her to my favorite scenic overlook. The small car park was surrounded by trees, then it was only a small walk to a clearing with a few picnic tables. A stone half wall separated us from everything below. City lights brightened the summer night sky. It was quiet, and Hollis made it all the more beautiful.

I took her churro and stole a bite. "Why are you so shocked? Am I not fun, or happy now?"

She raised a brow. "You mean to tell me you have a scowl permanently etched into your face because you're happy?"

"It's only there because I'm old. Wrinkles come with aging."

"If telling yourself that makes you feel better than by all means, I won't stop you." Hollis held up her hands in defense, then stole her food back.

I laid back onto the table and stared at the night sky. "In high school, my parents were supposed to show up for a hockey tournament. They promised to be on their best behavior." I remembered that night like it happened yesterday, not sixteen years ago. "Well, they ended up getting kicked out because they couldn't stop fighting. My dad threw a chair, and it ended up hitting the other team's coach."

Hollis's expression was serious when I turned to face her.

"It happened a few more times, the fighting, and eventually I stopped talking to them altogether. And in turn, I also stopped expecting much of other people. Kennedy was the only person I felt like I could rely on."

She was quiet for a long moment before she crawled on top of me. Her legs straddled my hips as she leaned down and looked at me with pity.

I hated that look…but I couldn't hate who it was coming from.

"You've been by yourself for a long time huh?"

My hands ran along the sides of her legs until they rested on her hips. I shrugged. "I haven't been for a while actually.

It's made things easier to manage."

I wasn't sure words could ever express the change I'd felt living with Hollis. Even though our marriage wasn't technically real, there was something about being tied to her that changed me. I'd find myself less anxious leaving Hayley to travel, and I was looking forward to what new thing each day brought with it.

Hollis blushed, and lowered her head until her hair was a curtain around us. "I want you to know that I like all the parts of you Townes. The grumpy bits, and the anxious ones. Then the bit where you pour milk before cereal."

"Hey, it makes more sense to ensure a maximum cereal to milk ratio," I said–my hand climbing up and over her ass.

She hummed as her nose brushed along mine. "Sounds like something a psychopath would say."

When her mouth brushed against mine, my grip turned to steel as I crushed our lips together. Hollis moaned into my mouth as her hips rolled, and I was helpless beneath her. Our tongues clashed as I bucked against her, my hand in her hair as her hand trailed down my chest.

All week this was what I'd thought about; her on top of me–though with far less clothing. I'd imagined how she'd look with her head thrown back in pleasure as she rode my cock.

I wanted it now. I didn't care where we were; now or ever. The only thing coursing through my veins was the need to strip her bare and help her climb on top of me so I could fuck her into oblivion. My aching cock twitched against her, and Hollis pulled back to smirk.

"As much as I love kissing you, I can't help but think you need some attention elsewhere," she said as she stroked a hand over my jeans.

I reached down to still her wrist before she could move it again. "What do you think you're doing?"

"Having some fun, of course." Her face was innocent, but the way she moved her fingers against my cock was anything but—we needed to go home. Neither of us needed a ticket for public indecency.

I sat up, and gripped Hollis's ass so she wouldn't fall when I stood. Then, I carried her to the car, kissing her neck with every step. "Where are we going?"

"Home."

43

Hollis

Screw going home.

"Hollis, I have to drive," Townes bit out as I started kissing his neck. I dropped my hand down to the taught denim and reveled in the way the fabric scratched my palm as I stroked his cock. His breath turned labored as he white knuckled the steering wheel. "I'm serious."

"No one's telling you to stop," I said as I started working on undoing his belt, then the button.

Townes continued breathing hard, and I heard the engine accelerate. Adrenaline coursed through me as I shoved my hand down the waistband of his underwear and wrapped my hand around him. He was thick and heavy, and he let out a shuddering breath when I gave him a firm squeeze. We came to a stop, and Townes lifted his hips so he could help me tug his jeans down. His cock sprung free, and I took my time admiring it.

When we had sex, sure it felt amazing, but the moment was so heated I wasn't able to appreciate it. I stroked my hand over the swollen tip before dragging it down the thick shaft.

Townes bucked into my hand, and I ran my thumb over the bead of precum that leaked out.

"Either put me out of my misery or stay on your side of the car," Townes commanded in a voice that was equally pissed and filled with pleasure.

I lowered my head and kissed the tip before I took him in my mouth. Townes groaned and placed a hand on the back of my neck, he never squeezed or forced me to move. It remained a steady pressure as I explored him—sucking as I went as far down as I could without gagging, then dragging my tongue over his shaft on my way back up. I kept a slow, sensual pace, and each moan that escaped Townes's lips sent a zing of pleasure down my spine until I was soaked between my legs.

"Fuck baby," Townes said with another buck. "Th—this is better than I imagined."

A wet sound echoed throughout the car when I removed my mouth and started stroking him. "You've thought about this?"

"I tried n—not to for a long time." He flipped on the blinker and started pulling off the road. I wasn't sure where we were, but I knew we weren't close to the house. We parked, and Townes pulled me into his lap before he lowered his seat as far as it would go. He palmed my breast as he kissed along my collarbones. "But you just had to weasel your way into my brain, you know that?"

He removed my shirt, and I gasped when he lowered my bra and pinched my nipple. His other hand wrapped around my neck, and he pulled my face closer. "Fuck, I love looking at you like this."

I did my best to arch into his touch when he finally kissed

me, but it was hard when the hand around my neck was keeping me in place. I moaned and rotated my hips, desperate for any friction that could ease the pounding between my legs. Townes pulled back and let me go.

"Take off your fucking pants."

Frantic, I threw myself off him and stripped while he fished out a condom and removed his own clothes. Then, when we were both naked–the windows fogging up–he pulled me back into his lap. I grabbed his cock and lined him up against my entrance.

I paused.

"Are we really having car sex? What if someo–"

"I can't wait til we get home, and you sucking me off isn't helping," he said as his hands gripped my hips.

"What about getting caught?"

Townes leveled me with a heated stare. "I'll deal with it. Now sit."

He pushed up into me as I sat down, and my hands instinctively found his chest. We both groaned as I adjusted to him once again, then he stilled. With wide eyes, I looked down, worried I had done something wrong.

But Townes just stared up and ran his hand along my side before settling it on my thigh. "Use me."

"What?" I asked, my chest full of something I wasn't familiar with.

"You're on top. Do what you need to get yourself off."

It was silly, but I'd never been given that kind of control before; never had the opportunity to do what made me feel good. Because to most men I'd slept with, their pleasure came first–and often fast.

I leaned down and kissed Townes again before I started

moving my hips in circles. There wasn't much room, so the movements were short and stunted, but that didn't mean it didn't feel good. Townes tightened his grip and supported me when I started moving up and down. We were a mess of heavy breathing and soft noises as the windows continued to fog.

"Townes," I breathed.

"What is it baby?" His voice was pained, and I knew he was holding himself back. I just hadn't realized how much.

"I need more."

"Fuck, okay," Townes licked his lips and worked a thick swallow. "Put your hands on the door and the console."

I did as he said, supporting myself by holding onto the car. Then, I felt Townes widen his legs as far as he could before his thumb landed on my clit. I whimpered when he started moving it in slow circles.

"Ready?" he asked.

I nodded, and Townes let go. He bucked his hips up in a fast, steady rhythm that worked in sync with how he circled my clit. The only thing holding me up was my flimsy grip on the car, but that wasn't going to last. Not when heat bubbled in my stomach that made my limbs go numb.

Townes moved faster. "Let it go for me, baby."

I gasped when the pressure on my clit increased, and my orgasm slammed into me. My hands grappled for something to grab onto when I fell forward. The head rest, Townes's hair, anything to keep me grounded as he followed soon after.

We were a sweaty mess as I laid on him, my arms tucked between us. Townes traced his fingers over my back while our hearts slowed to their usual steady beats. Then, he started running his fingers over my scalp.

"We need to get going."

"Mm, but I'm comfortable," I said, snuggling closer to him.

I felt his chest expand before he chuckled. "Yeah, well–I've noticed a few cars pass by and I don't want to risk someone thinking we've broken down and come offering to help."

My cheeks heated with embarrassment, and I threw myself off of him. "I thought you pulled over somewhere secluded," I said as I tugged my clothes back on.

"You overestimate my ability to think clearly when your mouth is on my dick."

I shook my head as he put on his shirt, then I laid my head on his shoulder as we started driving once again. He grabbed my hand, and laced our fingers together, and I felt like I was going to explode. There was an emotion hiding in my chest, waiting until it was safe to come out–and while I was sure it could, I had to wait a little bit longer before I could promise it wouldn't get hurt.

My head fell onto his shoulder, and I kept my eyes on the road. "I have a silly question."

"I'm all ears," he said, his voice low and full of content.

There was a part of me that didn't want to ask, for fear of shattering whatever was happening between us. This was real, but asking about it seemed daunting.

"You fall asleep?" Townes asked as he squeezed my hand gently.

I shook my head. "I know we both want each other, and we even went on a date. A nice one by the way, but–what are we? Are we putting a label on us? Boyfriend and girlfriend? Or is this a friends with benefits kinda thing? Not that we have to label it, but it might help my brain not get too attached to anything, ya know?"

"Last I checked, we were husband and wife."

The words sent flutters loose in my stomach, and I kept my eyes forward as a blush broke out over my cheeks. "I'm serious Townes."

He sighed, and we didn't exchange any other words until we got to the house. I let go of his hand first and stalked inside. Townes was right behind me as I went to feed Bilbo, and he stopped me with his hands on my arms when I tried to walk past him. I gazed up into those soft brown eyes and waited.

"I'm sorry if you didn't like my answer, I didn't mean to brush off your feelings. I know you were asking for clarity, and I didn't help." He brushed away a stray curl, then cupped my face. "I've never asked anyone to be my girlfriend before, but I'd like to extend that experience to you."

My breath hitched.

"So, Hollis—my fake wife and wonderful roommate—would you be my girlfriend?"

I bit the inside of my lower lip and looked him over. "What does being your girlfriend entail exactly?"

He smiled. "Lots of dates, and me being less of an asshole. Other than that, it won't be much different than how things are right now."

My hands crawled up his chest until they wrapped around the collar of his shirt. I tugged his closer as I went on my toes. "Do I get more kisses?"

He dropped his hands to wrap his around my waist, and his nose brushed mine. "You can have whatever you want."

44

Townes

S weat dripped down my chin as the crowd roared, and my team huddled in the middle of the rink. Another game won, and we were more than halfway through the playoffs. It was bittersweet this time around, this was the last chance I had to go all the way with my team before I put this life behind me, and it left a hole in my chest.

If we kept winning, we had only a few games left to get to the finals.

A month before retirement, but also, a month before I could put all my energy toward the little girl whose future I worked so hard to secure. Money set aside for college, a stable home life–and the woman I was certain would be there for every step of the way.

Things between Hollis and I had been going well this past month; aside from sneaking kisses and late-night activities from Hayley. A part of me felt wrong for hiding the relationship from her, but I was worried about getting her hopes up. Because I wasn't sure the kinds of questions that would follow.

Everyone started heading toward the locker rooms, and I braced myself when Scottie came barreling my direction. He stopped at the last second though and threw an arm over my shoulders.

"You've been in a good mood lately," he said as he waved to women in the stands.

I attempted to shrug him off, but it didn't work. "What have I done to indicate I'm not more pissed than usual? Maybe I've finally cared enough to hide it."

The laugh Scottie let out had people's heads turning, and I shook my head when Case raised a brow.

"Man, a good mood and you're funny? Hollis must have really done a number on you, huh?"

Heat seared across the back of my neck, but I tampered it down as I shook my head.

"You're imagining things," I said, brushing Scottie off.

His grin widened and I kept my eyes forward as we walked into the locker room.

"Besides, if Hollis and I are doing anything it's none of your business," I bit out. I wasn't opposed to people knowing her and I were together, but they didn't need to be loud about it.

"So you are sleeping together?" Scottie's voice had dropped to an almost whisper, but the excitement was clear. "Seriously, so are you guys together or what?"

"What does it matter to you? Really, you're being weird about it."

Case came between us, a nervous smile behind his words. "Come on guys, let's just get ready to go home? This conversation can wait."

"Hold on, why are you being weird too?" I asked.

Scottie bumped shoulders with Case, and leaned in. "Are

315

you and Hollis together? I need to know for personal reasons."

"And what personal rea–"

Case groaned and smacked Scottie's chest with the back of his hand. "See what you did pushing him?" He faced me and crossed his arms. "Scottie bet me a hundred bucks you and Hollis would get together–in one way or another–before we made it to the finals."

I balked at them–not at all surprised they bet on my relations status–but surprised I hadn't seen this coming.

"You guys bet on it?"

Case held up his hands. "To be fair, Basil was in on it too."

I scoffed and turned to walk toward the showers. Tonight was tiring enough, and I needed to go home and ice my knee. I could talk to them later about them betting on my love life, then I could suffer while they boasted about how right they were–even though Case was out of money.

After a shower and a fresh pair of clothes, I headed to the family room. I'd convinced Hollis to start watching the games in there, because I knew if I saw her in the stands I'd get distracted. She'd smile, and wave, and I wouldn't care anymore that I had a job to do. The door was already open, and a few of the guys were already in the room hugging their partners and kids.

In the crowd of bodies, and kids running around, I locked onto the one person I wanted to see.

Hollis stood there, talking to Basil with a warm smile. The ache in my chest eased, and the pain in my knee didn't matter anymore. She was here, standing ten feet away, but she belonged in my arms. I started moving, and warmth surged through my chest when she directed that smile at me. She held out her arms, and I wrapped my arms around her waist.

"Great game," she whispered as her fingers trailed down my back.

I pulled away and laced our hands together. When I looked at Basil, she was smirking, and I shook my head. "How much do the guys owe you?"

"Case owes me a batch of brownies, and Scottie owes me three hundred bucks."

"Why do they owe you stuff? And why three hundred dollars?" Hollis asked, looking at us both with a curious pout of her bottom lip.

I squeezed her hand. "They all bet when we'd get together."

Hollis whirled on her friend. "Seriously? When did you think, since you obviously won."

Basil shrugged, and spotted something behind us that pulled her attention away. "Scottie thought it was going to happen after the carnival, so that's when we made our bets. I bet you"–she pointed a finger at me–"would be too much of a gentleman to fuck her brains out and call things official. So, I thought it would take at least two weeks for things to settle down."

"B!" Hollis's face was pink, then turned to a deep red when people looked at us.

Basil smiled and started to walk past us. "Anyway, I'm richer now, all thanks to you guys. Go home and celebrate, we'll catch up later."

We watched her skip to Case, who had averted his gaze.

Hollis tugged on my sleeve, and my annoyance melted with her soft gaze. "Come on, if we don't hurry up and get Hayley, Marion is going to chew me out."

I started leading us out of the room and to the parking lot,

I raised a brow and couldn't contain the shock in my voice. "What are you talking about?"

She stiffened and tried to walk past me with a wave of her hand. "It's nothing, promise. Can we get some food too? I'm sure Hayley's already eaten, should we get something before or after? Probably after, ya know?"

Hollis continued to ramble as she dragged me out to the parking lot, then to the car. The parking lot had cleared out, so we didn't fight any traffic as I made my way to the main road.

I knew Hollis hadn't been on Marion's good side in a while—she was still holding a grudge from when Hollis was sick and didn't ask for help. But that was so long ago—she should have gotten over it.

"What did Marion say to you?" I asked as I flipped on the blinker.

Hollis stopped humming to look at me. "I don't think I want to tell you. I'm afraid you'll yell at her or something and send her into a medical episode."

I chuckled. Marion was the epitome of health, plus she wasn't that old. Besides, I wasn't going to destroy my relationship with her because Hayley needs her. She was the only grandmother she had, and without her parents—I wasn't going to take away what little family she had left.

"I promise not to yell." I held out my pinky and waited.

"What are you doing?"

"Ever heard of a pinky promise?

Her smile was gentle, and barely tugged on the sides of her mouth, but it was beautiful all the same. She interlocked her pinky with mine, and I dropped our hands to her lap.

"When I dropped off Hayley, I may have given her the

318

smallest kiss on her head. She wanted a hug, and I don't know—it felt normal. I asked if she was okay with it right after, and she said yes because you do the same thing. Anyway, Marion saw and made a comment about how I don't need to act like her mom just because you and I are technically married."

My blood rushed to my ears, and my heart pounded in my chest.

"Has she said stuff like this before?"

If this wasn't a one–off thing...and I'd been letting Hollis drop off Hayley all this time...

"No. Usually, she just stands there when I drop off Hayley."

That lessened the anger I was feeling, but I knew the only way to make it go away, was to have a little chat with Hayley's Nana. We pulled into the driveway a short while later, and I slammed the door harder than I intended when I got out. Then, I opened Hollis's door and helped her out. We walked together, the backs of our hands brushing against each other with every step.

I knocked and entered a second later. Hayley was sitting on the steps with her bag, and a concentrated scowl on her face.

"What are you thinking of?" Hollis asked as she went to sit next to her.

I let them talk, and wandered to find Marion, who was in the kitchen nursing something dark pink in her glass. I crossed my arms when she glanced at me, and I raised a brow.

"How was she?"

"Fine, as always. She's a bit tired though, could you do me a favor and make sure Hollis doesn't keep you too long after a game next time? You know how important it is that Hayley keeps her routine."

My arms went slack at my sides. "Are you fucking serious?"

Hollis and Hayley's voices went quiet.

This wasn't the time for this conversation, not with them in the other room and anger being the only emotion in my chest. I turned on my heel and grabbed the bag off the steps. "Time to go," I commanded as I headed to the door.

I held it open as the girls filed out, and let it slam shut when I let go. They were both quiet as we walked, got into the car, and even on the ride home. There was no humming from Hollis or bad jokes from the backseat. It killed me–knowing they were quiet because of how I was feeling. I was affecting them, but there wasn't anything I could do about it.

Go home, get some air, and start again tomorrow with an apology bright and early.

I glanced down and noticed Hollis's pinky twitch in my direction. I wanted so bad to reach for her, to steady myself. But it was too risky with Hayley in the backseat. It had to wait, and I might have pushed on the accelerator to get home sooner, putting myself out of that misery.

45

Hollis

Townes shut his door harder than normal, then went around to take Hayley's bag from her. All with a deep scowl that told me everything–he was trying not to spiral.

I never should have mentioned what Marion said, because I knew he wouldn't take it well–but I did it anyway. Hayley was surrounded by so many people who loved her, and no one hid their affection for the little girl, so I didn't think I was doing anything wrong.

When we got to Marion's, I even double checked with Hayley that I hadn't made her uncomfortable. I hadn't, but she also didn't elaborate as to why she wasn't in a good mood. We followed behind Townes as he walked up the porch steps and opened the door. Once we were inside, he tossed the bag onto the couch and stalked to his room. I rubbed Hayley's shoulders when she sighed.

"Come on, let's get you to bed."

Her dark eyes met mine, and she shook her head. "Can I have some hot chocolate first?"

"I don't think we have any." Her head dropped, and a knot formed in my stomach. "But you know what? I don't think all the stores have closed yet."

Hayley's face lit up, and I grabbed her hand before leading her back through the door. I made sure to send Townes a quick text before we left, so he knew what we were doing. Hayley was quiet again as we made our way to the store, every time I looked in the mirror she was staring out the window. Her head thumped lightly against the glass, and I itched to ask what was on her mind. But she was a lot like Townes, she wasn't going to tell me what was wrong until she was ready.

We made it to the store a few minutes before closing; she and I made a mad dash and grabbed four different boxes of hot chocolate. Now wasn't the time to think over our options–I refused to be the reason people stayed at work late.

The cashier gave Hayley a small strip of stickers with a warm smile, then we headed back home.

She examined our selections in the back as I continued through the empty streets, and when we got home, she planted herself at the table while I grabbed mugs from the cabinet. Townes was still in his room, and he hadn't responded to my texts. So, either he was sleeping, or was sulking–either way, I'd sneak in later and make sure he wasn't spiraling.

The microwave beeped, and Hayley looked marginally better when I placed her Mickey Mouse mug into her hands.

"Thank you," she said before taking a small sip.

I nodded and tapped the table while I waited for my drink to cool. When Hayley finished, she let out a content sigh and leaned back into the chair. "That really hit the spot." She patted her belly.

"So, does a warm belly mean you're in a better mood to open up about what's been bothering you?"

Her face fell. "No," she mumbled.

I waited a beat, taking in how her shoulders slumped in and noticing how her voice dropped in shame. Then, I leaned in, and reached for her hand. "You know you can talk to me, right? About *anything* that's bothering you."

She sighed and raised a brow when her eyes met mine. "Will you tell Uncle T?"

I leaned back and held up my first two fingers on my left hand. "Scout's honor, I won't tell him if you don't want me to." When she nodded though, I dropped my voice on the off chance Townes had his ear to his door and was listening. "But you know, sometimes hiding things from Townes can do more harm than good. He loves you and would do anything to make you feel better. I won't tell him, but I wanted to remind you. Okay?"

"Okay," she said, and a smile finally made an appearance. It was small, and filled with nerves, but it was enough for me to keep my mouth shut.

I took a sip of my hot chocolate and patiently waited.

"Sometimes, Nana asks me a lot of questions; like what you make me for dinner or what kind of rules I have at your house."

"Alright?" I wasn't sure where she was going with this, because in my mind, all those questions were valid. Marion wanted to make sure Hayley was being taken care of when she was with me, I couldn't fault her for being curious.

"And tonight, Nana brought up Mama, but I didn't like it."

My heart pulled in two as I pulled back to look at her. "Why not?"

323

"Cause she said you guys were different, but I don't think so. I don't remember my mama a lot, but I think she was a lot like you, and that makes me happy. Nana said you didn't care that much though, and th–that made me cry."

I was going to buy a bag of crickets from the pet store and let them loose in Marion's house.

Hayley's tears spilled over, and I hugged her again. "Oh honey–I hope you know that's not true. Hey, look at me," I pushed her away by her shoulders, and wiped away a tear. "I want you to promise me something, can you do that?"

She nodded.

"Promise me, that you'll never *ever* forget that I love you, okay? I love you just as much as your uncle Scottie and your uncle Case does. The only people that love you *more*, were your parents, and Uncle Townes. Do you understand?"

Hayley hiccupped and nodded again with more force. "I understand."

"Okay," I pushed a hair out of her face. "Are you sure you want me to keep this from Townes? I think he'd like to know if Nana is telling you things that hurt your feelings."

"No, I don't want to keep it a secret from him. But Hollis? Can I tell him?"

"Of course you can, but it'll have to wait til tomorrow. You're going to bed after your hot chocolate is finished."

Hayley dove back into silence as she emptied her mug before placing it in the sink. I busied myself with wiping down the counters as I listened to the bathroom faucet. It wasn't until her bedroom door shut that I put the rag down and walked to Townes's door.

I raised my hand to knock, but the door opened before I even moved. Townes stood there, in a plain blue T-shirt and black sweatpants. His hair was sticking up on either side, and his eyes were half open as he scowled down at me.

Definitely sleeping.

"I didn't mean to wake you, I can le-"

He tugged me toward him, cutting me off as I was surrounded by him. Strong, warm, and smelling like fresh linen mixed with pine. My hands traveled up his back, and I ran my fingers between his shoulder blades in a soothing movement. Townes had so much on his plate, both with work and now with Marion—and I'd never wanted to be a point of contention. If our relationship, however new, was going to be a problem then—

I never meant to cause issues, I'd just wanted to help.

"Townes we-"

"Sleep with me," he said with his head in the crook of my neck.

Instead of waiting for an answer, Townes pulled back and led me to his bed. His hand never letting go of mine even as he tugged back the comforter. I laid down, and he followed soon after. Once he was comfortable, he reached down for the blanket, then he let my hand go to wrap his arm around my waist.

I laid there and listened as Townes drifted off to sleep, my mind wandering to all the possibilities to fix this problem I'd created. Because...would Marion stop saying things to Hayley to try and pit us against each other? If she didn't, then what would happen between Townes and me? Marion is her grandmother, and has been a key character in Townes's support system.

I was used to not getting what I wanted. So, I let a small tear slip out as I drifted to sleep.

46

Townes

ase hauled his duffle over his shoulder, and Scottie threw his arm over mine as we walked out of the locker room. We weren't scheduled to have practice today, but I was woken up to Scottie blowing up the group chat—asking if Case and I would be willing to tag along to his impromptu strength training session.

I only went because Case agreed, and I didn't want to hear any shit from Scottie for not showing up.

"So, how are things with your new lady?" Scottie teased.

I rolled my eyes and tried to shrug him off. "Hollis? Why can't you just say her name?"

"Because then it sounds too serious, and I want to bask in the fact you actually have a girlfriend for a little while longer. Pretend I don't know her–I'm a stranger actually. Tell me everything you secret keeping, scowling grump."

Case snorted and shook his head. "Keep it up, and Townes is going to revoke his friendship, dude."

"Ah, no he won't," Scottie said as he finally let me go. "So come on, details. Have you guys actually gone on a date yet?

Or is she only into you for the tattoos and *daddy energy?*"

All I could do was shake my head at the ridiculousness spewing out of his mouth. I'd never been an open person, and I wasn't going to start now, especially when it came to Hollis and me. Everything about her; her smile, the way she lit up a room when she walked in it, and her stubbornness–they were all mine–and I wasn't keen on sharing.

"Of all people I would talk about my relationship with, why do you think it would be you?" I asked, my voice clipped as we continued to the parking lot. We'd had an early practice today, and there was enough time to get home and start making breakfast before the girls woke up.

I hesitated leaving Hollis sleeping in my bed this morning, but I wouldn't have to be torn between leaving her and going to work much longer. As much as it pained me, I just had to suck it up for another month. Then, I could hold her to me until other responsibilities pulled us away.

Like Hayley.

I was still pissed at Marion for what she said to Hollis, but was more worried about Hayley and why she was so upset last night. Even though I wasn't in the headspace to talk to her about it–I didn't feel as guilty as I usually would. And it was all thanks to Hollis–she was there when I couldn't put things back together.

I'd have to thank her for being there when I couldn't.

Scottie elbowed my side and winked. "Because I'm a ladies' man, in case you didn't know? The more I know about your relationship, the more advice I can give if things go south."

"Pretty sure the only advice you're qualified to give is what condoms are the best," Case said as he fished out his keys from his pockets. "Let the man do his thing, okay? I'm sure if he wanted to talk to us he would."

I nodded and grabbed my own keys. "Thanks man. I'll see you guys later," I said in parting before they both walked away.

The drive home was quiet, and I hated it. Before Hollis, I sought it out, but after months of listening to her soft humming—I realized just how lonely I was. I used to see the silence as an escape from the world; an escape from my responsibilities as a single guardian, a professional athlete, and from pretending everything was okay. That the anxiety didn't exist, that my sister was still alive.

Hollis though—I didn't need to escape anymore. She was the reason I was able to stay and face things head on. I didn't have to run away and pretend anymore when I knew things would be okay.

The house was quiet then I opened the door, save for the new wind chime Hollis bought the other day. The music danced through the windows, along with the morning songbirds chirps and thrills. I quietly took off my shoes and placed my things down before I headed toward my room. When I passed Hayley's door, I paused and listened for any signs that she was awake. It was still early, almost eight, so I wasn't surprised when I didn't hear anything after a long moment.

I continued on, my blood rushing to my ears with every step closer to the woman of my dreams.

She was sprawled on the bed, her curly hair draped over the pillows as her chest rose in slow, shallow breaths. I took my time admiring her—the soft cupid's bow of her lips, her freckled nose, and soft skin that disappeared below the sheets. Blood rushed to my crotch as I let my gaze continue to travel down, over the miraculous body that was shamefully hidden from me. I took a tentative step forward and paused when Hollis moved.

"Mm, morning," she mumbled before she turned over and shoved her face into the pillows. She peeked out, her eyes half open. "Have a good practice?"

"How'd you know I had practice?" I asked as I got into the bed next to her, making sure to keep my hands to myself. I could at least let her wake up before I started ravaging her.

Once I was settled, she rolled over again, and threw her arm over my lap. Then, she shoved her face into my neck. "Your phone woke me up, and I got a blurry glimpse of a message from Scottie." Her soft breath tickled my skin. "I missed you."

I chuckled and ran my hand through her hair. "Missed you too."

"What time is it?"

"Almost eight," I said, my fingers never stopped moving.

Hollis groaned and moved to stretch. The sheet fell down her chest as her arms moved over her head, and I felt my cock harden at the sight of her perfect breasts.

"Mm, we should get ready for the day. Was Hayley up?"

I reached over and drug my fingers over the softness of her stomach. Hollis's breath hitched as I continued my path over a perk nipple. I shuffled down until my face hovered next to hers, and my hand started going south. Hollis's blush was bright red as she reached out to still my hand.

I stopped moving in an instant and placed a kiss on her cheek.

"You okay?" I asked as that familiar, anxious feeling wrapped its sticky hands around my chest. If I ever made Hollis uncomfortable, I'd never be able to live with myself.

She nodded. "I just don't want to risk a repeat of last time. Now let's get up and make some food. I'm starving and if Hayley isn't up by now, then my stomach's going to wake her up."

I reached for her hand as she threw her legs over the side of the bed, and I waited until I had her full attention. "Are you sure? Because if I pushed you or–"

"Never." Hollis leaned down and kissed me. I threaded my fingers through her hair and pulled her close. I licked along Hollis's bottom lip, a question–but she pulled back. "Food. Let's go."

When she stood from the bed, I found myself watching her, and wondering what was going through her head.

* * *

"During the summer, can we go camping?" Hayley asked from the table as she colored away in her new coloring book.

We'd spent most of the day out running errands and getting her some new things for summer. A swimsuit and goggles, a bike–without training wheels because she was a big girl–and a ton of art supplies to keep her busy.

Hollis glanced toward me, and the anxiety that crawled into my chest this morning gave me another squeeze. All day, Hollis had been…somewhere else. Despite her smiles and laughs, I could tell something was off.

She was sitting across from Hayley while I finished the dishes. I cleared my throat. "What kind of camping are we talking about, Haybug?"

"Well, what kind are there?"

Hollis leaned forward, took a blue crayon, and started

coloring. "Well, there's something called glamping. We could stay in a nice cabin with air conditioning and have easy access to a toilet."

"Oh, like last time? With the treehouses?"

"Exactly like that," Hollis said. Her eyes darted up toward me when I took the empty seat next to her. My hand found a spot on her thigh under the table, and I relaxed a fraction when she moved toward me.

Hayley shook her head. "That's fun, but I want real camping. My friend Mario said his parents make a tent and they use leaves when they poop."

"Ah—I don't know about leaves," I said as Hollis snickered. "But we can go regular camping if that's what you want. We'll need to get supplies and everything, though. Maybe when the season's over."

"Okay! And Papa said he would buy me a pink tent. I picked it out and everything."

Hollis smiled. "I guess that means your uncle and I are going to have to get a matching one then, huh?"

"No, Uncle T doesn't like pink. He likes green cause it's a boy color."

"There's no such thing as boy and girl colors." Hollis laughed and placed the crayon back on the table. "Come on, we have school tomorrow. Go get ready for bed, and one of us will be there to tuck you in, okay?"

Once Hayley rounded the corner, Hollis stood from the table, but I pulled her back into my lap. She stared at me with wide eyes and flushed cheeks. I could hear her nerves lacing her soft words when she spoke. "Everything okay?"

"Why don't you tell me, baby?" I ran my hand down her spine before I drew circles on her lower back. "You've been off all day, and I keep wracking my brain to figure out what I did wrong."

She bit her lip, and I had to place my finger under her chin to keep her gaze on mine.

"Talk to me."

Hollis blinked back a tear, and I felt my heart start to rip in two.

"It's stupid."

"Not if it makes you cry." I placed a soft kiss on her collarbone and waited as she gathered her thoughts. Of course, she didn't have to talk if she didn't want to, but I hoped she sensed how badly I wanted to make her happy. I'd do anything to chase away her worries.

She took in a shaky breath. "I just–Hayley told me something and it got me thinking about stuff that made me sad."

"Like what?"

"She wants to tell you, and I promised I'd let her." She wiped away a stray tear, and I kept up those circles on her back.

"So you're sad because you're keeping a secret from me, that you made to my eight-year-old niece?"

She scoffed. "No, you big dummy. I'm sad, because I got stuck in my head, and convinced myself that–this wouldn't work." Her voice dropped off, and the last word was barely a whisper. But I heard it loud and clear, and it sent panic rushing through me. She was wrong–this would work...it *was working*. I had never made a decision I wasn't confident in–and besides taking in Hayley, being with Hollis was the one thing I'd never questioned.

"Why?"

She blinked, and I stared into those baby blues as if they'd give me the answer.

"Because ever since Marion found out I was sick, and didn't ask for her help, she's been judgy. Like–I didn't know her enough to feel comfortable asking her anything, and what if I did and she got mad and thought I wasn't capable of looking after Hayley at all? And now, she's accusing me of acting like her mom, when I'm not–and she's such a big part of your lives. I don't want to ruin your relationship, because that's not fair to anyone. So, I don't know what to do. She doesn't like me, and if we have to break up to keep the peace, then it's okay–I've come to terms with it–I'm used to not getting what I want all the–"

I kissed her. I could have done anything else to stop her rambling, but I needed her to know that in his moment–she was the only thing I cared about. She cupped my jaw as I deepened the kiss, and as much as I wanted to stay here forever, I couldn't ignore the anger that settled into my stomach. I pulled back and gripped onto her hips.

"There is nothing that's going to keep me from you. I will talk to Marion–and I'm sorry it's taken me this long to realize what's been going on between you two."

"You don–"

"I do. On my list of the most important people in my life, you and Hayley share the top spot, and Marion doesn't come close to my top ten. I will get to the bottom of it, okay?"

Hollis nodded, and I could see her fighting a smile. "Okay."

Footsteps sounded behind us, and I felt all the blood rush from my face. Hollis and I turned to face the doorway and found Hayley standing there with an excited smile.

"Uncle Scottie *totally* owes me twenty bucks!"

47

Townes

Hollis laughed and buried her head into the side of my neck while I groaned.

"Seriously? What did you and Scottie bet? And why are you betting to begin with?"

Hayley giggled. "That you guys would kiss, and I won. Can I call Uncle Scottie now?"

I shook my head, and gently patted Hollis's waist–a silent command to move. She did, and I stalked up to Hayley, who still had that mischievous glint in her eyes. I held out my hand for her to take it.

"You can call him tomorrow for your money, and then I'm going to have a nice chat with him about how bad it is to encourage a gambling addiction in kids. Come on, bedtime."

"Wait." Hayley tore her hand from mine and ran past me toward Hollis. Something cleaved open in my chest when Hollis embraced her, and I wanted to join them–wrap my girls in my arms–but I felt this embrace should stay between them. Hollis whispered something in Hayley's ear, before she placed a kiss on the top of her head. Hayley spun on her heel and took my outstretched hand when she reached me.

I took one last look at Hollis, who gave me a nod before I walked Hayley to her bedroom. With every step, I could feel her excitement, and it only turned worse when she finally laid down in her bed. She bounced as I pulled the pink blanket up and smiled.

"Does this mean you and Hollis are boyfriend and girl-friend? Oh wait"–she tapped her chin–"Does kissing mean you guys get married? Oh! Can I be the flower girl?"

"Slow your roll Haybug, let's get to tomorrow before we start having big talks like that okay? Besides, who even said you get to know that kind of stuff. It's our relationship, not yours," I teased, which earned me a scrunch of her nose.

She then crossed her arms, and gathered all the attitude her little eight-year-old body could hold. "If you don't get married, I won't forgive you Uncle T. Cause who else likes those deep lines in your face? I have to be a flower girl, please don't ruin this for me."

If only she knew.

"Lay down. Bedtime." She finally laid down, and as I tucked her in, she rolled onto her side and rested her hands under her cheek. I sighed when I noticed the dazed look in her eyes. "What's up?"

"I think you love her, Uncle T," she said it with such confidence, and the words hit me square in the chest. Directly in that little spot I'd been ignoring for months.

I worked through the tightness in my throat. "What do you know about love Haybug?"

She shrugged. "Not much. But you look at her how daddy looked at mommy. And I think that's love. Looking at someone with a sparkle in your eye."

Words escaped me as I wracked my brain to understand how she knew—the photo album. The one full of her parents before Hayley was born; evidence of how strong their love was, and a reminder what we all lost. And the fact Hayley noticed that tiny similarity…

I never meant to do anything different; look at Hollis a certain way, smile at her, or even touch her. I tried so hard to keep my distance for fear of getting Hayley's hopes up, that my longing ended up on my face. When Hollis looked at me, I could feel how badly she wanted to be close—but had Hollis seen it too? If Hayley noticed, then surely Hollis did too.

Hayley was fast asleep by the time I glanced down, which worked in my favor considering I still didn't know what I was going to say.

I got up and made sure the door was shut completely before I walked back toward the kitchen. Hollis was still sitting at the table with Hayley's coloring book in front of her. Her brows were furrowed in concentration as she shaded the flowers on the page purple. I watched her and relaxed into the silence.

"How many questions did she have?" she asked, only pausing to grab the green crayon.

"Too many for me to answer tonight." I kept watching her and kept fighting the urge to pull her close. So we sat there until the flower was done, and Hollis leaned back and smiled. When she finally glanced at me, I reached for her hand and asked her the question I'd kept to myself; for fear of a certain someone catching us.

"Ready for bed?"

Her smile dropped to a smirk, and I couldn't wait to get her alone. "My room. My bed's better."

I scoffed and followed her movement to stand. I towered over her and took a step closer so I could cup her face and tilt her head up. "Your bed's tiny."

"I never said it was big, but it's more comfortable."

"Hm, comfort over practicality. Let's go to my room, at least then I know my feet won't be dangling off the bed."

Hollis rose onto her toes before she leaned in, her hands bracing on my sides for stability. "Practically speaking, if you're going to fuck me into the mattress, I'd rather be comfortable." She leaned back and took her hands away to raise them in front of her. "But hey if you're really tired, then by all means, your room it is."

I knelt down and grabbed the back of Hollis's thighs before I lifted and tossed her over my shoulder. She giggled as I carried her down the hallway and to her room. Bilbo ran between my legs when I walked into the room, and I waited until her tail disappeared before I shut the door. Hollis continued to giggle as I placed her on her feet, and she bit her lip when her eyes met mine.

"Someone's eager," she quipped.

I leaned down and gripped her waist before I moved close enough to brush my lips against hers. "Just trying to finish what we started this morning."

My mouth met hers, and Hollis melted into me. It didn't take long before her hands were gripping my hair, and her fingers were raking through my beard. She moaned into my mouth, and I took the chance to lick into hers. I followed her as she tilted her head back and wrapped one hand around her neck. She gasped against my mouth, and I pulled back to take her in; swollen lips, heavy lids, and her heaving chest. The sensible thing would be to take my time admiring her, the way she feels under my grasp, and how pretty she looked before I fucked her.

But I wasn't feeling very sensible at the moment.

I laid her against the bed and used my knee to spread her legs before I trailed one hand down to her jeans. I undid the buttons, and she helped me shove the fabric off her legs. When my fingers trailed up her legs, I found her dripping, and I kissed down her neck to bite the sensitive skin on her neck. Hollis bucked her hips against me, but I kept my fingers a whisper away from where she wanted me.

She bucked again, then groaned when I moved my fingers up her stomach and under her shirt.

"You're such a tease," Hollis hissed as my hand cupped her bare breast.

I gave her another kiss, this time lower on her collarbone. "I don't know what you're talking about," I glanced up at her and smirked. "If there's something you want, just tell me."

"What I want" –she wiggled under my grasp–"Is for you to put your hand back where it belongs."

"I don't know what you mean baby." I pinched her nipple and stared at her as her lashes fluttered. I leaned in, and my lips brushed the shell of her ear. "If there's something you want, fucking take it."

I felt her hesitate for a split second before she was grasping my wrist and yanking my hand back to her pussy. Then, I felt her tug on my fingers, and I knew what she wanted. I claimed her mouth and swallowed a moan as I inserted a finger, her hips started to roll, but stopped when I hadn't moved. She pulled back and creased her brows together.

"What are yo–"

"Ride my fingers, baby."

A deep blush crawled over her cheeks, but then she closed her eyes and started rolling her hips in earnest. I continued to pepper kisses over her exposed skin as she squeezed around my finger.

"More," she whispered.

And since I could never deny her anything, I inserted another finger and groaned as she stretched around me. Her hips bucked faster, and I felt her tighten. As her breath hitched, and she reached down to grip my wrist—I pulled away.

"Wa—what? I was so close," she whined.

I placed a gentle kiss on her lips before I licked my fingers clean. "I said to ride my fingers, not get off. Because when you come, it'll be around my cock."

She had a dazed look on her face, but bit her lip when I unzipped my pants. I could stare at her forever—engrave this scene into my mind so it would stay with me long before I was gone. I wasted no time grabbing the condom from my pocket and putting it on, then I lined up against her entrance. With one last kiss to her lips, I rolled my hips, and groaned when I felt how tight she was.

"How are you so perfect?" I asked as I pulled out. "These fucking tits." I tugged her shirt down to expose a perk nipple. "And your pretty fucking face."

I fucked into her until I was buried to the hilt and threw my head back with a groan. "And this perfect pussy. All for me." I picked up the pace, unrelenting with how hard and how deep I fucked her. Each moan that escaped her lips was music to my ears—a never ending symphony composed just for me. I was the conductor, and she was my instrument, and boy did she sound pretty.

Her eyes rolled back as I felt her tighten around me again, so I reached down and cupped the back of her neck. Then I lifted her slightly and placed a kiss on her forehead. She fought hard to keep her eyes open.

"That's right baby, look at me while I fuck you."

"Townes I–I'm so cl–"

"I know baby, you're doing so good for me." I captured her mouth with mine as her body went taught. She shattered around me, moaning and clawing at my back until I followed soon after.

Breathless, I dropped my elbows and caged her under me. As she caught her breath, I pulled out, and quickly cleaned up before I threw my pants on to grab her a water. By the time I got back to the room, she was walking out of the bathroom. Her eyes widened when she saw me.

"What's that?"

"Water?"

"You got me a drink?"

I hated the uncertainty in her voice, but instead of asking any questions right away, I walked over to her and grabbed her hand. Then, I led her to the bed, pulled back the covers, and gave her the drink before pulling them back up. I went to my side–strange, calling it my side when it was only the second night I was sleeping in here–and crawled under the blankets next to her. I kissed her exposed hip and threw my arm over her lap. "It's called aftercare, sweetheart."

"I know what it is, but I haven't–"

"Shh, just let me cuddle with you until we fall asleep."

Hollis placed her fingers in my hair, and I fell asleep with scratches on my scalp, and a heart full of an emotion I was almost ready to face.

48

Hollis

Townes and I underestimated how Hayley would take the news of our new relationship. Our worries of her being upset, confused, or having any sort of resentment were put to rest the morning after she caught us in the kitchen. For the past few weeks, she's been asking questions about how we fell in love, and Townes had stiffened every time. I couldn't be upset by his reaction–things were still new, and it was an awkward question to be asked. Especially by someone who was still too short to ride in the front seat.

We'd managed to avoid the topic and have steered the conversation elsewhere for now. Like, how things are going to change at the end of the season; what Townes is going to do, if I'm going to go back to the bar over the summer. But a change we weren't expecting came with a single question from Hayley over lunch.

She poked her salad with a fork as her brows furrowed. I was going to ask if she was okay, until her utensil clattered in her bowl, and she placed both hands on the table.

"Does this mean I'm getting adopted?"

Townes choked on his water, and I spent a good two minutes patting his back while he collected himself. I handed him a napkin, and his face was red as he cleaned himself up. Hayley sat there, innocence on her face as she stared between us.

"Carmen is adopted. She said she had a different mommy before, but she never met her. So, her new mommy bought her when she was a baby."

"Uh—she didn't buy her Haybug."

I cocked my head. "Well, technically—"

Townes shot me a serious look, and my mouth clamped shut. Then, he sighed and leaned forward on the table. It was late June; families were out together, the sounds of children laughing filled the air, and Townes was gearing up for his last game this weekend. He'd been so busy with practice and doing publicity for the Peaks, Hayley and I hadn't seen him much. So we planned to spend the day together before—if only we had been prepared for this conversation.

"Why are you asking about adoption?"

Hayley fell back in her seat, and her voice dropped. "Well, since I don't have a mommy or daddy, I thought maybe I could get new ones. And since you two are in love, I thought maybe you could do it."

I glanced at Townes, and waited—how was he going to address this? He and I hadn't had any conversations about the future; about what would happen if things ended between us. About what would happen if things didn't end, we hadn't included Hayley into the equation because we needed to make sure our shit was together first.

Now here she was, asking the hard questions while I was

342

still thinking about how I was woken up this morning.

With Townes's head between my legs.

Hayley's eyes darted between ours. "Can I get adopted?"

Townes took deep, steady breaths, and I knew this conversation wasn't going to go anywhere. I placed my hand on his back again and started rubbing circles between his shoulder blades as I smiled at Hayley.

"You know, that's a really big question. And to be honest" –I leaned in and scrunched my nose–"I don't even know if I like your uncle that much. Besides, I don't think you'd want me as your mom."

"Yes I do."

The truth of her words hit me square in the chest, and I forgot how to breathe for a moment. Townes lifted his head to something behind her, and I felt him stiffen under my hand. I followed his line of sight, and steeled myself as Marion walked toward us, bags filling her arms.

Hayley turned around and jumped out of her seat before she ran to her grandmother. "Nana!"

"Hi hon." She reached down to hug her. "Fancy seeing you here."

"I could say the same thing," Townes said through gritted teeth. His hand landed on my thigh beneath the table, and I breathed a little easier. We'd both been avoiding Marion; dropping Hayley off from the car instead of taking her inside, keeping all conversations short. Townes planned on talking to her after their last game–to keep a level head and not be anxious about anything that might be said.

"Uh, well it's nice to see you. Are we still expecting you two at the game later?" I asked. Marion's eyes darted toward me, and I could feel the tension in the air. She didn't want to

343

talk to me, and frankly I didn't want to talk to her either, but I wasn't going to air out our issues with Hayley in front of us.

She smiled down at Hayley. "Of course I am, considering it's the finals and Hayley's coming home with me." She lifted her head and pinned me with a stare. "Will you be going? Or will you be watching from your house?"

"Hollis is going! She said she would show me the family room, cause they have snacks and it's quiet," Hayley said before sitting back at her seat.

"How come I've never been in the family room?" Marion looked at Townes with a raised brow.

He shrugged and leaned back in his seat. "Maybe if you came to more games, I would have shown you."

I could feel the tension of unspoken words between them and did my best to ease it. I smiled and cleared my throat. "Well, we don't want to keep you. Hayley and I will meet you outside tonight, and we can walk together."

"Fine." She turned on her heel without another word, and Hayley was graciously oblivious as she shoved food into her mouth. Townes kept his hand on my leg, and despite his usual scowl and aura of grumpiness, I could tell he was getting anxious. It was the way he squeezed my leg while his other bounced, and how his brows seemed to pulse together as he stared at his niece.

I leaned in and whispered, "Hey, it's fine."

"No, it's not. I hate how she talks to you."

I tapped his leg with my free hand, offering a distraction. "You can deal with it later, after you guys win, okay?"

He rolled his head to look at me, and even though he never smiled, I could feel his appreciation. "Okay."

"So how much do you think I'll cost? I think five dollars

cause I'm short," Hayley rambled as she ate, and Townes sat there shaking his head at the things that came out of her mouth. Meanwhile, I wondered what would happen when we eventually talked to Marion, and the clusterfuck that might happen afterwards.

* * *

"Wait so, she insisted on taking Hayley into the stands? Why? It's wild out there," Basil said as her brows creased.

I shrugged and took a sip of my overpriced beer. "She wanted the full experience with Hayley and felt it was better to do it out there. Besides, god forbid she's around me for more than five minutes. At least out there she can't make any judgmental comments."

"Honestly, Hol, I can't believe Townes has let this go on for so long."

I tossed my head back and groaned. She was right, of course, but if I let Townes talk to Marion, then their conversation would be stuck in his head, and I didn't want it to affect his game tonight. I wanted to keep the peace–no matter how fragile it was. I took another sip and ignored how it burned my throat.

"To be fair, I didn't mention anything until a month ago. Since then, he's been so busy I haven't pushed the topic."

"Why'd you keep it from him?" she asked.

"Because before, I didn't know what we were doing so I didn't think it mattered."

Basil shook her head and let out a heavy sigh that told me how dumb she thought I was being. "But you were helping with Hayley, of course it mattered."

345

"It's whatever. Townes is going to talk to her after the game. So let's just focus on having a good time."

We fell into silence as we watched the game. Everyone in the room was quiet as they watched their husbands and partners go back and forth on the ice. Meanwhile, the crowd in the stands was roaring with excitement. As my eyes tracked Case and Scottie going back and forth, I couldn't help but keep snapping them back to Townes. His last game; what was he thinking, was his knee bothering him, was he still caught up about earlier?

I wished I could pick his brain, figure out exactly what he was thinking, so I knew how to approach him after the game.

"So, wedding stuff. What's up with it?" I asked Basil.

She smiled and kept her eyes on her soon-to-be-husband. They finally decided on a date in the fall, right after Halloween. "Sometimes I wish we just went to the courthouse or something. I want to be married already."

"If you don't stop being sappy, I'm going to cry," I said, wiping away a fake tear.

"Stop being dramatic," she quipped.

I laughed, then turned my attention back to the game. The next hour was filled with cheers and excitement so thick it was suffocating. Then, when Scottie made the winning goal, the screams become suffocating. The sound carried from the arena into the family room–people around us jumped and embraced as the players on the ice piled onto each other.

I grabbed Basil's hand and rushed out to the hallway. We could wait closer to the locker rooms for the guys and avoid most of the crowds. As we walked however, we ran into Marion, with Hayley in tow. Her small smile was wide, and she was dressed head to toe in Townes's jersey number.

"Hollis! Did you see that! They won!" She moved to rush toward me, but Marion held her back.

"Basil, is it? Would you be a dear and take Hayley to get a drink? I need to have a conversation with Hollis for just a second."

I glanced at Basil and nodded when she gave me an unsure look. Hayley went willingly to her, chattering away about her time in the stands. When they rounded the corner, Marion adjusted a bracelet on her wrist. "How much longer?"

"Excuse me?"

She scoffed. "The season's over, Hollis. How much longer are you and Townes going to put on this little act?"

"What are you talking about?" I knew that Marion was aware of our initial agreement, and she knew how long we planned on being together so we wouldn't raise any flags with the immigration office.

"This dating thing you two are trying out. Better to end things now before it gets messy and causes problems later on."

I took a step back. "Uh, what are you on? Our relationship is none of your business."

"It is when it involves my granddaughter thinking you two are actually together. She's asking me about adoption and if she can call you mom. I'm not okay with it."

I hadn't realized...

"And how is that my problem?"

Marion took a step closer, and I could feel something thick and heavy radiating off of her. It wasn't anger like I expected, and the longer I stared at her, the clearer that emotion became.

Hurt. Fear.

Where was it coming from? I hadn't realized she'd been on the verge of tears until she was standing in front of me. "I've already seen that little girl and Townes be destroyed once. When her parents passed away. And I'm not going to stand by and risk it happening again."

I cleared my throat, shocked by the tightness blocking it. "You have a lot of assumptions about someone you don't know."

"I don't want to know you, Hollis. I want to make sure my granddaughter doesn't get hurt again."

I blinked back the tears that were threatening to flow over. I needed to leave, go anywhere else to collect myself–but as I turned around, I came face-to-face with a sweaty, red-faced Townes. He was holding Hayley's hand, and when his eyes met mine, his smile fell. That beautiful smile was wiped from his face, and it was because of me. He took a step, and I turned the other way and ran toward the doors.

I couldn't face him. Not right now.

49

Townes

"Uncle T, are you mad?" Hayley asked from the backseat.

I gripped the steering wheel and glanced back to her, then to the car following behind us. Tonight was supposed to be great—we won the Stanley Cup, and I had planned on spending the night with my girls.

So, when I saw Hollis standing in the hallway, with tears in her eyes, nothing else mattered. I wanted to hold her close and ask her what was wrong, but she ran the opposite direction. Leaving Marion standing there with no remorse for what she had done. I was going to find out what she said to Hollis, then I was going to make sure it never happened again. My original plan to confront her before the game kept being thwarted by Hollis.

I got so distracted by her presence that I wanted to bask in it as long as possible. Yes, I knew that was a me problem, but I was a weak man.

I never thought I would be distracted by a pretty smile and kind heart.

My eyes shifted to Hayley, who was both concerned and confused by my silence, and the situation. After Hollis left, I went to confront Marion but stopped when she insisted we talk at her place. I turned and walked out with Hayley before either of them could protest.

"Uncle T?"

"I'm not mad Haybug, just need to talk to your Nana about something," I told her, returning my attention to the road.

She sighed, and even though I wasn't looking at her, I knew she had her arms crossed and a brow raised. "Well you look mad, like how you did before Hollis."

"What are you talking about?"

She shrugged and wiped away a stray curl. "Before we moved in with Hollis, you looked mad all the time. Now, you don't, so I can tell."

I tried to think of what exactly was different, how could I have changed so much that it was noticeable to Hayley? Was it noticeable to everyone else too? How much did Hollis change me, or did I change for her?

The thoughts continued until I pulled into Marion's driveway. Hayley jumped out of the truck and waited patiently for her grandmother to park next to us. Marion got out of her car, slow and elegant–as if nothing was wrong and smiled at Hayley. "Get your bag honey, it's in the backseat."

"Actually, Hayley, I'll grab it," I said, keeping my eyes locked with Marion's.

Oblivious to the tension between us, Hayley nodded and ran to the door. She put in the code on the keypad and walked inside. Marion went to follow, but I stepped in front of her, blocking her path. She raised a brow.

"Was there something you needed?"

I hated her tone, it was too calm. Did she have no remorse? I clenched my fist and stared down at her. "What did you and Hollis talk about?"

She scoffed, and I had to focus on outside stimuli to try and keep myself in check. The warm breeze against my skin, how the crickets were really fucking loud. Anything to suppress the pounding in my chest.

"I told her that she had no business being involved with you more than she needed to be."

"Our relationship is none of your concern, Marion," I said, my throat growing tight. "Why on earth do you think you can dictate what anyone else does with their life? Huh?"

She raised her chin, and I could feel her frustration–but it wasn't an excuse for what she said to Hollis. What she had ever said to the woman I loved.

"I was fine with you getting married so you could stay here with Hayley, Townes. Okay? I had gotten over the fact that my son chose you to be her guardian over me–"

"You said you were fine with it." When we looked over the paperwork after the accident, Marion never showed any resentment over me being named Hayley's legal guardian. All she did was offer support.

She scoffed. "I lost my son, and the last connection I had to him went to you. A hot-headed athlete with no parenting experience. It was a slap in the face."

My blood boiled, and I had to keep distracting myself before I crumbled. The grass danced in the wind, and Marion's neighbor drove by in his car with a modified muffler. It crackled down the street, but I needed more.

"So, you're being an asshole to Hollis because–what? If you couldn't have Hayley, then no one else could? You expect me to be by myself forever?"

"I'm protecting my granddaughter, Townes. I don't expect you to be alone forever, but I did expect you to find someone because it was what you wanted. You found Hollis out of obligation to Hayley, and what's going to happen when your little honeymoon phase ends? One of you is going to wake up and feel resentment over the whole thing. She's going to leave you and Hayley, and it's going to destroy you both."

Silence drifted between us, and Marion let out a single tear. "Hayley's already lost one mother, and I refuse for her to get her hopes up just to lose another one. Fake wife, or real one, that little girl looks up to her and shame on you for not putting her first."

I snapped.

"Not putting her first?" I took a step forward, but Marion didn't move. "What do you think I've been doing for the past five years? Huh? You think I've been sitting on my ass, wallowing in the fact that my life got put on hold? No. I've been doing my damnedest to take care of Hayley, all while putting my wants and needs aside. So god forbid I do one thing that makes me happy."

I stepped away and took a few deep breaths. Then, I turned back toward Marion. "I think it's best that Hayley stays at home for a while. At least until you accept the fact that Hollis isn't going anywhere."

I left Marion standing there, with her mouth open, ready to say something I wasn't in the mood to hear. I couldn't, not with how my heart was pounding hard enough to block out everything else. When I got to the doorway, I called inside. "Hayley! Change of plans, we're going to go home."

It was quiet for a long moment, and I took a step inside

when I didn't hear her. "Hayley?"

* * *

Hollis

Carly sat across from me, a mug of tea in her hands while I bounced Michael on my lap. He gurgled and clapped as I kept my focus on my sister-in-law. After talking with Marion, I didn't know where else to go–who else I could talk to.

"She sounds like a bitch," Carly said.

I tried not to snort. "She's…concerned. And part of me can understand her protectiveness, but I don't know how to get through to her. How can I convince her that her worries are misplaced?"

Carly shook her head and leaned back in the beige lounge chair. Michael reached his arms down, and I gently sat him on the laminate so he could grab whatever toy he was pointing to. I called her from the parking lot–crying and needed someone who might offer some sage advice. And she seemed like the best person, considering my parents weren't a huge fan of her when she got pregnant with my brother. They were worried she would derail his plans of becoming a doctor and forbade him from seeing her.

After months of fighting, Lionel decided it was better to cut ties with them if they couldn't get over their own biases. It was hard, them not having support while Carly was pregnant.

Then, Michael was born and our parents decided they wanted to meet their grandson. I wasn't sure what conversation they had–when I was helping Carly get laundry done and

Lionel went to lunch with our parents. But I did hear them apologize to Carly, then cry tears of joy when she handed them Michael, wrapped tightly in a green swaddle.

"You can't," she said. I glanced at her and noticed the worry between her brows. "I wish I had better advice for you Hol, but her worries aren't your responsibility. All you can do is make the best of it, and look, I don't want to tell you to avoid her. Because that all that's going to do is raise questions from Hayley that you might not be able to answer. She's the only reason I'm telling you to keep things civil. You all love her, and none of you want her to get hurt just because her grandmother can't keep her mouth shut."

I nodded and took in her words as I tried to think of something I could do. It wasn't possible to avoid her forever, but maybe I could talk to her–earn her trust.

Michael waddled over on unsteady legs and placed a red block into my lap.

"Ed," he said, drool dripping off his chin.

"You got it monster, red." I smiled as he clapped and walked back to his toy chest. "So what should I do?"

Carly picked up her legs and tucked them into the couch. "Go home and make a plan with Townes. Navigate this together."

I nodded and reached for my bag. I shouldn't have bolted when I saw Townes earlier, but better late than never. When I pulled my phone from the side pocket of my purse, my brows furrowed.

"Everything okay?" Carly asked.

I scanned through the text messages and stood when I got to the last one. I was too busy slinging my purse strap over my shoulder and grabbing my shoes to answer Carly's question.

Panic coursed through me as I got to the car and started driving home, the last text from Townes burning in my mind.

Townes: *Hayley's missing.*

50

Townes

Marion and I had torn the house apart looking for Hayley, and when she didn't show up–I called Hollis. She was the only person I needed to talk to–to try and bring down the panic that was rising in my throat. But she never answered her phone and it made that sticky, suffocating feeling worse. I understood if she needed space, but to ignore my calls?

We figured Hayley had overheard parts, if not all of our conversation, and it understandably made her upset. However, running off was a new thing, and not something I ever thought I'd have to worry about with her. When we couldn't find her in or around the house, I started calling everyone I knew, while Marion stayed inside searching for her phone.

The police were on their way to get a description while I drove around the neighborhood, hopeful to find a crowd of people if someone noticed Hayley walking around.

My phone rang, and when I registered Case's name on the screen, I answered. His voice was full of the same panic I felt, but he spoke with an even voice. "Hey, Basil and I are leaving the house now."

"Okay, I'm going to the park around the corner from Marion's, since it's not far." It was the same park we had gone to hundreds of times, and one I hoped she'd be at. But after another five minutes of searching the entire area from top to bottom, I was back at square one. I got into the truck and hit the steering wheel. "Where the fuck are you?"

I took a second to gather myself before I started driving again–I wasn't any use to anyone if I couldn't keep my emotions under control. It didn't matter that my vision was turning blurry around the edges, that my head throbbed with each echoing pound of my heart. My hands turned sweaty, and I had to keep wiping them on my jeans. Anxiety attacks were something I was used to, they were quiet and left me to address my spiraling thoughts.

But I was on the verge of a panic attack, and it was new–I wanted someone to help me through it.

My phone rang and pulled me back to reality for a second, and when I saw Hollis's picture on the screen, I answered it with more enthusiasm than I thought I could manage. "Where are you? Why didn't you answer my calls? Hayley's missing and I've been driving arou–"

"Townes, she's at Scottie's. I'm with her and he's on his way."

She hung up the phone, leaving me with more questions, and feeling more panicked than before–if that were possible. How had she found Hayley before me, and why was she at Scotties? I flipped on the blinker and continued to the townhouse, calling everyone to let them know Hayley had been found. Case offered to go back and tell Marion, since she hadn't found her phone.

Hollis's car was sitting in the driveway, and I pulled in at the same time as Scottie. He shut his door, and his expression was pulled taught with the same anxiety I was feeling. "Man, I'm sorry. I didn't know she came here til I got an alert," he said.

Ah yeah. We installed a security camera last summer so we could catch a porch thief, it wasn't supposed to be used for looking out for an eight-year-old runaway. I pushed past Scottie and walked inside, then when I saw Hollis sitting with Hayley on the steps, I nearly fell to my knees.

But instead, I walked and knelt in front of Hayley, whose eyes were red-rimmed and her cheeks were streaked with dried tears. For the first time tonight, I felt like I could breathe. My head fell as I gathered myself, but it was too late. The panic attack was still there, and it was only getting stronger with every thought that passed through my mind. I looked at Hollis, and it killed me to see how sad she looked.

"Townes–"

"Why didn't you answer any of my calls? And why didn't you at least text me back? You knew what was happening, so where were you?"

Scottie took a step closer. "Let's not jump to any conclusions."

Hayley spoke up, her voice tired and cracked. "Uncle T–"

"Where were you, Hollis?" I asked her.

She was quiet for a moment as she looked between me and Hayley, then, she cleared her throat and did her best to smile. "Let's get Hayley home, then we can talk."

"Fine." I stood and stormed outside. Then, when the girls were in the truck, I started for the house. No one spoke as the yellow from the streetlights dashed across our faces. At some point, Hayley fell asleep, and I carried her inside when we got home. Hollis wasn't far behind, but she kept her distance and her head down. She was still standing in the living room when I came back, and the panic had subsided thankfully. The only evidence of it was the headache behind my eyes, and how tired I was.

In its place however, sat anger, and I wasn't sure who I was angry at–myself for putting Hayley in a position to overhear a sensitive conversation, or Hollis for not calling me when we needed her.

I crossed my arms and leaned against the far wall. "How did you find Hayley?"

Hollis crossed her arms over her middle, and it didn't escape me how her lip quivered when she looked at me. "She called me from Marion's phone. I talked her through the process of sharing her location so I could get her somewhere safe. It just so happened Scottie's was the closest place."

It clicked. "That's why you didn't call me back, because you were busy."

Hollis nodded, and I felt like an asshole. For not only assuming she had been ignoring me all night, but for fighting in front of Hayley–it was my fault she ran off and I was too busy pointing fingers to realize it. I shoved off the wall to take a step closer to Hollis, but she backed away.

"We need to talk, Townes."

I waited, uneasy about where this was going.

Hollis sucked in a breath, and when she looked at me again, I saw them. The tears that were threatening to spill over. "I don't think we can keep doing this." It was like all the air in the room disappeared and I couldn't breathe even if I wanted to. "The marriage thing, sure. But not us."

"What are you talking about?"

Her breath was ragged, and wet. "Us being together is causing more problems than either of us thought Townes. I mean, Hayley ran off because you and Marion were arguing over it. Do you know what she told me when she called? She was terrified of me leaving, Townes. Just the thought of it was enough for her to run off. What would happen if things actually did end? Marion was rig–"

"Don't you dare finish that sentence, Hollis." I took another step toward her, but she backed away again and it broke me.

She wiped away a tear and did her best to put on a reassuring smile. "I love you both too much to risk putting either of you through his again, Townes. I know it destroyed you when you couldn't find her, and it was my fault. I put you in that position and I'm sorry."

Those three little words looped in my brain, and I did my best to latch onto them. So I could say the words back, but it was too late. Hollis had backed up to the door. "I'm staying with Basil tonight, we can talk more about this later."

I couldn't move. She was leaving. "When is later?"

She shook her head. "When *this*" –she pointed between us–"Doesn't hurt as much as it does right now."

I watched her walk out the door, and remembered how I felt when I got the call Kennedy was gone. How much it hurt.

This pain was just as terrible.

51

Townes

It was only quiet for a moment when the floor creaked behind me. I didn't want to face Hayley, not with my emotions all over the place. She deserved to see me when I wasn't about to fall apart.

"Uncle T?" Her voice was small, and it broke another piece inside of me.

I turned around and saw her shuffle her feet across the wood floor, her head down as she fiddled her fingers together. I fell apart for a different reason then, seeing how fragile Hayley looked–I could've prevent that. If only I wasn't so distracted with Marion, with Hollis, I could have kept Hayley safe, and tonight would have never happened.

"What's up Haybug?" I asked as I moved to sit on the couch, exhausted and ready to sleep.

She paddled over and took the spot next to me, nerves radiated off her as she remained quiet. I dropped my hand to her head and leaned mine back. "Are you okay?" I asked.

"Maybe," she whispered. It was quiet for another moment, before she took in a shaky breath. Then, she turned toward me. "Nana said you married Hollis, is that true?"

I dragged my hand over my face and sighed. There was no getting out of this, I had to come clean and hope I didn't cause irreversible damage from lying to her. Hayley blinked, and it was shocking to find nothing but curiosity in her eyes. I was expecting to find hurt, confusion, anger...*something*.

It didn't do anything to quell the anxiety filling my chest though, not knowing how she felt was worse than seeing her hurt.

I nodded. "Yes."

She pulled in her brows. "When did you do it?"

"It was right before we moved in, Haybug. I uh–I didn't have any other choice?"

"Because Hollis is so pretty?" she asked.

I chuckled, because while she wasn't wrong, it wasn't the full truth. The first time I laid eyes on her, I knew I had to keep my distance. Because that much beauty didn't deserve something so harsh and jagged.

"I did it because otherwise, I would have had to leave and go back to Canada."

"That's the place that makes your favorite maple syrup right?" She blinked, and I chuckled again.

"Yes, it is." I rubbed her head, and she giggled. "I couldn't do that though, it's not my home anymore."

Hayley tilted her head, and a few curls bounced with the motion. "What do you mean? You're from there."

She must have seen the shift in my expression. The one where I realized–how do I explain it to her?

"What do you think of when you think of home?" I asked.

Hayley sat with that question for a moment, tucking herself under my arm. The house was quiet, and it only made me feel more guilty than before—why did Hollis leave? It's her fucking house, she should have kicked *me* out. I just stood there and watched the door shut without even trying to convince her otherwise.

I didn't deserve her, not after everything I put her through.

"I think of you," Hayley said, her voice soft and full of warmth. She tilted her head up and smiled. "And I think of Hollis, Basil, and Uncle Casey."

"What about your uncle Scottie?"

"Yeah, him too." She smiled. "Is that your home too, Uncle T? Is that why you wanted to stay?"

I nodded, because it was all I could manage. Hayley let out a heavy sigh and turned her head up to look at me. "I'm sorry I ran away, Uncle T. I was just upset."

There wasn't anything I wanted to say about that, not right now. But the conversation had to happen, and it was better to have it now when the mood was already heavy. "Why'd you do that? You scared us."

She shrugged. "I think it's cause I was upset."

"That I kept the truth from you?"

Hayley pushed herself up and looked at me with furrowed brows. "What? No. I was upset I didn't get to be your flower girl, Uncle T. That was my dream, and I may have overreacted."

I blinked at her, stunned by her honesty. Yet, incredibly confused by her logic. "Haybug. You ran away because you didn't get to be a flower girl?"

"Well yeah, Uncle T. Cause I love you guys, and I was mad I missed the wedding."

I scoffed and shook my head. I wasn't sure I'd ever understand how kids think. I glanced back at her and found the smallest smile growing on her face. She reached out and took one of my hands. "I'm sorry."

"Listen." I tugged her back into my side and rested my cheek on her head. "Don't *ever* do that again. I don't care how upset you are, running away from your problems doesn't solve them. If anything, it just creates more of them. Okay?"

Hayley was quiet for a moment, then asked in a soft voice. "Did Hollis run away?"

"No. She didn't run from anything."

She glanced up. "Are you going to get her?"

God, I wanted to. But I wasn't sure if that's what she would want, I had made her feel like the wasn't important–the most important thing in my life. How could I fix that? Hayley pulled away and stood in front of me. Her bare feet hit the floor, and I made a note to get her a pair of slippers so her feet wouldn't be cold. She crossed her arms and raised a brow.

"Uncle T, in all the old princess movies, the prince always runs after the princess. And that's what you need to do."

"You think so?" I tried to keep from smiling at her enthusiasm.

She threw her arms out. "Of course! You love her and that's what you're supposed to do. Plus, I love her too and I want her here."

I huffed out a breath and leaned forward. I wasn't sure how I'd get her back–but it was going to happen one way or another.

"Haybug, I don't know how, but we're going to get my wife back."

She grinned. "Yeah!"

52

Hollis

"I say this with so much love, Hol. You're being ridiculous. Just go home," Basil said over our shared basket of fries. It had been a week since I'd seen Townes, and a week of Hell. I missed being around him, waking up next to him, seeing the smallest smiles of his when he laughed at my bad jokes. A week ago, it made sense to keep my distance, because I stupidly thought my feelings would simply wash away and things would go back to how they were before.

That wasn't the case though, if anything, staying away only made things worse. And telling him I loved him didn't help. It wasn't how I pictured saying those three little words–when I was willing to walk out the door to save him and Hayley from potential heartache in the future. I wanted to get it over quick, leave now before I got more attached.

It wasn't until the second day of sleeping in Basil's guest room that I realized I was already too attached, and I gave up the two most important people of my life because I let Marion's words get to me.

I fucked up, and I knew there was no going back. Even

if I crawled back to Townes and apologized, begged, it was done. The best thing I could do was wait until I could face him, then discuss where we went from here. We still needed to be legally married for a while, maybe he and Hayley could get their own place but have it be under someone else's name. I was sure Case or Scottie would be willing to help with that, and if anyone needed to do a home visit, then they could just come over. We could pretend to be a happy family–we were one until I screwed everything up.

When Hayley called me, crying and asking if I was really leaving them, it broke my heart in two. She didn't go too much into detail, partly because she hadn't heard the whole conversation, but mostly because I was too busy trying to get her to a safe place to entertain anything else.

I leaned back into the booth and ignored how the faux leather chafed against my legs. It was hot outside, and the air conditioning in the building was on its last leg. I wanted to go back to Basil's and continue to stuff my face with ice cream that would send me to the bathroom.

You know that saying? That hot girls have tummy issues? Well, I've got that and then some, but maybe if my tummy issues were at the forefront of my problems, then I could forget everything else for a while.

"I'm processing a breakup, B. Cut me some slack."

Basil sighed. "Hol, go and talk to him."

"How do I know he won't turn me away, B? Huh? I didn't just hurt him, I hurt Hayley too and I can't imagine he'll forgive me."

She tilted her head and glanced around the room for a moment. Then, she got out of her seat and walked around to slide into mine. Basil slid an arm around me, and I was ashamed of how hard I let my head fall to her shoulder. I'd always been the rock for others; for Emma when she failed an audition, for Lionel when his high school girlfriend cheated on him. For so long, I helped put people back together and put aside my feelings, that now, as I let someone do that for me, I felt the mounting pressure behind my eyes.

I needed a shoulder, and as much as I loved Basil–I wanted it to be Townes.

My phone rang from my purse, and for a moment I contemplated letting it go to voicemail like all the other calls had done. But something about it made me pick up my head and fish it from my pocket. It was an unknown number–I answered anyways.

"Hello?"

"Um–Hollis?" Hayley asked, her shy voice was backed by a wall of excitement.

I sat straighter and reached for my purse in case I had to leave. "Hayley? Where are you? Is everything okay?"

"Yeah, I'm okay. Uncle T said I could get a phone so if I got lost again, he could call me." She was silent for a moment. "When are you coming home? Uncle T is really sad."

I ushered Basil out of the seat and made my way to a far corner. With my arm tucked across my middle, I glanced around. "IS your uncle there? Can I talk to him?"

"Nope," she said, popping the p. "I'm at Uncle Scottie's, and he's making me pancakes."

"Perfect, let me talk to him please."

There was a rustling sound on the other end, and when Scottie finally came on the line, my heart sank at how upset he sounded. "Hey, Hol."

"Hey, why is Hayley with you?"

"Oh, uh, yeah Townes needed a minute. She's been staying here the past few days."

My blood ran cold, and I rushed back to the table, where Basil was already paying the check. She glanced up at me with a raised brow, and I shook my head. "Is he okay?"

Scottie was quiet for a moment while I gathered my bag and gave Basil an apologetic wave.

"He–he's pretty broken up, Hol. He dropped Hayley off and no one's really spoken to him since."

I opened the car door and went into autopilot. I didn't remember turning it on, or looking into traffic before I started driving to the house. All I could focus on was Scottie, and the things he was telling me. A tear spilled over as I hung up the phone. It was my fault–all of it.

And even though I wasn't ready to face Townes yet, to talk over everything that happened and where we went from here–I was ready to offer him comfort the only way I knew how. It was the least I could do after screwing everything up.

53

Townes

If I was a better person, I would feel bad about how I convinced Hollis to come home. But after endless calls going to voicemail, and unanswered texts, I felt hopeless and reached out for help.

This was, of course, after I talked to Hayley about the dangers of what she did and asked her why she did it. As it turned out, Hayley had only caught the beginning of the conversation, and had only heard Marion's discontentment that Hayley had gone to me after her parents passed. Sure, Hayley loved her nana, but I was her home.

Hollis was too.

Hayley running away had nothing to do with Hollis, but I couldn't talk to her to let her know that. So, I decided to do the one thing I could think of to ensure Hollis knew where I stood. Then, after I confessed all of my feelings, and told her what she meant to me—if she still wanted to walk away, then I'd learn to deal with it.

It would be painful, and I would end up more of an asshole than before—but at least it would happen without regret.

I had been planning all week, and when Scottie sent me the code word, I knew she was on her way over.

Scottie: *The blonde chipmunk is in route with the acorn*

Me: *...what's the acorn?*

Scottie: *Her love for you dude. Expect the acorn soon*

Scottie: *And a lil somethin else if you know what I mean*

Me: *You expect way too much from me when it comes to my sex life*

Scottie: *;)*

Me: *Shut up.*

Me: *And...thank you.*

I made sure everything was in place before I stood in the middle of the living room–surrounded by peonies from the garden, and her favorite candles she gets from the small boutique downtown.

If I was going to confess my love for her, and beg her to come back, I was going to do it in style.

A few minutes later, Bilbo awoke from the windowsill and looked out the window. Then, the cat stretched and wandered off into a different room just as the front door opened. Hollis came in fast, her breathing ragged as she glanced around the room. I watched as her eyes caressed over the flowers, the candles, and the small path I made leading up to me.

"It's not the best wedding aisle in the world, but I hope you like it?"

Hollis dropped her bag and took a small step forward. It wasn't much, but it was progress. "What is all this?"

"Well…" I cleared my throat and widened my stance. "I figured now was as good a time as any to recite a few vows. That is, if you'll hear me out?"

She let out a breath and cocked her head to the side. "Vows?"

"Yeah, well, the ones in Vegas were good in the moment, but now I have a few more things I'd like to say."

I watched as Hollis shook her head, and tears welled in her eyes, making them appear darker. She shook her head and kept a sob at bay when she spoke. "You don't have t–"

"Yes, I do. Or–I would like to." I waited a moment for any indication she was going to walk closer, but when I didn't get one, I reached out my hand. "Please, baby. If you don't like what I have to say, then you can leave. I won't stop you, but I just–I need you to hear this."

She walked over, but didn't take my hand.

It was progress.

I straightened my shoulders and filed through the notes I'd been making all week. But they became jumbled, and if I wasn't confident in my abilities to express my thoughts before...I sure as hell wasn't now.

"Townes?" Hollis asked, tilting her head to the side.

I cleared my throat, and finally looked at her. "There are a lot of things I want to say, but we both know words aren't my strong suit so just–bare with me okay?" She stayed silent, but nodded, which gave me enough confidence to continue. "I'm a simple man, Hollis. I was good at my job, and I'm a good parent to Hayley. I didn't care about being good at anything else, and didn't care if people liked me. Because I had what I needed, then I met you. I'm not sure when it happened, but at some point I started taking note of small things. When you'd smile at me, when you challenged me, and I let you win–"

"Sure you did," she quipped.

I smiled. "You started becoming important to me, Hollis, and I had another thing to care about. I started thinking of ways I could get you to smile, laugh, and jus–I wanted to do everything with you. And I'm grateful for you. I'm grateful for the joy you've brought into our lives, and I'm grateful you decided to give me a chance once I pulled my head out of my ass."

Hollis started tearing up again, and I reached out to tilt her head up, while my other hand wrapped around her waist and pulled her closer to me.

"And I am so sorry I couldn't show you how much you mean to me. I love you, and I'll love you for however long you'll let me. I want you here, Hayley wants you here. Please. Stay."

Silence descended on us as we stared at each other, both holding our breath. If she wanted to leave, I'd let her. I would pack up my shit and leave tonight so she could be in the comfort of her own home. Whatever she wanted, I'd give it to her. She wiped away a tear, and my arm tightened around her when she stepped closer to me.

Then, she smiled, and I knew if I died in this moment, I'd be okay.

"Scottie freaked me out. I thought I was going to walk in here and see you how I did on your birthday."

"You came even after you thought you should stay away?"

She shook her head. "I realized the day after I left that I couldn't stay away. Ever. But I did because I thought that's what you wanted."

I leaned in close, I wanted to kiss her so bad. "I'm sorry I made you think that, baby. I would never want you to stay away. You're my *wife*. I've got you. Now until forever, don't forget that."

A smile crossed her face as she closed her eyes, and I felt

her fully relax into me. "I'm sorry. Can you kiss me now?"

She didn't have to ask twice. I closed the distance between us and kissed her like I'd been drowning and she was the first gasp of air. Hollis threw her arms over my shoulders, and I reached down to pick her up. I turned around, ready to take things into a bedroom when the door burst open. We broke apart to see who the fuck interrupted us.

Scottie leaned against the doorway while Hayley stood next to him–her arms crossed as she tapped her foot.

"What the fuck are you two doing?" I asked.

"Swear jar," Hayley whispered.

"Well, we were waiting for you two to tie things up so we could all get some food. But you guys got distracted, and well–do you want to explain this to her or should I?"

Hollis raised a brow as she moved to untangle her legs from my waist, and I begrudgingly let her, but my hand never left the small of her back. "You were snooping?" she asked.

"Uncle T said I couldn't be the flower girl, so I wanted to watch."

Hollis turned. "Why couldn't she be the flower girl? That would have made this grand proclamation of love so much cuter."

"Because then everyone would have wanted to come," I argued.

Scottie laughed. "Do you have performance anxiety? It's okay, it's normal."

"See? You wanted that in the background while I confessed my love?"

"You love her!" Hayley jumped. "I knew it!"

Hollis giggled and reached for my hand before starting for the door. "Come one, we can tell you the story over ice cream."

54

Hollis

Townes placed a firm hand on my shaky leg, and his touch only quelled the nerves for a second. We were meeting with Marion, it was the first time I'd seen her since Townes's last game, and I wasn't sure how to feel.

We'd kept Hayley at home since she ran off, and told Marion that when she was ready to sit down and talk, she'd be able to see her again. It wasn't what I wanted–keeping Hayley from her family–but Townes was worried about what she might hear from Marion if she went over. He wanted to protect us both, and I wasn't going to stop him from what he thought was right.

The cafe was unusually busy for a Sunday morning, but we didn't have any problems finding Marion in the crowd. She wore a huge sunhat that flopped at the edges. Her expression was guarded as she walked toward us and took a seat, then she tilted her head in greeting.

"Townes. Hollis." I kept quiet as Townes's hand tightened around my still shaking leg. Marion folded her hands. "How are things? How's Hayley?"

The way her eyes lit up at the mention of her granddaughter made my stomach twist. How could someone–family–be so resentful and prideful, they would be willing to hurt someone they loved so dearly? Marion didn't have to like me, but she had to put Hayley first and accept I wasn't going anywhere.

Townes sat straighter. "She's fine. She misses you, actually."

"Oh! Well feel free to bring her over anytime! How about this weekend?"

I glanced at Townes, who gave me a reassuring nod before I took a steady breath. "Actually, Marion. Hayley isn't going over without a few ground rules."

She raised a brow. "Is that so? And why do you think you have any authority to make a decision like that?"

"She is my wife, Marion. Either you treat her with respect or we're leaving, and we will try this again when you learn to grow up."

Marion balked. "Fake wife."

Townes went to stand. "It stopped being fake a long time ago. I'll call you later and we can try this again, for Hayley's sake. Not yours." He grabbed my hand and led me out onto the downtown streets.

He rubbed his free hand over his jaw as we walked back to the car, and I ran my free hand over his forearm. I knew there wasn't much I could say that would make things better. Townes wanted what was best for Hayley, and Marion, being unable to respect our relationship, really threw a wrench into things. But as much as I wanted to focus on cheering him up, I couldn't get over what he said to her.

It stopped being fake a long time ago.

"Did you mean it?" I asked, unable to help myself.

"Hm? Mean what?"

My cheeks burned and for a second I considered brushing it off, but I needed to know. When did the man I love realize he wanted to keep me forever? "About me being your wife. When did it start being real? I mean, if you were just saying that to get her off your ass then that's fine. You know what, maybe I shouldn't have asked, is it too personal of a question? Is there even such thing as too personal? I mean, we are dating, and you've had my–"

Townes stopped walking and yanked me until I was nestled in the safety of his chest, and I felt him smile when he placed his head into my hair.

"Baby," he whispered.

I wrapped my arms around him and soaked in the way I felt in his arms.

When he pulled back, he took a long moment to look over me, and I flushed under his gaze. "You don't have to answer, it was a silly question."

"No, it wasn't." He pushed a hair out of the way, then moved to interlock our hands before we continued walking. "Do you remember that morning when you had to do Hayley's hair? Because she was complaining how rough I was being?"

"She's tender headed, but yes, I remember."

"It was then that I realized I wanted it to be real. I know I may not have shown it, but that was because I was still fighting that reality. Hollis, you fit in perfectly into our lives and it doesn't make any sense to start from the beginning."

We had stopped walking, and I glanced around. We weren't anywhere near the parking lot, instead we stood outside an old brick building. I could make out a few people through the frosted glass, but I didn't recognize any of the signage.

"Where are we?" I asked.

Townes turned and placed a gentle kiss on my forehead before he opened the door. "A jeweler, I think it's about time we got some rings. Don't you?"

"Oh, no we don't have to."

He stared at me, then blinked. "I know we don't have to, but I'd really like to. Let's just go look."

I took one looked inside the pretty, ornate shop and then nodded. Townes and I spent the next hour looking at the rings–they were all beautiful, and I had my sights set on one. A stunning solitaire oval ring, with a gold band. It was simple–but it was too much.

I set it back down in the display box and smiled at the employee. "Thank you."

The man nodded and walked off as I faced Townes, trying to hide my disappointment. "I'm ready to go, you hungry?"

He eyed me with hesitation before he nodded, then we walked out of the store, and I made sure I kept the longing from my face. The ring was beautiful, but that was too much of an ask from someone who'd given me everything.

* * *

"Uncle T! Hollis said we can have cookies for dessert!" Hayley stood in her chair and yelled as Townes walked through the front door. He'd been tasked with grabbing dinner, and I was busy convincing Hayley that we didn't need another pet.

Bilbo was more than enough–at least for the moment. Townes and I were going to discuss if we wanted to sell the house and move somewhere out of the city. However, that was a decision for another day, right now I wanted to spend time with my little family.

It felt good–being a part of one.

Townes set the bags onto the counter and furrowed his brows. "You're not getting any cookies if you don't sit down. What'll happen if you fall and get hurt?"

She sat down and tapped her chin. "Hm, well you'll make a fuss. And Hollis will tell you to calm down, but that might make you more upset." She smiled at him, then raised her hands. "What? I'm sitting down *now*."

Townes rolled his eyes, and I moved to help get the food, but he stopped me by grabbing my hands and turning me around.

"I have something for you, go sit."

"For me?"

Townes wasn't the kind to give gifts, so to say I was confused was an understatement. I did as he asked though, and sat back down at the dining table. I watched as he took the food from their containers and transferred it to plates. Then, when he placed mine in front of me, I expected him to move. To get Hayley's plate, or his, considering he only came over with the one.

I watched as Townes reached into his pocket and grabbed a small black box. I glanced up at him, not caring about the bewildered look on my face.

Hayley sat there giggling as Townes placed the opened box on the table. I stared at the ring I admired earlier, and felt my eyes fill with tears–my vision went blurry.

"It's only fair that we match," Townes said, grabbing my hand with his left–a smooth gold band around his ring finger.

I let the tears fall as I stared up at him, and the smile on his face–I didn't know what to say. The man who challenged me, who got me to open up and admit my desires when I didn't think anyone would listen. The man who gave me a family he built from tragedy.

"Are you going to put it on, or do I have to?" I asked through a wet sob.

I saw the tension disappear from his shoulders before he picked up the ring and placed it on my finger. Hayley came between us and hugged our legs.

"Does this mean I get a sister?"

We laughed–unsure of how to respond to that particular question–but elated we had all the time in the world to figure it out.

55

Epilogue

T ownes
Four years later...

I watched from the table as Hayley wandered around the kitchen, her apron covered in flour and icing covering the counters. She insisted on baking a cake, and I was helpless to do anything but watch. Ever since she started helping in the kitchen, my blood pressure's been on a constant high.

At the old house it wasn't much of an issue, Hollis had taken the liberty to teach Hayley the basics. But then, we moved into our new home and switched from electric to gas.

Was my worry about the oven exploding if the cake overflowed and touched the bottom, excessive? Of course it was, but it was my job to worry so I could keep everyone safe.

So the girls could suck it up.

"Do we have one of those long, flat knives?" Hayley asked as she opened drawers just to close them.

"A long, flat knife?"

"Yeah, you know. The ones bakers use to frost cakes. I

could use a butter knife, but I'm worried it won't come out good."

I sighed and went to stand, but Hayley stopped me with a finger. "I've got it pops, just tell me where it is."

"In the drawer next to the fridge," I said, settling back into my seat. Hayley had started calling me pops when she turned ten after asking if it was something I was comfortable with. Yet, every time she did, I couldn't help but feel a pull in my chest. I wasn't sure why–Hayley was too young when her father passed, and I was really the only one she had. It made sense, and honestly, it warmed my heart.

"So, when are you going to tell me what the special occasion is?"

"What makes you think there's a special occasion?" she asked with a smile.

I leaned back and crossed my arms. "You've been in the kitchen all day watching videos to make sure that cake is perfect. Something's up."

The front door opened, and Bilbo ran out of the kitchen when Taco, our adopted three-legged mutt ran toward the door. Amidst the dog's nails clicking against the floor, I heard it–the wonderful sound of laughter that seemed better than the first I'd heard it.

Then came the babbling.

Daisy rounded the corner, and her brown eyes lit up when she spotted me. "Daddy!" She held out her hands as she ran toward me, and I picked her up and set her in my lap.

"Hi, Mamas," I said as I poked Daisy's side. "Have fun with mommy?"

Hollis walked into the kitchen and eyed Hayley with a smile as she frosted the cake. "So much fun, well, except for the potty accident inside the store. That's never fun." She walked over and placed a kiss on my cheek. "How have things been here?"

"Fine, except for the fact that Haybug won't tell me why she's being so secretive."

Hollis shrugged. "I'm sure she has her reasons." Then she turned to our smallest daughter, and my heart swelled. "Come on, let's go change."

Daisy wrapped her little arms around my neck and shook her head. "No! Daddy."

"Yeah, well too bad. Little girls who don't listen don't get cake."

She turned her head and whispered, "Cake?"

Hollis nodded, then whisked our daughter off into a different room. Sometimes it was overwhelming–thinking about where we started, and how far we'd come. Never in my wildest dreams did I think I'd be lucky enough to be where I was today; a wife, two daughters, and coaching a little league hockey team in the small town we'd moved to last year.

"Okay, done," Hayley proclaimed. I looked over and noticed the simple white cake sitting on the counter. She had her hands on her hips and was smiling wide.

"Great, now, are you cooking dinner too?"

She turned and raised a brow. "After seeing how much I stressed you out, I think I'll let you cook tonight. Besides, Nana asked me to call her when I was done."

I nodded, which Hayley took as permission to leave. I walked into the kitchen and started prepping dinner, and tried not to listen as Hayley talked to Marion in the other room. She'd come a long way–her grandmother–and things had mellowed out. While she and Hollis weren't best friends

383

who hung out together, things were cordial and that was all I wanted.

By the time dinner was done, Hollis had set the table, and Daisy was ready to eat in her high chair. She tried to yank off her pink bib until her mom gave her *the look.* We ate dinner how we did every night. We took turns talking about our days, the wins and the losses, if there were any. When dinner was done, I was ready to settle into bed, but Hayley insisted on having dessert right after.

I wasn't going to say no to cake.

Hayley brought out the cake, and I saw her nerves in the way her hands shook. Once she placed the cake down, and moved one of Daisy's hands so she didn't touch it, she placed a hand on my shoulder.

"I have to grab something first, no eating."

She ran out of the room, and I glanced at Hollis. "Do you know what's going on?"

She shook her head, but I didn't believe her. A minute later, Hayley walked back into the room with a letter sized yellow envelope. She handed it to me, then sat in silence next to me. After a moment, she nudged my arm. "You're supposed to open it."

I knew that, but I was overcome with nerves. I took my time pinching up the sides of the metal tab, then gingerly removed the stack of papers. "What's this?"

"Just read it," Hayley said, her voice laced with nerves.

Daisy babbled in the quiet room as I scanned the papers–it was a lot of legal jargon–and I hadn't fully comprehended what I was reading until I got to the last page. My eyes welled with tears despite my attempts to keep them at bay, and I looked at Hayley.

Then, I looked at Hollis, who was smiling.

She'd been in on it this whole time.

"Adoption papers?"

Hayley nodded. "I did a lot of research, and I'm old enough now to make the decision. I also have some for Hollis." She turned toward her. "If you'd like them?"

Hollis gave her a teary-eyed smile, then placed a steady hand on my arm. I knew that when I took Hayley in, I could never replace her parents. It wasn't something I aimed to do, but knowing she saw me as more than just her uncle T–

I grabbed Hayley's arm and pulled her into a hug. And I remembered the first night I had her, when she was tiny and wearing a pink nightgown. She hadn't realized her parents had passed, and I remembered the way she looked up at me–with her hair a mess and her eyes heavy with sleep.

I vowed I wasn't going to replace them, but that I'd make sure to give her the best family I could. Just the two of us. Then along came Hollis, then Daisy, and the animals. I had fulfilled the promise to myself that she would never go without, and that I would always be there for her.

It just so happened that we found more people along the way that felt the same, and our little family grew from there.

About the Author

Ashlynne has loved writing from an early age but stopped when motherhood became her priority. In January 2021 she re-kindled her love of reading and in April 2023 decided it was time to start writing again.

She writes sweet stories, filled with tension that will have you reading until the early morning.

Also by Ashlynne Kristine

The Captain and The Coach
Basil Andrews knows three things are Rhonda's brownies are elite, love leads to heartache, and she's the best youth hockey coach at her facility.

So, when Basil is forced to take on an assistant coach, she's more than confused. Things only get worse when she shows up for practice and is faced with the unexpected. The tall, handsome man she yelled at the week before–who also happens to be the captain of Denver's hockey team. She's determined to keep things professional, despite his intent on being in her life. Because Basil can't promise anything more than friendship, even when her heart starts to beg for more.